IN SEARCH OF PEACE

A Prequel to The Horses Know Trilogy

LYNN MANN

Coxstone Press

For Darren and Braveheart

Chapter One

I winced as my axe landed with a thud on the chopping block. The pain in my shoulder was getting worse with each swing, but I had no intention of stopping any time soon. I needed the pain; it replaced the rage that I normally embraced but from which, every now and then, I needed respite. In addition, the sound of each log splitting and the sight of its two halves falling away in opposite directions gave me satisfaction – it wasn't just me who could be broken.

I began to sense that I wasn't alone, but still I continued to chop; there was a whole lot more pain that I needed to feel. It was only when I couldn't lift the axe any higher than my waist that I let it fall to the ground. I wiped the sweat from my face with the bottom of my unbuttoned shirt and then lowered myself to sit on the chopping block, exhausted.

A woman's voice began to hum and the pain in my shoulder eased. I looked over to my right.

'STOP THAT,' I shouted over to where I knew Morvyr must be standing, presumably behind one of the huge trees that surrounded my home. She stepped into view, still humming. My pain continued to diminish.

'HOW DARE YOU HEAL ME AGAINST MY WILL?' I stormed and got to my feet. As I began to stagger towards her, her humming ceased.

'I'm just doing what Bronwyn would have wanted, which is more than you are,' said Morvyr.

I gasped as if she'd hit me with far more than just words, and stopped in my tracks, staring at her.

'I'm a Tissue-Singer, Adam. Healing people with my voice and intention is what I do, just as healing with herbs is what you used to do. You're the most gifted Herbalist in living memory, yet you're hiding away in the woods where most of those who need your help can't find you, and when those suffering badly enough to keep searching for you do actually manage it, you hurl abuse at them until they leave you alone. You actually turn away people who are ill or injured, because you think that losing your wife and child gives you the monopoly on suffering. Bronwyn would be ashamed of you. I've kept bringing you food and clothes because I thought you just needed time to come to terms with your grief, but now I'm not so sure I've been doing the right thing. Look at yourself, you're even thinner than the last time I saw you, you're dirty and what's more, you smell. Do you think you're honouring my sister's memory by wasting away like this? Because I can tell you that you're not. Three years to the day this has been going on and I've come to tell you, Adam, that it has to stop.' Morvyr's chest heaved up and down as if she'd been running. She reached up and tucked her long, wavy blond hair behind both ears, just as Bronwyn used to when she was anxious. Bronwyn. My beautiful wife. No. I couldn't think of her. Anger was easier.

'Don't pretend you come out here and bother me for your sister's sake, you've always been a nosy, interfering pest of a woman and I've no doubt that you relish entertaining everyone back in Greenfields with all the gossip you take back about me.'

Morvyr took a step backwards, her brown eyes, so like my late wife's, widening in shock. I didn't allow myself to feel the pain that recognition brought with it. I found rage instead and hurled it at her. 'I never asked you to bring me food or clothes, and where I choose to live is my business and nobody else's. Why don't you just concentrate on finding a husband of your own, instead of hankering after your dead sister's? Have you no shame?' I was now in front of my sister-in-law, stabbing my pointed finger in front of her face. She flinched each time and a tear ran down her face, but she stood her ground.

'You know, those green eyes of yours were all Bronwyn could talk about when she first starting seeing you, Adam. She was captivated by their sparkle, their kindness, the love they held, not just for her but for everyone, for life itself. But it's as if they belong to someone else now. They're dull and empty one minute, and flashing sparks the next, and they don't even look green anymore, not really, it's as if all the colour has just leached out of them.' She peered more closely at me. 'Where are you, Adam? I know the man my sister loved is in there somewhere, but he's hiding behind all that anger and, try as I might, I can't seem to bring him back.'

I lowered my hand and scowled. 'Like I said, I never asked you to. Go away and find your own man, Morvyr.'

'You think you're hurting me by accusing me of betraying my sister's memory, but the truth is, you're only hurting yourself, which I know pleases you almost as much, sickening as that is. And not that you'll care, but I already have my own man. Felin and I were married eighteen months ago. I didn't tell you because I didn't want to bring back memories of your own wedding, I knew it would only cause you more pain and I knew you'd never allow yourself to be happy for anyone else anyway. I came out here today to tell you that this will be my last trip to see you. I'm pregnant, you see. It won't be long before I'll be uncomfortable walking this far.'

I looked down to where Morvyr was unconsciously rubbing her rounded belly. Pain stabbed through me and my legs buckled as I saw in my mind for the millionth time, my very beautiful but very dead newborn baby daughter as I cradled her in my arms before they wrenched her from me.

'Adam, I'm sorry, but I had to tell you. I need you. There was nothing anyone could have done to save Bronwyn after her problems in childbirth, or to save your little girl, everyone but you accepts that. I know it's unlikely that it will happen to me, but something else could, something you can help with. Having been through losing my sister and niece, I have this... this terror that my baby and I will die too. Please come back to Greenfields, please be there in case I need you,' pleaded Morvyr, taking hold of my arm to steady me.

I wrenched it from her grip and summoned my old friend, the only one on whom I could rely to give me relief from the agony of losing my wife and child – and fury was quick to answer my call. 'LET GO OF ME!' I screamed and staggered backwards. 'DO YOU HONESTLY THINK I HAVE ANY INTEREST IN HELPING YOU, WHO MEANS NOTHING TO ME, WHEN I COULDN'T SAVE THE TWO WHO MEANT EVERYTHING TO ME? GO AWAY AND FOR THE LAST TIME, LEAVE ME ALONE!'

Morvyr stood where she was for a few moments, tears streaming down her face. Then she turned and stumbled away. I saw her pause and reach a hand out to an oak tree, bending over slightly as if in pain. Unbidden, the man I used to be almost fought his way out. I almost felt concern for the only person I had allowed anywhere near me during the past three years; the only one who had persisted in caring for me however foul I was to her, the only one who, until that day, had never given up trying to bring me back from the place of pain and anger in which I was choosing to reside. I almost went to her. Then she straightened, took a deep breath in and out, and walked steadily away. I let her go.

Unsteadily, I made my way back to my axe and chopping block. I placed a log onto the block and took a swing. It wasn't long before I had replaced the pain that Morvyr had taken away from me. I proceeded to add to it with fervour.

When my shoulder was screaming and I could barely lift the axe, I let it fall to the ground and sank down beside it. I leant back against a tree with a grimace, wiped the sweat from my eyes and brow and surveyed my home.

The tiny log hut that I had built three years ago needed its walls restuffing with moss, and its roof was sagging. The line that I had strung from the hut to a nearby tree, on which to hang clothes, was snapped in two and covered with green slime; I had given up washing my clothes in the nearby stream many months ago. My cookfire crackled merrily just in front of the door to my hut, but no pot hung over it. It had been days since I had bothered to cook, and longer since I had found the will to hunt. I spotted a back-sack that Morvyr must have brought. It would contain food and probably the clothes that had disappeared after her last visit, now washed and mended. I had a good supply of logs piled near to where I sat, but judging by the steadily increasing heat of the last few weeks and subsequent drying out of the woodland floor and undergrowth, I would soon have to limit my use of fire lest I burn down the forest.

My stomach rumbled in anticipation of the food in Morvyr's back-sack. I would have to find the plate, bowl and mug that were wherever I had thrown them in temper because there was no food easily available when last I felt hungry. I wasn't sure I could be bothered, even if I could get myself up with the stabbing pain in my shoulder.

A chittering made me look up into the branches of the beech tree against which I was leaning. I sighed. That flaming squirrel was back. I had taken him in months before, when his flopping around outside the door of my hut as if he were dying got really annoying. I had made up an unguent to heal the wound on his back and fed him until he was well enough to survive on his own, but that didn't mean I wanted his continued presence. A piece of tree bark landed on my forehead and bounced off, landing in my lap.

'So, Squirrel, you're not only intent on annoying me with that stupid noise, you're intent on killing the trees around my campsite?' I called up to him and was rewarded with more chittering and another, larger strip of bark landing in my lap. I hurled both pieces away from me. 'I should have let you die from that wound, at least I'd have had some peace,' I muttered.

Peace. That was all I wanted. It was why, a few months after my wife and daughter had died, I left the interfering people of Greenfields village, to go and live in the forest by myself. At least there, I didn't have to suffer their continual lecturing about how I would get over my loss, how I still had a life to live, how important I was to the advancement of herbalism. There, they couldn't pester me to treat them; the few that found me soon thought better of it. I wasn't fit to treat anyone except that annoying little git above my head.

I had thought I was invincible. Early on in my herbalism apprenticeship, I found that I could tweak the dose and usage of known herbal cures to achieve better results, add new herbs to improve the efficacy of existing combinations and even, sometimes, diagnose and cure underlying conditions that were the cause of the more obvious symptoms for which patients were currently receiving treatment. I just found it easy. It was as if I had done it all before and the training was just jogging my memory.

Once I was qualified, people came from far and wide to see the new, ground-breaking Herbalist who could cure just about anything. But I couldn't cure Bronwyn or Alita – I hadn't even picked up the fact that there was a potential problem that might need curing. When Alita came early to this world and then Bronwyn began fitting, I just went blank, numb, as if it were happening to someone else. The intuition I had learnt to trust when diagnosing and treating patients completely deserted me and I just stood there, looking at them both, my mouth opening and closing in horror. Morvyr tried to save them, but in vain. Bronwyn was gone, followed a few hours later by my beautiful baby girl. They died while I did nothing but stand there and watch. I knew then and there that I didn't deserve anybody's trust. Never again would I let someone put their faith in me, only to be let down. I wasn't the genius everyone said I was. I was a pathetic, useless coward and I loathed myself.

When another two pieces of bark landed on the top of my head, I roared up at Squirrel to get himself gone. He just looked down at me and chittered furiously, as if trying to prove that his temper was easily a match for mine. I looked down at the scars from the bite marks he had left on my hands during his last few days of treatment, and thought that maybe he had a point.

I pushed myself up and away from the chopping block, swearing at the pain that lanced through my shoulder. I gathered my crockery from where it was strewn about the forest floor, then threw it all back down to the ground in a pile by Morvyr's back-sack in my haste to see what food she had brought me. I found a huge loaf of bread first, and began tearing off huge chunks of it with my teeth. My stomach groaned at the smell of the ham that I found next. I pulled my knife from the trunk of the nearest tree where I had thrown it the day before for lack of anything else to do, and carved slices of ham and bread to make a rough sandwich, from which I threw the odd morsel to the brat of a squirrel who now sat on his haunches in front of me, waiting expectantly.

When my stomach was full, I lay back, leant my head against the sack and dozed. The next thing I knew, the sun was low in the sky, my fire was almost out and the rustling coming from within the sack meant that Squirrel was inside it, helping himself to whatever he fancied.

I leapt to my feet and with a howl at the pain in my shoulder, turned the sack upside down. Squirrel tumbled out clutching a net full of nuts, and scampered up the nearest tree.

'From the look of you, you don't have the luxury of food to spare, to be throwing it all over the ground,' a man's voice said from behind me.

I spun around to see a slim, dark-haired, dark-eyed man of middle years riding a tall, slender, black horse into my campsite. The man wore a brown, wide-brimmed hat, white shirt, brown leggings and brown boots, all immaculately clean.

'I don't remember inviting you to invade my home, let alone to pass comment on how I choose to live,' I said coldly.

'I didn't ask the woodlice, birds, mice, rabbits, or any of the other animals who live here, either, yet none of them seem to be objecting,' the man said, looking around himself. 'You've been living here a while.'

'And I'll say the same to you as I've said to everyone else who has tried to impose their presence upon me while I've been here. Go away, and don't come back. And you can tell Morvyr that I meant what I said,' I snarled.

The man jumped down from his horse and rubbed her face

affectionately. 'Thanks, Risk,' he told her. 'Give me a minute and I'll fetch you some water.'

'Don't plan on making yourselves comfortable,' I said. 'You may be used to adoration wherever you go because you're Horse-Bonded, but I couldn't care less who or what you are. I don't want you here, either of you, so you can get lost. Do you hear me? GET LOST.'

The man ignored me and began to undo his horse's girth. I stormed over to him, waving the hand of my good arm and shouting, 'GET LOST, I TELL YOU!'

The horse put her ears flat back against her head and snaked her neck at me but the man merely looked up from underneath the saddle flap, and raised an eyebrow. 'What's wrong with your other arm? Why are you holding it against yourself like that? I'm no Healer, but the Herbalist of the last village I passed through gave me some preparations if you need respite from pain?'

'You don't know who I am, do you?' I said. 'So Morvyr didn't send you?'

'Not a clue, no, and sorry, never heard of her.' The man returned to unsaddling his horse.

'Who are you then? And why are you here? Not that it matters, because I want you to leave,' I said.

'I have every intention of leaving once Risk has drunk and eaten as much as she needs to, and once you've received our message.' The man placed his saddle on the ground, then reached into one of his saddlebags for a brush, with which he began to groom his horse's back.

I shook my head. 'It never flaming well stops, does it? However hard I try to remove myself from know-it-all do-gooders, however remote a place I choose to live so that I can just be left alone, so that I don't have to hear the advice of everyone who knows how to live my life better than I do, it just goes on and on. I DON'T WANT YOU HERE AND I DON'T WANT YOUR HORSE'S ADVICE.'

'Her name is Risk. Mine is Devlin. I'm pleased to meet you, despite your lack of manners and regardless of whether you decide to tell me your name in return. Now, where can I find water for Risk?

She's brought me a long way in the heat to find you.' Risk turned and nuzzled Devlin's shoulder as he groomed her, and I was shocked by the sudden envy I felt at their bond.

Like all people of The New, I grew up learning about the people of The Old, with their enormous cities, their machines and their desperate need for safety and control. They eventually obliterated themselves, leaving behind small communities of people who'd had the courage to leave the insanity of The Old regime before it imploded. Those communities were vulnerable and would never have survived had the horses not helped them; the horses chose human Bond-Partners with whom they communicated telepathically and through whom they reminded the people of The New of abilities long forgotten by humanity. Rock-Singers remembered how to use their voices and minds to move rocks and build houses. Tree-Singers remembered how to influence the growth and vitality of trees and crops. Earth-Singers remembered how to move huge volumes of soil to aid building and farming. Weather-Singers remembered how to sing up a breeze to blow rainclouds away or call them in. Bone-Singers, Tissue-Singers and Herbalists remembered how to heal. The communities of The New survived and then flourished under the ongoing guidance of the horses and their Bond-Partners.

But that didn't mean I wanted any of them here, ramming their contentment, companionship and irritating self-assurance down my throat.

I turned and stormed into my hut, slamming the door behind me. The door latch was broken, so the door bounced against its frame and then hung back open. I turned in fury to see Devlin and Risk watching me with matching expressions of relaxed interest. I picked up the empty water bucket by the door and hurled it at them.

Devlin bent his knees, caught the bucket and cradled it to his stomach. 'Thanks,' he said. 'I take it that's a water barrel jutting out from behind your shed? I'll just help myself, shall I?'

Risk sniffed the bucket and looked back at me, her ears pricked forward and her dark brown eyes soft and...warm. I actually felt warmth from her. No. I didn't want to feel that. Anger and pain were safer. I slammed the door and held it shut with my hand while I looped my foot around the leg of my stool and pulled it over to wedge the door closed.

I squeezed around my small, rickety table to sit on my narrow, wooden bed with its mattress of moss. I put my face in my hands and tried to summon up my anger once more. I heard Devlin removing the cover of my water barrel, and then the sloshing of water as he lifted out a bucketful and offered it to Risk, murmuring to her all the while. I put my hands over my ears to try to block out the bond between them that I could not only hear in Devlin's voice, but that I could somehow feel, as if it were wending its way through the wall and into me, taunting me as it prodded me somewhere very deep and very sore inside.

I began to rock backwards and forwards, trying to give myself something else on which to focus. Devlin and Risk weren't in the least intimidated by me, so I wasn't going to be able to get rid of them in the same way I had everyone else. I had to think of another way, yet I couldn't think at all. The feeling of contentment that practically oozed out of Risk and Devlin, the comfort they drew from one another, and their calm sense of joint purpose all reminded me of the partnership I'd had with my wife. It was as if my skin were burning as their bond continued to touch me. It was unbearable.

'AAAAAAAAAAAAAARGH! AAAAAAAAAAAAAAARGH! AAAAAAAAAAAAAAARGH!' I screamed over and over and over until I had exhausted myself. I remember feeling a brief moment of relief as I drifted off to sleep.

Chapter Two

$\mathcal{I}$ woke to the smell of something savoury, cooking. My stomach gurgled noisily and saliva dribbled out of the corner of my mouth. I sat up with a start, just as the first birds began to call their greetings to the morning. That flaming Horse-Bonded was helping himself to my food!

I leapt to my feet, kicked my stool out of the way and flung the door open. Devlin was sitting cross-legged by the fire but Risk was nowhere to be seen. At least I would be spared having to witness their connection on an empty stomach.

'Just in time, I was about to dish up,' Devlin said. 'Rabbit stew okay for you? I managed a little hunting and gathering before I put my head down last night. I helped myself to a little of your salt, I hope you don't mind?'

'Would it matter if I did?' I growled.

'I gathered your food parcel back together and hung it from that branch over there, else there would have been nothing left by this morning. Mind you, that squirrel has been busy gnawing at the draw-string for the past few minutes, so you might want to take it inside and store it somewhere he can't get to it.'

'Well, I'll just do that then, shall I?' I stomped past him, winced as I reached up with both arms to retrieve the back-sack, and then stormed back towards my hut.

'That shoulder still troubling you? Shall I add some of the painkilling preparation the Herbalist gave me to your portion of stew? It really will help,' Devlin called after me.

I ignored him and busied myself in my hut, distributing the contents of the various food parcels into my purposely squirrel-proof storage containers. When I had taken as long as I possibly could over it and could bear the griping in my stomach no longer, I stepped hesitantly back out of my hut.

Devlin indicated with his spoon to where a bowl of steaming stew waited tantalisingly for me on the ground. 'I washed all your crockery and found various pieces of cutlery lying around and cleaned them as best I could, and I promise you I haven't poisoned the stew, so go ahead and eat, I'm not a bad cook.'

He almost had me. I almost sat with him and ate his annoyingly delicious smelling stew. But then Risk appeared. Devlin glanced up at her and smiled one of those smiles that comes unbidden when a loved one enters the room. I didn't move quickly enough to avoid seeing the eye contact they shared; he was listening to her, hearing her in his mind as only the Horse-Bonded can, I knew it. Their bond seared at my very soul. I ran, and didn't stop running until I was free of... what? Just free of them. I couldn't afford to think any more deeply about it.

It was a blisteringly hot day and I was glad of the shade provided by the trees. As I tramped around, trying to find food, dry leaves crunched beneath my feet. I realised I had seen them drifting to the ground around my campsite too. If the trees were dropping leaves, then they were feeling the effects of drought. I thought back and realised that I couldn't remember the last time it had rained. I would need to be vigilant in keeping the area around my cookfire clear of leaves, and I would need to have it alight only when necessary, much sooner than I had envisaged. That was if I ever managed to take possession of my home again.

When I found myself at the stream from which I hauled my water, it was late afternoon. I drank deeply from cupped hands and then lowered my head, splashing my face and rubbing away the sweat and grime. When I opened my eyes, I saw my reflection and gasped.

Whenever I had caught a glimpse of my face over the past three years, I had recognised myself. Sure, I had gradually become thinner, I looked a lot older than my twenty-nine years and I wore a permanent scowl, but I had known who I was. If I'm honest, I was pleased with what I saw. I looked how I felt and my obvious wrath had let people know that when I told them to get lost, I meant it. Now, the layers I had wrapped around myself had all been stripped away and I looked gaunt, scared and vulnerable. I felt the need to get back to my hut, back to where I felt safe, where I could hide from the world. If Devlin and Risk were still insisting on outstaying their welcome, I'd throw them out, physically if I had to.

With each step back to my campsite, my thoughts fuelled my anger. How dare that man and his horse impose on me the way they had? How dare they flaunt their bond and make me feel so terrible? They could leave my camp and take all of their happiness and self-assurance with them. They could... I reached my camp and looked around me. Felt around me. They were gone.

Thank the light for that, I tried to tell myself, yet I couldn't completely ignore the sense of loss I felt. No. Not loss. It was relief, that was all it was. I didn't need their like, I just wanted what I had wanted ever since three became one – to be left alone.

The stew pot was missing from where Devlin had hung it over the fire and I felt a surge of hope for which I hated myself, that he may have left me some. Sure enough, the pot was on the table in my hut, lidded and half full of stew. My crockery was arranged around it, including the bowl that Devlin had filled for me, now empty of stew and containing instead my cutlery, a white parcel, and a folded piece of paper. I wanted to hurl the note into the barely flickering fire, unread, yet I knew I would read it.

Risk tells me that you have received our message, so we will
bother you no longer. The parcel contains the herbs I was telling
you about. I doubt you will use them, but I'm leaving them for
you just in case – the dosage is written clearly on the front of
each preparation. When next we meet, I truly hope that you will
be happier to see us.
Devlin

Message? What flaming message? They came here, made me feel
like they were worth everything and I was worth nothing, and then
disappeared. I thought the Horse-Bonded were meant to pass on
advice from their horses that would make situations better for people,
not just arrive and depart having made things a hundred times worse. I
felt like taking my axe up again but having barely eaten all day, I
didn't have the strength. I needed to do something, though.

As if on cue, Squirrel appeared in the doorway. I picked up the
mug that Devlin had so meticulously scrubbed free of dirt, and threw it
at him. He leapt to the side, chittering furiously, then turned tail and
fled.

I sank onto my stool and ladled cold stew into my bowl until it was
full. I ate the lot, then a second bowl, and then lay down on my bed,
exhausted.

I dreamt of Risk. She was walking away from me, but kept
stopping and looking back, as if she wanted me to follow. To begin
with, I refused, but eventually, I took a single, halting step.
Immediately, Risk disappeared and in her place was… who? I couldn't
see anyone, yet somehow, I knew another horse was there, one whose
attention was wholly on me, as if I were all that mattered. I felt drawn
to this ghost of a horse, as if nothing were more important than finding
him. As if everything would be alright once we were together.

I sat bolt upright, shaking and sweating profusely at the intimacy I
had just shared with the dream horse, an intimacy that was terrifying
because of the comfort it gave me – comfort I neither wanted nor

needed, I told myself. I drew in a deep breath. It was okay, I was still on my bed, in my hut. It was just a dream. Yet, I suddenly realised, I was still feeling drawn towards the invisible horse. His pull on my mind had followed me from my dream into wakefulness. A cold dread stole over me as comprehension dawned. The horse actually existed somewhere. And he was trying to pull me to him because he had chosen me as his Bond-Partner.

Chapter Three

I cursed Risk and Devlin with every word I could think of. This was happening to me because of them. They had tricked me. Trapped me. By showing me what was possible, by inflicting their bond upon me until I couldn't help but be affected by it, they had drawn me into this trap. If I succumbed to this maddening tugging on my mind and went off to find the horse who was doing it, I would become Horse-Bonded, just like Devlin. My mind would be linked to that of my horse and we would share our thoughts, our feelings, our lives... No. There were two people with whom I had wanted to share my life, and they were both dead. I would never love anyone else and I didn't want anyone to love me... except I could feel that my horse – no, not my horse, THE horse, for goodness' sake – already did. His love reached out to me, enfolded me and drew me to him. It felt as if my mind were blistering, even as a part of me, somewhere deep inside, tried to reach back and embrace that which was being offered. No. I wouldn't succumb. This wasn't what I wanted.

'I JUST WANT TO BE LEFT ALONE!' I shouted as if the horse could hear me, even though I knew there were days of travel between the two of us. I shook my head and put my hands over my ears. I didn't want to know of the distance between us. I didn't want to know anything about this horse who was torturing me. I needed to occupy myself, that was what I needed. I would block the horse out and eventually, he would get the message and leave me alone.

I stood up and went outside. My fire had long since gone out, which was just as well because dead leaves had continued to fall and could well have taken the flames to the rest of the forest. I cursed myself for an idiot, grabbed my broom and began to sweep a wide circle around the fire, wincing at the pain in my shoulder. Then I relit it, burning myself in the process because my hands wouldn't stop shaking with the incessant distraction of my mind being continuously yanked off somewhere else.

'Just keep busy,' I told myself out loud, as if my voice could drown out what was going on in my head. I practically ran into my hut to get the pot of stew, hung it over the fire and stirred it manically as it heated.

I was almost relieved when Squirrel came bounding along to sit just out of arm's reach, and then, right in front of me, proceeded to eat one of the nuts he had stolen from me the previous day.

'You have a nut? Good for you, I have several bowls of stew, and I'm going to eat the lot. Then I'm going to... to...' My mind was pulled with a sudden urgency and I shook my head vehemently, forcing my attention back to my conversation with Squirrel. 'THEN,' I shouted, determined not to be interrupted again, 'I AM GOING TO... FETCH... MORE... WATER.... AND... AAAAAAAAAAARGH! JUST LEAVE ME ALONE!' I sank to my knees. 'Please,' I begged the horse, 'just leave me alone.'

I could feel his unshakeable conviction that we would be Bond-Partners, his unwavering love for me that I didn't want, but that continued to draw me to him. I couldn't shut it out. A flash of anger shot through me. Since when was I so weak? I just had to try harder. When I had food inside me, when I felt stronger, I would be able to block the horse out of my mind and get on with my life. I wiped my face on the filthy arm of my shirt and drew in a deep breath. Squirrel's bright eyes peered up at me with a total lack of concern as he continued to nibble on his nut, and I drew strength from his confidence. I could do this.

I got to my feet and hurriedly stirred the stew, which had begun to stick to the bottom of the pot. It was nearly ready. I fetched my bowl, scraped the remains of my previous meal out of it with my spoon, and flicked them across the small clearing. When the stew was steaming hot, I raised the pot to a higher peg on its tripod so that the food would keep warm without burning, filled my bowl and settled down to eat. The tugging on my mind eased a little; my horse – flaming lanterns, THE HORSE – had recognised my need for food. That was big of him. Or her. I realised that despite the horse presumably having enough information about me to choose me as Bond-Partner, I knew nothing at all about... it. That was how I would refer to the one who was so intent on torturing my mind.

I hummed to myself as I ate my breakfast, all two and a half bowls of it, and practised focusing on the sound I was making to the exclusion of all else. I convinced myself that if I concentrated hard enough, I could increase the volume of my humming once the tugging on my mind returned to its previous strength, as it surely would, and that by focusing on my voice, I could keep my mind wholly with me.

As soon as I swallowed my last mouthful, the pull on my mind re-intensified and my mind was flooded with the knowledge that the horse was closer than it had been. The fact that I knew unwanted information about an unwanted horse who was intent on forcing me to make an unwanted journey brought my temper to the surface afresh. I hurled my bowl and spoon away from me and increased my humming to such a degree that my throat hurt. I cast about for something – anything – to do, and spotted my axe. I leapt to my feet and began splitting logs. The searing pain in my shoulder was a welcome diversion from the increasing discomfort of staying put when every part of my body wanted to move in the direction from which my mind was being pulled, and I put everything into creating more of it.

I chopped wood until there were no logs left to split. Then I set about the nearest tree trunk. A tiny part of me recoiled at the damage I was inflicting on such an old and beautiful tree, but by far the greater part was occupied with the pain of a now torn muscle in my left shoulder, the concentration necessary to hurl the axe at the tree with my remaining good arm, and anger at my failure to block out the relentless tugging on my mind.

I could no longer hum; I had neither the voice nor the breath. Blood pounded in my head and everything suddenly seemed very far away. Still, I continued to flail at the tree. Eventually, I passed out.

When I came to, Squirrel was sitting directly in front of my face, clutching another nut and chattering away urgently at me. Immediately, I felt the horse's concern for me. It knew of the agony I was experiencing in my shoulder, the pain I felt just about everywhere else, my fatigue and my extreme thirst. It knew all of that and... something else, but it did not cease its pull on my mind, in fact it increased it even further. If I'd had the energy to cry, I would have.

I sat up and found that the pain in my shoulder obliterated any desire to move further. Then I heard a crackling and smelt smoke. I shuffled painfully around the base of the tree and cursed. That flaming horse had distracted me to the degree that I had failed to put out my cookfire once I had finished eating and, as I had foreseen, falling leaves had caught in the flames and been taken on the breeze, spreading fire to both a nearby clump of brambles and to my hut; flames licked up one side of it, rapidly catching on the dry moss that stuck out between the logs.

I shot to my feet with a roar, adrenaline blocking out the worst of my pain. I ran to the water barrel, dunked my bucket in with my good arm and flung it at the brambles, extinguishing the fire there in one attempt. Cradling the arm attached to my bad shoulder as much as I could, I retrieved the bucket, refilled it and flung it at the wall that was alight. There was a lot of hissing and smoke, but then orange flames reappeared. I raced back to the water barrel and repeated my attempt to put the fire out, again to limited effect. It took five more buckets before the flames were completely extinguished and then another to put out those that had appeared in another patch of undergrowth a short distance away. When I had emptied a final bucket over my cookfire, I sighed with a relief that was short lived as my physical pain and mental torture returned.

The horse's concern had intensified and it was moving in my direction at increased speed. I spat on the ground in fury at knowing it. I staggered over to the water barrel with my bucket and found the strength to haul out another half bucket. I quenched my thirst and then sat leaning against the barrel, pondering my predicament. I had injured my shoulder beyond my ability to either relish or ignore the pain. My hut now needed urgent repairs and judging from the smoke billowing out of the doorway, I would need to retrieve the food stored within urgently, before it spoilt. The water barrel was now almost empty and there was no way I could fetch more from the stream with my shoulder this painful and the rest of me not much better. I sighed wearily. With the little piece of my mind that still belonged to me, I knew what I needed to do.

I took off my shirt and immersed it in the remaining water in the bucket. Putting the wet shirt over my head and holding the arm of it to my mouth, I staggered into my tiny hut and one by one, grabbed the food containers from the foot of the bed and hurled them out through the doorway. Then I felt around on the table for the parcel of herbs that Devlin had left, and emerged from the hut, coughing, my eyes streaming. I threw the parcel on the ground and sank to my knees beside it. When my coughing had subsided and I could see clearly, I opened it and sorted through the packets of herbs within. I grimaced at the simplicity of the herb combinations chosen by the Herbalist who had prepared the various remedies, but they would have to do. My life practising herbalism was behind me and I had no intention of ever taking it up again.

As if intent on providing proof to the contrary, Squirrel bounded past, chittering happily. I realised that if it hadn't been for him rousing me, the fire could have spread beyond my ability to put it out. I might even have died. It wouldn't have mattered, I decided as I threw my head back and poured the entire contents of two brown packets of herbs down my throat, ignoring the recommended doses written on the front. Nothing mattered.

The horse disagreed with my observation and I almost overbalanced in the direction from which it suddenly increased its pull on me. I didn't have the strength to be angry. I didn't have the strength to do anything. As the herbs began to exert their painkilling and soporific effects over me, I shuffled back to lean against the unburnt side of my hut. Before long, everything went black.

The horse was galloping to me, its body lathered in sweat and its eyes wide... yet it was still invisible to me. How could I know these things when I couldn't see it? Suddenly the horse took form and became a black mare. Risk. She was also galloping in my direction. I only knew it because my horse knew. My horse. I sighed and then was furious. IT was NOT my horse. I lashed out with my mind and the image of Risk shattered into a thousand pieces, leaving only the infuriating impression of the invisible horse still galloping in my direction. I lashed out with even more force, but all of my anger, my frustration and my resistance were absorbed by the horse's energy, as if they had never existed. The horse didn't even check its stride but merely continued to gallop... and then became Risk again. She was closer to me than the invisible horse, and she was coming for me.

I tried to get up and run from them both, but my legs wouldn't obey me. It felt as if I were trying to move through mud that was thigh deep and sucking all of my energy out of me. I realised that I liked the sensation. I didn't have to struggle any more.

Chapter Four

I was being slapped hard. Then all of a sudden, I was cold, wet and choking. I opened my eyes briefly as my head was lifted back out of the water. I was slapped again. I smiled and sank back down into oblivion. Then I was choking again. There was a tube in my throat that was quickly removed. I was flung on my front just in time before I vomited herbs and salt water.

'Don't you go back to sleep. Don't you dare,' Devlin's voice warned me. I was hauled to my feet and made to walk around and around for I don't know how long. Then I seemed to be moving through the air. I was sitting on something that was moving, rocking from side to side as it moved continually forward. I was being held firmly around the waist as I swayed with the movement, which went on and on and on.

When I was finally lowered to the ground, I fell instantly asleep. The invisible horse was exhausted and resting somewhere close by. I tried to find the mud that had drained me before, that had given me relief from being who I am, that had taken it all away and just let me be. How had I found it before? I had tried to run, that was it. I had tried to run from Risk and the invisible horse. I tried to run again, but I only found myself moving closer to where the invisible horse was resting. I lashed out with my mind, trying to hurt the horse, to stop it from pulling at me, but as before, my blows were absorbed as if they had never existed.

When I opened my eyes, I was propped against a tree and sitting in long, dry grass. I felt as if my skin had been scrubbed and when I looked down, I found myself to indeed be free of the dirt and grime that had been my second skin for so long. I was wearing clean, unfamiliar clothes, and the arm of my injured shoulder was bound tightly to my chest. My other arm had the handles of a very large, very full back-sack draped over it. I shifted slightly. My stomach felt delicate, but other than that, the only discomfort I had was a dull ache in my injured shoulder. I left the back-sack where it was and got awkwardly to my feet. I looked all around myself, squinting in the high, midday sun. I frowned. Last thing I remembered, it had been afternoon. The forest in which I had made my home was nowhere in sight, there was just the odd lone tree poking up from the grassland that surrounded me and stretched for as far as the eye could see. I had absolutely no idea where I was, or even what day it was. Devlin. And Risk. They did this. They couldn't just let me be.

Movement caught my eye. A long, thick, white tail with a black streak flicked flies from the body of a large, stocky, white and brown horse, who was busy snatching at grass nearby. I left the shade of the tree and began to walk towards him. Definitely a him, I knew now with certainty. How did I know? The pulling at my mind was absent, leaving… something else in its place; something I couldn't define but which left me curious. I approached the horse on weak, shaking legs. I couldn't seem to summon up the anger I had felt towards him. I didn't feel anything really, apart from hunger, weariness and, suddenly, calm. As if something inevitable were happening that made any opinions or feelings superfluous.

As I got closer to the horse, I could see that his coat was caked in dried sweat, from his dark brown ears and face to his white neck and body with light and dark brown patches, all the way to his tail. There

were light brown streaks down his white legs, where dirt particles had
been lifted from his body and carried away by rivulets of the sweat
that had drenched him as he raced to get to me.

When I was ten paces away from the horse, he stopped grazing and
looked up at me from under a shaggy black forelock, his soft, warm,
brown eyes welcoming me and drawing me in. All at once, I felt his
extreme thirst, his exhaustion, the itchiness of his sweat-caked coat,
and his total acceptance of his discomfort. I felt his contentment at
having me near him, his relief that help had reached me in time, and
the total, unswerving love that he felt for me.

He knew all of me. He knew me at my best and at my worst. In his
eyes, I saw myself stealing kisses with Bronwyn outside her parents'
house, walking through the fields with her, sharing picnics under the
stars, dancing with her at our wedding. I saw myself barricading
myself into our cottage after her and my daughter's deaths, screaming
at anyone who knocked on the door to leave me alone, regardless of
whether they were there to offer or ask for help. I saw a young couple
arrive at my home, only to turn and walk back down my front path in
tears minutes later, to begin their week-long journey back home
carrying the sick infant I had refused to even see. I saw each and every
one of those who had tracked me down at my hovel in the woods to
beg me for help, only to run from my temper before they had managed
to utter a word. Swirling around all of the images that I saw in the
depths of the horse's eyes, was his calm, loving acceptance.
Everything was, and always had been, alright.

I felt as if I had been stung. I stepped back away from him as fast
as I could, catching my heel and sitting down in the long grass with a
bump. I used my unbound arm to support myself as I scuffled
backwards along the ground, desperate to get away from this... this...
madness. Everything was not alright and it never would be. I didn't
want reassurance and I didn't want whatever this was between the
horse and me.

A bond. It is a bond. The words arrived in my mind as if I had
thought them, yet I knew I hadn't. The horse continued to look at me,

his dark, almost liquid eyes calm and reassuring. My heart began to race as I felt something that had been insubstantial between us, akin to the beginning of an idea, unfurling into something solid and real, irreversibly joining our minds. Our very existences here.

'NO!' I screamed. 'I DON'T WANT THIS. I CAN'T STAND IT. I CAN'T STAND YOU. WHY ARE YOU DOING THIS TO ME? WHY COULDN'T YOU HAVE JUST LEFT ME ALONE? HAVEN'T I SUFFERED ENOUGH?'

You have indeed chosen to suffer greatly. It is time to choose differently.

'Chosen?' I whispered. 'CHOSEN?' I shouted.

It has been convenient for you to choose rage and isolation over acceptance and inclusion. The former choices have been less uncomfortable. Their benefits have been overtaken by their shortcomings however. The time has come for you to make new choices.

You think... No. I would not be drawn into this way of communicating with him. 'You think I can just choose to forget my wife and child? To forget they lived? TO FORGET THEY DIED?'

You choose to forget them every time you use anger as a barrier to grief. Most of your memories of them are inaccessible to you because you fill your mind with rage at their loss instead of love for their memory.

My head was spinning. I didn't want to hear this, if hearing was even the right word for how I knew that flaming horse's thoughts. I didn't ask for his advice, I didn't ask to be here, wherever here was. I didn't ask for any of this.

You did. In time you will understand but for now merely accept that you and I are here by mutual agreement. We have much work to do to ensure that you are in a position to fulfil your life's purpose. We will begin now.

The words that appeared in my mind were so unexpected, so out of the ordinary, so... unfathomable, and delivered in a way that was so assured and so all knowing, that I couldn't find the wherewithal to argue. I merely sat where I was in the grass under the hot sun, feeling confused and miserable.

You should eat and rest. I will return once I have located water. The horse turned and walked away. I resolved to be gone by the time he got back.

Chapter Five

$\mathcal{I}$ ate from one of many food parcels that I found tightly packed within the back-sack Devlin had left for me. Each time I took a swig from the large water pouch he had attached to one of the handles, I felt irritated with myself for feeling guilty that the horse had not yet found water for himself. I had never asked him to get himself into that state. I had certainly never asked for the ability to know how he was faring.

As I ate, I unpacked the back-sack and found two plain white shirts and another pair of brown breeches that matched the clothes I was wearing and also those that Devlin had been wearing. My anger flared at being indebted to him. I had noticed that he travelled light, so by the look of everything that now lay strewn in the grass in front of me, he must have given me all of his food, clothing, and hunting gear. The cook pot, bowl, plate, cutlery and some of the food packets were mine, but everything else was his. Well, he flaming well owed me, I decided. All of this was his fault. His and his horse's.

Instantly, I remembered the sense I'd had of Risk galloping to save me. My Bond-Partner – I gritted my teeth at thinking of him in that way – had brought my overdose to her attention, and she had not hesitated in turning on her heel and coming to me. She hadn't even wasted energy informing Devlin where they were going or why, she had focused all of her attention on bringing her Bond-Partner to me, knowing that he would know what to do when he found me. The two of them had turned my life upside down and then saved it whether or not I wanted to be saved. Then they had dumped me here, where I couldn't help knowing everything that had happened, because I was now bonded to a horse that knew it. I felt fury at them afresh for their unwanted intrusion into my life, and began shoving everything back into the sack. I needed to get moving before the horse came back. I would find my way home and live the life I had chosen, not the one that was being forced upon me.

As I repacked the clothes, I found a brown, wide-brimmed hat folded up between the two shirts. It was either the one I had seen Devlin wearing or more likely, a spare. Not having left the woods for years, I was unused to being in direct sunlight for any length of time, so I donned it and unrolled the sleeve of my shirt down my unbound arm to prevent sunburn. I heaved the back-sack onto my good shoulder and then realised I had no idea in which direction to head. I tried to think back to how I got there, but other than the sensation of riding Risk with Devlin behind me, I could remember nothing.

The horse. He would know where we were. I tried not to feel relieved at the knowledge that he was now swallowing long draughts of cool water. Once he had quenched his thirst, he rolled in the mud around the watering hole, then got up and rolled again in the parched grass a short distance away. Feeling entirely more comfortable, he moved back nearer to the water and nibbled on the greener, lusher grass there. I could feel from him that he didn't know where he was and he had no need to know. His only reference point, the only location that was important to him, was where I was. Not because he needed me for his survival, his comfort or his happiness, but because we were partners. We had lessons to learn, experiences to share and a life to live together.

Emotions that I hadn't felt for a long time flooded through me and a lump formed unbidden in my throat. Instantly, I swallowed, and then swallowed again and again until I had succeeded in forcing both the lump and my emotions away. I didn't want this partnership. The partnership I had wanted and the life I had wanted to live had been taken away from me. This bond that had been forced upon me could never replace what I had lost.

Change is constant. If you continue to use a single set of circumstances to define yourself then you will always be vulnerable to the feeling of loss of which you are so fearful.

GET OUT OF MY HEAD.

It is easier to be angry than to feel all of the hurt and fear that is waiting for you if you allow your anger to subside. But it is not helpful.

I AM NOT AFRAID. I hurled my anger at him, but it felt as if he reached out to it and welcomed it into himself, where it quickly became something else.

You are afraid. You fear life without your wife and child. You fear having to live a different life from that which you expected. You fear even contemplating the change of direction. But most of all you fear your emotions. You believe you must choose anger in place of all of the others lest they overwhelm you. It would serve you to feel those which you avoid. To learn their roles in your life as a human. Then you will be in a better position to find what you seek.

What I seek is TO BE LEFT ALONE. I began to march in the opposite direction from that in which the horse had headed. I stumbled over tussocks of grass in my haste to get away, and soon fell flat on my face, unbalanced as I was by carrying the heavy back-sack on one shoulder whilst the other arm and shoulder were bound. I briefly considered removing the binding, but there had been no herbs in the back-sack – presumably I was no longer trusted with any – to keep the pain at bay that I knew would result from my arm hanging loose. Curse Devlin, curse horses, and curse this place, wherever it flaming well was.

I got back to my feet, hauled the back-sack onto my good shoulder once more, and began to walk more carefully. Sweat poured off me and my shirt was soon soaked through, but I didn't dare remove it. I had treated sunburn in the past and had no wish to suffer it myself.

I knew I was being foolish, walking in the hot sun – I should have rested and then travelled in the cool of the evening, night and early morning – but I had to get away from that horse. I had experienced no pulling on my mind when he walked away from me, and felt confident that I could walk away, too, without it happening, so all I had to do was to keep moving and hope that his need for water and grazing would stop him following me. I looked around at the grassland that stretched for miles. Okay, grazing might not be a problem, but his need for water would stop him coming after me. I refused to consider the fact that I had a need for water too. I made for a tree in the distance, promising myself that I would stop for a few minutes under its shade to slake my thirst.

The tree was much further away than it had seemed and by the time I reached it, I was suffering. The strap of my back-sack was causing my sweat-soaked shirt to rub my shoulder and I was dizzy from the heat. I threw my load to the ground and collapsed beside it in the shade, lying flat out on my back in the grass. The branches above me seemed to be spinning as if unattached to the trunk of the tree, and I felt sick. Birds chirruped as they hopped between the branches, as if scolding me for being so stupid. I reached out and pulled my back-sack to me so that I could drink from the water pouch that hung from it. By the time I had finished, it was only half full. I undid the buttons of my shirt and peeled it away from my chest and stomach, leaving only my sling to trap heat and moisture next to my skin. Then I waited for everything to stop spinning.

I opened my eyes to the sound of munching nearby. I shot upright to see the grassy plains shimmering with heat in front of me. The munching continued from behind me and as I turned around, a white tail with a streak of black flicked around the tree trunk.

'So, I'm not the only one stupid enough to travel during the heat of the day,' I sneered. 'You'll have sweated out all of the water you drank, so you'd best be off again to find more.'

The munching continued unabated and the tail flicked around the tree again, presumably dislodging the biters from the horse's side on the way.

I got to my feet and rounded the enormous tree trunk. The horse was caked in light grey mud, and had an enormous dried dollop of it lodged in his forelock. It swung from side to side as he grazed, and when he lifted his head to clear his nostrils and then dropped it back down to the grass, the dollop hit him in the forehead with a clunk. He grazed on, completely unconcerned.

'You must know that I'm not going to accept you, that I'm going to keep running from you, so why don't you just give up now? Go and find someone else to bond with? Someone who wants this? Everyone wants to be Horse-Bonded, there are thousands upon thousands of people who would love to be chosen by you as a Bond-Partner, can't you just go and annoy one of them?' I said.

The horse stopped grazing and moved his front feet a couple of steps so that they and the front half of his body were turned in my direction, while his back feet and hind end were still turned slightly away. He peered down his nose at me and snorted, and the clod of mud lifted and then clonked down on his forehead again. I felt a smile twitch at the corners of my mouth at the ridiculous sight he presented, and then instantly frowned.

You yet choose anger over other emotions even when the emotion that wants to be expressed is joy, the horse noted.

'I don't have anything to be joyous about,' I retorted.

The horse continued to peer down his nose at me for a while and then returned to his grazing, his front feet still pointing in a different direction from his back feet. I shook my head. I was not only bonded against my will, but to an ungainly buffoon. I decided that there was nothing for it; I would have to move on again.

I did the buttons back up on my shirt, wincing as it shifted across the spot where the strap of my back-sack had rubbed my shoulder. That was only going to get worse without something to cushion and protect it. The thought flitted across my mind that there was a time when I would have had an ointment ready prepared that would have speeded up its healing. Those days were long gone.

Only until you decide otherwise.

'There is no decision to be made. I'm not fit to be a Healer, so I refuse to be one.'

Learn the lesson instead of focusing on the mistake.

'MY MISTAKE COST MY WIFE AND DAUGHTER THEIR LIVES,' I yelled.

You missed a symptom that would merely have warned you of what was to happen. It would not have enabled you to change the outcome. Your failure to diagnose is not the mistake to which I refer.

'What? Then what was my mistake?'

Concentrate on the lesson.

'Which is?'

The appropriate use of emotion. Your failure to diagnose in that situation was inconsequential but the reason for it continues to be a problem that you must overcome. Your talent for healing is unparalleled due to your unusually high degree of sensitivity to everything around and within you. Other Healers must concentrate in order to attune themselves to the ailments of their patients and the herbs with the potential to cure. You have an innate sense of both but your sensitivity is dampened by the heightened levels of emotion to which it also leaves you vulnerable. What you perceived to be the absence of a problem when your wife was nearing her time was in fact the absence of your natural ability to detect one. You have refused to heal those who need you when your only refusal should have been to heal in situations when you are distracted by extremes of emotion. That is the lesson.

'How dare you refer to what happened to my family as "a lesson"! And for your information, Horse, I experience extremes of emotion whenever people come looking for me, asking me for help that I don't want to give, so according to you, my refusal to heal them has been entirely correct,' I spat.

Horse continued to graze. *There is less strength to your anger than previously. That is progress.*

Without a word, I stormed over to my back-sack, pulled out a spare shirt and draped it over my rubbed shoulder to act as padding, then heaved the sack into place. I replaced my hat from where it had fallen while I slept, and strode out into the heat without looking back.

Chapter Six

$\mathcal{I}$ couldn't decide which angered me more – the fact that Horse had provoked me into walking in this infernal heat, or that I had no idea where I was going. For all I knew, I could be walking further and further from my home with each step I took. Well, as soon as I found more woodland, I would just make a new home for myself, I decided. At least if I had no idea where I lived, then no one else would either.

I made for a tree in the distance, and this time I allowed myself sips of water as I walked, instead of risking dehydration by the time I got there. My water pouch gradually became lighter and lighter, and a feeling of unease began to wash over me. Shallow streams and bodies of water would have dried up in all the heat we had been experiencing, meaning that opportunities to refill my water pouch would be few and far between. What if I ran out of water? I allowed a grin to spread across my face at the thought that at least if I died, I would have defied the scheming of Devlin, Risk and Horse. But I couldn't make the grin last, however hard I tried. I also couldn't ignore the feeling that something inside me had shifted since I had overdosed. I was no longer ambivalent over whether I lived or died; I definitely wanted to live. I wondered what it was that had changed.

Our bond.

I shuddered, unable to discern whether the thought had originated with Horse or me, but knowing it was true. Whether I had asked for it or not, being Horse-Bonded was having some sort of effect on me.

I steeled myself. I didn't want this. I would deny the bond that had been forced upon me until I was finally, blessedly, left alone.

When I reached my next source of shade, I turned to look behind me. All I could see was the heavy shimmering of hot air above the still grass that was shorter here than where I had rested, and dotted with wild flowers. I could see no sign of Horse, so I allowed myself to sit and rest awhile. I took my shirt off, apart from the arm that was still bound within my sling, and inspected the rub mark on my shoulder. It was no worse, but it needed cleaning with water that I couldn't spare, easing with ointment that I had no intention of making, and dressing with something more appropriate than a spare shirt. I sighed. Fresh air would have to do what it could for now.

I ate sparingly from my food supply, dozed until the sun was nearly down and then set off again into the cooler air of the twilight. This was the way forward, I told myself. I could walk so much faster when the heat wasn't sapping all my energy out of me, and I would consume less water. I would carry on until the sun was well up, find shade and then rest until the following evening.

The moon was bright in the sky, making it easy to see my way and illuminating the hordes of rabbits that hopped out of their burrows in the cool of the night to nibble the grass. Unlike those amongst which I was accustomed to living in the woods, they appeared to be comfortable in my presence. They weren't used to predators. At least if my food supply ran out, hunting for meat would be easy.

I stopped often to rest, but by the time the sun's rays broke over the horizon in front of me, I felt as if I had made good progress. The landscape was still dominated by grass with odd trees scattered about as if some giant had once upon a time cast a handful of seeds at random, but in the distance, I could see that the land undulated more and was dotted with bushes.

I was just approaching the tree for which I had been aiming ever since it had broken the flat outline of the moonlit plains, when I nearly stepped on something, the sight of which almost stopped my heart. With huge effort, I diverted the course my foot had been taking, and put it down to the side of the wildflower with bright pink, ragged petals that hung down delicately around the flowerhead like a shredded bell, its leaves lobed with slender fingers that made them look like little green hands. The flower was rare, yet I had made it my business to seek it out on many occasion, usually to make Bronwyn smile but the last time, three years ago, to lay on her grave. Her favourite flower.

Yesterday, I would have stamped on it, but I found I couldn't summon the rage that always served me when I needed to avoid feeling anything else. I sank to my knees, cradled the flower gently in my hands without removing it from its stalk, and began to sob. As my sobs turned into howls, there was a pounding of hooves and then hot air blasted onto the back of my neck. Horse breathed his presence onto me and, it felt, into me, until eventually, I quietened and stopped sobbing. Then he removed himself before I could summon up anger at him for his intrusion. Curse him, I couldn't even be left alone to grieve, I decided as I got to my feet. I frowned in disbelief. I had just grieved. Unable to summon the anger that usually shielded me from it, I had just felt that which I had been avoiding for so long.

I stormed over to where Horse was now standing, resting a hind leg under the nearby tree.

'WHAT HAVE YOU DONE TO ME?' I raged.

Horse closed his eyes and began to snooze with a total absence of concern.

I poked his shoulder. 'Don't ignore me,' I hissed. 'What have you done to me? I can't be like this. I can't... do this.'

You can. You must. Horse sighed a long, deep sigh. *You have done well. Rest.*

'Done well? DONE WELL?' I felt weak at my lack of control over every aspect of my life. I was stuck out in the middle of the light knew where, with an animal who always knew what to say to confuse me, who always seemed to be one step ahead of me, and was somehow changing the way I felt. Emotions against which I had guarded myself so carefully from feeling were spilling out of me at the slightest thing and I could see no way out of my predicament.

You see it. You have merely to accept it.

Never. I silently cursed myself for answering him via our bond and then marched back out into the rapidly rising heat.

It was a stupid thing to do and I knew it. I was exhausted, very low on water and could see no source of shade for which to aim. But I needed to feel as if I were in control of something, even if it were doing something foolish and dangerous.

I started at a sound just behind me and turned to see that Horse was following me.

'What are you doing, you stupid horse? It's blisteringly hot and you have no water.'

I would be with you. His dark brown eyes held mine and much as I didn't want to, I felt his love for me and his commitment to look out for me. The clod of mud still attached to his forelock swung from side to side as he walked. It had seemed comical when I first saw it, but now it irritated me. Before I could stop myself, I reached out, took hold of it and pulled it off.

'I don't need you to look out for me,' I grumbled. 'I can look out for myself.' I took a swig of water and a pang of fear shot through me. My pouch was now empty.

I know where there is water.

'You go and drink, then. I'll find my own.'

Horse merely continued to walk behind me. I turned to him. 'You haven't drunk since yesterday. Your need is greater than mine. Go to where you know there is water, then just keep walking, anywhere but after me,' I told him, trying not to look in his eyes. Sweat ran down his face in tiny streaks, and dripped to the ground, each tiny bead of water a threat to his continued existence. I flapped my hands at him. 'Go!'

He merely stopped walking for a few seconds, then continued at a slightly increased distance behind me.

'Okay fine, kill yourself. At least I'll be rid of you.' My bottom lip quivered as I said it, so I set my mouth in a hard line. I meant it. I did.

I walked slowly onwards. When I staggered, Horse appeared by my side. Without thinking, I put a hand to his shoulder to steady myself. It seemed like such a natural thing to do, to reach out to him. Through my dizziness, I noted that he wasn't sweating as much as he had been. There were damp streaks but much of the sweat had dried, making his fur stand up in stiff tufts. He was dehydrated and now that he was running out of fluid with which to sweat and cool himself, his temperature would quickly rise. He was in danger.

'Horse, go to the water. You'll die if you don't,' I whispered, my lips cracking.

I would follow you.

You don't want to follow me. It will be the death of you.

I felt his conviction that I would never find water without him. That if he left me alone, I would die. I felt his acceptance of everything that could befall him as a result of his determination to stay with me. Either we would both find water or neither of us would. We were Bond-Partners.

Anger flared in me. He had trapped me yet again. 'Okay, fine,' I croaked. 'Take me to where there's water. I hope it's not far because otherwise we'll both be dead before we get there.'

Horse turned to our left and I walked alongside him, my hand still on his shoulder. We hadn't gone far before I tripped on unsteady legs, fell, and couldn't get back up under the weight of my back-sack. My hat had fallen off and the sun's rays beating down on my head were causing it to thump painfully. There was a disturbance in the grass, and white fur appeared beside me.

You should lift your leg over my back and hold tightly to me, I was advised.

I didn't have the strength to argue. I felt around for my hat, replaced it on my head with a shaking hand, undid my sling so that both of my arms were free, and then did as I was told. Through the onset of delirium, I marvelled as Horse found the strength to heave himself to his feet with me and my gear on his back. I barely registered the pain in both of my shoulders as I clung to him and my back-sack clung to me.

The added heat from his body should have been unbearable, yet I found it oddly comforting. I leant forward, bracing myself against his neck with my hands so as to remain vaguely upright. As I weakened further in the relentless, all-consuming heat, I scented water. It wasn't me scenting it though, was it? I realised. It was Horse. I could smell it with his nose. He tripped beneath me and I almost slid off the side. I grimaced as my back-sack shifted on my shoulder, and saw in my mind's eye the layer of skin that had just been torn away. Then I croaked what would have been a scream if I'd had the voice, at the pain in my other shoulder as I hung on with what little strength I had left while Horse righted himself. I felt what it cost him to keep going. He was nearly spent.

When he tripped again, I went straight over his head. All of a sudden, I was underwater. Gloriously wet, cold water. And I was sinking. The cold rejuvenated the ability to think straight that the heat had sapped from me and as I hit the sandy, silty bottom of whichever body of water this was, I realised that if I didn't escape from my back-sack, the weight of it would hold me there.

Just as I was struggling to get my arm out of the strap, I was thrown to one side by a sudden movement in the water next to me. I could just make out a hairy white leg. I grabbed it with the hand on the side of my torn shoulder muscle, bubbles spouting out of my mouth in place of my scream. I clung on despite the pain, using not just my own strength, but that which radiated from Horse to me. I could feel his encouragement, his calm confidence that I would make it and I believed him. I stopped struggling and calmly felt my way out of the strap until I was free. Then I took hold of Horse's leg with both hands to steady myself, put my feet to the ground and stood up.

My head just cleared the surface of the dark blue water of the river that was flowing slowly over and around Horse and me, taking our sweat, our heat and our dirt with it as if washing away all the hardship of the last few days and leaving us to start afresh. I took hold of a handful of long, white mane and Horse stood fast in the current as I coughed and spluttered until my throat and lungs were clear of water, and then drank until I could drink no more.

When I had finished, it dawned on me that I would need the contents of my back-sack. I took a deep breath and, keeping a hand in contact with Horse, crouched down in the water. I was relieved beyond measure to find that the gentle current had let my back-sack be and it was exactly where I had left it. I heaved it up through the weight of water that seemed intent on holding it down, until my head broke the water line – and then realised that I didn't have the strength to do anything else.

Horse looked around at me, the tip of his muzzle just touching the water. *Take a hold of me and do not let go.*

I did as I was told. I wrapped a big handful of his mane around my hand and held on as he walked the short distance to the river bank, towing me and my back-sack with him. As I was pulled through the water, I felt the imprint of his instruction on my mind, and realisation struck me. He had not just been telling me how to escape the river.

Chapter Seven

*O*nce he had pulled me out of the river and up the steep bank down which he had tripped and thrown me, Horse dropped his head and began to graze the lush, green grass that grew there. His white and brown coat, now completely free of the mud in which he had previously caked himself, sparkled as the sun's rays bounced off the moisture that clung to each and every hair. The long, thick, white tresses surrounding his lower legs ran with water, as did his tail, which he flicked at the biters that were already descending on him, sending an arc of droplets into the air.

All I wanted to do was sleep, but I knew it would be dangerous to do so in the sun; I may be cool and hydrated now, but that situation could reverse very quickly. I settled for rebinding my arm against my chest and then emptying out the contents of my back-sack onto the river bank. The food packets were sealed and so, hopefully, still dry within. I squeezed as much water out of my spare clothes as I could with my one free hand, before laying them out under the hot sun, along with my hunting and cooking gear.

With my immediate concerns attended to, I realised that I was ravenous. I opened a food packet and was relieved to find that its contents were indeed dry. They were unappetising – a ration of travel bread, four strips of jerky, some very nutty biscuits and some dried fruit – but nutritious nonetheless. When I had finished eating, I stood up in my rapidly drying clothes and paid proper attention to my surroundings.

The river was wide enough that the deer I could see drinking on the far bank appeared the size of rabbits. There was only one river that size within a few days' ride of the forest I called home; I knew where I was. At least, I knew beside which river I was standing – the River Plenty was named for the reliable volume of water that it provided to its many offshoots regardless of the weather or season, including the River Gush that flowed past my home village of Greenfields.

I remembered following the Gush upstream to the Plenty once, when I was looking for new herbs with which to experiment. I had found myself in grassland very much like this, although it had been much greener then and the Plenty had been much fuller in its banks. I looked upriver. I could see the same undulating ground, dotted with bushes that I had seen in the distance when I had been walking earlier. I cursed as I realised that I must have been walking parallel with the river, albeit some distance away. So then, if I needed to stay in the grasslands in order to find the mouth of the River Gush, I needed to turn back and walk downriver, in the direction from which I'd come.

I reached down, picked up a pair of rapidly drying breeches and then slammed them back down to the ground in frustration. At least I knew where I was now, though, and what I needed to do; I would follow the river downstream until the River Gush branched off, then I would have my bearings and could head back towards the woods where I had made my home, leaving this whole sorry nightmare behind me.

Something pulled inside me, as if my gut had twisted around on itself into a less comfortable position. I ignored the sensation. Once I was home, I would be fine.

I felt a prickling down the back of my neck, and turned to see Horse watching me with interest, his lower jaw moving from side to side as he munched the ends of the long grass that hung out of his mouth. Then I realised that he wasn't just watching me with his eyes; I could feel him observing my thoughts and… something else; he was noting changes that were occurring in me. And it interested him that I was aware I was changing and yet still denying it, still fighting it. Too right I was. But sensing Horse's observations made it more real somehow, and even more difficult to deny.

'Devlin and Risk tricked me, and now you're doing it too. STOP IT, JUST STOP IT,' I shouted at him.

They did not trick you. They prepared you. Their bond reminded you what is possible. It touched you and carved a path through your anger along which I could reach you.

'So that you could manipulate me.'

So that I could help you. Already you are beginning to accept your grief instead of using anger to hold it apart from yourself.

'And you're making me do it. I don't know how, but you're making me feel things I don't want to feel.'

Do you think I can make you feel joy? Horse's sudden challenge was so at odds with everything else I had felt from him, that I just stood there, staring at him.

'No, of course not,' I snarled eventually. 'There are only two people capable of that and they are no longer here.'

And yet you choose to believe I can make you feel other emotions. I do not have that power over you and neither does anyone else. You indulge yourself with the belief that it is possible because it allows you to avoid taking responsibility for your own thoughts and emotions. Horse's eyes bored into me and I stepped back with the force of his rebuke. The thoughts that followed were softer. *My presence merely stimulates the part of you that knows of your purpose here and encourages it to remember its voice.*

Something stirred within me. It reminded me of how I had used to feel when I was diagnosing disease in my patients and somehow knew to look deeper than the ailment that initially presented itself; when I somehow just knew that a herbal preparation needed tweaking so that it would be more ideally suited to an ailment, even though the standard preparation had been used successfully many times; when I just knew that the recommended dose needed altering to levels that were deemed either ineffective or dangerous, because something inside me was so sure of it. Intuition, that was what it was.

The voice of your soul, agreed Horse.

The voice that failed me when it mattered most, I thought to him before I could stop myself. 'The voice that I will never listen to again,' I whispered, trying to mean the words but being prevented from speaking them out loud by the stirring inside of me that seemed to be gaining strength.

I felt as if everything were spiralling out of control. I needed to do the only thing that I appeared still able to choose to do – move.

The sun was beating down ferociously on the top of my head now that it was dry, and I had lost my hat in the river. I selected the shirt that I had been using to pad my rubbed shoulder, stood on it and pulled at it with my good arm, tearing it up the length of the back. I stepped carefully down the river bank, keeping my feet facing sideways so as to not overbalance or slip, and dunked the rag in the water. Then I wrapped it around my head, draped its other, dry, half over my shoulder, packed up my back-sack and hoisted it into place atop the makeshift pad. I walked past Horse, trying not to grimace at the pain on my shoulder where skin used to be. I sensed his calm satisfaction as he continued to graze, and the flare of anger I managed to feel towards him pleased me no end. I would wrestle back control of myself yet.

Chapter Eight

*T*his was better, I decided. Sure, it was still hot, I was still in need of sleep, I was still pouring with sweat and I still needed to drink often, but most of those things could be eased by a careful descent down the river bank to splash water over myself and refill my water pouch. The water was clear and cool and as it hit the bank and folded back on itself with a gurgle, it almost seemed to speak to me, to reassure me of its ability to sustain me as it led me in the direction of home.

Home. I thought of my tiny, fire-damaged hut with its sagging roof, bare earth floor and meagre contents. My table, stool and bed would all reek of smoke. I wondered if my food containers were still strewn all over the ground outside where I had thrown them, and decided that Devlin would have been sure to tidy them away. The man had probably fixed my roof and refilled my water container too, just to be even more annoying. I sighed. It wasn't much to go back to and I hated to admit it, but where before I had viewed it as my safe place, now I felt as if that place were somewhere along the bank behind me, and not even a place.

Take a hold of me and do not let go. The words didn't come from him this time, but from where they had become lodged, deep within me. I shook my head sharply, trying to free myself from them.

'Are you alright?'

I jumped and looked up. A man and woman in what I guessed to be their early twenties were standing in front of me, each laden with a large back-sack, and dressed in matching clean, white, loose-fitting shirts and trousers, and white sunhats.

'By the wind of autumn, you nearly made me jump in the river. Do you always creep up on people like that?' I snapped, and then frowned as I realised that there was no way they could have crept up on me in this flat expanse, had they tried. As they both stared at me, clearly taken aback, I realised further what a sight I must look with one arm bound to my chest, blood running down the other from my raw shoulder, and half a shirt tied around my head, dripping water down my face. Well, no one asked Mr and Mrs Squeaky Clean for their opinion.

'Um, I just asked if you were alright because you were shaking your head as if you were in pain, and you appear to be carrying several injuries,' said the man. 'Is there anything we can do to help?'

Those words, that had been asked of me so many times by countless happy, self-satisfied people who only wanted to make themselves feel even better about themselves by being the ones to sort out "poor old Adam", were the quickest way to activate my temper. I felt it rise and swell, and relished the feeling of strength it gave me after having felt so weak and out of control for the past few days. Just as I opened my mouth to batter the young couple with my choicest words, the woman looked past me and gasped, 'Ooooh, look, isn't he beautiful.'

I turned to see Horse moving at speed along the river bank behind me, his thick, black forelock and bushy white mane lifting and then softly falling in time with his canter. The long hair that swathed his lower legs swirled about as he extended his limbs, accentuating the length of his strides. He moved with a level of grace that was at total odds with his substantial build and weight. He was breathtaking, right up to the point that he was almost upon us, whereupon his elegant canter became an ungainly bounce on all four feet at the same time. He came to a heavy, snorting stop, his legs splayed out in all directions.

A smile twitched at the corners of my mouth as I watched the sublime become the ridiculous. I turned back to Mr and Mrs Squeaky Clean to find them taking a few rapid steps backwards in alarm. I allowed my smile to form fully as they gawped at Horse, who had moved close enough to peer at them over my shoulder, still breathing hard.

'He's...' began the man, and then didn't seem able to find the words to continue.

'So, you're, um, well, you're Horse-Bonded,' said the woman, looking from me to Horse, clearly unable to believe the sight in front of her. My smile broadened at the realisation that Horse and I presented a very different picture from the normal capable, self-assured image of unity and decorum that people had come to expect of the Horse-Bonded and their Bond-Partners.

'Oh, I'm flaming well Horse-Bonded,' I said. 'You are currently having the misfortune to meet Adam Belson, the most reluctant Horse-Bonded ever to have lived, and his Bond-Partner, Horse, who is, as you just saw, an idiot.' I started to laugh and was instantly horrified. I hadn't laughed in three years. How was this happening? My laugh turned into a horrible, manic cackle and the couple's eyes widened in horror. Then the woman frowned and peered into my eyes.

'You're Adam Belson? The Herbalist who had a breakdown and... er, who...'

I stopped laughing. 'Who what?'

Horse chose that moment to clear his nostrils. A shower of green and brown droplets flew through the air and sprinkled the two sets of bright white clothes in front of me. The anger that had flared in me dissipated instantly and my mouth twitched as the couple looked down at themselves in dismay. I was taken back to my mischievous schoolboy days, when I had enjoyed nothing more than carrying out a good prank with my best friend. I glanced sideways to where Horse still stood with his head over my shoulder, the picture of gravity and wisdom as he stood calmly watching the young couple with his large, brown eyes. I noticed that sweat had begun to drip from his face; he would need to get back into the river to cool down. As soon as I framed the thought, he moved his eye a fraction in my direction and then turned and launched himself down the river bank, landing in the water with a splash. The river may have been low in its banks, but Horse was a large animal and displaced a correspondingly large amount of water. I enjoyed the soaking myself, but Mr and Mrs Now-Not-So-Squeaky-Clean were less appreciative.

'I told you he's an idiot,' I said, not even trying to suppress my grin. 'He's done you two a favour, though. I'm wandering around in the heat because I have no choice, but stupidly, you appear to be doing it on purpose.' Something pulled uncomfortably in my gut, and I acknowledged to myself grudgingly that my current predicament was entirely my choice. Flaming lanterns, what was happening to me?

'There is no such thing as bad weather for travelling, only inappropriate clothing and lack of planning,' said the woman, bending over and wringing water out of her flared trousers in an attempt to unglue them from her legs.

'We're travelling to see my parents over in Smallbrook,' said the man as he watched Horse standing in the river, eating grass from the bank just below us. 'When it's hot, we take the longer route along the river, so that we can use the water to keep cool and hydrated. We've done it lots of times. Er, why are you out here, if not by choice?'

'To find my way back home.' Unwittingly, I glanced down at Horse, who was still intent on tearing at the lush grass of the river bank. I stepped back, the image of him suddenly too much for me to bear as I realised that my words had taken on a different meaning from that which I had intended when I began speaking them.

'You don't still live in the woods now that you're Horse-Bonded, do you? I heard that...' The woman stopped speaking at a nudge from her husband.

I scowled. 'What? What gossip have you heard?'

She scowled back. 'It isn't gossip. My brother and his wife came to find you. They wanted to ask you for help and you chased them away, even though my sister-in-law could barely walk. They said that you were living like an animal.'

'Well, if that's what they said, then it must be true,' I replied quietly. Flaming people, they were all the same – either nosy do-gooders or needy gossips. I could feel the embers of my anger being fanned by the avid look on the couple's faces as they hoped for more tittle-tattle to spread around.

There was a grunt and Horse launched himself up the riverbank, flinging water ahead of him, this time brown with silt.

The woman exclaimed loudly and turned away, brushing ineffectively at the brown water dripping down her front. The man merely looked from Horse to me with interest. 'Is he really just called "Horse"?' he asked.

'I have no interest in repeating myself,' I told him, 'any more than I have in talking to you any longer.' I made to step around the two of them, but the man stepped in front of me and held out his hand.

'But wait,' he said. 'It's been ages since any of the Horse-Bonded visited Manysprings, I need your horse's help.'

'Then feel free to ask him for it,' I snapped and pushed past him, taking enormous pleasure at the look of shock on his and his wife's faces.

'But I won't know if he's understood me and I won't be able to hear his reply, I need you to tell me his counsel,' the man called after me.

I walked on, expecting Horse's rebuke at any moment. I was astonished when he merely trotted up behind me and then slowed to walk beside me, still dripping.

'So you're not content with just sullying what it means to be a Herbalist, now you're dishonouring your responsibilities as a Horse-Bonded as well?' The man's voice carried angrily after me.

I stopped and turned around, but before I could say anything, Horse spoke in my mind.

You owe him no explanation.

I... I don't? I mean, no, I don't. I wasn't going to explain, I was just going to give him a piece of my mind.

Which would have told him what he wanted to know. Come. We will continue our journey.

Our journey? No. I'm going back to where I live in the woods, without you.

That is not the journey to which I refer. Come.

I turned away from the now dirty, wet couple, both of whom stood with their hands on their hips in outraged astonishment, and found myself walking in confusion beside Horse. *You made them wet and dirty on purpose,* I observed.

Their condition is merely a consequence of their proximity to you.

So you were trying to make me wet and dirty?

You were those things already.

Err, yes I was. I frowned. *So why did you behave the way you did towards them? I mean it was funny and all, but aren't you supposed to be helping people now that you've chosen a Bond-Partner?*

I am helping someone.

I gulped at the all-consuming love that accompanied his thought, and with great effort, pushed it away from me. *But aren't we supposed to help others? I expected a lecture for walking away from those people when they wanted your counsel.*

Rules and expectations are fabrications of the human mind. I am not bound by either. Neither are you.

Not for the first time, his responses to my questions were so unexpected that I couldn't help being intrigued by them. By him. I shook my head. What was happening to me? How was I going along with this? With him? I didn't want it, any of it. I didn't want to converse with him, I didn't want to be fascinated by him, I didn't want his thoughts in my head, I just wanted what I had always wanted – to be left alone.

The wants of your personality are not necessarily the same as those of your soul. When the two are in conflict you will experience discomfort and confusion. When the two are in harmony you will be at ease.

At ease. There was something about the words, about the way he placed them within my mind, that resonated with me deep inside, as if there were nothing more important than being able to feel that way. But no, wait, that would mean that I was okay about Bronwyn and Alita not being here. About the fact that I had let them down. I wasn't and I never would be.

We will rest, Horse announced before I could organise my thoughts enough to argue with his latest statement.

I looked up to see that a tree had become visible through the hot waves of air. I almost fell asleep on my feet in anticipation of the respite I would soon have from having to think and feel.

We will rest, I agreed, too exhausted to correct "we" to "I".

Chapter Nine

The call of an unfamiliar animal woke me. The last sight I had seen before I fell asleep was the flickering of sunlight as it defied the canopy of leaves above me to reach the ground where I lay. Now, all above me was darkness. The cool night air that had crept up on me while I slept was a welcome relief. My head rested comfortably on my back-sack and the flattened, long grass on which I lay cushioned me from the hardness of the ground. Despite one arm being bound to my chest and the throbbing of my raw shoulder, I was comfortable in the way that extreme tiredness tends to allow.

I could hear the faint rustling of leaves, the repetitive call of the night animal, and the long, slow, deep breaths of something else. I sat up and felt warm air on the top of my head. I tilted my head up and then looked off to the side slightly, so that everything above me was in my peripheral vision and therefore potentially visible to me in the dark. The moonlight gently rebounded off Horse's muzzle and hit the multitude of receptors in my eyes that allowed me to see in various shades of black and grey.

I craned my neck to the side so that I could see more of him. He appeared to be asleep, but the flicking of his ear at each call of the increasingly distant animal to her young, and the fact that I now knew, through him, what the noise was all about, told me otherwise. He was standing sentinel and had been since I fell asleep. Predators large enough to bother either of us were rare out here, but the instincts of his species would not allow him to fully sleep until there was another to relieve him of his watch.

How foolish, I thought to myself, but couldn't quite bring myself to be irritated by his stupidity. He had been standing guard over me, and the only reason I knew about it was because another animal had disturbed me. Horse needed sleep too, proper sleep, more than the light doze with which he was satisfying himself in its stead, yet I could sense that he was more than content to watch over me so that my body and mind could recharge. We were Bond-Partners. Members of our herd of two. He supported me so that as a herd, we were strong. He needed no recognition, no appreciation nor anything in return. He was just Horse being... a horse. Well I was awake now, and hungry. He may as well sleep while I ate and kept watch for a while.

Immediately, he folded down onto his knees and then allowed his body to gently collapse to the ground. He rested his nose on his front leg for a few moments, then with a grunt, lay flat out, his belly a large mound in the moonlight. He sighed and then was asleep.

'Oh, no worries, you're welcome,' I grumbled, frowning at his lack of response; his neglect to even acknowledge my gesture. As I began to fumble around in my back-sack for another food packet, I frowned even harder as I couldn't seem to find any justification for my irritation. Horse clearly had no use or need for manners in either direction and that should have pleased me, frustrated and furious as I had become by the way my fellow humans used them as camouflage for their refusal to respect my need to be left alone. So why had his behaviour annoyed me so much?

As I began to chew on a strip of jerky, I looked past Horse so that I could once again pick him up in my night vision. His belly rose and fell slowly and, it appeared, not without effort. He was a big animal and I supposed that there was probably a lot of weight exerting pressure on his lungs when he was in that position. I pushed away the thought that I could know that for certain if I allowed myself to have a sense of his body through our bond. No. I may have been forced into this position for now, but I wouldn't encourage it by exploring what being bonded enabled me to do. A little voice whispered that I could know about his body by tuning into it with my mind, as I had done so many times when diagnosing ailments in patients, but I slammed down hard on the voice, quashing it and giving it no opportunity to resurrect itself. Horse's behaviour towards me and my irritation about it – that was safer territory, I would ponder that.

I didn't want this bond between us and would escape it as soon as I could – I ignored the knotting of my insides at the thought – so whether he acknowledged my efforts to help him or not, I didn't care, I told myself. But something pushed at me, not letting me stop there; my musings had disturbed Horse's sleep and he was monitoring my thoughts, not letting me get past them until I delved further.

'So it's not enough that you interfere in my life when you're awake, you even flaming well do it when you're asleep?' I complained to his prone body. His breathing remained slow and steady. No one except me would have had any idea that he wasn't as dead to the world as he appeared to be.

I tried desperately to think about other things, but it was as if he kept moving in front of me in my mind, refusing to let me pass. Trapped with the lie that I wanted to be true, I went around in circles, reaffirming to myself over and over that his behaviour towards me was of no consequence. Eventually, I exhausted myself and could ignore the truth no longer. I had been irritated with his lack of acknowledgment because I had wanted his approval. Instantly, Horse let go of me.

'AAAAAAAAAAAARGH!' I shouted, holding my head in horror. I stood up, wanting to run away and leave my tormentor behind, but I couldn't seem to make my legs move; I couldn't leave him. If I left, there would be no one to watch over him. He wouldn't be able to sleep, to get the rest he needed. BUT WHY DID I CARE? This was intolerable. Horse was forcing me to care for him, to feel things I didn't want to feel, to face things I didn't want to face, and I couldn't seem to flaming well escape it.

I would wait until he was awake, and then I would push on for the woods, I decided. Woodland was not a comfortable environment for horses. He would have to leave me once I entered the trees. That's what I would do, I would force him to leave me. The knotting in my stomach was something to which I would just have to get accustomed.

I woke with the dawn and immediately cursed myself for having fallen asleep when I was supposed to have been on watch. Not that it mattered; Horse was awake and grazing nearby. By the look of the wet mud that caked his lower legs, he had already been down to the river for a drink.

His dirty legs were completely at odds with the rest of him. His white coat shone in the early morning rays of the sun, broadcasting his health and vitality. The large brown patches that broke up his white outline, camouflaging him in the plains in which he was born, were the rich hue of ripe conkers. The black of his forelock and streak in his tail was the blackest of black, refusing to reflect even the tiniest amount of the light that might weaken its effect. Everything about Horse was bold and extravagant, from his colouring to the curtain of long hair around his lower legs, the thickness of his mane and tail, and the sheer size of him. Everything except his soft, brown eyes. They were half closed at the moment, his attention concentrated on his other senses as his whiskers told him where it was safe to graze, and his nose and tongue told him which grasses and herbs to select. But I knew that when he looked at me next, I would see the same unconditional acceptance of me and my actions that I had seen every other time I had met his gaze.

I blinked. Well, I wouldn't have to see it for much longer. As soon as we reached the woods, he would leave me. He would have to. Horses spent as little time as possible in woodland, everyone knew that – they were animals of the plains, where they could see potential dangers from a mile off and had the space to run.

I finished the packet of dried fruit I had begun during the night, then made my way down the river bank to the water to wash my face and refill my pouch. The water was beautifully cool and I wished I could splash it up to my raw shoulder to ease its constant throbbing and stinging, but I knew that would just make it worse. I needed boiled water to clean the wound and ointment to soothe it and help it to heal. I had neither, so I would just have to pad it as I had the day before, and ignore the pain.

I felt Horse observing my thoughts and prepared myself to defend my decision of inaction when, even with a bound arm, I was more than capable of lighting a fire, boiling water and making the ointment I needed from the plethora of herbs with which we were surrounded – but he ventured no counsel. For a moment, I was surprised but then I felt his observation that all was well.

'It flaming well is not,' I called out to him. 'I have a torn muscle in one shoulder, the other is rubbed raw and I can't help making it worse with every stride I have been forced to take as a result of being dumped out here with you.'

Horse lifted his head and gazed at me as he continued to munch. Again, he offered no thoughts but I sensed that he felt no sympathy for my injuries. They were merely irritations to be borne, irrelevant in the scheme of things. Charming.

The scheme of things. The bigger picture. What was that, exactly? I wondered.

The need for the advancement of humanity. Life will not continue here for much longer without it.

It won't?

Horse turned his attention back to grazing. I scrambled up the river bank and marched over to him. 'You can't just drop that into a conversation and then carrying on eating as if you had just told me that the sky is blue,' I told him.

He ignored me.

'Horse, tell me what you mean? Please?' When he continued to ignore me, I shouted, 'ANSWER ME, DAMMIT!'

I shall answer when you ask the fundamental question.

'Which is?'

He was silent in my mind and I could glean nothing through our bond. I seethed as I repacked my sack and tied the water pouch to it. Life wouldn't continue here for much longer if humanity didn't advance? We already had advanced. We lived in peaceful communities. We cooperated with one another; those qualified in the Skills of the mind exchanged their services for goods and foods provided by those in the Trades so that everyone had what they needed. We lived in harmony with our environment, allowing it to slowly recover from the damage inflicted by the greed and excesses of The Old. We had the Horse-Bonded to resolve any disputes, using wisdom provided by their Bond-Partners. We had progressed immeasurably since the people of The Old annihilated themselves. How could we possibly be putting life at risk?

'How are we putting life at risk?' I demanded.

Horse barely registered my question before dismissing it.

I thought it all through again. We were peaceful. We cooperated. We lived according to our intuition, the very thing that had caused our ancestors to leave the vast cities of The Old before they were destroyed. We embraced the help of the horses, without whom our ancestors would never have survived. How could we be going wrong? I repeated the words over and over, trying to find the flaw in the ways of The New that could possibly be a threat to the existence of life. As I continued to repeat the words, I became uneasy. Gradually, I found myself substituting "we" for "they", as I realised that I was conforming to none of the ways that defined The New. Eventually, I knew which question to ask.

'How am I putting life at risk?' I whispered, afraid of the answer because I suspected that I already knew it.

You are a small part of an interconnected whole. When a small part agitates with enough force it cannot help but disrupt that whole. Your demonstration of how easy it is to revert to the ways of The Old opens a pathway for the rest to follow.

'So why didn't you just let me die then? You, Risk and Devlin? Why insist on prolonging my misery when I'm jeopardising everything the people of The New have strived for?'

The human race has indeed advanced but that advancement is precarious. The time has come for it to be rendered irreversible.

'So why didn't you let me go?' I repeated. 'Surely it would be a whole lot easier with me, the agitator, out of the way?'

One who is capable of creating disturbance to the extent that you have done is capable of creating harmony to the same degree. You are unusually sensitive for a human. This we have discussed. You hear the voice of your soul far more than most and as a result you are far ahead of your peers in your ability to provide not only physical but emotional healing.

'So if you can somehow make me into good citizen again, then life on earth will be assured? Because my sensitivity and intuition means I'm a good Healer? That's just ridiculous.'

As is your assumption that this undertaking concerns only you. You must become more than the man you once were because then you will be in a position to help those capable of finishing what your ancestors began.

'Become more than I once was? What's that supposed to mean?'

Feigning ignorance is a habit that does not serve you.

'And avoiding questions is one that doesn't serve you, but I'm guessing we'll be letting that slide, and just concentrating on my faults? Wait a minute, what am I even saying? I have no intention of concentrating on whatever you think are my faults. I didn't deserve to lose my family, I can't help how I feel about it and I'm going home.' I hoisted my back-sack onto my shoulder, draped my makeshift hat over my head and shoulders, and stomped off into the rapidly rising heat, leaving Horse grazing contentedly behind me.

Chapter Ten

$\mathcal{I}$ stamped down hard on a tussock of grass that threatened to trip me. How dared he drag me from my home, even enlisting the help of others to do it, tell me what I should do and how I should feel, and then, the final insult, tell me that if the people of The New reverted to the ways of The Old, life on Earth would fail, and it would all be my fault. "You must become more than the man you once were." What did that even mean?

Unbidden, memories flashed through my mind of being thrilled when new herb combinations I had prepared proved successful in curing the lingering illnesses – instead of merely keeping their symptoms at bay – of patients who had travelled far to see me in the hope of help. More memories followed in their wake. I walked the cobbled streets of the village of Greenfields, smiling at those who passed by in a hurry and stopping for those who had the time to chat. I was in my healing room, writing up patient notes with excitement as I thought of ways to further improve the treatment I was providing. I was collecting herbs in pastureland near the village, and Bronwyn was with me, placing each sample carefully in her basket as we discussed our wedding plans. I felt a pang of something that I didn't want to feel, that was too painful to feel, yet I couldn't seem to tear myself away from the memory. Bronwyn had been looking at me with love in her eyes as we chatted. Would she even recognise me now? I wondered.

I remembered Morvyr's words: "Bronwyn would be ashamed of you." I stifled a sob.

Do not block out your grief any longer. Feel it in its entirety for with it will return all of the memories that you have denied yourself. Horse flowed through my mind, jumbling it into one fluid mass of thoughts and preventing me from being able to close off the portions of it that I didn't want to face. He was like the barest whisper in the wind; so soft and insubstantial that I couldn't grasp hold of him to expel him. *Embrace your grief. Welcome back your memories of your wife and child.*

I can't. I flitted about within my mind in panic, trying to avoid the parts I had successfully closed off for so long, but which were now roaming free. *It's too painful.*

I am with you. You are safe to feel your pain in its entirety. You must. Only then will you remember what it is to feel love.

The words he had spoken in my mind when I had been at risk of being taken by the river came to me once again. *Take a hold of me and do not let go.* I found him still easing his way around all of the thoughts in my mind, and I did exactly that. I latched onto his calm strength and hung on for all I was worth as I allowed my thoughts to catch up with me.

Instantly, I saw Bronwyn, her blond hair soaked with sweat, her eyes half closed and her lips the palest pink in her ashen, almost grey face as she smiled down at the baby daughter in her arms. She died with that smile on her face. I remembered that now. She was happy.

I sank down into the grass and howled. Within seconds, Horse was by my side, his warm breath on the top of my head an additional assurance that I wasn't alone as I allowed myself to feel all of the shock, hurt and sadness of losing my family.

I remembered Bronwyn in the minute detail that grief had kept from me; the sound of her voice, the shape of her face, the wave in her long, blond hair, the warmth and laughter in her eyes. I remembered her reaching out to me in between her seizures, squeezing my hand

and telling me that it wasn't my fault. That she would be okay. I remembered the moment my daughter was born, how beautiful she was, how tiny her fingers and toes were, how her little face was all screwed up, how she had Bronwyn's cute, turned up nose. I remembered everything about my wife and daughter, detail by tiny detail.

When the heat began to affect me, the breath on my neck disappeared. The next thing I knew, Horse was sidling into place above where I sat, streaming with water from the river, soaking me and cooling me down. He remained in place, his belly just above my head, shading me from the hot sun as I continued to wail my grief out to the plains. As I continued to remember.

When I had finally exhausted myself of both tears and emotion, I felt weak and insubstantial, as if I had shed most of who I was, leaving only emptiness behind.

'I j...just w...want them b...ack,' I whispered hoarsely.

You cannot regain that which in truth you have not lost, Horse told me gently, interlacing my mind with his own, holding me together so that I couldn't unravel.

'But I saw them both die. I've lost them forever.'

It merely appears that way whilst you continue to take human form and they do not. Your soul and theirs incarnated together as humans for a brief spell. Now that the souls of your wife and daughter have relinquished their bodies your human interpretation of the situation is that a loss has occurred when in truth loss is not possible for we are all one.

'I am here and they are not. I have lost them,' I insisted.

There will come a time when you will know the truth for yourself. In the meantime you will need to find the courage to accept that all is well even when it seems as though the opposite is true.

'All is well?' I looked up to Horse's belly in disbelief. 'You got your way. I'm feeling all of the pain that I've spent the last three years trying not to feel. I no longer have the energy to scream and shout at everyone who crosses my path. But accept that all is well? When I'm here and my family are not? I'll never do that.'

You have achieved much. Rest. I will protect you from the heat.
Horse gradually, gently, disentangled his mind from my own, leaving a
quiet sense of love and assurance behind him. I lay down and within
seconds, was asleep.

When I woke, it was dusk. I sat up, water dripping from me. I was
surrounded by wet, flattened grass and four circles of mud; the run-off
from Horse's legs following his trips to the river, I supposed. He had
been as good as his word. I had slept practically the whole day out in
the sun, yet had clearly been kept shaded, wet and cool. Protected. I
frowned in confusion; that no longer rankled with me as it once would
have. It felt strange to be looked out for and it was still not my choice
to be close in any way to someone who was not my wife, but I no
longer felt the need to push at my bond, to try to hold it away. I didn't
have the strength. Despite my hours of sleep, I felt as tired as if I'd had
none.

The effect of your sadness, observed Horse. *It will continue for
some time.*

'How do you know? You who have never suffered loss because
you don't believe in it? How could you possibly know?' I challenged
him.

*Belief has no part in what we do here. I possess knowledge that
you do not. You would be wise to accept my counsel until such time as
you know the truth for yourself. It will save you much time and effort.*

'Fine, whatever you say. I suppose we'd better head on to...'
Where? Where was I going now that I had been browbeaten into being
Horse-Bonded?

To your home village.

'Nooooooo,' I groaned, slapping the ground like a child. 'I can't
stand them all there, with all their sympathy one minute and demands
on me the next. And I'm sure the feeling is mutual now, after how I've
behaved.'

That is why it is the perfect place for healing to continue.

'Healing?' I croaked, getting to my feet. 'Continued torture more like.'

You should converse using your mind. Your voice requires the rest.

'And I require the privilege of conversing however I flipping well please,' I replied petulantly.

I drank from my water pouch until it was empty, then climbed down the river bank to refill it before the light failed completely. I cursed as I slipped and slid down the mess that Horse had made of the bank during his repeated trips up and down to cool himself and bring water to cool me. I knew that I was being unreasonable and ungrateful, but I felt irritated nonetheless. The effect of my tiredness, I supposed, which, apparently, was the effect of the sadness that I hadn't even wanted to feel.

I sighed. Horse didn't deserve my irritation, not really. It wasn't as though he was affected by it, however, I observed as I reached the top of the bank. He was grazing contentedly, his long, full tail flicking rhythmically from side to side, keeping the biters at bay. He was the image of serenity – and not just the image. Tranquillity oozed from him in all directions, including down our bond. For a split second, I felt envious that he could feel that way. It was alright for him, he was just a horse, with none of the complications of being human.

Instantly, I felt his amusement, followed immediately by a sense of hundreds, no, thousands, of experiences. He had felt pain, hurt, fear, love, sadness, rejection, frustration, curiosity, loneliness, wonder... his reminiscing went on and on, giving me the opportunity to appreciate the depth of who he was, without allowing me to focus on or even remember any of the incidents to which he was exposing me. The whole time, his sense of serenity never wavered. Regardless of everything that had happened to him, and anything that would or could happen to him, all was well as far as he was concerned.

My head was spinning by the time he had finished. I sat down in the moonlight and opened a food parcel, not even sparing a thought for the fact that this one had let in water the previous day and the contents were soggy. I shovelled a handful of somewhat revitalised dried fruit into my mouth, and chewed thoughtfully.

How old are you, Horse? I asked him.

This is my fifth summer.

So you're four? Then how is all of that possible? How have you managed to experience it all in just a few years?

You are beginning to realise that your view of reality cannot always provide the answers to your questions.

Don't you ever let up? I mean you look content, you feel content, and yet you can't resist hammering your many and varied points home at every opportunity that presents itself, I complained, turning my nose up at the mouthful of wet traveller's bread that I was forcing myself to chew.

The opportunity did not present itself. I created it.

Give me strength.

Horse stopped grazing, and I felt rather than saw the intensity of his stare as his thought settled in my mind. *Always.*

Chapter Eleven

$\mathcal{W}$e plodded on through the cool night air. I had found myself too tired to be in a hurry and had waited for Horse to finish grazing, then without comment, we had taken our places side by side and continued our trek alongside the river. At times, a stray memory would hit me full force and I would sob for a while as I walked, all the while holding on to Horse within my mind and not letting go of him until the memory passed.

When the first rays of light streamed across the plains, casting long shadows in front of us that made me look taller and Horse appear even more physically imposing than he was, I heard the sound of water moving apace ahead of us. As our shadows gradually became less exaggerated versions of us both and I was forced to put my rag over my head and shoulders to prevent the sun's rays from burning my neck, I was able to make out splashes of water leaping into the air in the distance.

The River Gush – named for its conversion of the peaceful, meandering flow of water fed into it by the Plenty, to an urgent, ferocious surge – roared across our path. It was far narrower than the Plenty and its bed was lined with enormous rocks that hurled water between them, causing much of it to be flung into the air before rejoining the swirling, churning mass that made its way south towards Greenfields.

Horse and I turned in concert to walk alongside it. I squinted at a dark mass on the horizon in front of us, and realised that it was the edge of the forest in which I had made my home for the past three years. We would have to pass through it where it butted up to the river, but that should only take half a day, so Horse wouldn't be too long without grazing and the comfort and safety awarded him by open space.

I found my steps slowing and not just from fatigue; we were only a day's walk from the village where Bronwyn and I had made our home, and returning there was bound to spark fresh rounds of grief now that I was no longer employing anger as a weapon against it. All of the memories that I had held away from myself would come flooding back – happy, beautiful but excruciatingly painful memories.

Your memories are part of who you are. When you shy from them you diminish yourself. Embrace them. Welcome them back so that you can be whole. Feel the pain that accompanies them and then you will be able to release it. It is necessary.

I was too tired to argue. *If you say so. We'll keep going until we reach the edge of the forest, shall we? There'll be shade and we can rest more comfortably.*

I felt Horse's assent.

By the time we were halfway there, I was having trouble putting one foot in front of the other. The banks of the Gush were too steep for either of us to risk slipping into the turbulent current below, so I made do with drinking sparingly from my water pouch, occasionally offering to cup some water in my hands for Horse – which he refused – as we trudged on in the heat, both sweating profusely. My misery was added to by the blood now flowing down my arm from my abraded shoulder, and the pain that accompanied it.

I will carry you and your load, offered Horse.

You're as hot as I am.

But neither injured nor as weary.

It's okay, I can make it.

Then I will carry your load. Lay it across my back. I will not allow it to fall.

I don't think I have the strength to heave it up there.

Immediately, Horse dropped to his knees beside me. *Hold it in place as I rise,* I was instructed.

I laid my sack across his broad back, with the side where my clothes were packed next to him so that he would be protected from anything hard. I held on to it as firmly as I could with my free arm as he got back to his feet.

Support yourself against me as we continue. You are close to falling with every step.

I put a hand to his shoulder and was surprised to feel a little stronger and more stable, just as I had when I held on to him in the river. If I concentrated, I could feel his strength permeating through me from my hand, down my arm to the rest of my body and then back to him, as if by being in physical contact with him, I had somehow become part of him. *Er, thank you, Horse.*

He did not reply. He was focused on getting us both to our goal of shade that, however far we trudged, always seemed the same distance ahead of us in the sweltering, shimmering air.

When we finally reached the shade of the trees, I was relieved to see that the bank of the river there was shallower, as if it had been crumpled and trampled down. It probably had, I realised. This was a convenient watering point for the animals of the forest. There were fewer rocks in this part of the river, so it was less turbulent than at its mouth and there was a small beach of shingle, presumably deposited there following the action of the water grinding against the rocks further upstream.

I dragged my sack down from Horse's back, leaving a trail of foamy sweat in its wake. He turned and trotted down the shallow river bank, grinding to a halt in the shingle by the water's edge and sniffing the water before taking long draughts of it.

I sank down into the grass where I was, and allowed myself to drink until my water pouch was empty now that I had the means to replenish it. I used the rag that had padded my shoulder to mop up the trail of blood down my arm, then made my way to the river to wash it. I chose a spot downstream of Horse so that I wouldn't disturb the flow of clean water from which he was still drinking, then splashed water over my face and neck. I washed my rag and scrubbed the dried blood from my arm, all the way up to the wound itself which was now oozing more than just blood. It smelt terrible. I supposed that once I was back in my cottage in Greenfields, I would be able to clean it properly.

You can do that now. Everything that you need to clean and heal it is within your reach.

Except the will to do it. That's waaaaay out of reach.

Eat and rest then it will not seem so. I will keep watch.

There's no need to keep watch. I lived in the woods for three years and was never troubled by anything bigger than Squirrel. We both need to eat and sleep.

Horse's ear flicked towards the forest and back and I felt his unease. *I will keep watch,* he repeated.

Suit yourself.

I opened the last of my food parcels to find it – thankfully – dry. Devlin really didn't vary his diet much, I observed as I poured water from my pouch over the strips of jerky and left them to soak, having found those from the previous, water-logged parcel much more palatable. By the time I had polished off the bread, fruit and jerky and washed it all down with nearly a full pouch of water, I was feeling better. I undid my sling, noting with satisfaction that I could rest my arm on the ground next to me without it being quite so agonising as the last time I had tried it, and feeling all the more comfortable for allowing air to reach my chest. I nestled back between the roots of the outermost tree of the forest, and dozed to the sounds of swirling water and the tearing and grinding that accompanied Horse's grazing.

We could just stay here for a while, I decided. We had reached a level of accord where I could tolerate Horse's presence and our bond, while he satisfied himself by telling me how to live my life and then ensuring that I did it – that was enough for now, wasn't it? I frowned as I realised that I couldn't pinpoint the exact stage in our relationship that I had begun to succumb to Horse's "counsel" as he seemed to enjoy referring to his iron grip over my life. I felt him observing my thoughts as I thought them. Further, I felt his lack of need to venture an opinion. He had laid out both our immediate and long-term futures and had every confidence that that was what would happen.

I opened my eyes a fraction, feeling irritated, and felt a sudden sense of kinship with the drops of water I could see being flung in the air as a result of coming up against the rocks; Horse and rock were both as solid and unyielding as the water and I were subject to their influence.

I dozed on and off through the heat of the afternoon and early evening. Horse grazed his fill and then sauntered over to where I lay. He dozed alongside me, his head low, his eyes closed and one hind leg resting. It irritated me that he refused to sleep, especially since he knew I was only just short of being fully alert.

I came to with a start, immediately even more irritated that I had proven Horse right in being distrustful of my ability to remain awake, but then curious at the behaviour he was displaying and that had woken me. He was thundering back and forth along the narrow stretch of grass between the forest and the river, his paces exaggerated and the long hair of his mane, tail and lower legs airborne as a result. Every now and then he would slow to a halt and gaze off into the distance with a whinny – a shrill noise that went right through me and was so at odds with his size and bulk that it was almost comical.

I stood up, squinting in the direction in which he had been staring. The far bank was almost as low as the one on our side of the river. It gave way to a brief stretch of grassland that merged seamlessly into scrubland dotted with rocks and bushes, among which I spotted movement; I could just about make out a dark mass moving in our direction, leaving a cloud of dust in its wake. Before long, I could hear the pounding of hooves and shrill whinnies replying to those being emitted by Horse. I looked back at him and felt his affinity with the approaching horses. This wasn't just any herd of wild horses. This was his maternal herd.

As he watched his family approach, I felt the sense of him on which I had learnt to depend being absorbed by them all so that I couldn't make him out in my mind. *Take a hold of me and do not let go.* That was what he had told me to do, that was what I had been doing, that was the only reason I was coping with this whole situation in which he had put me, and now he was like a raindrop being reabsorbed by the sea and I couldn't find him. I found myself rooted to the spot in panic, unable to think, let alone decide what to do.

Horse stood still, facing the horses who had fanned out on the far bank to watch him. There were mares with foals, older, greying mares, youngsters of various ages and colours and a tall, black and white stallion. Horse's neck was rigid and almost upright, his nostrils flared and his ears pricked forward towards them all. He quivered as he looked down at the water and then back to them. Panic flared in me as I realised that he was considering wading through the deep, fast-flowing current to go to a stocky, brown and white mare with a black mane and tail who had made her way to the water's edge and appeared to be considering doing the same thing. She had to be his mother. They would never make it.

'NO, HORSE, NO! THE CURRENT'S TOO STRONG AND THERE ARE ROCKS IN THERE THAT YOU CAN'T SEE,' I shouted, and ran to him. He ignored me and put a front foot into the water.

I put a hand to his shoulder. His coat was sticky with sweat and he was still quivering. He suddenly looked smaller than he had before. I saw for the first time that his head and legs looked a little too big for his body. He was still a baby, really. A baby horse who clearly still felt a draw towards his mother. I was hit full force by emotion as I realised that I wasn't the only one to have been separated from my family.

Horse relaxed suddenly and took a step back from the river. He reappeared in my mind as the constant sense of reassurance I had grown used to being there, and I blinked as I once again struggled to see him as such a young horse. He turned his head and nudged me gently.

Your pain is your own. Do not allocate it to me for I suffer not.

Just like that? You're back to lecturing me? How is it possible that you can be such a baby one minute, and... like you are now, the next? And how can I not feel for you that you live apart from your family?

I left my family when it was time. Had I not done so by choice my sire would have forced it upon me. It is the way of my kind. Remember what you perceived when they welcomed me. I am one with them and can experience it any time I choose. I have relinquished nothing by being apart from them.

When you were one with them, I couldn't find you.

That is the reason for their presence here. To remind me to focus on whom I chose to be.

I frowned. *What, so your mother was testing you? Seeing if you'd forget your bond with me and go to her?*

She was reminding me of my choice. I chose you once, when I left my bachelor herd and came to find you. In so doing I focused my energy away from that of purely being at one with my kind. My mother sensed an imbalance in me. A part of me that had not quite adjusted to my choice. She gave me the opportunity to choose you for a second time. In so doing my energy has become more defined as that of an individual. It is how I must focus myself in order to be of ultimate assistance to you and your kind. She has corrected the imbalance. I will not see her again.

He felt no sense of loss whatsoever. No sadness, no hurt, no yearning for his family. All I could feel from him as we watched the herd drink from the river, three or four at a time, and then wander away, was a sense of renewed commitment to me.

A suspicion crept over me. *Was that little display really just about you reaffirming your choice to yourself? Because I'm feeling like I've just watched you showing me how you think I should be dealing with the loss of my own family.*

It is a human trait to assume that all that occurs is for your benefit.

Don't avoid the question. Was that scene to help you commit yourself fully to being my Bond-Partner, or was it to highlight to me how badly I've been dealing with my loss? I'm asking you a direct question and I expect a direct answer.

My mother sensed and corrected an imbalance in me. She also sensed an imbalance in you and did what she could to help you. All is well.

I frowned. *All is NOT well and it never will be.*

Never does not exist in the here and now. We are both here and now. All is well.

NO, IT ISN'T. Flaming lanterns, Horse, you think if you run my mind around in circles, I'll just give in, don't you? I don't know why I'm calling you Horse, I should be calling you Mountain, you're every bit as immovable. What is your name, anyway?

That is for you to decide.

Huh?

Names are a human custom. As such it is for you to look within me and choose a name for what you see.

How do I do that?

You should sit down.

Chapter Twelve

I sat down on the river bank at the edge of the beach. The backs of my legs brushed against tough, brown tree roots growing out of the bank in their quest for water. Here, unlike where I had been living in the depths of the forest, there were no dead leaves drifting to the ground from the trees. The leaves that danced on their branches in the breeze were a vibrant green, perfect for capturing the sunlight and transforming its energy into the sugars that would feed the growth of the roots towards the river for the water that was so lacking everywhere else.

Right, I'm sitting. What now? I asked.

By way of response, Horse blossomed within my mind, expanding until he filled it, and then expanding further until I was completely lost in a gentle, loving silence. It was as if I had stepped away from all of the turbulence, the drama, the confusion, indecision and insecurity that accompanied being human, and floated into a place of calm knowing. A place where I felt nothing other than utter, all-consuming peace.

Peace. Your name is Peace. It's... incredible. Bliss. It's the only way to be. It's... wait, no, this is wrong. I can't feel this way. I killed my wife and daughter with my ineptitude. I have no right to feel this way, I don't want it... 'YOU TRICKED ME,' I shouted, leaping to my feet and pointing my finger at him. 'You made me feel as if everything that happened was somehow okay. As if it's just something that can be brushed to one side, of no consequence. How dare you? You know that's not how I feel, but you tricked me into feeling it.'

Peace stood on the shingle beach in front of me, resting a hind leg and calmly watching me with his knowing brown eyes. *You asked for my name. I told you how to choose it. I showed myself to you in my entirety and you clung to the aspect of me that you need the most. The aspect that you will feel for yourself if you allow me to help you.*

'I DON'T WANT IT! HOW MANY MORE TIMES DO I HAVE TO TELL YOU? GET AWAY FROM ME, YOU'RE POISON.' I winced at the pain in my shoulders as I flung my arms at him. He merely stood watching me with that soft, implacable gaze of his. I saw the peace that I had felt and was drawn towards it, wanting to lose myself within it once more. 'NOOOOOOOO!' I screamed. I bent down and grabbed a double handful of shingle and flung it at Peace. He flinched as a piece went in his eye and the rest hit him on his face, neck and chest.

I felt his pain, his distraction from me and I revelled in it. Finally, I had found a way to stop him battering at me with his "counsel", his influence, his tricks. Ignoring the searing agony in my shoulders, I reached for another double handful of shingle and flung that at him too. He spun around on his heels, and I flung another lot at his backside. I heard the cracks as some larger stones made contact with the bones of his hind legs. The instincts of his species took over and he bolted away from me, into the trees.

I stood on the beach, cradling my arm as I listened to the sound of Peace crashing through the forest. As my temper receded and the manic grin slowly disappeared from my face, I opened my mouth in horror at what I had done. I felt my Bond-Partner's agony. There was still a small piece of shingle in his eye and he had numerous wounds where he had been struck everywhere else. All four legs had been lacerated by shingle and stones, and the injuries were being made worse as he bolted through the snagging, thorny undergrowth.

I couldn't reach him to tell him I was sorry, to tell him to stop and come back to me and I would make it up to him; all he was aware of was pain, terror and the desperate need to run. The flight response that served to remove him and his kind from danger would keep him bolting for some time yet. It would make sure he removed himself far away from the threat to his safety. From me. My legs felt unsteady.

I staggered back to the river bank and sat down, feeling revulsion at myself. All of the times I had shouted and railed at those who had insisted on coming to find me when I had made it abundantly clear that I wanted to be left alone, all of the times I had lost my temper and stomped around, waving my arms in fury until my tormentors ran from me, I had never been violent. Oh, I had made sure that my demeanour threatened it, countless times, but I had never physically harmed anyone. And it had never entered my head that I ever could. Now I knew exactly of what I was capable.

Despite the heat, a cold dread flooded through me and I shivered. I didn't cooperate with my fellow humans. I didn't help anyone but myself. I denied my intuition, the voice of my soul as Peace called it. I lived in anger, self-loathing and self-pity. And now I was violent. I had taken the final step onto the pathway back towards The Old and I would lead everyone onto it eventually. I could see that now, for, as I had so ably demonstrated, one deterioration in conduct led to another. Peace had told me that my behaviour was infectious. I had already infected those who had come to me for help with my behaviour, and if I didn't heal that damage, they would be the first to follow me onto the path to The Old. I began to panic. Peace had been right about everything. I had to fix the mess I had made, but how would I do it without him?

I got to my feet, manoeuvred my arm back into its sling and heaved my sack onto my shoulder, grimacing at the pain but feeling like I deserved it. I would follow Peace. When he calmed down, I would be able to reach him in his mind, to persuade him to turn around and come back to me. I would make this right. But what if he didn't trust me anymore? What if he... what if he feared me? My lower lip began to tremble. He had cared for me. Looked out for me. And I had hurt him in return, just like I did with everyone who got close to me.

Maybe I should turn in the opposite direction and run? Or maybe I should do intentionally what I had failed to do accidentally, and end it all? Take myself out of the picture where I couldn't cause any more damage? A churning in my stomach reminded me that wasn't what Peace wanted. He wanted me to heal. I marched into the forest.

It wouldn't have been hard to follow his trail even had I not been able to sense his mind with my own; he had left a trail of crushed and torn greenery in his wake and I shuddered at the drops of blood with which it was spattered. His panic had taken him roughly in a straight line, only deviating slightly to avoid the trees directly in his path. I could feel that he was tiring now but his terror and pain drove him on. My heart sank as I realised how far he was in front of me. I bit my lip and stiffened my resolve. I had caused this, and I wouldn't stop until I had made it right between us.

I walked as fast as I could, hampered as I was by the weight I was carrying and the pain it was causing. By the time darkness fell, Peace had thankfully also slowed to a walk. He was tired and sore, but he was also extremely thirsty, and I could feel him trying to scent water. Then he scented something else. He stopped and sniffed the air. There it was again. All of a sudden, a deer ran across his path, followed by another. Then I smelt it with my own nose. Smoke. It was coming from my left, but also from in front of me.

I let my back-sack fall to the ground as a cacophony of thoughts struck me at once. The forest was on fire. If both Peace and I were able to smell it, the fire must be huge. For it to be between him and me as well as off to my left, it must be being spread in multiple directions by embers as well as following its own path, meaning that we were unlikely to be able to outrun it. We would have to find water or a space clear of undergrowth, get as low as possible to avoid the smoke, and hope it went around us. Not me, I realised – us. But I could feel panic rising in Peace as more animals bolted past him. I couldn't let him panic. If he did, if he tried to outrun the fire in this tangled mess of woodland that would snag hold of him and impede him every bit as much as it had done on his journey to where he was now, the fire would probably catch him. He would die.

I began to run along the pathway he had left in the undergrowth, looking slightly to the side so that my night vision could pick the way out of the dark in front of me. I knew I was running towards the fire I could smell in front of me, but I didn't care. I was consumed by the notion that if I could just get closer to Peace, I would be better able to get through to him. *PEACE!* I shouted in my mind. *Peace, please stay calm. Focus on trying to find water, just as you were. You need to find water, get in it and lie down. There are lots of streams that run through the forest, and even a few ponds. Find one!* I tried desperately to punctuate his rising fear with my thoughts, even as I realised that although there were indeed lots of streams and ponds, many were running either low or dry because of this flaming drought. *PEACE!* I hammered at his mind but my fear for him was just adding to his own as he began to spin around, trying to decide in which direction to run.

I stopped running and drew in a deep breath, trying to ignore the fact that the smell of smoke was getting stronger. I had to calm down if I were to help Peace to stay calm and follow my instructions. It was too late. I felt him bolting alongside all of the other animals of the forest, and there was nothing I could do to get through to him. He was going to die and it was all my fault.

I staggered off to my right, the only direction that would take me away from the fire but not further away from Peace. I battled my way through the undergrowth, the smoke getting thicker all the time. I began to cough. I held my unbound arm in front of my mouth and nose and crouched down lower, which made it even more difficult to move at anything resembling speed. Soon, I could hear crackling behind me and realised that I no longer needed to look slightly away from where I was heading in order to be able to see; a warm, orange glow gave enough light for me to be able look directly in front of me and see in colour. Being able to use my day vision was hardly a good thing, I thought to myself, my own panic rising.

I was rapidly overtaken by deer bounding along at breathtaking speed as if there were nothing in their way, foxes tearing through the undergrowth alongside the rabbits they would normally have been hunting at this time of night, and squirrels leaping through the branches above me or tearing along the ground where the trees were spaced too far apart. They left me in their wake as if I were standing still, as did the birds flying up to the night sky in front of me, screeching their alarm to one another and to the world at large.

The crackling became louder, the orange glow brighter and the smoke even thicker. My eyes streamed so that I could hardly see and I couldn't stop coughing as I stumbled on, trying to stay below the worst of it. Peace wouldn't be able to do that. He was a big horse. A big baby horse. I sobbed out loud as I felt him tearing through the forest, faster than I but much closer to falling as a result of exhaustion, dehydration and smoke inhalation. *Peace!* I tried one last time, hoping that being close to collapse would mean his terror had less of a hold on him. *Peace, please, find water and lie down in it. Concentrate on scenting for water. You can do it, you can sense it through the smoke if you try. Find it, and lie down in it, please, Peace, please.*

I just about felt him register my advice and then I was tumbling. It was as if the forest floor had just disappeared and I was rolling head over heels, so fast that I couldn't even take a breath to scream at the agony in my shoulders, and then twisting to roll lengthways even more excruciatingly. I took in huge lungfuls of cleaner air and then smelt the pungent odour of stagnant water seconds before I landed in it. A deer bounded into the water next to me and then ran on without pausing, her panic taking her away from the only thing that could save her.

I was lying on my back in a pond that would, judging by how far I had tumbled, normally have been many feet deep, but in fact just about lapped over my thin frame, and didn't quite cover my head. I decided that it might, though, if I wriggled down into the soft bottom of the pond in which I had landed in such a well-timed fashion.

All is well. The words reverberating in my head were suddenly all that mattered.

Peace?

He had collapsed. I could feel that he was lying down, exhausted, as smoke drifted over him. He could hear the crashing of branches and weakened trees in the distance as they fell into the ravenous flames that barely paused to consume them before racing on apace to where he lay just a short distance from the water I could scent with his nose.

Peace, get in the water. It's right there. I know you're tired but you can get up and move just a tiny bit further and you'll be in the water. Please, Peace, move, I begged him. *You just have to get in the water and then you can lie back down. Please, for me?*

I cannot move.

Yes you can. Take a hold of me and don't let go. Do you hear me? You told me to do that, and now I'm telling you. I'm strong enough for both of us. Do you feel that? That's my strength. Take it and don't let go until you're in that water. Peace! Move!

I could feel the heat that was almost too fierce for him to bear as the fire got closer. No, that was me. The flames were almost upon me and the brief respite I had enjoyed from the smoke as a result of falling so much lower than the ground over which it stole, was coming to an end. I wriggled frantically from side to side, digging my way deeper and deeper into the soft silt. I took a deep breath from the shallow layer of air between me and the smoke that was now billowing down the steep bank towards me, and submerged myself just as the fire appeared at the top of the bank, in all its fury.

Dirty as the water was above my eyes, the luminescent orange of the flames still reached through it to me as they passed around the lips of the pond. Luckily for me, the water level had dropped too quickly for the plants of the forest to have yet taken advantage and spread down the pond's banks, so the fire had no means of reaching me but I knew the air would be thick with smoke that would choke me in seconds. I held my breath for as long as I could, and soon my lungs were screaming for oxygen that I wasn't sure the air would be able to provide.

I felt strangely calm. I had the choice of risking death by drowning if I stayed as I was, or by smoke inhalation if I took the chance and breathed the air above the surface of the water. How was I so sanguine about my predicament? I wondered to myself. Surely panic should be setting in? Yet I was calmly considering my options as if time were of no consequence and neither was the outcome of my decision.

All is well. I nodded my head as much as the silt below it would allow, at Peace's reminder. Yes, that was it. All was well, that was why I wasn't panicking – his words had touched the part of me that knew he was right. Peace. He needed me, I remembered suddenly.

I sat up, gasping, and was amazed to find that clean, fresh air filled my lungs even as it irritated my sore, smoke-damaged airways, making me cough. How was that possible? I shook my head, clearing my ears of water. Then I heard the wind. Not just wind, I decided, it sounded more like a hurricane as it belted over the top of me. I looked up to see fresh, unburnt twigs and branches flying in the direction from which the fire had come, their path lit by the glowing embers that accompanied them. Then the rain began to fall.

Giant splats of water landed on my head and shoulders and I opened my mouth to drink those that landed in it from the dark sky above. For the first time in months, I couldn't see any stars. I couldn't even see the moon. All above me was thick, black darkness, howling wind and huge drops of water that were steadily increasing in frequency. This was either the biggest, most fortunate of coincidences, or, more likely, I realised, the work of the Weather-Singers. They must have been alerted to the glow of the forest fire in the night sky, and sung up the mother of all rainstorms to put it out. The wind they had created had driven the flames back towards the parts of the forest that were already blackened and stripped bare, and no longer provided them with anything upon which to feed. Now that the rain they had summoned was quenching the embers and soaking the ground, the fire would have no chance of resurrecting itself.

Grief washed over me at the thought that there would have been a time when Bronwyn would have been leading the weather-singing. Not that she would have needed to lead it though; her strength would have allowed her to sing up a rainstorm like this by herself. A smile of pride stole across my face, even as I sat sobbing in a dirty pond in a rainstorm. It was because of Peace that I could smile. Peace! His name shook me back to myself. I had to find him.

I put my unbound arm behind me and tried to push myself up, but the silt at the bottom of the pond pulled at me, refusing to let me go. I leant forward and tried to free my legs, intending to curl them to one side and get to my knees, but they wouldn't budge. I lay back down and rolled from side to side until I had loosened the mud's grip on me, then tried again, this time with success. Once I was on my knees, I got to my feet.

The rain was now torrential. It hammered down on me, and I could feel the thick sludge that had been clinging to me and my clothes being washed quickly away. I couldn't see a thing, but judging by the fact that my head was the only part of me being battered by the wind, I deduced that I would have a bit of a climb to get out of the pond. I was forced to gasp in order to breathe as the air roared past me with so much force that I was unable to draw much of it in at any one time. None of that mattered. I needed to get to Peace.

I had lost my bearings completely. In which direction was he? I should just know, yet I found that I didn't. *Peace?*

He didn't respond. We had been bonded for such a short time, but I had become used to a constant sense of him; where he was, how he was feeling. I searched every last corner of my mind for him, but he wasn't there.

'PEACE!' I shouted as loudly as I could, setting myself off coughing again. The sound of both my words and my spluttering were swept away by the wind so quickly that I couldn't even hear them myself.

All is well. A forest grows back stronger for having come close to destruction. His thoughts were faint and insubstantial but the love and pride that accompanied them convinced me that I hadn't imagined them, and that his observation was about more than just our surroundings.

I knew in which direction he lay and I knew that he was unable to get up. He was injured, very weak and urgently in need of help. *Peace, hang on, I'm coming. I'll find you. Please, please, hang on.*

I felt him lose his grip on my mind as he slid back into unconsciousness.

Chapter Thirteen

*G*etting out of the pond seemed an impossible task. Water was pouring down the bare earth banks, making them slippery, and there was nothing to grab hold of in order to pull myself up with my one good arm; all I could feel as I cast about with my hand on the ground around the edge of the pond, was wet, rapidly cooling ash. I couldn't see anything through the dark and the sheeting rain and I couldn't hear anything above the wind.

My mind flicked back to the dream I'd had when I had accidentally overdosed. Then, I'd relished the feeling of my energy being sucked out of me by the mud that wouldn't let me move; I had been delighted at the notion of not having to struggle anymore. But now that I was not only standing in, but surrounded on all sides by energy-sucking mud for real, my mood could not have been more opposite. Now, I would fight against it with everything I had. Now, I realised, I had something for which to fight.

After several failed attempts to scramble up the bank, I decided to try a different tack. The mud was so soft now that I wondered if I could poke my fingers and toes into it, to gain traction. I tore off my boots and hurled them up and over the brim, hoping that they hadn't been caught by the wind and either blown back in again or carried off.

I poked the toes of one foot into the muddy bank at knee height, then dug in with my fingers. I put my weight into the foot that was dug into the bank, and slammed into the bank with the toes of my other foot. Their hold was good and allowed me to release the other foot and dig into the bank high enough that I could push myself over the edge onto the ground. Immediately, residual heat from the fire seeped up into me from the sodden ash on which I lay, warming me and almost eliminating my shivering.

Once I had finished another bout of coughing, I held my face up to the sky and allowed water to pour down my throat, soothing the stinging and cooling the swelling. Then I crawled around the edge of the pond until I found one of my boots, followed shortly by the other. As soon as I had them on, I began to walk blindly towards where I had last felt Peace. I was tentative at first, reaching out in front of me with my good arm and with each foot before putting it down, in case something tripped me or stood in my way. The further I managed to walk without falling, the more I increased my pace, hoping that I wasn't being reckless. I would be no good to Peace if I broke my leg or knocked myself out from running into the remains of a tree. I would also be no good to him if I were too late, I realised, and was soon almost jogging through the tempest that the Weather-Singers had created, only stopping when my coughing became too violent to carry on. I hoped that the fluid I was coughing up and spitting out wasn't blood. When I started on my way again, I had to hold a hand to the side of my head exposed to the wind, so that the missiles with which I was frequently struck didn't knock me out. I chose not to worry about the dozens of minor wounds they were inflicting on me.

By the time dawn broke, the rainstorm had finally passed. My boots were in tatters due to the hot ash I had scuffed up from beneath the wet, surface ash, and I was reduced to a staggering, coughing, bleeding, exhausted mess. I was also hopelessly lost.

The fire had been blown back into its own path soon after it had passed over me, and Peace had been further in front of it than I had been. I had reasoned, therefore, that the fire wouldn't have reached him, and that if I kept the wind coming from my right, as it had been

when I began to follow the sense I'd had of him, then once it got light
and I could see the boundary between scorched ground and untouched
forest, if I kept that to my right, I should, at some point, be able to see
Peace just on the other side of it. All I could see about me, however,
was blackened ground punctuated by charred, branchless trees and the
odd jagged tree stump. I cursed loudly. The wind must have blown me
sideways as I jogged, further into the path the fire had taken. Now that
the wind had dropped, I had lost all sense of direction completely.

I spun around repeatedly, trying to identify any tiny part of the
black, dripping landscape that I might recognise, or that might give me
some clue as to roughly where I was. There was nothing.

I was so tired that part of me wanted to just drop where I was, but
panic gave me focus. I had to find Peace. I had no sense of him
whatsoever. What if I were too late and he was already dead? He had
been weak before he had lain unconscious all night in a rainstorm. No,
he wasn't dead, I would know. I didn't know how I could be so certain
of that, but I was.

I sank to my knees and looked up to the sky that was slowly
clearing of the clouds that had spent the night discharging themselves.
Now that there were no trees left standing, there would very soon be
nothing to impede the sun's rays. What if Peace wasn't in the shade?
He had been dehydrated when he collapsed. If I were right and by
some miracle he was still alive, the sun would definitely finish him
off. Where was he?

Take a hold of me and do not let go. Peace's words almost seemed
to vibrate so that I felt where they had lodged themselves within me –
within my heart.

I leapt to my feet. I might not be able to find Peace with my mind,
but my heart would take me straight to him. He was my Bond-Partner.
The link that had settled into place between us joined us by far more
than just our minds, it joined us heart and soul.

I turned and began to walk, knowing absolutely that I was going in
the right direction. That knowledge gave me the energy to increase my
pace to a jog, and the ability to ignore how hungry and sore I was.
Bouts of coughing still forced me to stop from time to time, but at

least now that it was light, I could see that what I was spitting out contained no blood. My airways were irritated but not too badly damaged and, as it happened, increasingly soothed by the vast steam bath in which I now found myself as the sun's rays, combined with the residual heat in the ground, caused the rainwater to evaporate.

I poured with sweat as I continued to jog in the direction my heart led me, stumbling frequently as my boots gradually fell apart. The ground rose steadily and, just as I was beginning to wonder how much more running my legs had in them before they would finally give way, I topped the incline. I paused, panting as I looked down a blackened slope to the green of trees and undergrowth that stretched as far as I could see. My heart leapt. Peace was close by.

I stumbled down the slope and into the trees, instantly unsure whether the relief at finally escaping the blackened remains of the forest was worth the extra energy demanded by negotiating the undergrowth. I came to an area where it had been flattened. Peace had lain here when he first collapsed, I could feel it. I had sent him every bit of strength I could muster to enable him to get up and reach the water that he had scented close by, and it appeared that he had managed it. I followed the trail of ripped undergrowth and blood until I found him lying prone, his head drooping over the bank of a stream that was only a few paces wide and so shallow that it would barely reach my shins. It would never have saved him from the fire, but it had kept a nearby oak tree densely packed with leaves, and sustained a thick mass of brambles, both of which had sheltered Peace from the worst of the storm and from the heat of the sun as he lay beneath the former and in the lee of the latter.

My heart thumped almost painfully in my chest as I dropped down into the stream and crouched beneath Peace's head, cradling it in my lap. I stroked his cheek with a shaking hand, feeling hollow inside, as if the greater part of me had just fallen out and disappeared. I wanted to sob, yet I couldn't. All I could do was stare at my horse in disbelief at what I had done.

Now that his mind didn't assure mine of his wisdom and competence, he looked once again like the very young horse he was. A baby horse, covered in blood. A line of it ran from his nostrils and dripped into the stream. It pooled around his eye, which was also swollen, I assumed due to the piece of shingle that must still be lodged in its corner. It matted the hair around the many gashes on all four legs and oozed, along with other fluids, from several large burns on his back and one on his ear, presumably where embers had been flung ahead of the fire and landed on him as he bolted. Blood also ran from the deep, open wounds on the back of his hind legs, caused by my stoning of him.

Despite all of his wounds, it was his breathing that scared me the most. In place of the long, slow breaths of a healthy horse were rapid, shallow wheezes. Peace had inhaled smoke from the fire as he ran and then, unlike me who had found relief in the depression of the pond and then its water, he had continued to breathe it after he had collapsed and until the wind had blown it away. The lining of his airway would be far more damaged and swollen than mine. If the swelling continued, his airway would collapse and he would lose the ability to breathe at all. I needed a Tissue-Singer but by the time I got my bearings, made it back to Greenfields and persuaded one to come back with me, it would be too late. I had to do something now.

I looked around me for the hollow reeds that often grew along the banks of streams and rivers, thinking that I could maybe feed one or two down Peace's throat to keep his windpipe open and buy me some time. I refused to listen to the voice inside that reminded me it wouldn't just be his throat and windpipe that were inflamed; the lining of his lungs would be too. I couldn't think of that, I had to focus on what I could do and hope it would be enough. The alternative was too painful to bear.

My heart sank. There were no reeds in sight. My eyes rested instead upon what looked like an old, wooden bucket whose hoops were missing. Its panels were falling outwards and away from one another as a result, and one appeared rotten through. It was my old bucket. When it had developed a leak months ago, I had taken the hoops off it to use for a new one, and then hurled it away from me in disgust.

I stood up, ignoring the protests of my legs as I straightened them. My surroundings fell into place. The spot where I fetched water would be just downstream from here, and the exact distance I could hurl a bucket. So, my hut would be just over there. Somehow, Peace had managed to collapse only a short walk from my home. Not that it helped, for there was little there; Devlin had made sure of that when he packed up my stuff into the back-sack that would now have been burnt to cinders. I knew exactly where there was a dense patch of the reeds I needed – a day's walk downstream from here. Peace didn't have two days. I doubted he had two hours.

To have ended up so close to the place that gave me the best chance of being able to help to Peace, and then to realise it was of no help at all, was worse than being lost. I sank back down into the stream, letting it flow over and around me as I sobbed and coughed my guilt and remorse into Peace's thick, black forelock. My sobs turned into wails and then into shouts and screams that irritated my own airways further and made my coughing much worse. If Peace was going to die, then I was going with him. I was a blight on humankind and I had no chance of being otherwise without him.

A voice punctuated my screams. 'Adam? Oh, thank goodness, Adam, is that really you?'

I looked up to the bank to see Bronwyn peering down at me.

Chapter Fourteen

I blinked. Bronwyn couldn't be here. I was hallucinating, that was it; I had finally succumbed to exhaustion, hunger and the aftereffects of smoke inhalation and I was seeing a vision of the person I needed the most. I buried my face back into Peace's forelock and sobbed. It wouldn't be long now. Soon, we would both leave the bodies that I had wrecked. Unless – maybe we were already dead?

There was a splash beside me and then the light pressure of a hand on my shoulder. I flinched and looked up to see Bronwyn's brown eyes looking concernedly into my own.

'Adam, let me help you and... whoever this is.' The woman had Bronwyn's eyes, but spoke with Morvyr's voice.

'Morvyr? How can you be here?' I croaked.

There was another splash and a broad face that I recognised as Felin's appeared over his wife's shoulder. 'She's here because she insisted that we leave home at dawn to come and see if you were alive, dead, or injured and in need of help,' he said. 'Not that you deserve it.'

I looked back at Peace and slowly shook my head. 'You don't know the half of it,' I said sadly. All of a sudden, my brain caught up with what was happening. Morvyr was here. Morvyr was a Tissue-Singer. 'Please, Morvyr, please help Peace, he's dying,' I begged her.

She nodded. 'You both are. He's much closer to it than you are, though, so I'll help him first.'

'Morvyr, you can't give too much of yourself. Think of the baby,' Felin warned, his dark eyes full of concern.

Morvyr took her hand from my shoulder and rested it on his arm. 'Always, love. I'll do what needs to be done to get these two out of danger and then I'll rest before healing them further.'

'You don't need to heal me. Felin's right, I don't deserve it,' I said, barely managing more than a whisper. 'Please, do everything you can for Peace before you need to rest. I'll stay here and support his head.'

'No, you'll let Felin help you out of there, so that you can rest while I work on... Peace, is it?' Morvyr said firmly but kindly.

I shook my head emphatically. 'No. I'm not leaving him.'

Strong arms appeared under my armpits and then Felin heaved me to my feet, leaving Peace's head to flop back over the bank. I struggled, but Felin was a Baker and had the strong arms and shoulders typical of those in his occupation. I would have been no match for him had I been fit and healthy, let alone in my present condition.

'I'm not leaving him.' I coughed violently and then began to sob again. 'It's my fault he's like this. I can't leave him. I can't.'

'Adam, calm down,' Morvyr said gently. 'Felin, set him down on the bank there, next to Peace. Okay, Adam? Will that be okay?'

I nodded. 'Thank you. Yes.'

I was hauled up the bank and then lowered to the ground beside Peace's rump. I put a shaking hand to a patch of white fur that had been beaten into clumps by the overnight rain. The tree and brambles may have sheltered him from most of it, but this part of him protruded past both. At least there was a part of him, however small, that wasn't streaked with blood, I thought to myself and began to sob again.

'Morvyr will save the horse. And you. You know that, don't you?' Felin said gruffly, crouching in front of me, his dark, almost black eyes scrutinising my own from behind the ringlets of black, curly hair that hung down in front of them.

I nodded as Morvyr began to hum. 'She'll save him,' I agreed, and passed out.

The sun was just sinking behind the tree tops when I came to. I sat up to find myself bare chested, my arm newly bound across my chest with what appeared to be the shirt I had been wearing. Despite the heat, I was shivering. I was in a considerable amount of pain and I was covered in flies. I immediately pushed my discomfort to one side. Peace was the only one who mattered.

His huge, white and brown body lay next to me, in the same position as it had been when I passed out. I leapt to my feet and went to his head to find that it now rested upon a pillow of branches that had been laid across the stream, lashed together with vines and covered in soft moss. He was breathing normally. I knelt on the side of the pillow and lowered my hand to just in front of his nostrils, so that I could satisfy myself that I wasn't imagining the sound of him drawing air into his lungs in long, deep breaths, and then expelling it just as easily. Relief flooded through me as I felt the warmth and strength of his breath on the back of my hand. It was only as I stroked his face that I realised I was breathing normally too. Curse Morvyr, I had told her to concentrate on healing Peace.

A quick pinch of his skin that took too long to disappear told me he was very dehydrated. I stood back and took an inventory of the rest of his body. His eye was still swollen, but it looked as if it had been cleaned and it was no longer bleeding. It appeared that there had been some sort of attempt to clean all of the injuries on his exposed side, his back and his legs, but they were nowhere near clean enough and they were jammed full with flies. The shallower wounds should have been smeared with healing ointment and fly repellent by now, and the deeper ones should have been packed with poultice to draw out potential infection. This wasn't good enough. I had been out cold for hours, what on earth had Felin and Morvyr been doing, to have given Peace's wounds so little attention? He needed far better care, otherwise infection could still take him from me. Or me from him, I realised, for the first time allowing myself to pay attention to the pain of my own wounds as I swatted at all the flies swarming around them.

I had cuts and bruises down my right side, inflicted by the unseen missiles hurled at me by the wind as I had run through the night. A couple of the cuts were deep. Like Peace's injuries, the worst of the blood and dirt had been cleaned away, but they would soon be infected. I had shallow scratches and deeper lacerations from where the undergrowth had torn at my legs, and I was surprised to see that, like Peace, I had several burns which had gone unnoticed as I fled from the fire but which were making themselves very painfully obvious now. The raw sore on my shoulder was the worst of all, though. I winced as I remembered the fetid water in which I had immersed myself in order to survive the fire. It had certainly served that purpose, but judging by the shivering that was rapidly taking me over, it had made my already infected shoulder much, much worse and the flies at which I was now slapping manically wouldn't be helping either.

I turned irritably at the dull thump of footsteps on the soft forest floor. Felin was approaching with something draped over one arm.

'Here,' he said, 'put this around your shoulders, you're feverish.' He handed me an armful of greenery. 'It's ferns woven together and then interwoven with moss, it's the best I can do. We brought food, water and some basic herbal preparations with us, but we didn't think to bring blankets or clothes. What happened to all your stuff? We found a few bits of rusty cutlery lying around and a beaker hanging in a bush, but that's it. No clothes, food or cooking gear. What happened, Adam?'

I took the improvised blanket and did as I was told, ignoring the extra pain it inflicted on my raw shoulder. 'Peace, that's what happened. He made me go to him. I didn't want to, I tried to avoid it, but he had help from another Horse-Bonded.'

'Another Horse-Bonded? What do you mean another... wait,

you're Horse-Bonded? You?'

I glared at him. 'Yes, me.'

'So Peace isn't just a horse who got himself trapped in the forest and injured by the fire, he's your Bond-Partner?'

'Yes, he is. He's my Bond-Partner, and he could still die. I can see that you and Morvyr have helped him a bit, but it isn't enough. His wounds need cleaning more thoroughly and then poulticing. Then they need healing ointments, particularly the burns. I would have thought you would already have left for Greenfields to fetch a H... Herbalist?' My teeth began to chatter.

'You're welcome,' said Felin, putting his hands to his hips. 'Being Horse-Bonded may have taken the edge off your temper but it hasn't reminded you of your manners, has it?'

'Manners are an indulgence I'll be able to enjoy once I know Peace will be okay,' I snapped. 'Why isn't he awake? I can hear his breathing is back to normal. We need him awake so that we can get him to drink.'

'He has woken a couple of times, and has drunk from the bucket that we found by your water barrel. It's now in the stream just below his head, full and waiting for when he wakes again. Morvyr did as much as she could to get you both out of danger before she was forced to rest, and even then she didn't rest for long because she insisted on helping me to clean the two of you up. And we're well aware of the need for a Herbalist. It's just as well there's one already here, isn't it?' Felin's furious glare should have warned me to choose my next words carefully, but I hadn't been capable of that when it was just Peace's health praying on my mind. Now that Felin had poked at the wound of mine that was the deepest and by far the most painful, it was impossible.

'Clean? Is that what you call clean?' I said, pointing at Peace. 'You don't just clean around wounds, you have to get all of the dirt OUT of them. He needs a proper Herbalist, and you should have been well on your way back to Greenfields to fetch one by now. You've always been a bit slow, but I didn't think you were lazy as well.'

Felin's enormous hand clasped my neck and propelled me

backwards, ramming me against the tree that sheltered Peace. All the air was knocked out of my lungs and I gasped for breath.

'Let me make one thing very, very clear to you,' Felin said between his teeth. 'Morvyr has tolerated your vileness for the past three years because she wants to believe that the brother-in-law she loves will one day come back, and she believes she owes it to her sister's memory not to give up on you until you do. I have neither her patience nor her beliefs. I came with her because she was adamant that she had to make sure you were alright and there was no way I was going to let her travel or suffer your abuse on her own any longer. She's done everything she can for you and your horse, and she'll no doubt do a whole lot more as soon as she's able, whether I want her to or not. So here is how it's going to be. You are going to agree to show her courtesy and gratitude, or I am going to bash your head against this tree, throw you in the stream and leave you there. Got it?'

'Felin? Felin, put him down, what on earth do you think you're doing?' Morvyr appeared and began to wrestle Felin's arm away from my neck. He instantly released me, and I dropped to the ground, gasping and shivering, beside a pile of sandwiches and a wooden beaker full to the brim with what smelt like a herbal preparation.

'Those are for you, Adam, you need to eat,' Morvyr said. 'Felin, what's got into you? You won't swat flies, yet you nearly throttled Adam.'

'Someone has to stand up to him. His behaviour towards you, towards everyone for that matter, is contemptible and you've all taken it from him for long enough.'

'And you think that standing up to him means choking him? I never would have believed it of you...'

Morvyr's words swept over me as my shivering became a hundred times worse – and not because of my fever. Peace's counsel came back to me, word by excruciatingly painful word: *You are a small part of an interconnected whole. When a small part agitates with enough force it cannot help but disrupt that whole. Your demonstration of how easy it is to revert to the ways of The Old opens a pathway for the rest to follow.*

Everything of which Peace had warned me was happening, right in front of me. Felin – whom I had known ever since I had moved to Greenfields in the hope of courting Bronwyn – was one of the mildest men I had ever met and yet he had employed violence against me. Morvyr was every bit as kind and loving as her sister and I doubted that she and her husband had ever argued, yet their voices were steadily rising as they continued to disagree about Felin's treatment of me.

I managed to get to my feet. 'Stop ar...arguing,' I stammered.

'I NEVER ASKED YOU TO COME OUT HERE WITH ME. I'M MORE THAN CAPABLE OF WALKING BY MYSELF, AND OF HANDLING ADAM. I'M PREGNANT, NOT ILL,' Morvyr shouted.

'SOMETIMES, I THINK YOU CARE MORE ABOUT HIM THAN ABOUT ME,' Felin retorted and turned as if to walk away.

'ST...STOP!' I managed to shout, my teeth now chattering furiously. 'Please, F...Felin, Morvyr, stop arguing. I'm s...sorry. This is all my f...fault. I'm a d...dreadful person, I know th...that. P... Peace is trying to h...help me not to be. He's very sp...special and I've hurt him even m...more than I've h...hurt y...you b...both. Don't let me h...hurt you anymore. I'm s...sorry. So, so s...sorry.'

Morvyr turned to me, her soft, brown eyes, so reminiscent of Bronwyn's, searching my own. 'You're coming back to us,' she whispered eventually. 'I can just about see you in your eyes again. You're coming back. And Peace is trying to help you? How is he doing that?'

'He's m...my B...Bond-Partner.'

'Your Bond-Partner? You mean he's with you? So you didn't just find him in the fire and bring him home, then? You're... you're...'

'Horse-Bonded.' I nodded. 'And P...Peace isn't just my Bond-P...Partner. He's my h...heart. He's my...my... he's my...' my teeth were chattering so much that I stopped and tried to clamp them together.

'Your what, Adam? What is he?' asked Morvyr gently.

'He's m...my life now,' I managed to say. 'He's my way f... forward. I'm s...sorry for my b...behaviour, Felin. I'm just so w...

worried about h…him. He's h…hurt, it's all my f…fault and I t…took it out on y…you.'

Morvyr looked back at Felin, whose face softened. He gave a short nod in my direction.

'Sit down, Adam, before you fall down,' he said. 'Eat the food Morvyr's brought you and while you're doing that, I'll go back to your cookfire to get the next beaker of water, which should be boiling about now. It's lucky we found it, it's the only metal container we have. It's small, so it's taking us a long time to boil enough water to clean all of your and Peace's wounds properly, but we're slowly getting there. While you're eating, you can think about which herbs you want us to gather so you can make the poultices and ointments that Peace needs.' His tone left no room for discussion, and I didn't have it in me to argue anyway, so I did as I was told. He turned to go.

'Um, Felin?' Morvyr called out uncertainly.

There was a pause before he answered, 'Yes, love?'

'Please would you have another sweep around the cookfire while you're there, in case more leaves have dropped? One forest fire is plenty to be going on with.'

'Will do.'

Morvyr sank down beside me and handed me the wooden beaker. I noticed that the sleeves of her blouse were missing, torn off at the shoulder. She followed my gaze. 'We've been using them to clean Peace's wounds. He's beautiful, Adam, such a gentle soul. I'm so happy for you.' She nodded at the beaker in my hands. 'Drink that, it'll bring down your fever. Oh, why am I telling you that? You'll know what it is by the smell, and knowing you, you can identify each and every herb in it, even though it isn't one of your preparations.'

I took a long draught of it and shuddered. 'It's d…disgusting. Would have been b…better with h…honey.'

Morvyr's face dropped. I just couldn't seem to help myself. How had I come so far from the amiable, likeable man I used to be, to one who couldn't pass more than one sentence without being objectionable? 'I'm s…sorry. Peace tells me I need to be more than the m…man I once was, but I can't even see how to be h…half of him.'

Morvyr managed a smile. 'Well, at least your shivering's calming down, we'll take one improvement at a time, shall we? Keep drinking, Adam, and then eat. I need to sing your shoulder muscle back to health and then we'll tackle your other shoulder. You're going to need your strength.'

I took another draught. 'Don't worry about me, please just help me to get Peace better.'

Morvyr looked over at my unconscious horse. 'He's stable for now,' she said. 'I've healed his throat, his windpipes and his lungs but I don't dare sing his wounds back together, I'll just trap infection inside. My best chance of helping him further is to get you right. It's your help he needs now.'

'I'm not a Herbalist anymore, Morvyr, you know that,' I said, unable to help my voice from sharpening. 'I won't let Peace down the way I did Bronwyn and Alita. He needs a proper, practising Herbalist. Just not the one who prepared this concoction I'm drinking, it's crude and it's foul.'

'You are a proper Herbalist, and the best there is, Adam,' Morvyr said gently. 'You say you want another to come and tend to Peace but you won't be happy with what they prepare for him, any more than you are with what you're drinking right now. You'll feel what they can't. You won't be satisfied with the standard preparations and doses, you'll know where they need altering to suit Peace's wounds and predicament exactly. I've seen you at work, you don't even prepare the same medicine for members of the same family who all have the same cold. Are you really going to ask another Herbalist to treat Peace, knowing that whoever it is and however good they are, they won't be the best you can offer him?'

Part of me knew that she was right but the bigger part of me was terrified to act on that knowledge. My failure to diagnose my family had resulted in their loss. I wasn't going to lose Peace too. I set my mouth in a firm line and shook my head. 'Martha prepared the disgusting mess that I've just drunk, didn't she?' When Morvyr nodded, I continued, 'I never did manage to teach her any degree of subtlety during her apprenticeship with me. My temperature seems to have come down nicely though, so she'll have to do. At least she won't kill Peace.'

Morvyr sighed. 'Neither will you, Adam. You've lost your confidence, that's all. What better reason could you have than healing your Bond-Partner to get yourself over it?'

I shook my head firmly. 'No. I can't do it. I won't risk letting him down.'

I could feel Morvyr's eyes boring into me as I occupied myself with swatting at some of the flies hovering over Peace. Finally, she spoke. 'I'll go and ask Felin to go back to Greenfields now. He can describe the extent of Peace's injuries to Martha so she'll know what to bring, and he can pick up a set of clothes and some boots for you while he's there. If he goes now, he'll be there by nightfall; he may be big, but he's fit and an excellent runner.' Her voice was full of love and pride for her husband.

'Morvyr?' I said as she got up to go to him.

'Yes?'

'I'm sorry for everything. What I said to you the last time I saw you was unforgiveable. I'm glad that you have Felin and I'm trying to be happy for you both about the baby. I'm sorry that's all I can offer at the moment, but when Peace is back in my head with me, I might be able to do better.'

'Nothing is unforgiveable, Adam,' she whispered, and then was gone.

I finished my sandwich and felt a little better. I got up, keeping my blanket of ferns in place to help keep the flies off me, and went and sat on the bank of the stream, my bare feet dangling in the water as I stroked Peace's swollen eye very gently with my fingertips. A fresh pang of guilt swept through me at what I had done to him. 'Help is coming, Peace,' I told him. I put my palm to his cheek and imagined my newly gained strength flowing into him, the way he had done for me when I had needed it. He blinked and then shook his head with the pain, still only half-conscious. The piece of shingle was still in his eye! It was far too swollen for Morvyr and Felin to have been able to see anything in there when they cleaned around it, they couldn't have known anything was lodged there. I cursed myself for an idiot and guilt surged through me, accompanied by such strong self-loathing that I could hardly bear to be in my own company. I pushed it to one side. I needed to get the little stone out, right now.

I jumped down into the stream so that my face was level with Peace's as it came back to rest on his makeshift pillow. The brief flare of consciousness that my strength had given him had winked out again. Good. I didn't want him to feel what I was about to do.

I peeled his lower eyelid down, wincing at the pus that came out and ran down his cheek. All I could see was bright red, inflamed tissue, and pus that seemed to be coming from between his third eyelid and his outer eyelid. Thank goodness, the piece of shingle must be wedged down there and nowhere near his eyeball; his sight should be safe. Now, how to get the stone out? I put my finger below the swelling and pushed upwards. A jet of pus shot out, propelling the stone out with it. I sighed with relief and continued to massage the swelling, easing as much fluid out as I could. When fresh blood appeared, I stopped, relieved that all the foulness was out. I cupped some water in my hand and washed the mess from Peace's cheek.

A familiar chittering caused me to glance upwards. Squirrel was sitting brazenly on Peace's shoulder as if it were perfectly reasonable and normal, holding a small piece of bread that must have fallen from my sandwich.

I shook my head. 'It didn't take you long to reappear once there was food around, did it, Squirrel? I'd tell you I've missed you, but I'd be lying.'

He chittered back at me.

'Don't get too comfortable there, Peace won't tolerate it once he's awake,' I said, immediately knowing that it wasn't true. Peace had already tolerated far, far more.

A small cough made me look over the swell of Peace's belly. Morvyr was standing there, a steaming beaker of water in one hand and strips of what used to be her blouse sleeves in the other. She was looking from me to Squirrel and smiling.

Chapter Fifteen

I climbed out of the stream and held a hand out to Morvyr for the water and rags. She shook her head and said, 'I've already told you, I'm going to heal your torn muscle first.' She looked from me to Squirrel, and back again. 'Are you going to introduce me?'

'This is Squirrel, and he's a thief,' I said. 'Anything you have that's edible will need to be either shut in squirrel-proof containers or guarded at all times, otherwise he'll take it and then eat it where you can see but not reach him. He's a little git and he has a temper.'

'Which would explain why the two of you clearly relate to one another,' Morvyr said. 'That's a hefty scar on his back. I wouldn't expect a wild animal to survive a wound that would leave a scar that size.'

I had no intention of following the conversation where I could see she was trying to lead it. 'Are you going to heal my shoulder so that I can get on and clean Peace's wounds more thoroughly, or not?' I snapped. 'Just look at the flies on him.'

'Did you heal Squirrel, Adam? Is that why he trusts you?' Morvyr said.

'Okay, never mind healing my shoulder then, just give me the rags and water,' I said. I swallowed hard, trying desperately to hang on to

my temper. Then I looked down at Peace, the just-about-living proof
of what my temper could do. Instantly, I took a deep breath and
calmed myself. But I knew that as soon as Morvyr spoke again, or
Felin, or anyone, I would get angry again, I just couldn't seem to
help it.

I wished with all my heart that Peace were in my mind with me,
giving me the counsel that I had resented so much, I had forced him
from my side.

Take a hold of me and do not let go. He hadn't stirred but I knew
that the words that had had a profound effect on me from the first time
he thought them came from him again now, albeit very faintly. He left
the barest sense of himself with me as he faded from my mind again,
but enough that I was reminded of his strength, his calm and his peace.
I held on to it with everything I had and as it faded away to nothing, I
knelt down, put a hand to his mane and held on to that. The effect was
the same. Relief and gratitude washed over me, followed by guilt as I
realised that Peace had used strength he didn't have to counsel and
comfort me. But I did as he had instructed. I held on tightly to a
handful of his mane, and the guilt flowed out of me and disappeared.

I nodded to Morvyr, who was now crouching down in front of me,
apparently unsure what to do. 'Yes,' I managed to say. 'I healed
Squirrel.'

'So then, you can heal Peace,' she said gently. 'Please don't be
angry with me for keeping on at you, Adam, I'm just trying to do the
best for Peace, the same as you are, and the best thing for him is you.'

I focused on holding on to Peace. His strength emanated from the
thick, white hair in my hand, his warmth from his neck below. I
listened to his breaths – slow, deep, calm breaths and I breathed along
with him. Only then did I allow myself to speak. 'I'm not the best for
him, Morvyr. Even if I could get past what happened with Bronwyn
and Alita, I can't be trusted. Peace told me so himself.'

Morvyr put one hand on her rounded belly and the other on the
ground behind her, and lowered herself until she was sitting on the
ground. She crossed her legs in front of her, arranged her brown, full
skirt over them and then pulled her long, wavy, blond hair back over

her shoulders so that her face was free of it. 'May I ask what he said to you, exactly? Because I doubt it was that.'

I wanted to shout at her that she knew nothing, that she couldn't possibly know what had passed between my Bond-Partner and me, but I held on to Peace. I focused again on his warmth. His strength. His calm. When I had control of myself, I took a deep breath, looked up at Morvyr and said, 'Peace told me to stop focusing on my mistake and learn the lesson.'

'What mistake? What lesson?'

'When Bronwyn was nearing her time, I made the mistake of practising herbalism whilst my ability was clouded by emotion.'

Morvyr was quiet. Then, she said, 'Peace wasn't saying that it was your fault, what happened to Bron and Alita, surely?'

I clenched my handful of Peace's mane so tightly that my hand went white. Warmth. Strength. Calm. 'No,' I replied. 'He said that even if I had picked up that something was wrong, the outcome would have been the same. I don't know how he knows that, but I can feel from him that he does. He wants me to learn from what happened, though. The lesson is not, as I thought, to refuse to treat anyone. It is to not attempt to treat anyone whilst experiencing extremes of emotion. And right now, extreme emotion doesn't even cover what I'm feeling. I'm only just about managing not to lose the plot entirely. I'm no more use to him than I was to my wife and daughter.'

Morvyr shuffled closer to me and put a hand on my knee. 'So, then we're fine! You're in a state because you're worried about Peace, but you can relax, Adam. Peace is young and strong. He has infection to fight, sure, but with the right herbal preparations – and by that, I mean yours – he'll be fine. You've healed worse than this, you know you have. He's only out now because he's still recovering from what my healing took out of him on top of everything else, but it won't be long before he's up on his feet and grazing the bank of the stream. It's a good job you got him here before he collapsed, it really couldn't have happened in a better place. All you need to do is calm down enough to tune into him and do your thing, and he'll be back to normal in no time.'

Take a hold of me and do not let go. I released my grip on his mane and fished through it until my hand found his neck underneath. Warmth. Strength. Calm. I had to tell her, to make her understand that my state of mind was down to far more than purely worry about Peace, otherwise she wouldn't let it go, and heal me so I could clean his wounds, which I knew, despite Morvyr's optimism, were beginning to bring him down.

'It wasn't me that got him here,' I said. 'I can't fathom how he ended up here, but it wasn't because I helped him. It was because he was running away from... away from...'

Morvyr squeezed my knee. 'Away from what?' she whispered.

'Away from me.' I squeezed my eyes shut, as if that would stop me from being able to see the images replaying through my mind of what I had done to Peace.

'From you? But why?'

'Because I hurt him. I lost my temper with him and I threw shingle at him. I stoned him, Morvyr, and not just when he was in front of me, but when he was running from me. He bolted in terror, the undergrowth ripped his legs to shreds and then he ran straight into the forest fire. It herded him this way and he collapsed here, right near my hut. It took me all night and into this morning to find him. It's my fault he's like this. He said he could help me to find peace and I stoned him for it.'

Morvyr's eyes widened in horror. She opened her mouth as if to say something, and then closed it and chewed at her lip as if to make sure she kept it shut.

'I loathe myself,' I said. 'I'm terrified that every time I open my mouth, I'm going to infect you all with my hatefulness more than I already have. I'm grieving for the family I've lost and the family I'm about to lose. And the only reason I'm not taking all of that out on you right now is because Peace told me to hold on to him and not let go, and that's what I'm doing. As long as I'm next to him, touching him, holding on to him, I can keep trying to be the person he wants me to be. But it's taking all I've got, Morvyr. In the meantime, the least I can do is to learn my lesson as Peace instructed me, and not practise herbalism when I'm emotional, that's if I can ever bring myself to do it again at all. I'll clean his wounds, I'll try to keep the flies off him, I'll hold the bucket for him to drink out of when he wakes and I'll watch over him while he sleeps, but I can't be trusted to treat him.'

'Oh, Adam,' Morvyr breathed.

I opened my eyes to see her looking at Peace and then at me with pity on her face.

I shook my head. 'Don't feel sorry for me, there's no excuse for what I did. None whatsoever. Just heal my shoulder, please, so I can clean his wounds properly. Felin said you brought basic herbal preparations with you in case you found me injured. They won't be enough for him but we'll use them to begin fending off infection until Martha gets here. We need to make another draught of that preparation you gave me, and get him to drink it the next time he wakes...'

It was Morvyr's humming that stopped me talking, but it was the steadily decreasing pain in my shoulder that kept me silent. She adjusted the tone of her humming as the muscle knitted back together, until it was a soft, smooth, uplifting sound, signifying that the muscle was whole and healthy once more. I undid my sling and stretched my arm out in front of me, up, down and to the side. I sighed, relieved to have its use again.

'Thank you,' I said to Morvyr and almost managed a smile. 'Now you rest while I see to Peace.'

'As I told Felin, I'm pregnant, not ill,' she said. 'And compared with what it took out of me to heal the parts of Peace I could heal, that was nothing.'

Deep breath. Warmth. Strength. Calm. Another deep breath and then I managed to say instead of shout, 'Morvyr, let me clean Peace up. It's the one thing I can actually do for him. Please.'

Morvyr reached behind her and then passed me the beaker of boiled water and the rags. 'Okay, fine. Pour the water into my wooden beaker that you drank from earlier, then I'll take the metal one back and boil more water. I'll make up the draught for Peace in Felin's beaker. Do you want to come and see what else we brought with us? You might not want to prescribe and mix herbs yourself, but you can choose which of Martha's to use, surely? Their use and dosage are all marked up ready.'

'I'm not leaving Peace, both for his sake and mine. Could you fetch the herbs here? And if you see a branch on your way, or something else we can use to waft over him and keep the flies from settling, that would be really helpful too.'

'Of course.'

I helped Morvyr to her feet, transferred the boiled water that she had brought with her as she suggested, and gave her back the metal beaker. She turned to go, but then hesitated and turned back to me.

'You've given yourself a rough time, Adam, but you're doing better than you think. Just keep going. Okay?'

I opened my mouth to rail at her, to ask her if she'd been listening when I told her what I'd done to Peace, to demand that she explain how I could possibly be doing better than I thought when I was a hideous excuse for a human being – but just then, Peace flicked his tail. I dropped down to my knees and peered at his face, but he was still out cold. Just a twitch, then. I stroked his cheek. Warmth. Strength. Calm. I looked back up at Morvyr, bit my lip hard, and gave a sharp nod.

She nodded back, a look of relief on her face, then left me to see to my horse.

I started with his eye. I pulled back his lower lid and was relieved to see that the fresh blood that I had stimulated no longer flowed. I gently wiped all around the eye until the soft, dark brown hair glistened. Then I tended to all of the little cuts down the front of his nose and neck, before moving on to the larger tears and gashes on his front legs. Every single wound I had inflicted on him, either directly by my stoning of him, or indirectly as he bolted from me, tore at my heart and increased my self-loathing in equal measure.

The rags I was using hadn't been boiled, they weren't as clean as I would have liked, and as soon as I moved on to clean the next wound, flies swarmed back to the one I had just finished cleaning. It all felt so hopeless. There were so many wounds, so many entry points for the infection I was convinced would take Peace from me. I felt so utterly,

utterly useless, just as I had when I stood and watched my wife and daughter being taken from me.

When I ran out of boiled water, I perched by Peace's head to wait for Morvyr's return with more. I stroked the fine, downy hair of his muzzle, then the rougher hair of his cheek, and finally the white blaze down the front of his face, talking quietly to him all the while. 'Peace, I'm sorry. Truly, truly sorry, for everything; for fighting you when you called me to you, for running from you, from almost allowing the heat to kill you because of my obstinacy, for ignoring you when you tried to help me, for hurting you in as many ways as I've managed to. I'm doing my best to remember what you've been trying to teach me, and to act as I think you want me to. I'm holding on to you, even though I don't deserve to have you as my strength. Someone is coming who can heal all of the wounds I've inflicted on you, and then I'll try to be more than the man I was, just like you said. I'll try, Peace, but I can't do it without you. I can't do any of it without you.' I paused for a while as sobs took me over. Then I continued, 'I don't know how you've managed to get to me the way you have, but somehow, you've pulled me out of the life I was living and into this one. I don't know where to turn, I don't know how to function, because everything looks so different. I won't survive here without you, Peace. I don't want to survive here without you. Please, fight the infection that's beginning to taking hold of you. Fight it, the way I fought you. Please, Peace.' I put my arms around his neck, lowered my face into the thick, white hair of his mane and held on to him for all I was worth.

Dark was falling when I felt a hand stroke my hair. Morvyr was crouching down beside me, holding a steaming metal beaker in one hand and a wooden beaker in the other. My stomach turned over at the smell of the herbal draught that would bring down Peace's temperature if he turned feverish, as I was sure he would.

'Shall I take over while I can just about see?' Morvyr asked.

I shook my head. 'No, thank you.'

'Right, well I'll go and make us something to eat, then.'

'Morvyr, you've done enough, you should rest. I'll go and fetch the food once I've done this.'

'Already going. Back soon,' she called out.

I cleaned the burns on Peace's back and the lesions on his back legs, and then, since the heat of the day was dissipating, I wafted the blanket of ferns and moss that Felin had made for me over Peace's body, dislodging the flies, and laid it over him to keep them off.

I had done as much as I could. Felin would be back at Greenfields by now. If Martha left with him straight away, she could be here during the night, but I knew she wouldn't. She and Felin would have a lot to carry, and they wouldn't do it through the forest in the dark, when they risked straying from the paths created by all of the others who had sought me out over the past three years. I just had to hope that Peace's strength would keep him stable until she arrived in the morning.

As I sat down by his head once more, I allowed myself to notice the toll my own injuries were taking on me. The relief I had felt at having one shoulder healed and healthy was a distant memory due to the burning, throbbing pain in the other. All of the smaller wounds down my right side were mere irritations compared with the stinking mess that I had allowed to fester from my first day of being rubbed by my back-sack. My first day of being Horse-Bonded. I almost grinned; it was symbolic, really. Peace had come along and irritated me, pushed me, provoked me, until I had snapped and all my nastiness had come pouring out. I was pretty sure that there was a whole load more to come, so maybe it was right that my injury was there to remind me just how foul I could be.

When Morvyr returned, we ate in silence and then I tried to persuade her to return to my hut and sleep on the bed there.

'But where will you sleep? You are going to sleep?' she said.

'I don't know if I can, but I want to be close to Peace, so I'll know straight away if he needs anything.'

'Then I'll stay here with you both. I'll be perfectly comfortable lying back against that tree, so wake me if you need any help. Goodnight, Adam.' She stared at me, daring me to argue with her.

I sighed, knowing that Felin would be unhappy with the situation, but too tired to see what I could do about it. 'Goodnight,' I said and lay down alongside Peace's neck so that my head was near his. His slow, deep breaths assured me that for the moment at least, he was indeed still sleeping off the exhaustion of having been so badly injured and then healed. I hoped he was still breathing like that come morning. I tried to stay awake, to make sure that his breathing didn't quicken with fever, but eventually, I succumbed to the needs of my own body and I slept.

Chapter Sixteen

*W*hen I woke, I thought it must be morning due to the amount of light reaching the ground in front of my face, but then I realised that the light was coming from the moon, so bright in the sky that everything was illuminated, albeit with a pale blue tinge. There was rustling nearby as an animal of the night scampered through the undergrowth, but other than that, the only sounds I could hear were the pounding of blood through my head, and a rhythmic grunting. Peace! I sat up and winced at the throbbing in my head. I put my palms to my temples and pressed hard, giving me enough relief that I could process what was happening.

Peace was awake and trying to get up. He had his front legs out in front of him, and was rocking forward onto them with grunts of effort as he tried and failed to push himself up with his hind legs. I needed to lean into his back, so that when he tried to gain traction with his hind legs, I could help him to push up and forward, instead of some of the momentum being lost out to the side.

Peace, wait, I'll help you, I told him. He stayed where he was until I was in position, my hands on his back, one foot on the ground and the other braced against the tree under whose branches Morvyr lay sleeping. *Okay, push now. Give it everything you've got, and I'll try to support you.* I accompanied my thoughts with as much of my own strength as I could muster.

Peace rocked forward onto his front legs again, and pushed with the little strength he had in his hind legs. The foot of mine that was on the ground began to slip, so I threw it back against the tree trunk alongside my other foot, and pushed against him with everything I had. All of a sudden, there was nothing to push against. Peace had heaved himself to his feet, leaving me to fall to the ground. My first thought was that I needed to fetch the waiting bucket from the stream, as Peace would need a drink and the stream was too low in its banks for him to reach easily – but I couldn't seem to get up. I began to shiver.

'Stay there, Adam, I'll see to Peace,' Morvyr spoke by my ear. 'I'll make sure he has a drink and can eat okay, and then I'll come back and see to you.'

I couldn't reply. All I could do was lie there on the hard ground that seemed to amplify each painful throb of my head, and watch as, sideways in my vision, Morvyr lowered herself into the stream, hoisted the bucket onto the bank and offered it to Peace. His legs quivered, their shaking accentuated by the ripples travelling down the long hair below his knees and hocks. His body looked fragile and thin, his head and legs far too large for him. His coat was matted with blood and sweat, and his forelock, mane and tail, all previously so full and lustrous, hung limply, their vitality drained away.

He lowered his head and must have drunk all of the water that Morvyr offered him, because she took the bucket back, refilled it and offered it to him again. I wanted to shout out, to remind her to add the draught she had prepared for him, but I couldn't find the strength. Tears leaked out of my eyes at my lack of ability to do anything to help. A pregnant woman was heaving water about for my injured horse, and all I could do was lie there like a helpless baby.

I could give him encouragement, though, I realised. *Eat, Peace. There's lush grass all along the bank of the stream. As soon as you're strong enough, we'll go to the pastures of Greenfields. They're irrigated with water from the river, so the grass will be much richer than you've been used to on the plains. You'll be back to yourself in no time.*

All is well. His thought was faint but steadfast.

I beg to differ, but it will be.

Peace dropped his head and began to graze, his white legs still trembling in the moonlight. *You must alter your perspective.*

It took me a moment to comprehend the fact that Peace was counselling me. I couldn't get up and very possibly had blood poisoning, Peace was so weak from his injuries and healing that he could hardly stand, and yet he actually deemed it an appropriate time to counsel me?

Our bond will never have the opportunity to make a difference should you choose not to listen.

What do you mean? Wait. Do you mean one of us will die? Or that we'll both die?

Death is not what you currently believe it to be. It is never an end but often a delay. In our case that delay would be unnecessary and pointless.

Peace, I don't understand. I don't know what you want me to do and my head is pounding so hard, I can't think straight.

Then remember this for when you have improved clarity of thought. All is well. Always. Peace is not something that you acquire as a result of your external circumstances being to your satisfaction. It is a state of mind that endures regardless of circumstance. I will soon need assistance that only you can offer. For you to be able to give me that assistance you will need to trust that what I have told you is true. You will not know it for yourself. Not yet. But you must trust me.

I do trust you, Peace.

Then remember.

I tried to nod as I lay on the ground, but it was too hard. Everything seemed too hard. I closed my eyes.

When I tried to open them again, they seemed to be glued together.

I rubbed one of them and managed to free its lashes enough that it opened a crack, but then I clamped it shut again, wincing at the stabbing pain in my head as light flooded in. Something warm and wet was wiped across the eye I had opened, and then across the other one.

'Can you sit up?' said a voice I hadn't heard in a long time.

'Peace. How's Peace?' I coughed, my throat dry and a little sore.

'Take it easy. I had to run a tube down your throat to get the tinctures down you. Morvyr's healed the, err, damage I caused, but she said you might feel a bit uncomfortable when you woke.'

I tried to sit up. A strong arm appeared around my shoulders and helped me. I rubbed my eyes and squinted as I opened them a tiny amount. A small, blurred face framed with short, black hair was directly in front of mine. Bright sunlight forced its way above and around her but to both sides of me, it was dark.

'Martha? Where am I? Where's Peace?' I croaked. *Peace?* There was no response.

'You're in your hut. Adam, stop, don't try to get up, Felin hold him down,' Martha said. She waited until I had stopped struggling and then continued, 'Peace is just outside. We had to bring you here so I could treat you more easily, I needed to be near the fire and I didn't dare light one anywhere else after recent events. Peace came of his own accord and he's… like I said, he's just outside.'

'Then why won't you let me up? Felin, let me up, I need to see Peace, I can't find him in my mind,' I said, trying to open my eyes further.

'First things first,' Martha said. 'You've been very ill. You're over the worst, now, but the infection took all your strength as well as everything I had to offer before it finally gave in, and you're still very weak. Drink this.' A beaker of what smelt like tomato soup was held under my nose. My stomach gurgled noisily, but I pushed it away from me.

'I have to see Peace.'

Felin sighed loudly. 'You won't talk any sense into him, Martha. Just let him do as he wants, it'll be quicker.'

There was silence and I suspected that there was sign language going on over my head. 'Fine,' Martha said eventually. 'Let's get his boots on, then you take one arm and I'll take the other.'

They pulled me to my feet and then each arranged one of my arms over their shoulders before supporting me as I walked on wobbling legs towards the light, squinting. They turned to walk sideways so that we could all get through the doorway without them having to let go of me, and then we all walked forward a few paces.

'Bend your knees. He's right in front of you,' Felin said.

I did as I was told and then had to shut my eyes completely, blinded by the sunlight reflecting off of the white of Peace's coat. Why did I have to kneel down? Why was he on the ground outside my hut? I stretched out my hand and even before I touched him, I could feel the heat coming off him. When my hand found him, I discovered that his coat was wet. I opened my eyes slowly, and just about made out Morvyr leaning over him, brushing his coat with a wet sponge.

'Morvyr? What are you doing? He's feverish. Didn't you give him the draught you prepared to bring his temperature down? Oh, never mind that now Martha's here. Martha, you'll have brought something stronger for him. He needs it now, and he needs his wounds cleaning on the side I couldn't get to when he was lying down, and he has wounds that need poulticing and others that need healing unguent and fly repellent. As soon as I can open my eyes properly, I'll help you.'

There was silence. I managed to open my eyes a little more, to see Morvyr looking worriedly at Martha and Felin.

'What are you all doing just standing there? Didn't you hear me?' I said.

Morvyr crouched down so that her face was level with mine. 'Adam, Peace drank the draught I prepared for him, two days ago. Martha has given him several stronger ones since, and she's cleaned, poulticed and applied healing ointment to all of his wounds.'

'Two days ago? I've been unconscious for two days? Martha's been treating him for two days? Then why is he so hot? Why is he lying down? And why can't I find him in my mind?' I pushed Peace gently with my hand. *Peace? What's happening to you? Peace?*

There was no response.

Martha crouched down next to me. 'I've done everything I can for him, Adam, but he isn't responding to my treatment. None of his wounds are anything major, but it's as if I've done absolutely nothing for them. They're all seriously infected, and the infection has brought him down, the same way yours did with you. He's been unconscious for several hours now. I'm so sorry.'

I couldn't believe what I was hearing. Peace couldn't die. *Death is not an end but merely a delay.* The counsel he had given me before I passed out reverberated through me. I frowned, desperately trying to remember what else he had told me. It was important, I remembered that much. What was it? I shook my head violently, then held my hands to my ears to block out the questions being fired at me by Martha and Morvyr. *In our case, that delay is unnecessary and pointless.*

'He doesn't want to die,' I said out loud. 'Peace knew this would happen and he doesn't want to die. He needs me to save him, but I can't remember how. I need food. Please, give me food. I need to be able to think straight.'

'I told you,' said Felin, 'there's no telling him anything but when it's his idea, he'll do it.'

'So not unlike yourself, then, Felin?' Morvyr said, her gentle tease revealing her affection even through the worry in her voice.

'Here,' said Martha and the beaker of soup appeared back under my nose, accompanied by a hunk of bread. I tucked into them both with fervour, as if each mouthful would somehow transform into the memories I needed so desperately.

A soft chittering next to me made me tear off a piece of bread and toss it to the ground without thinking.

'Felin, Martha, meet Squirrel,' said Morvyr.

'He just ran over my foot!' said Felin.

'He's very tame,' said Morvyr. 'Adam healed him.'

'Adam WHAT?' said Martha. 'He refused to heal all of those who came to him for the kind of help only he can offer, he won't even heal his Bond-Partner, but he healed a squirrel?'

'Shhhhh, this isn't the time,' Morvyr replied.

Martha's words swam around in my mind; "help only he can offer". *I will soon need assistance that only you can offer.* That was what Peace had told me.

'Peace needs it to be me who heals him,' I said. 'But why? Like Martha said, none of his wounds are that severe, there are just a lot of them. They should be responding to even the most rudimentary preparations.'

'Thanks a lot,' said Martha.

'He doesn't mean it like that,' said Morvyr.

'Yes, he does,' said Felin.

Their words washed over me as I tried to remember everything else that Peace had told me. It was something to do with trusting him. Trusting that something he told me was true even though I didn't know it for myself. What was it? I shovelled bread into my mouth and took great gulps of soup, ignoring the discomfort as my already sore throat was further irritated by sharp crusts and hot fluid. What did I have to trust was true? What had he been counselling me about? Thunder and lightning, what was it?

I finished the soup and threw the beaker to the ground so that I had a hand free to shield my eyes from the sun filtering between the leaves above me. I took in the sight of Peace lying on the ground in front of me. The last time I had seen him, he was standing, just about. He had been trying to graze on wobbly legs and he had told me, *All is well.* I had doubted him and he had said... what had he said? Something about needing to change my perspective. What was it? I finished the last of the bread and put both hands to Peace's back.

What do I need to change my perspective about, Peace? I asked him. He didn't respond but it was as if he reached out of himself and held my words still in my head, so that I couldn't let them go. *What do I need to change my perspective about, Peace? Perspective about, Peace?*

The last three words stuck and repeated over and over. *Perspective about Peace.* That was it! I had to change my perspective about peace! All of a sudden, I was free to think again.

'If I'm to help him, I need to change my perspective about peace,' I muttered.

'He's becoming delirious again,' said Felin.

'I'll get some more tincture. We shouldn't have let him get up and we shouldn't have told him about Peace, he's not strong enough,' said Martha.

'I just need more food,' I said. 'I'm not delirious, I'm just trying to think.'

'In your case, the two tend to be much the same thing,' Felin said.

'Here.' Morvyr shoved a cheese sandwich under my nose. 'Keep thinking, Adam, you're the only chance Peace has got. How do you need to think differently about him?'

'Not about him, about peace itself,' I replied. 'I was thinking that everything would be okay once he was well again but he was insisting that all was well, regardless of the circumstances. Circumstances! That was it, that was what he told me! Peace is not something that I achieve just because my external circumstances are to my satisfaction. Then how do I achieve it? Aaaaaaaargh! Why can't I remember?'

'Let's think about it logically,' Morvyr said. 'What's the opposite of thinking you have to be happy with everything around you in order to have peace?'

'Having peace regardless.' I said. And I remembered. 'That's it. Morvyr, that's it! He told me that peace is a state of mind that endures, regardless of external circumstances. And I have to trust him that that's true.'

'But why? What difference does knowing how to be peaceful make to you being able to heal him?' Martha said.

'Because he also told me that I should only attempt to heal when I'm not experiencing extremes of emotion. Only then can I hear the voice of my soul.'

'The voice of your soul?' said Felin. 'Martha, are you sure he's not delirious?'

I shook my head. 'I've never thought more clearly. I have to trust my Bond-Partner that it's possible to find peace, regardless of the fact that he's dying in front of me. Because only if I can do it will I be able to hear the voice of my soul, my intuition, and know why he isn't healing and what I need to do.'

'You have to find peace in order to save Peace,' breathed Morvyr. 'Adam, I'm sorry to point it out, but you don't have long.'

Chapter Seventeen

*P*anic flooded through me. Morvyr was right. I had but hours to not only change my whole view of the world, but to then use my potential new viewpoint to discover why Peace wasn't responding to Martha's preparations, and find those to which he would respond. I'd never do it in time, if at all.

Take a hold of me and do not let go. It seemed to be a habit, now, for those words to come to me when I was panicking. Immediately, I put both hands to Peace's back. Warmth. Strength. Calm.

I searched within myself for more of the counsel Peace had given me. *All is well. Always.*

I shook my head, still not able to understand. *All isn't well,* I thought to him. *How can it possibly be?*

His reminder came not from him as he lay in front of me, but from the version of him I could see in my mind's eye, grazing on wobbly legs as I lay helpless nearby. *You must trust me.*

I felt panic beginning to rise again, but quickly remembered to hold on to him. Warmth. Strength. Calm. He was always that way – apart from when the instincts of his species took over to ensure his survival, he was always, always that way. I had named him Peace, because that was who he was.

I found myself reliving the experience of naming my Bond-Partner. I remembered the all-consuming, blissful serenity that I had experienced when my horse had revealed his essence to me, the feeling that peace was all there was, that there was no reason to ever feel any differently. And then I remembered how I had responded. How I had refused to allow myself to feel that way. I still couldn't allow myself to feel that way. I didn't deserve to be that untroubled, not when I had done absolutely nothing to stop my family from winking out of existence.

Death is not what you believe it to be. It is never an end but often a delay. Peace's counsel echoed around in my head as it came back to me. Not an end? What could he possibly have meant?

You will not know it for yourself. Not yet. Trust me.

I put my hands to my ears as if I could prevent the memories of his thoughts from flooding my mind and confusing me.

'Adam?' Morvyr's voice was right by my ear and full of concern. 'Adam? Can I help? Talk to me. Maybe we can work through this together, like we did before.'

I shook my head. I couldn't break my line of thought, I didn't have time. Everything I needed in order to be able to help my horse was in the words he had given me, I knew it. I felt it. He had delivered them to me with his usual calm conviction that his counsel was necessary and the truth. So why couldn't I accept what he had told me?

I will soon need assistance that only you can offer. For you to be able to give me that assistance you will need to trust that what I have told you is true. You will not know it for yourself. Not yet. But you must trust me.

Trust him. I trusted him. I couldn't believe what he had told me, because I couldn't make it fit with my experience of the world, but maybe I didn't have to. Maybe it was as simple as just trusting him. Something lightened inside me. I was on the right track. I couldn't understand him, but I could trust him.

Trust him. Trust him. I repeated it over and over in my head. *Trust him. All is well. Always. Trust him. I can be at peace regardless of external circumstances* – resistance began to rise within me at the very idea, but I focused on the words that I needed – *because I trust him.*

I dug my fingertips into my horse's fur and held tightly to him. Warmth. Strength. Calm. Trust. *Peace is a state of mind that endures regardless of circumstance. Trust him. Trust Peace.* I allowed myself to feel again his calm stillness, the tranquillity that had invited me to feel the same way, that had allowed me to feel the same way when I had named him. I felt a hard knot of resistance trying to form in my mind, but I cast it aside with a firm thought. *I TRUST HIM.*

I flexed and relaxed my fingers in Peace's fur so that I had a constant reminder of his presence, his counsel, his strength, his warmth, his calm, his... peace. It was something that he was and that we were together. It eased its way through me. Whenever the slightest resistance to it arose, I clung to my Bond-Partner with my fingers and with my heart. I trusted him. That was all that mattered. Trust. Peace. Love.

Love. As soon as I felt it as part of our bond, it was as if it began to break up and fall away from me. Peace and trust, I had a hold of. But love... it was like water soaking away into the ground where I couldn't reach it. However hard I tried to grab hold of it, to bring it back to me and to the bond I shared with my horse, it just carried on sinking further away.

All of a sudden, I understood. I knew why Peace wasn't responding to Martha's herbal preparations. The wounds I had inflicted when I stoned him were filled with my fear, my hate, my grief, everything I had hurled at him along with the handfuls of shingle. It wasn't merely bacteria that had infected him and brought him down – it was me. My vileness. My hate. And the only way to heal festering negativity was with something that was far more powerful.

I knew what I had to do. I had no knowledge of it ever having been done before, but intuition assured me that it was both possible and necessary.

I turned to Martha. 'Get me herbs that we don't use for healing, any herbs growing nearby that have no curative properties. Fresh plants, as many as you can, we don't have much time. Do you have much left of your poultices and ointments?'

'Ointments, yes, poultices a little…'

'I'll use them as a base and add to them what Peace needs. Morvyr, we need to clean his wounds of everything Martha's applied, it's all useless.'

'Now look here,' began Felin, 'you don't just order people…'

I got to my feet and glared at him. Flushed with anger, he rearranged himself on his feet and folded his arms, as if to make sure that he could absorb anything I dealt out to him, and then return it tenfold.

Warmth. Strength. Calm. I took a deep breath. 'Okay, look, I'm sorry, but I don't have much time.' I turned to Martha. 'Martha, please do as I asked, like I said, I don't… what I mean is, Peace doesn't have time for me to explain why. Please?'

She nodded and rushed off. I looked back to Felin and found myself trembling with fear that he wouldn't do as I asked, that Peace would die because I couldn't undo the damage I had caused and was still causing to those around me. 'Felin, by the look of that huge boiling pot over the fire, I can guess that you have a ready supply of boiled water, and I'm sure that Martha will have brought clean rags with her. Please would you pour water into a beaker for Moryvr so that she doesn't have to lift anything heavy, and into one for me, because I don't think I have the strength to lift much either – we need to clean everything out of his wounds, ready for the new preparations I need to make. I know I'm rude and objectionable, but please don't make Peace suffer for it?' I turned to Morvyr. 'Will you help me?'

'Of course,' she said. 'And Felin will too, won't you, love?' She looked to her husband, who dropped his hands to his sides, lowered his shoulders and nodded. She smiled at him and they held one another's gaze, their eyes soft. Then Morvyr blinked and looked at me. 'While Felin sorts the water, you need to eat more, Adam, or you won't have the energy to do whatever it is that you need to when Martha gets back. Sit back down beside Peace, before you fall down.'

'Thank you. Both of you.' I sank down beside Peace and rubbed his back, hoping that he could hear my thoughts. *I understand, Peace, I know what I need to do. Now you hold on to me and don't let go. Do you hear me? Don't you dare let go.*

A hand held a huge pile of ham slices in front of me. 'Eat this, and then wash it down with the last of the soup,' said Morvyr. 'Felin and I will start cleaning out the wounds again, and you can join us when you're ready. What about the ones he's lying on?'

I hadn't considered that. Worry and panic tried to grip me again. Instinctively, I put a hand back to touch Peace. Warmth, Strength. Calm. Trust. Peace. All was well. Unencumbered by confusion, worry or fear, the voice of my soul reverberated through me with a firm certainty. What I had planned would work. Everything would be alright.

'We'll sort them out when he can stand. Once I've treated all the wounds I can get to now, it will be enough to pull him back,' I said confidently.

There was silence and then Morvyr said, 'It's, um…it's…' I looked up at her. She took a deep breath and stared straight down into my eyes. 'It's good to have you back, Adam.'

I nodded, my mouthful of ham saving me from having to answer her; I wasn't sure that I was "back". I didn't think it was possible for me to be the man I used to be.

You must be more than the man you were. I was becoming used to Peace's counsel bounding into my mind at opportune moments from wherever I had stored it. It was as if his mind and mine were in cahoots, as if they had conspired somehow to keep his advice right where I needed it. Not our minds, I realised. Our souls.

I was learning that his advice was timeless; it was relevant when he dispensed it, and then time and time again afterwards, yet it meant something slightly different, slightly more, each time it re-entered my consciousness. When I had first heard the latest piece of counsel in my head, it had seemed an impossibility. This time, as I was about to attempt something I had never done before, it reassured me that I was on the right path. Even when unconscious, Peace continued to influence me.

I quickly finished off the ham, downed the soup and then burped loudly. Felin sighed in disgust.

'Sorry,' I said, and held my hand out for the beaker and rags he was using. He gave them a little shove as he put them into my hands. Then he gently took Morvyr's beaker from her to refill from the boiling pot over the fire. He swept around the fire first, as I knew all three of them would have been doing whenever they went near it; no one would risk endangering more of the forest in the unabating heat.

I set about cleaning all of Martha's unguents out of Peace's wounds, wrinkling my nose at the smell of them. Martha had been apprenticed to me for four years and in all that time, I had never managed to disabuse her of the idea that for something to be of good, it had to smell bad. She had never seemed able to grasp the fact that there was more to herbalism than just selecting the right herbs and dosages for a condition; that there were subtleties – including having a smell or taste that made them more acceptable to the senses – that may have seemed so insignificant as to be of no use, but which in fact made a healing preparation many times more powerful.

As I removed the poultices, I found that they contained dirt and pus; they were doing a decent job of drawing out that which normally contaminated a wound, yet they were no match for the foulness with which I had infected my horse.

All the time I worked, I spoke to Peace in my mind, telling him over and over to hold on to me and not let go, telling him that I would heal him, that he would live to boss me around again and that now, I would listen to him. We would live our lives as Bond-Partners and I would cherish our bond.

When Martha arrived with her arms full of plants, I handed my beaker and rags back to Felin and rushed into my hut, beckoning her to follow me. 'I'm going to need to reduce them all myself. You brought a grinding bowl and a grinder?'

Martha nodded. 'On the table, there.'

'Good. And your mixing bowl is clean?'

'No, it's got the remainder of the last batch of poultice in it.'

'From when?'

'Yesterday.'

I shook my head. 'That's no good. Make some more from scratch, please, and then I'll mix into it a portion of the paste I'm just about to make. Then, while I'm applying the new poultice to those wounds that need it, you can be mixing in more of the paste to your healing ointments, ready for me to apply to the rest of his wounds.'

'But that won't do any good. All you'll be doing is applying the same preparations that we already know are useless for Peace. Adding herbs that have no healing properties to the preparations I've already tried isn't going to make them work better. Adam, are you sure you're not delirious again? You're making no sense.'

'These plants may have no healing properties at the moment, but by the time I've made them into a paste to mix in with your existing unguents, they will do. I haven't the time to explain, Martha. Just do as I ask, okay?'

She sighed irritably. 'Okay, fine, whatever you say. I'll go and make the new batch of poultice now.'

'Martha?'

She stopped in the doorway of the hut and looked back at me. 'What?'

'Thank you.'

She rolled her eyes. 'Better late than never, I suppose.' She turned away.

'Martha?'

'WHAT?'

'I know you don't believe that it's important, but I wouldn't ask you if it wasn't – please add anything you can find that is sweet-smelling but not toxic, obviously, to everything you make. It will help.'

'There is no evidence for that whatsoever, as we've discussed many times.'

'And yet my preparations work better than yours. I know you're qualified and not my student any more, Martha, but discounting so much of what I tried to teach you isn't sensible.'

'Whatever you say.'

When Martha had left, Morvyr appeared in the doorway. 'You may be adept at using intuition to heal, but you're amazingly lacking when it comes to using it in other ways,' she said.

'Are all of Peace's wounds clean and ready?' I said.

'No, but what I have to say will only take a moment. Adam, does it ever occur to you how difficult it is for Martha to be in your shadow?'

'Huh?'

'She trained with the best there is. It won't have escaped her attention that while she's competent, she doesn't have the ability that you do. In order to remain near her family, she practises her craft in Greenfields, where people also have access to you. Or did, anyway. Martha can't do what you can, so she tries to separate herself from how you do things, to find her own way. You might not think that what she does is good enough, but while you've been turning away the people who have travelled far and wide to see you these past three years, she's been taking them in. She's tried to help them, all the while knowing that they see her as second best, and usually not succeeding any better than the Herbalists in their home villages did. And now, she's dropped everything to come out here and help you, she's saved your life, and all you can do is put her down and lecture her. She's the best person you could have at your side while Peace is in his current state, so just be a bit more sensitive to her feelings, okay?'

'Okay.' I sighed. Here I was, about to try to heal the wounds I had inflicted on Peace, whilst apparently unable to help inflicting them on those around me. But I needed to focus on undoing the damage I had done to my horse first. Once he was healthy, I would do whatever he told me to do to be a better man.

I glanced out of the doorway at where Peace lay. Images flashed through my mind of him cantering to catch up with me as I walked away from him, standing over me to shelter me from the sun, carrying me to water when my obstinacy had nearly killed us both, choosing me over his family, standing watch as I rested, spraying the young couple we had met with the contents of his nose and the river, walking companionably by my side even when I was ranting, grazing peacefully in the moonlight... affection for him flooded through me.

I hadn't thought I would ever be capable of feeling love for anyone or anything ever again, but as I began to grind the plants that Martha had gathered, I found that all I had to do was to think of the bond I shared with the magnificent, wonderful, amazing horse who lay just a short distance away, and infusing each stroke of the grinder with love was easy. I held nothing back of myself and soon discovered that the more love I gave out, the more I felt, and the more there was to infuse into the herbs. By the time Martha came back with a large bowl of freshly prepared poultice, the grinding bowl was full to the brim with green paste.

'What did you put into it to make it that colour? It's such a vibrant green, it's almost vomit-inducing,' Martha said as she put her bowl down on the table next to mine.

'The most powerful ingredient there is,' I said. 'Thank you for making the poultice so quickly, and for making it smell nice. I'm going to add half of this paste to it and then go and apply it to the wounds that need it. In the meantime, would you be so kind as to add the other half of the paste to your healing ointment, and then I'll apply that too?'

'Er, sure. But I can apply the ointment, I know which wounds need what,' Martha said.

'I know you do. I know how capable you are, Martha, and I'm very grateful for your help, but please, trust me, it has to be me who applies everything to Peace's wounds.'

Martha frowned. 'Why?'

'Because it was me who infected them. I'll explain once Peace is okay but for now, please just help me by mixing the paste to your ointment?'

Martha shrugged and then watched in silence as I poured half of my paste into the poultice she had prepared, and mixed it in. 'Right, I'll go and apply it. Do you think you could have the ointment ready for when I need it?'

'I can mix two preparations together, Adam,' Martha snapped.

I sighed, suddenly feeling very tired. 'Yes, you can. Thank you. I'll just go and apply this then.'

As I stepped out of the hut, Morvyr nodded and smiled at me. Felin ignored me but stood up and held out his hands to Morvyr. 'That's all of it cleaned out,' he said. 'Come on now, love, up you get, you need food and rest. You've done all you can.'

'Thank you both,' I said.

Felin nodded briefly without looking at me. Morvyr smiled at me as he pulled her to her feet. 'We'll be just over there if you need us.'

'Thanks, but I'll be fine.' I knelt down by Peace's back legs and took a deep breath. I couldn't allow any irritation, self-doubt or self-loathing – any of the negative aspects of myself that came to the surface when I was around people – to poison what I was about to do. I focused on the trust I had in my horse, our bond, and all negativity melted away.

I scooped some of the poultice – now also bright green as a result of the paste that ran through it – up with my fingers and pressed it gently into the deepest of the wounds on Peace's hind legs, with the intention that it would draw out anything noxious and allow my horse to heal. As I gradually added more and then moved onto the next wound, I focused on the bond I shared with Peace, on everything positive that it contained. Every stroke of my fingers was infused with it. It coursed through me as I worked, adding even more to the poultice that I knew would draw out and obliterate all the foulness currently residing in Peace's body.

When I had finished with the poultice, I stood up to take the bowl of now bright green healing ointment that Martha offered me. 'Thank you,' I said and smiled at her.

Her pale blue eyes widened as they looked into mine, and she took what looked like an involuntary step back. Then she smiled a smile that began at her mouth but reached her eyes. It had been a long time since anyone had appeared happy to be in my presence. I almost faltered at that realisation, but managed to stem the flow of memories that threatened to disrupt my newfound calm, by looking back down at Peace. He still needed me.

I set about smearing all of his shallower wounds with the new ointment, continuing to infuse all of my actions with my feelings for him and with my knowledge that he would heal. The voice of my soul sang to me that he would, and I couldn't stop smiling even as I felt the heat coming off his body, and heard the quickness of his breath due to the fever that raged through him. It had no chance against what I was employing against it.

When I had finished, I knelt down by Peace's head and stroked his swollen eye. I gathered his limp forelock together and twisted it around on itself so that it would stay down the centre of his forehead and out of his eyes when he woke up. Then I stroked his dark brown cheek and his soft, pink muzzle. 'You're going to be okay, Peace,' I whispered to him.

Chapter Eighteen

I sat with Peace for hours, stroking his face and sponging him with water to cool him as his fever continued to rage.

The weak rays of light managing to penetrate the leaf canopy overhead were still strong enough to add to the heat of the hot summer air that pressed down on us all, so Morvyr, Felin and Martha moved into deep shade to rest away the hottest part of the day. Occasionally, one of them would bring me food or water, and then pause to stroke Peace's face before retreating back to the relief of the trees. Morvyr would bend over him awkwardly, her long, wavy blond hair falling about her as she stroked him gently with the back of her fingers. Felin crouched down, his large, powerful frame hunched over as he rubbed my horse's face with his palm. Martha, slight of build and athletic, was as efficient in her movement as she was with her affection. She would pause to tuck her short hair behind her ears so that her vision wasn't in danger of being obstructed, and then touch Peace's face with her middle three fingers, checking his pulse at the lower border of his jaw before turning her assessment into a stroke of his cheek. It made no difference to her that I was sitting right next to Peace and monitoring him constantly, and remembering Morvyr's words to me about my treatment of Martha, I chose not to make an issue of it.

It was late afternoon, when the heat seemed to be at its most oppressive and whilst Felin was bending down next to me, offering a beaker of water and an apple, that I noticed Peace's breathing had slowed and deepened a little. And he felt a little less hot!

You put your trust in me. In our bond. There is much we can now achieve. Peace's thoughts were so faint, I could barely make them out amongst the myriad of my own thoughts. He lay still, but his eye moved beneath its swollen lid.

'Peace?' I whispered, unable to stop a tear from sliding down my cheek.

'What is it? Has he died?' Felin said, kneeling down beside me and putting a hand to Peace's shoulder.

'No, just the opposite. I just heard him in my mind, the preparations are working, he's getting better!'

'He does feel a little cooler,' said Felin. 'Come on, lad,' he said to Peace, 'keep fighting.'

'What's happening? Is he alright?' Martha called out from amongst the trees.

'He will be,' I called back. 'His fever is lifting.'

There was the sound of running feet and then Martha dropped to her knees on the other side of Peace and put her hands to his back. Then she looked up at me. 'His breathing is slower and his temperature is dropping! Adam, you made my poultice and ointment work, but how?'

Morvyr knelt down beside her and looked at me expectantly.

'Your preparations were already working in the way you intended, Martha. If Peace's wounds had been sustained accidentally, he would have been well on his way to healing by the time you brought me around. Unfortunately, the worst of his wounds were inflicted on him intentionally. They were full of spite and malice, which brought him down and prevented him from healing. It was the antidote to those that we added to your poultice and healing ointment – and it's working.'

'The most powerful ingredient there is. That was what you said you added to the paste to make it that bright green. That was the antidote. But I don't understand what it is,' said Martha.

'Love,' I said simply.

Martha narrowed her eyes at me.

'All ailments have their own, very particular energy vibration, you know that,' I said. 'That's how those of us trained to tune into them can get a sense of which particular illness or condition is presenting, and which herb or combination of herbs has an energy vibration that will cancel that of the ailment and therefore cure it. Peace was infected with my negative emotion, so I used an emotion with an energy vibration that would cancel out and cure the negativity in the same way we do with normal illnesses. And not just cancel it out, actually, but obliterate it.'

'How wonderful,' whispered Morvyr.

Martha shook her head. 'I still don't understand. Finding a herb that already has the ability to cure an illness is one thing. But you took a mixture of herbs with no curative properties whatsoever, and you're saying that somehow, you gave them a different energy vibration? One that meant that they could then act as a cure? I mean, that's just not possible.'

'It is if you have an open mind,' I said.

'Adam,' Morvyr warned me.

Peace chose that moment to heave himself onto his elbows. *You need not argue your point.*

'Peace,' I said, a broad smile stretching across my face that only seconds earlier, had been about to scowl.

He shook his head and tried to blink, but his swollen eye would barely open. *A mind can only accept that for which it is ready. Merely state your truth and then allow others to recognise it at a time of their choosing if they choose to at all.*

It's like there's nothing wrong with you, isn't it? You just carry on dishing out advice as if you weren't lying on the ground, barely able to see and just having been hours away from death.

That is in the past. It is the present with which we are concerned.

I threw my arms around his neck and hugged him. In the short time that he and I had been bonded, I had largely resented his thoughts, but now that he was back in my head with me, I couldn't have been happier to have him there.

Martha stroked his back. 'Can he get up?' she asked me. 'I suppose we still need to clean the wounds he's been lying on and then apply your bright green concoctions to them? I must go and pick some more of the plants I brought for you to make it. I was so sure they had no healing properties, but maybe I was mistaken.'

I let go of Peace, and gently stroked the wide, white blaze down the front of his nose that was usually concealed by his forelock as I looked at Martha until she returned my gaze. I would try one last time.

'Martha, while I was grinding those herbs into a paste, I was remembering everything that Peace has told me, everything he's done to help me, to protect me, to keep me alive in the short time we've been together. I was thinking of the bond we share, what it entails, and how he's achieved the impossible and filled my heart. I poured all of my feelings for him into the paste as it formed and when I applied it to his wounds, I added even more. Hate and anger almost took him from me, and love has brought him back, nothing more and nothing less. You won't find any healing properties in those plants, because they don't have any other than that which I gave them.'

Martha shook her head and rolled her eyes. 'Fine, whatever. Felin, could I trouble you to fetch more water from the stream? Peace will be thirsty and I'm hoping he'll stand up soon so he can have a good, long drink.'

Felin nodded and, with an unexpected clap of solidarity on my shoulder, left to do as he was asked. Morvyr looked at me with trepidation on her face, clearly expecting me to press my point with Martha, but I merely shrugged and grinned. Peace was right. It was down to me to say what I knew to be true, and then let her do what she wanted with it. I felt almost giddy with the relief of not needing to be right.

I felt Peace's approval just before his thought arrived in my mind. *Getting up.*

'Mind out, he's getting up,' I said to Morvyr and Martha. *Do you need me to lean into you like I did last time?* I asked Peace.

He heaved himself to his feet by way of reply and then stretched his now scrawny neck, then each of his seemingly over-large legs, in turn. He wasn't nearly as wobbly as he had been the last time he was on his feet, despite not having eaten or drunk for several days. His ribs were visible, though, and his coat, previously so shiny, so bright where it was white and so rich where it was brown, was dull and matted with sweat, blood and traces of poultice and ointment that had run with the water I had applied to keep him cool. My heart sank.

Peace turned his head and peered at me through his good eye. His gaze was as soft and knowing as ever but there was a sparkle in his eye which I hadn't noticed there before.

I would have my remaining wounds tended, he told me and I felt, rather than heard, an echo of his previous advice. *It is the present with which we are concerned.*

I jerked out of the downward slide towards guilt and self-loathing on which I had been in danger of embarking. That was of no help to Peace whatsoever. I rubbed his neck in gratitude and accepted the beaker of boiled water and handful of rags that Martha offered me.

I worked on Peace's head, neck and chest, Morvyr worked beside me on his torso and Martha occupied herself with his rump and hind legs. Then they stepped back and let me apply the remainder of the poultice and healing ointment in the same way I had done before. By the time I had finished, Peace's breathing was almost the slow, deep breathing of a healthy horse at rest, and he felt hot merely as a result of the summer air and sun, rather than with the burning fever that had raged through him less than an hour previously.

Can you walk into the shade where it's cooler? I asked him. *You'll be more comfortable there.*

I would drink first. Peace's ear flicked back towards the sound of Felin returning from the stream. Unable to see the approach of the one who carried water on the side of his swollen eyelid, he craned his neck around in order to see through his good eye, almost losing his balance. I thought my heart was going to break.

I'm sorry, Peace. For everything I did to you.

A forest grows back stronger for having come close to destruction, he reminded me as he lowered his nose into the bucket Felin placed at his feet, and began to drink.

I stroked his neck as he swallowed huge mouthfuls. *Are you the forest in this scenario, or am I?*

There is no you and me. There is only our bond.

I could feel that Peace had no concept of us being two separate beings; as far as he was concerned, we were two halves of the same whole. I felt his agreement with my assessment.

My external wounds were merely an expression of those that you have been suffering internally, he told me. *Once you could see them you could heal them. In healing me you have healed yourself. All is well.*

I've remembered how to feel positive, how to feel love, I agreed. *But Peace, I still don't feel that all is well. That sense of peace I found through trusting what you told me, it doesn't feel real to me. I can find it through you, through our bond, but it doesn't feel like it's mine. I still miss my family. I still feel grief and that's only going to get worse when we get to Greenfields.*

You believe you found peace through me but you cannot find that which you do not already have. You are not in a position to accept that yet. We have much work to do.

Work?

You have already discovered that healing another cannot help but bring healing to oneself.

Not just another, it was you, the other half of me.

In truth we are all other halves of one another. Our bond allows you to accept in a small way that which is true on a much larger scale. You rediscovered love within yourself by giving it to me. You will find your peace in the same way.

By giving it to you? But you already have it.

By being a source of it for others.

How can I possibly be a source of peace for other people?

It is possible because you have it within you and you share a bond with me. It is necessary because the damage you have done to yourself and to others must be healed. Yet it will not be easy.

No, it won't. I had abused so many people both with my temper and my refusal to heal even the most desperately ill over the past three years. I didn't even know who most of those people were, or where they lived, and they would have taken all their hurt and outrage at my actions – which went against and threatened everything upon which the communities of The New were built – back to their villages where it couldn't help but have festered and spread. How on earth was I going to find and heal all of the damage I had caused?

We will start at the beginning. Peace's thought was so calm, so confident that we could do what was necessary, that my rising panic halted where it was and then began to decrease. I remembered how I had come this far. I focused on the sense of Peace in my mind and held tightly to it.

Greenfields. We'll start there, I decided, but was soon corrected.

We will begin now.

Chapter Nineteen

*H*ow are we going to feed him?' asked Martha. 'I don't think he's strong enough to make the walk to the stream for the grass growing there, which wouldn't keep him going for long, anyway.'

'I suppose we could always go and pick what's there and bring it back here for him while we think of something else?' Morvyr suggested.

I shook my head and pointed in the opposite direction from the stream. 'The last time a horse was here, she took herself off over that way. I don't go that way much, but I'm pretty sure I remember there being an opening in the trees that has allowed grass to grow in a decent sized patch.'

'A horse was here? So another Horse-Bonded was here? When?' said Morvyr.

'Never mind that. How far is it?' Martha said. 'Peace needs to eat now.'

'It's much closer than the stream, and I'm well aware of what he needs, thanks, Martha,' I said. 'Right now, he needs more water and I don't think Felin will thank us for moving Peace so that he has further to carry it. In fact, Felin, sorry, you take a breather while I fetch the next one,' I told him as Peace slurped up the dregs from the bucket.

'You'll do no such thing,' Martha said, glaring at me. 'You'd barely be able to rip a leaf in two if I asked you to after all the work you did on Peace when you should have been resting. None of us need to have to come and find you once you've collapsed from the effort of carrying water, and carry you back here as well as having to fetch more water for Peace. Felin, are you okay to carry on?'

'Of course he is,' Morvyr said. 'He could go all day, couldn't you, love?'

Felin grinned at his wife and then flicked his eyes to Martha – who was bending down, her fingers to the inside of Peace's knee as she checked his pulse – and then to me, raising his eyebrows at me in warning not to argue with her. I nodded.

Peace reached around and snuffled in Martha's ear, dribbling water down her face and making her giggle. She reached up and stroked his muzzle as she continued to monitor his pulse. 'You big dafty, you need that water yourself, you don't want to be wasting it on me,' she said, warmth and affection replacing the sharpness that she had employed against me.

Her confidence has been shaken on numerous occasions by your ability to do what she cannot but this time it is worse than previously, Peace observed.

Understanding dawned on me of Martha's compulsion to boss me around and continue treating Peace as if he were her patient, as if I weren't even there. My irritation with her began to subside. *So, what do I do?* I asked. *How do I make her feel better? Keep telling her that she's good at what she does?*

You are responsible neither for how she feels nor how she views herself.

Hmmm. So do I hide what I can do then?

You must be the best you can be while helping others to do the same.

Okaaaaay, so…?

Peace did not reply. He seemed to be waiting for me.

That's it? I have to be the best I can be while helping Martha to do the same? That's great advice, Peace, but not exactly helpful in this scenario, I mean I thought I was doing that?

Consider more carefully. Peace had moved on to wiggling his nose around in Martha's hair, twisting it and ruffling it until it stood up almost straight. She had given up trying to concentrate on counting the beats of his pulse and was standing up straight, rubbing both sides of his face, still giggling. All of the tension had gone out of her face. I began to have an inkling of what Peace was trying to teach me, but I couldn't seem to grab hold of it, to put it into a thought upon which I could act. Help Martha to be the best she could be. I'd try harder to do that.

'Is his pulse rate okay, Martha?' I asked her.

She glanced over at me. 'It's fine.' She took a step back from Peace and looked up at him, her hands still either side of his face. 'Peace, lovely as this has been, you're going to need to stop now, or I'm going to end up as dishevelled as you are, and then I'll be of no help to you at all, will I?' She began running her fingers through her hair in an attempt to flatten it back down, and turned back to me. 'His breathing is fine too, and his temperature feels normal. He's sweating a lot though in this awful heat, and he's filthy. When he's had enough to drink, if Felin will agree to continue fetching water, I think we need to sponge him down. That will delay him being able to move to where there's grass, though. There's nothing for it, I'm going to have to go and pick some of the grass from the bank of the stream and bring it back here for him to eat in the meantime.'

'I'll come and help you,' said Morvyr.

'You'll do no such thing,' Martha told her. 'You need to rest until it gets cooler. You shouldn't even be out here in the middle of the forest in this heat, let alone running around after Adam the way you have been.'

'Peace can move deeper into the shade now,' I said. 'If you don't mind keeping an eye on him, Morvyr, you can both rest there together, and I'll go with Martha and get some grass.'

'Did you miss the part where I told you to stay here?' Martha said, her earlier sharpness returning to her voice. 'You may feel stronger than you did earlier, but that's just because you're still pleased with yourself at having healed Peace. As soon as you exert yourself, you'll become a liability to all of us, including him. None of us know where to take him to graze so he can regain his strength, so do us all a favour and rest so that when Peace needs to move, you can take him to this clearing of yours.'

Her reasoning and advice were sound, but her manner irritated me. Peace turned his soft, brown gaze towards me and I bit down hard on my lip as I remembered his advice. Be the best I can be and help others to do the same. I nodded to Martha and attempted to smile. 'Good point, well made,' I said stiffly. 'Come on, Morvyr, and you, Peace, we'll move over there where it's cooler, and rest like Martha said.'

I put a hand to Peace's shoulder and sent as much of my strength out of it, to him, as I could.

You do not have much to spare, he observed.

So, then, you can hold me up as we walk the ten paces necessary to get over there, I said.

He obliged me by shuffling one step at a time from where he had collapsed in front of my hut, across the tiny clearing. We passed the cookfire with Martha's huge boiling pot hung on the highest notch of the tripod above it, so that the water inside remained warm. We passed the pile of logs I had created when I was trying to ignore the pull that Peace had been exerting on my mind. Reflexively, I moved my arm around, reaffirming that the muscle I had torn in the process was indeed now healthy.

I was reminded all of a sudden of the condition in which my other shoulder had been the last time I had paid it any attention, and risked a glance at it. I noticed for the first time that I was wearing a clean shirt that was too big for me, its sleeves rolled up to my elbows, as well as a pair of oversized trousers, each leg turned up to reveal a worn but well-fitting boot. A large pad, which I knew would be smeared with one of Martha's poultices, held the shirt away from my infected shoulder. I moved the shoulder around a little. There was no pain, no throbbing, just a slight itchiness. She had done a good job. I turned my attention to feeling around within my body for any pain or throbbing, and could feel none. All of my injuries had clearly been expertly tended and were healing well.

When we reached the spot where the branches of two trees interlaced, providing an area of deep shade and little undergrowth, I felt Peace's relief at the slightly more comfortable air temperature. When he rested a hind leg and closed his eyes, I let out a sigh.

'Are you alright?' Morvyr asked, lowering herself to the ground and leaning back against one of the tree trunks.

'Yes thanks, just relieved that Martha has everything under control and that Peace is going to be okay.'

'And you, Adam? Are you going to be okay too?'

I sat down beside her and leant back against the trunk, suddenly feeling very tired. Martha and Peace had both been right; I didn't have much strength. 'Yes, I think so, eventually. I have a long journey ahead of me to undo all the damage I've done, but I also have him.' I nodded towards Peace. 'I don't deserve him, I nearly killed him, and yet here he is, still standing, still here and adamant that he can help me.'

'Because you saved him. Don't forget that, Adam. And in the process, you found a whole new way of healing. I mean, being able to use herbs that already have curative effects as precisely as you do, that's one thing, but using them to carry the energetic imprint of an emotion, that's something else entirely – it's huge!'

I smiled at her. 'It is, isn't it. If infusing a paste with love could overcome the vileness I infected Peace with, it must be able to overcome any negative emotion that might otherwise slow a patient's healing. I can't wait to tell the other Herbalists about this, it's going to make such a difference to the way we practise our craft.'

Do not underestimate the amount of pressure required for humans to alter the way they think. The sharpness of Peace's thought belied his restful appearance. I held a hand up to Morvyr as she began to answer me, and nodded my head towards Peace, hoping she would understand that I needed to listen to his counsel. *You have already encountered resistance to your discovery even though its efficacy could not have been more clearly demonstrated. Consider. Were it not for the risk of losing me you would not have been willing to push yourself to the point of challenging your belief of what was possible either. You will learn to recognise those who possess the openness necessary to accept and use what you have discovered but even they will need to come to the discovery in their own time and in their own way in order to truly believe it.*

But why will people not want knowledge that is useful to them?

Did you accept the counsel that I offered you before you decided for yourself that you had need of it? Your fellow Healers can already heal. The belief already exists that your abilities exceed theirs. They will not welcome that which they will consider to be further evidence of that.

But they'll be able to do it too!

Were they to attempt it that would be true. They will not.

But why?

They will not risk failure. They will not risk proving to themselves more than they already have that their abilities are more limited than yours.

So I just keep this knowledge to myself?

Be sparing with its theory but generous with its application. Those whose minds are open to its discovery will become obvious to you.

I nodded thoughtfully to myself.

'What did he say?' Morvyr whispered.

'He just opened my eyes to how complicated we humans are. He keeps doing this; turning my view of the world upside down. I feel as if I've been seeing everything slightly out of focus my whole life and Peace gives me a way of seeing some things with such clarity that it makes everything else seem even more out of focus. I don't know what to do or how to behave, and he's having to teach me, step by step. It's like being a child all over again.'

'How are we complicated? I mean, I know you are,' Morvyr nudged me and chuckled, 'but the rest of us?'

'I don't think you are, any more than your sister was. You accepted straight away how I altered Martha's preparations so that they could heal Peace, and I know Bronwyn would have too, but Peace says that I need to be sparing about how much I talk about it, as most of the other Herbalists won't welcome the information any more than Martha did.'

'Because they already feel inferior to you. Hmmm, I see the problem.'

'Peace should have chosen you as his Bond-Partner instead of me,' I said. 'You learn much quicker than I do and you'd give him far less trouble. Ouch!' A large piece of bark bounced off the top of my head and landed in my lap. 'Talking of trouble…' I looked up and a second piece of bark hit me on the cheek. 'Come down here and do that, you little monster,' I said and Squirrel chittered loudly in response.

Morvyr laughed. 'He's actually aiming at you, isn't he? Look at him, here comes another… oooh, was that your eye?'

It was a long time since I had heard her laugh, a sound so reminiscent of Bronwyn's that a sharp pang of grief pierced my heart. Instead of lodging there though, as it once would have done, it passed straight through me and was gone. Morvyr laughed even harder as another large piece of bark hit me, and I couldn't help but join in.

'Why is he doing that?' she said once she had her breath.

'He's hungry and obviously thinks I should feed him to save him having to bother finding food for himself. He enjoyed the nuts you brought the last time you were here, by the way.'

'You gave them to him?'

'No, in true Squirrel fashion he stole them and then tried to steal everything else. If Devlin – he's the Horse-Bonded who was here – hadn't tied your sack from a branch so that its weight held the drawstring tight, he would have done.'

Squirrel chittered his fury at my lack of response to his demands for food, and scampered off just as Felin arrived back with the next bucket of water. He put it down in front of Peace. 'Here you go, fella, drink deep,' he said softly and then turned to Morvyr. 'Want some tea, love? Or I can go back and fill this to get you some cool water, if you'd prefer?'

She shook her head and patted the ground next to her. 'Come and sit down for a bit, while Peace drinks.'

Felin wiped the sweat from his brow with the sleeve of his shirt, and then did as she said. Morvyr turned to me. 'So, when the Horse-Bonded was here with his horse, um, do you mind if I ask how that went?'

'The first time they were here, they came to open me up to Peace's influence. I would say that from their perspective it went well, and from mine, badly. Then they came back and saved my life and again, it was mission accomplished from their perspective, but from mine, it was an excuse to be even more angry with them. They're on my list of people to seek out, thank and apologise to.'

'They saved your life? You said that Peace did that, and Martha's done it for you too,' said Morvyr. 'I only saw you a week ago, Adam, how many times has your life been in danger since then, exactly?'

Martha arrived at that moment, laden with as much grass as she could carry. She had picked it right at the bottom of each plant so that Peace would benefit from the sugar reserves there, as well as from the more fibrous stem and leaves. As she dropped her burden next to the bucket from which Peace had just finished drinking, and looked at me for my response to Morvyr's question, I managed to smile at her. 'Thanks, Martha. Will you rest for a bit?'

Martha looked down at Peace, who was beginning to tuck hungrily into the pile of grass, and then back at me. 'Just for a few minutes, while he's eating. Then I'll go and get more. I'm as curious as Morvyr to know just how many times you've almost died before your most recent attempt?' She brushed soil from her green, cropped leggings, then sat down in front of the rest of us, crossed her legs and looked expectantly at me.

'Well now, let me see,' I said. 'I suppose I could count the first time as being when I set my hut and the surrounding undergrowth on fire, because if Squirrel hadn't roused me in time to put it out, I would probably have died then. The second time was when I accidentally overdosed on the painkillers and sleeping draughts that Devlin left me – Peace sensed what had happened and knew he couldn't help, so he alerted Risk and she brought Devlin back here. By the time I fully came around, they had dumped me out on the plains with Peace. The third time was when I got lost on the plains in the heat, and couldn't find water. Peace carried me to it in the end, oh yes, and threw me in the river, from which he then had to drag me out because I was weighed down by my back-sack. The fourth time was when I got overtaken by the forest fire – thank goodness for the remains of a pond that I fell in. And the fifth time was when you three saved me and Peace.'

Felin had shifted around to sit next to Martha as I spoke, and all three of my companions looked continually back and forth between me and Peace as I summarised my calamitous tale. They continued to do so after I had finished speaking.

'So, um, I realise how stupid I've been and how fortunate I am to have such good friends,' I said. 'I don't deserve all the help you've given me, any more than I deserve my bond with Peace.' I looked at Morvyr and Felin. 'Thank you for caring enough to come and see if I was okay and for looking after Peace and me.' I looked at Martha. 'Thank you for saving our lives. From the bottom of my heart, thank you.'

She swallowed hard. 'I may have brought you back from the brink, but it was you who saved Peace.' Her voice was laced with a bitterness that annoyed me. If she would just accept how I had done it, she would be able to heal that way herself, she had no reason to be jealous of what I had done. I wanted to try and convince her, but felt Peace gently nudging my mind, reminding me of his earlier counsel. I sighed. How could I help Martha to be the best she could be when she wouldn't allow me to?

Morvyr and Felin were both watching me, Morvyr with a concerned expression and Felin with one that dared me to be rude to Martha.

I shook my head in frustration and said, 'Martha, whether you believe it or not, it's down to both of us that Peace is standing, not just me. My paste healed the damage I caused, so that your preparations could heal everything else unhindered.'

'He's nearly finished that grass, so I'm going to go and get more.' Martha leapt to her feet and went to Peace. She stroked his neck and peered down into his water bucket. 'Judging by the fact that he hasn't licked quite all of the dregs from that bucket, I think one more might do it, when you're ready, Felin, and then we'll be able to move him to the glade,' she said and made off for the stream.

I glanced at Morvyr and Felin as I lifted my hands and let them fall back into my lap. 'I tried.'

Felin winked at me and made to get up.

'Before you go, Felin, could I have a quick word with you both?' I said.

He nodded and settled back down.

'I know Martha will have been keeping an eye on you, Morvyr, and as a Tissue-Singer you're more than capable of monitoring your own body, but the last time you came to visit me, you asked for my help. You said you were scared about losing your baby because of what happened...' I swallowed and then cleared my throat. 'Because of what happened to Bronwyn.'

Felin reached out to Morvyr, took her hand and squeezed it. She nodded at me, and looked desperately, searchingly, into my eyes as if to try and read from them what I was about to say.

Take a hold of me and do not let go. I couldn't tell with whom the thought had originated this time. It didn't matter. I allowed my sense of my bond with Peace to fill my mind and I recomposed myself. Calm. Strength. Trust. Peace. I turned my attention to Morvyr and extended my senses into her body, tuning into each and every organ in turn, confirming to myself that which, as a Tissue-Singer, she would also have known. Then I listened to my inner voice for the additional information that always came to me after my initial investigation of a patient, allowing me to know the exact adjustments that would ensure a herbal preparation was of ultimate efficacy, and to know of underlying causes of more obvious symptoms.

'Your baby may not be as large as his father, but he's every bit as strong and healthy,' I said. 'Morvyr, you're doing fantastically well.'

Morvyr grabbed my arm. 'He is? And he's... a he? You know that the same way you know all the other things you know?'

I nodded. 'I couldn't hear my intuition when Bronwyn was

pregnant, because I was so excited. I let my emotion drown it out and I missed what I should have known. I will never make that mistake again, Morvyr. I can tell you both with absolute certainty that all is well and there's no reason whatsoever why that shouldn't continue.'

All is well. What had made me say those words?

You allowed the part of you to speak that knows it is true. Move your attention elsewhere before you can resist the notion. It will settle within you and be the foundation upon which we will build.

Moving my attention elsewhere was no sooner requested than done, but not because of any effort on my part; Morvyr had thrown herself at me and was hugging all the breath out of me. When she finally released me, Felin put a huge hand on my shoulder, his face damp with more than just perspiration. 'Thank you, Adam,' he said. 'Now I'm going to pull myself together and go and fetch some more water for Peace.' He got to his feet and when he bent to pick up the bucket, he rubbed Peace's forehead and whispered something in his ear. I had a feeling I knew what it was.

'Bronwyn would have been so proud of you.' Morvyr's voice had a tremble in it. She chewed her lip as she rubbed her rounded belly. 'Last time I saw you, I told you that she would have been ashamed of you, but I was wrong. You've been to a very dark place, but you've managed to fight your way back and I can only imagine how much that's taken out of you. I can see you're still struggling, but you're back with us, Adam, and I'm so relieved, both for you and for my sister. She would have wanted you to be happy.'

'I'm not sure I ever can be, without her and Alita. It's down to Peace's influence that I've clawed my way back this far, and he tells me that I'll find the same level of peace that he has, but I can't see how, when I'm always going to want what I can't have.'

'Maybe you just have to keep doing what he says and eventually, everything will fall into place.'

I nodded as I watched my big, battered horse chewing long stalks of grass, pulling them slowly into his mouth before taking up the next mouthful. 'I trust him,' I said. 'I just miss Bronwyn so much. I wish I could share everything I'm learning from Peace with her.' A thought occurred to me. 'You know, when I used to pick wild flowers for her, she smiled every time she looked at them for days afterward. Now I'm wondering, was she just smiling because she loved how pretty they were, because she appreciated my having picked them for her, or was she also feeling the love that I felt when I picked them for her? The love which, looking back, I'm pretty sure I must have infused them with, albeit unintentionally?'

Morvyr smiled at me. 'All of those things, I should think. She's still with you, Adam, just like she's with me. When I feel my baby kicking and there's no one around to tell, I can almost feel her standing at my shoulder, smiling and sharing it with me. I don't think we ever lose the ones we love, not really.'

I wished I could believe her.

Chapter Twenty

*W*hen Peace had eaten his second helping of grass, Martha carefully sponged him down with water from her boiling pot that had been allowed to cool, avoiding his wounds but cleaning all of the blood, sweat and grime from him. By the time she had finished, he was much more comfortable, and ready to walk to the glade that Risk's disappearance had made me sure must still be there. Morvyr and I got to our feet, but Martha shook her head.

'You needn't think you're coming, Morvyr. The sun's going down and you've done quite enough. Felin has put a clean covering of moss on Adam's bed, and we've agreed that you're both going to spend the night there. Then in the morning, he's going to take you home. You've both done all you can, and it's time you looked after yourselves and that little one in there.' She pointed at Morvyr's belly.

'As I keep telling everyone, I'm not ill, I'm...'

'Pregnant,' we all finished for her.

'Yes, you are,' I said, 'and that means you have to rest far more than you have been. Martha's right, you've both done enough for me as it is, and it isn't just about you, Morvyr. Felin needs to get back to his baking, or my name will be even more hated in Greenfields than it already is. Martha, you should go too, for the same reason. I've managed to deprive Greenfields of both its Herbalist and Baker in one go, your apprentices must be rushed off their feet by now.'

Martha shook her head. 'Reeta is nearly qualified, she'll be fine without me for a bit longer. I'm not leaving you and Peace, you still have wounds that need tending, and you need help to tend to Peace's. I'm not risking you neglecting yourself as badly as you did before. I'll stay with you both until you can come back to Greenfields with me.'

Morvyr and Felin both looked at me uneasily, waiting for my reaction. Felin's lack of sternness reminded me that I had managed to be a source of peace for them, so surely I could do it for Martha? I had to bury my irritation and help her to be the best she could be. I knew there was more to it, I sensed it whenever I saw how Peace responded to Martha, but I couldn't put my finger on it so for now, this was the best I could do. I bit my lip hard and then nodded. 'Okay, thank you.'

Martha nodded and held out a cloth bag to me. 'You carry this. It's food for our evening meal, dressings and ointment for your injuries – I'll see to them before we lose the daylight completely – and beakers, as I'm hoping that Peace will allow us to share his water, which I'll be carrying.' She pointed to the bucket Felin had just placed at her feet. 'I'll come back in the morning for more water, and food, if you'll be so kind as to leave it for us,' she said to Morvyr and Felin, who nodded, 'and for the supplies we'll need in order to see to Peace's wounds.

I took the bag from Martha, and Felin held out his hand to me. 'We'll see you back in Greenfields soon?' he said.

I shook his hand. 'Thanks for everything, Felin. We'll be there in three or four days, I should think.'

'Yes, I should think so, but it will depend on you as much as Peace, Adam, we're not going anywhere until you're both strong enough,' Martha said. I took a slow breath in and then out.

'I almost feel sorry for you,' Morvyr whispered as she hugged me. 'Almost.'

I grinned. 'You take it easy walking back.'

'We will, we'll leave at dawn and be home before the worst of the heat,' Felin said. 'We look forward to welcoming you home, Adam.

And you, Peace.' He rubbed Peace's neck and Peace nuzzled his shoulder in return, leaving a green stain on his shirt. When Morvyr went to stroke his nose in farewell, he lifted his head and blew gently into her ear.

'We'll see you soon, Peace,' she said and kissed his nose. 'Thank you,' I heard her whisper.

'Come on then, let's get you to more grass,' I told him.

That would be welcome.

I put my hand to his shoulder, both so that I could give him strength if he needed, and in order to stabilise myself on legs that wouldn't seem to do exactly what I wanted them to. And, I realised, because I found it comforting that we could help one another by walking together that way. I felt Peace's agreement and was flooded with affection for him. He sensed from me where we were going, and we headed that way together.

The ground began to slope down away from us, and, both unsteady on our legs, we took it slowly. Martha walked behind us, cursing every now and then as water sloshed out of the bucket she was carrying.

Before long, we came to a grassy clearing in the trees, nestled in a large dip in the forest floor. Towards its centre there was a large puddle whose surface appeared to bulge periodically; an underground spring. No wonder the grass was lush and the ground was squelchy underfoot.

There were signs that we weren't the only visitors to the glade – the grass was growing at different heights due to the choicest varieties having been grazed, there were tracks leading to the puddle in the middle, and the bark had been stripped up to waist height from many of the surrounding trees; the deer that trod through the forest so lightly, so unobtrusively, had a heavy impact once they stopped to eat.

Peace dropped his head as soon as he was in reach of the grass. I felt his contentment as he snatched huge mouthfuls and began to grind it down with his teeth, releasing both sugar and moisture.

Martha put the bucket down beside me. It was only half full. 'Well, at least Peace can drink from over there,' she nodded towards the gently bubbling puddle, 'because there's not much left in here. Sit down, Adam, I need to see to your shoulder before it gets dark. Back from here a bit, or you'll get a wet backside.' She pointed to a spot just behind us.

I felt my exasperation rise again at her insistence on speaking to me not only as if I knew nothing about healing but as if I were a child, but I did as I was told and began to unbutton my shirt.

'Take your shirt off,' Martha said, upending the bag I had put down beside me.

'Already doing it.' I didn't quite manage to keep my annoyance out of my voice. Helping Martha to be the best she could be was wearing incredibly thin.

She ripped the dressing from my shoulder without warning and began to clean it. 'I soaked these rags in boiled water before we left,' she told me. 'The poultice has drawn everything out that it's going to, I think, so once I've got it all off, I'll put healing ointment in its place and put another dressing on it for the night. Tomorrow, I'll take the dressing off and let the air get to it. How are your other cuts and bruises feeling?'

'Fine, thank you.'

'I'll leave them alone for now then, but if you feel any soreness or throbbing, you're to let me know.'

'Yes, Martha.'

'Don't take that tone with me, Adam.'

I ground my teeth until I could be sure not to snap and said, 'I'm sorry. Everything is healing well, though. I really think it's only my shoulder that still needs attention.'

'You'll forgive me if I don't completely trust your judgement regarding what needs attention, after having found you in your previous state,' Martha snapped.

I couldn't help feeling that my tolerance of her need to be in charge was fuelling it, rather than softening it. I remembered the relaxing, calming effect that Peace always had on her but I still couldn't see how I could help her to feel that way. I felt Peace observing my thoughts with interest.

I'm not doing very well at this, Peace.

You are merely learning how not to be on your way to learning how to be, I was informed. His words seemed like a reproach, yet I could sense the importance Peace attached to them.

I frowned. *So my appreciating her efforts and leaving her to do her job unhindered isn't the right way to go?*

Peace transferred his attention to moving, one careful step at a time, further into the glade and selecting the grasses he preferred from the many different varieties that grew there. It appeared he had told me all that he was going to.

'Right, you can put your shirt back on, and then we'll eat,' said Martha.

The second I had finished buttoning my shirt, I was handed a ham sandwich.

'Eat that, and then there are another three here for you. Drink at least three beakers of water so you're well hydrated, and then you can sleep. I'll have you both strong and healthy in no time,' Martha said, gazing towards where Peace grazed in the twilight.

I had a strong urge to tell her to go back to Greenfields and leave us both alone; it felt as if all the good Peace had done me was slowly being unravelled as I became more and more annoyed with her, and I wondered how long it would be before exasperation turned to anger and I reverted to shouting at her. I looked back to Peace and instantly felt calmer.

'Hello there, little one, want some of my sandwich?'

Squirrel was sitting on his haunches in front of Martha, watching her expectantly as she ate.

'Have you been feeding him?' I asked.

'Of course. In case you hadn't noticed, half of the forest is gone and I wouldn't mind betting that his food stores went with it.'

'I was his food store,' I said. 'He didn't bother looking for food himself once he realised he could steal it from me.'

'That's all the more reason to feed him now then, isn't it? You can't just tame him and then abandon him.'

'He appears to have survived perfectly well in the time I was gone,' I said. 'Now it makes sense why he was so angry I wouldn't feed him earlier. The more you feed him, the more he expects it.'

'And what's wrong with that?' Martha laughed with delight as she tossed Squirrel a piece of bread and he caught it between his paws. 'We have enough to share, don't we, little man?'

'I'll remind you of that when it's you being pelted with bark because he's decided it's feed time,' I said.

'He wouldn't do that to me, would you, Squirrel? Oh look, Adam, how cute is he? He's holding his paws apart, ready to catch the next piece.'

I groaned. It was going to be a very long few days.

Chapter Twenty-One

*I*t transpired that Peace and I remained at the glade for three days. Slowly, the lustre returned to his coat, he put on weight, and his forelock, mane and tail regained their bulk and luxuriance.

He would eat for most of the night and then rest in the shade of the trees with me for much of the day, wandering off from time to time for a drink and then grazing his way back to me. Often, he would lie down by my side in my chosen resting place, at the bottom of a huge beech tree. He would snooze with his head resting on the ground, his muzzle all scrunched up as he blew away the leaves and dirt of the forest in two lines, one from each nostril. Then, with a grunt, he would lie flat, his head landing with a thump by my thigh, his breath creating a warm, sweaty patch on my leg. I never moved further away from him. It was as if his calm oozed into me with his every outward breath, helping me to feel at ease with myself and my situation, and soothing away my latest irritation with Martha.

I slept on and off during the nights, stirring frequently as a result of the many animals who visited the glade to eat or drink from the spring, and then staying awake long enough to check that Peace was okay. I knew he was from my sense of him in my mind, but I always stood up, waited for my eyes to adjust to whatever level of light the moon afforded, and did a visual double check. Every time I saw him grazing serenely amongst whichever other animals were also there, I felt as if everything was okay with my new world.

It was at the times during the day when he was asleep by my side and Martha was there and awake to keep watch, that I slept deeply and restfully. Falling asleep to the sound of Peace's long, deep outward breaths lulled me into a type of sleep that I had never experienced before. I woke refreshed and feeling stronger each time.

Martha slept soundly all night at the foot of a nearby elm tree which Squirrel appeared to have adopted as his home. She came and went during the day, fetching food, water and fresh plants for the herbal preparations she was constantly making for Peace's wounds, in between ordering me to stay still and rest. To her delight, Squirrel often accompanied her, either bounding around her or leaping through the trees above her head. Every now and then she would, without comment, dump at my feet an armful of the plants I needed to make fresh amounts of my paste. Her grinder and grinding bowl would likewise be deposited, and when it was obvious that the paste was ready, she would, still without comment, take it and mix it into her fresh batches of poultice and ointment and then place those at my feet, ready for me to apply to Peace.

I knew that he didn't really need my paste anymore from a healing perspective but I chose not to reveal that fact to Martha; I enjoyed applying preparations that had such a positive vibration, and could feel how much Peace appreciated them, so I continued.

When Martha and I cleaned out the poultice on the third morning, it came out clear of anything nasty.

'It's knitting together nicely in there,' Martha told me, as if I weren't capable of assessing that fact for myself. 'You can just use the healing ointment on everything now. He's almost strong enough to make it back to Greenfields. I'm not sure about you, though.'

'Thanks, I'm fine.'

'And you're still my patient, so I'll be the judge of that.'

That was it. My approach with Martha clearly wasn't working, and

I'd had a gutful of her. 'Martha, I appreciate everything you've done for Peace and me, you know I do, I've told you often enough, but you need to stop talking to me as if I don't know anything about healing.' I tried very hard to maintain a conversational tone, but didn't quite manage it. Instantly, I felt Peace focus his attention – which had previously been on his enjoyment of having the healing ointment applied to his rapidly healing and very itchy wounds – on our conversation.

'I know exactly how astonishing your knowledge of healing is, Adam, goodness knows, I'm never allowed to forget it, but while you're my patient, you'll do as I tell you.' The bitterness in her voice annoyed me further. I had tried to teach her everything I knew when she was my apprentice, but she had chosen to ignore some of it, was a less effective Healer as a result, and then resented me because of it.

Do not underestimate the importance of this moment, Peace told me.

I've had enough of her, Peace. I've tolerated all of her...

You have a choice between retribution and peace. One will offer you short term satisfaction. The other will help you to continue on the path you have chosen. The same choice will arise over and over and you must choose the same way over and over if it is to become the way you are.

But I don't know what to say to her. You said I have to help her to be the best she can be, but I tried that when she was my apprentice before I even knew you. I tried again by telling her how my paste worked, and I've followed her lead in your continuing recovery so she can see that I respect her knowledge and position as a Herbalist, but nothing helps. She's still feeling the need to assert herself over me, which means she's still feeling threatened by me. I haven't been a source of peace for her at all. Not even a tiny bit.

Your efforts have failed because you have focused purely on what to say and how to act.

What should I have been focusing on?

Peace moved his forequarters towards Martha whilst leaving his hindquarters where they were, so that his front feet faced in a different direction from his back feet. I remembered having seen him standing in that inelegant and comical posture before, and frustrated and annoyed as I was, I couldn't help a smile twitching at my mouth as he began to gently nuzzle Martha's shoulder. She reached a hand up and stroked his nose and her face softened.

How did you provide comfort to your other friends? Peace asked me.

By doing what I can do as a Healer. That's hardly going to help Martha, is it?

You trusted yourself to diagnose despite everything that has gone before.

Yes, because I remembered the lesson you taught me. I remembered that I had to be calm and clear of excess emotion, so I found my sense of you and held on to it... It was as if something cold landed on my head and then trickled down into my body as realisation dawned. *I used the peace of our bond to give peace of mind to others.*

Peace left my thought hanging there as he continued to stand in his ridiculous pose, now wiggling his nose on Martha's cheek and making her smile. It was hard to reconcile the gravity he attached to his counsel with the vision of tomfoolery in which he was currently engaged.

Will that work for Martha, though? I asked him. *I've already tried reassuring her, teaching her, thanking her...*

Whilst you were in a state of irritation. In doing so you have learnt the futility of attempting to say the right thing whilst being in the wrong frame of mind. The humans of this time are more sensitive to emotions than to the words or actions that accompany the emotion. In order to effectively deliver the truth you must be calm. You are in search of peace. To discover it within yourself you must be a source of it yet you believe you do not have it to give. But you are aware of it within me. I will be your source until you no longer have need. Take hold of me and do not let go.

And then tell Martha what?

The truth. Truth has a vibration which is comforting even when it may be uncomfortable to hear. When it is delivered by one who is at peace with himself it has power. Hold to your sense of our bond and you will know the words to say.

I nodded slowly to myself as I considered his counsel and recognised the truth within it; Peace had dealt out help and advice to me in the way he had just described, from the moment we had first met, and I was living proof of its effectiveness.

Peace had stopped showering Martha with attention and was standing normally, nibbling at the grass at his feet. Martha had reverted to scowling at me, and Squirrel was chittering angrily at me from a low branch just above her shoulder.

I looked away from her before my irritation with her could begin to rise again, and at Peace. I smiled as he snorted at a herb he didn't like and moved further into the grass to select something more preferable. I loved his gentleness, his strength, his ability to be profound and ridiculous simultaneously, his total lack of judgement of me or anyone else, his ability to be completely in the moment, the softness of his dark brown eyes, the sense of calm that oozed out of him. And I loved the sense of him in my mind. That quiet sense that there was no question to which he didn't know the answer, that nothing could shock him, that all was well. All was well. I held on to the feeling. And I knew what to say.

'You have absolutely no reason to feel threatened by me, Martha. None at all.' A small part of me registered that my voice sounded different from normal and I realised that I had sounded the same way when I gave Morvyr and Felin news of their child.

Martha's eyes widened. She flushed red and looked as if she were about to cry, but she didn't argue.

'You trained for four years to be a Herbalist and you worked hard in that time. If you had only ever healed one person, all of that work would have been worth it, but you've healed hundreds. You're a Healer, Martha. You ease pain, you speed healing, you cure disease. It's what you do and it's who you are. What I do, what anybody else does, is completely irrelevant to both your life and the lives of those you have helped and will help in the future.'

Martha stared down at the ground in silence. Squirrel was quiet at her shoulder, looking from her to me as if he were somehow involved in our conversation. Eventually, Martha sighed. As if that were all the proof he needed that I didn't need chittering at further, Squirrel bounded off up the tree trunk and disappeared into the branches above.

'I suppose I knew all of that, really. I don't know why you telling me makes me feel better, but it does. I've been silly, haven't I?' Martha said.

'Not silly, no, just bossy,' I grinned and she smiled back.

'I don't suppose there'll be a need for me in Greenfields once you get back there. I accept what you say. I can help people, and that makes my training worthwhile. It makes me worthwhile. But no one is going to ask for my help when you're around.'

'They will, just as they did before I left. I won't be staying there long, though. I need to make amends to those I've hurt, and then Peace and I will be moving on so that I can try to find all of those who came to see me and I chased away.'

Martha raised her eyebrows and whistled. 'That's a whole lot of people, Adam. Do you even know who they all are? I can't think you took the time to note their details down when you were busy screaming and shouting at them.'

I shook my head. 'Did you, by any chance? I know you took a lot of them in and helped them.'

'Their names, yes, but I don't remember where they all came from.'

'Well, I know it won't be easy to find them all, but it's what I have to do.'

She nodded slowly. 'I guess you do… ouch!' A small twig hit her on the head.

I grinned. 'Someone's hungry. You'd better step to it, Martha. Aren't ham sandwiches his favourite?'

She shook her head with a grin. 'You did warn me. I like him, though, he's a character.'

'That's one word for it.' I went to continue rubbing ointment into Peace's rapidly healing wounds.

'Adam?'

I turned back to where Martha still stood.

'Thanks,' she said.

I smiled. 'Not necessary, but you're welcome. Now go and feed that annoying little git before bits of tree start raining down on us all.'

She laughed. 'Squirrel, get down here, you little monster, it's breakfast time.'

By the time she reached the branch from which she had hung the food sack, he was at her feet, bouncing around in anticipation.

You chose well.

I chose the only way I could with you as my Bond-Partner, Peace. I don't really feel any different, though. I mean it's great to see Martha feeling happier, but having finally been able to be a source of peace for her hasn't meant that I feel it within myself.

Do not underestimate the length of the path on which we have embarked. We are far from our destination and you would be wise to avoid judgement of our progress. Merely hold on to your sense of me whenever you are presented with a situation in which you will struggle to be calm. There will come a time when you will not need to grasp it quite so tightly.

So what you mean is, one step at a time. I rubbed the ointment in a little harder since Peace's top lip was wiggling with enjoyment of the relief it provided to his itching. I grinned at him and realised that one step at a time would be fine.

Chapter Twenty-Two

$\mathcal{I}$ woke with a start. It was hot, but I was more comfortable than usual because I had taken off my shirt to allow my shoulder wound to air, and was using it as a pillow. I just about had the chance to register that I couldn't hear the sound of Peace breathing nearby, or feel his hot breath on my leg – both of which had been there when I went to sleep – when the sound came again that had woken me from my deep midday slumber. I sat up, rubbing my eyes as the memory came back to me of where I had heard it before; I had been snoozing near the bank of the River Gush, and Peace had sensed his family nearby. His squealing rang out for a third time and Martha, who was standing nearby, shielding her eyes from the sun, laughed delightedly.

I got to my feet and finally managed to clear my eyes enough to be able to focus on what was happening. Peace was in the middle of the glade, leaping from his front feet to his back feet alternately like a spring lamb, shaking his head as he squealed.

As we watched, he flung himself around to face the opposite direction and then reverted to leaping and squealing, with the odd buck thrown in for good measure. Then he launched himself back around again, ending up at the edge of the still bubbling puddle. His huge feet displaced a huge amount of muddy water, most of which landed on him. He squealed and spun to face me, Martha and Squirrel, who, I saw with a double take, was now sitting on Martha's shoulder.

Peace had mud all up his front legs and chest, it ran down his nose from where it had landed in his forelock, and it dripped from his muzzle. His brown eyes were wide, yet soft, his dark brown ears pricked yet relaxed. Mud dripped from the tip of one of them. He held his gleaming white tail proudly aloft and with the sun bouncing off the white of his coat, he was magnificent, despite his patching of wounds and the spectacle he was providing. He snorted and began leaping in the mud again, his bucks and leaps getting bigger and bigger until they connected together into enormous, powerful fly-bucks. I laughed, not just because Peace was fast disappearing underneath a coating of mud, but because of the sheer enjoyment I could feel from him.

'He needs space to run,' I told Martha when Peace finally came to a snorting, blowing standstill.

'Yes he does. Uh-oh, here he comes!'

Peace came squelching through the grass at a canter, flinging mud all about him. Squirrel leapt into the branches above us and Martha ran laughing into the trees. I stood with my arms wide open, welcoming all of the mud that landed on me as Peace bounced on all four feet to a halt in front of me.

'I get it, you're ready to go,' I said, smiling as I searched for a spot on him to rub that wasn't caked in mud. 'All you had to do was tell me, or just let me wake up properly, and I would have known. That wouldn't have been so much fun, though, would it? You really are a goon.'

Peace gave a little squeal in confirmation. It really was hard to reconcile the wise, knowing side of him with the side he was currently displaying. I was prevented from giving the matter further thought by Peace shaking his body from head to toe in an effort to dislodge the muddy water dripping from him, depositing much of it on me. I glanced at my shoulder, but I knew I didn't need to worry. The wound there had scabbed over as well as all of Peace's had. We could get as dirty as we liked and it wouldn't matter. Peace picked up on my thought and dropped to his knees and rolled, creating a soggy, flattened area of grass onto which I threw myself in solidarity the moment he got up. I wriggled around, scratching my many itchy scabs, just as he had done.

'I've seen it all now,' Martha called from her refuge in the trees. As I got to my feet and Peace dropped his head to graze as if nothing had happened, she emerged, flinching and then smiling in delight as Squirrel launched himself onto her shoulder from a nearby branch. 'You know, whenever I've come across the Horse-Bonded and their Bond-Partners before, it's always been obvious that they belong together, as if they are the equine and human forms of one another,' she said. 'With you and Peace, I couldn't see it. He's big and strong and his strength isn't just physical, he radiates it. He's always so calm and knowing, and there's a softness about him that puts people at ease…'

'Unlike me,' I interrupted with a wink.

'…but I have to say, having seen the two of you rolling around in the mud, one after the other like that, any doubts I had about the two of you being well matched have just been well and truly put to rest. He's bringing the real you out of yourself, isn't he? He's how you will be?'

She sees with her heart. She is relaxed about her role in life and so she is the best she can be, Peace noted with satisfaction.

I felt a lump rise in my throat. 'Thank you, Martha, for seeing what I can't at the moment. You have no idea what your observation means to me.'

Martha flushed with pleasure. 'Well, I should think anyone can see it. I mean, I should have seen it before, but this is the first time I've met Bond-Partners who are newly bonded.'

I nodded. 'Newly bonded pairs normally go to The Gathering once they've found one another, don't they, to learn from more experienced partnerships as they settle down together in their bond. Peace and I haven't had a chance to do that and I don't think we will for some time to come.'

'But shouldn't you make time?' Martha said and then peered

awkwardly at Squirrel as he began to nibble on a piece of apple, right by her ear. 'Must you do that now?' There was no hint of irritation on her face and when she looked back at me, she was smiling.

'I guess we'll end up there at some point, but I don't think my role as one of the Horse-Bonded is going to be the same as all the others. They're bonded so they can use what they learn from their horses to help people. I'm bonded so I can undo all of the damage I've done.'

You have already discovered that the two are not mutually exclusive.

'But you'll be able to help people at the same time, won't you?' Martha said.

I grinned. 'That's what Peace just said, so I guess I'll just have to do my best. I can't think anyone will want my help for a good while though, not until I've proved I've changed. I suppose there's no time like the present to start – he's clearly ready to leave here and we're both healthy and strong enough thanks to you, so I guess we should make our way back to Greenfields?'

Martha nodded.

'What will you do about him?' I nodded towards Squirrel. He had finished his piece of apple and was looking at Martha expectantly.

She handed him another piece. 'It's up to him, isn't it? He'll come with us or he won't.'

'Do you think Greenfields will be ready for him if he does?'

'More than it's ready for you, I'd say.' Martha grinned. 'We'd better stop by the stream so you can clean yourself off. Your return to Greenfields is going to be enough of a shock for everyone, without you appearing like some wild creature from a children's story book.' She bent down and began to gather the remains of our healing supplies into the bucket. Squirrel settled on her back and continued to nibble at his fruit.

'I'm a lot less filthy than Peace,' I said with a grin.

Martha handed me the bucket, flinching as Squirrel scampered up her back to his place on her shoulder. 'Peace can carry it off, Adam, you can't,' she said with a wink, and marched into the trees in the direction of my old hut.

Peace looked at me and blinked as mud dripped from his forelock onto his eyelid, now barely swollen at all. His soft, brown eyes drew all of my attention, as they always did when he looked at me that way. Martha was right. Peace's covering of mud was incidental to the whole majesty of him. Mine was all anyone would be able to see.

I put my hand to Peace's shoulder without even thinking about it and we followed the path that Martha had worn on her many trips between the glade and my home. When we stepped into the tiny clearing, I stopped suddenly. Peace halted beside me and waited for me to process my shock. How had I lived here for three years? My hut was tiny, smaller than the sheds that most villagers of Greenfields built by their back doors to house their outdoor clothes. What was left of its roof could barely be called that, it was so insubstantial. The clearing was littered with rotting clothes, parts of old tools that were rusting where I had thrown them in disgust when they were no longer of use, and piles of decomposing undergrowth I had ripped up as it attempted to encroach upon my dirty, pitiful life. How had I lived like this? And how had I not seen it before? How had I been so blind to the mess, the neglect, the filth? I had only walked this way three days earlier and even then, I hadn't noticed the aspects of my home that so shocked me now.

You have changed much, I was informed.

In three days? I picked up a stray log and threw it back onto the nearby pile. My axe was still stuck in the tree at which I had hacked away when I was trying to ignore Peace's pull on my mind. I remembered being that person, and yet I couldn't identify with him. Not even a tiny bit.

I was a mess, I thought to both myself and Peace. *What on earth must Devlin have thought when he was here? He must have been horrified at the thought of me joining him as one of the Horse-Bonded.*

He would have been advised against forming judgement. He and his Bond-Partner were here to help. They helped, Peace told me simply.

Martha poked her head out of my hut. 'You should come and see how much of these preparations you want to keep and how much we can leave behind,' she said. 'I'll see to packing up my equipment if you can sort out the herbal supplies. Felin's left you his back-sack, which was good of him.' She looked around the hovel that had been my home. 'I, um, I don't suppose you'll be coming back here?'

I rubbed Peace's neck and told him, *I won't be long and then we'll make our way out of here and you can run free.* Then I made my way over to Martha. 'No, I can honestly say that I have no intention of coming back here. In fact, I can't wait to get away and leave it behind. I'm sorry you had to see all this, this…'

'Mess,' she finished for me. 'I'm not. Seeing how low you had sunk helped me to be more patient with you.' She winked.

'That was you being patient?' I said.

'Touché.' We both laughed. 'Seriously, though,' Martha said, handing me Felin's back-sack as I joined her in my hut, 'isn't it amazing that I did get to see where you've been living? I mean, if Peace had collapsed anywhere else in the forest, Morvyr and Felin would never have found you both and Felin wouldn't have come back to fetch me. How lucky is it that Peace ended up within a stone's throw of your hut?'

Luck is a fabrication of the human thought process, Peace volunteered.

'You have that look on your face that you always have when Peace is talking to you,' said Martha.

I nodded and held a hand up to her to ask her to wait for my reply.

So how did you end up here? I asked Peace.

Even as my instinct to flee took me away from you my soul led me to where your energy lingered. You and I can no more run from one another than we can from ourselves.

I gulped and stepped into the doorway so that I could see my Bond-Partner. He was standing where I had left him and he lifted his head higher and pricked his ears as I stepped into sight. Love for him flooded through me. And gratitude such as I hadn't felt since Bronwyn had agreed to be my wife.

Martha stepped into place beside me. 'Adam?'

'Peace just told me that luck is a construction of the human mind, but I'm feeling pretty lucky right now,' I said, and told her what Peace had told me.

She took my hand, squeezed it and let it go. 'I'm pleased for you. You and he make sense. Oh, for goodness' sake.'

I turned to see that Squirrel had decided that Martha's head was a better vantage point than her shoulder. 'You know I could say the same about you and him,' I said with a chuckle, and began to pack.

Half an hour later, I was as clean as I could get myself, standing in the shallow stream and scrubbing myself with handfuls of wet moss. I had washed my oversized shirt and trousers, and wore them dripping wet, thankful for the cool they afforded me. We were ready to go.

I hitched Felin's back-sack onto the shoulder that Morvyr had healed, put a hand to Peace's shoulder and took a last look back at where I had lived for the last three years.

It is time to move forward.

I nodded. *It's time.*

Chapter Twenty-Three

Martha and I agreed that we would aim to be out of the woods and near the River Gush before we stopped for the night, so that Peace could enjoy being back in the open where he was more comfortable, graze to his heart's content on the plentiful grass of the outlying pastures of Greenfields and have access to plentiful water.

The trees that towered above us as we walked grew more densely than in other areas of the forest, offering a higher degree of shade and consequently a slightly more comfortable temperature in which to travel. Since less light reached the forest floor, there was less undergrowth to get in our way and trip us. Dead leaves crunched underfoot, however there were very few drifting to the ground afresh – the rainstorm had granted a temporary reprieve from the drought, enabling the trees to hang on to their leaves, at least for now.

We were making good time, I was informed after a few hours by Martha, who, having walked the path less than a week before, had a far better idea of where we were than I did. She walked at the front of the single file in which we were forced to amble as we twisted in and out of the trees, with Peace behind her and me bringing up the rear. Squirrel leapt around in the branches in front of us all, occasionally stopping to argue with other squirrels whose territory he was invading. Martha would stop and look up at him in concern when his screeching was especially loud, but it was always the other squirrel who backed down and allowed him to pass. I wondered at the tenacity of the animal who had managed to cause the injury I had healed on Squirrel's back, and couldn't help thinking that whatever it was would have been unlikely to have emerged from the encounter unscathed.

It felt very strange to be walking the path that Morvyr and so many others had travelled in coming to find me over the past years. Much as I wanted to leave my hovel behind me, I couldn't quite believe that I was doing what I had never expected to do again, and returning to Greenfields.

I had moved there in the hope of courting Bronwyn. She had brought her mother to see me for treatment in my home village of Springbank, and it was love at first sight, at least for me. When her mother's treatment came to an end and they returned to Greenfields, I knew I would have to follow. I remained in Springbank until the patients who had come specifically to me for treatment were healed, then packed up my things, exchanged fond farewells with my parents and brother and moved my practice to Greenfields, leaving everyone else requiring healing in the hands of the other two Herbalists in residence there, including the Master with whom I had served my apprenticeship. The resident Herbalist of Greenfields had been wanting to retire, so I was welcomed to the village with open arms. Bronwyn and I were married within six months, with her parents' blessing.

My heart sank as I wondered what they thought of me now. I had promised so much as a son-in-law and delivered so little. My feet felt heavier and heavier as the afternoon wore on, and I would have ground to a halt completely if it hadn't been for Peace's rhythmic plodding in front of me. His tail swung hypnotically from side to side, the black streak visible one moment and hidden the next by the enormous mass of white, wavy hair. I could feel his serenity, a constant reminder of his counsel that all was well. Whilst I didn't believe that, the sense of him in my mind and the sight of him in front of me reassured me that whatever I would face, I wouldn't face it alone. I may not have had peace, but I had Peace.

When we reached the edge of the forest, Peace immediately dropped his head to graze. Martha and I turned to walk along the treeline, towards the river Gush. Squirrel bounded along in the branches beside us, occasionally shooting up a tree trunk and leaping between the less substantial branches higher up, before coming, headfirst and at breakneck speed, down another trunk and resuming his journey alongside us. Every time he reappeared, Martha smiled and I sighed.

'Why do you pretend to hate him?' she said after a while.

'Pretend?' I said.

'Oh come on, Adam, he's been your only friend for, what? Months? Years?'

'Friend? He annoyed me until I gave in and healed him, then he refused to leave me be, instead stealing my food and throwing things at me.'

'From what you said, he also saved your life.'

'Probably because he was worried he'd starve to death without my food stores to pilfer.'

'So you're going to keep it up, then? This pretence of hating him?'

I considered for a while. 'He's rude and irritable. I suppose he reminds me of me. The me I'm trying not to be.'

'That's funny, because I don't see him that way at all. I think he's cute and cheeky. He should have a proper name, I mean you don't call Peace "Horse", do you?'

I was glad that she was walking beside me and so didn't notice my face flush red. 'Err, no, I guess not.'

'So, what shall we call him? You chose a lovely name for Peace, why don't you do the same for Squirrel?'

'Um, well it's not the same thing; Peace is my Bond-Partner. There was a process I had to go through to find his name. Why don't you choose a name for Squirrel? He seems to have attached himself to you, so it looks like it's going to need to be a name you can live with.'

Martha nodded. 'Am I allowed to know the process you went

through to find Peace's name, or is it something the Horse-Bonded keep private?'

'I guess you could do something similar – maybe just think of how you see him, and see which word comes to mind?'

Martha looked over to where Squirrel had leapt some way ahead of us. He was watching us, his eyes bright and inquisitive as we caught up with him. 'Hmmm, let's see. He's cheeky and clever. He's full of energy and determination. He decides what he wants and then he makes sure he gets it. He has grit. That's his name. Grit.'

I nodded. 'I like it. Rhymes with git.'

'Oh, Adam, no!'

I chuckled. 'Okay fine, Grit it is.' Then I said, 'Little git,' under my breath.

Martha punched my arm playfully and glanced behind her. 'Peace still hasn't moved. Do you think we ought to wait for him?'

'And deprive him of the mad gallop I can feel him building up to? No, we'll carry on. You won't want to miss what's coming.'

Minutes later, there was a pounding of hooves behind us. We both turned to see the white dot that was Peace, getting larger. He soon took form and I was thrilled to see that he moved with power and strength. His mane streamed out to the side of him, held aloft by the hot summer air though which he tore. His tail flowed out behind him, its bulk dissolved into fine lines of silvery white with a few strands of black. The long hair of his lower legs drew the eye to the length of his strides, each one terminating with a thud on the ground as his hooves gained purchase for the next leap forward.

Martha gasped. 'He's magnificent, isn't he?'

As Peace got closer, he gathered himself together and slowed to a canter. His footfall lightened and his mane lifted and fell in gentle harmony with his body. Gone was the weak, thin, baby horse whose head and legs had appeared too big for him. Here was a big, strong, powerful being who radiated joy and a zest for life and who moved with an elegance completely at odds with his size. He waited until he was almost on top of us before he sat his weight back a little and bounced on all four feet to an ungainly, blowing halt.

'Gosh,' was all that Martha could find to say.

I laughed. 'You're a dufus,' I told Peace, reaching up to rub his forehead, my hand coming away covered in hair and sweat. 'Feel better for that?'

I hadn't needed to ask and Peace didn't bother to answer me. He lifted his head and breathed in deeply. Water. The river must be just up ahead. I felt his agreement with my assessment of what we had both sensed – he with his nose, and I by interpreting what I could feel from him – and then he launched himself into a purposeful trot, his thirst and need to cool himself down driving on his tired body. His legs appeared to fly in all directions at once, again exaggerated by the long hair that curtained his lower legs.

Martha frowned. 'Where's he going? He looks like he needs to rest.'

'The river's just ahead and he's thirsty. He'll just keep moving his legs until he gets there. I imagine you're struggling to understand what you just saw?' I said as we began to follow him.

'It's like he's two horses, isn't it? Strong, composed and graceful one minute, and...'

'All over the place the next?' I finished for her. 'It's a gift he has.'

Martha chuckled. 'Does he just run out of steam?'

'I think it's partly that; he may be an old soul, but his body is so young still. But I also get the feeling from him that he enjoys making people gasp at his magnificence, and then doubt what they just saw when he acts the clown.' As I put into words for Martha thoughts that, up until that point, I hadn't organised into a definitive conclusion for myself, I knew I was right. 'Peace doesn't take life very seriously, and he's never going to let me, or anyone else, do it in his presence for any length of time, either,' I said thoughtfully.

Instantly, I felt Peace's assent. *It is a matter of dual perspective. Everything has a level of importance yet nothing is important for all is always well,* he informed me.

How can everything be important if nothing is important? That makes no sense.

There will come a time when you will wonder at how you could ever have doubted it.

And I'm guessing that time isn't soon? As in now, once you've explained it to me?

I felt his relief as he splashed into the river and began to drink. No further explanation would be forthcoming.

'I think it's a good thing if Peace can help you to not take life too seriously, it'll stop you from being overwhelmed by the task in front of you,' Martha said.

I nodded. 'I don't disagree with you, but it's his explanation of how he does it that has me stymied.' I told her of Peace's counsel.

She shook her head. 'Makes no sense to me either, and happily for me, I'm not you, so it isn't my problem. Grit and I have a much less complicated life, don't we?' she said to him as he paused on a branch nearby. He chittered in response and then held her gaze, his chittering getting louder.

Martha reached around to a side pocket of her back-sack and took out a crust of bread. Grit leapt from the branch onto her shoulder with incredible agility, but then dug his claws in to stabilise himself. Martha grimaced and gave him the crust.

'Looks like you're going to need shoulder pads in all of your clothes,' I observed. 'You actually had that crust ready for him, didn't you?'

She grinned. 'Of course. I save bits of food I think he'll like, either as I find them or while I'm eating, it's no bother.'

I sighed and shook my head.

'Don't be such a misery,' she told me. 'Oh, look at Peace!'

The river Gush was moving at a pace even this far downstream, but Peace had waded out, pitching his strength against the current until he was elbow deep, his belly dipping into the water. He stood facing downstream, almost sitting into the current to keep his balance. The water slammed into his backside and rose up in a spray, landing on his back and washing all of our herbal ointment off him. As was becoming a habit, he was a vision of strength, magnificence and buffoonery, all at the same time. We both laughed.

'I'm glad you're witness to this too, I don't think anyone would believe me,' I said, allowing my back-sack to drop to the ground.

'I'm just wondering whether all of the bonded horses are like this. When they come to the village with their Bond-Partners, they're the image of wisdom and dignity, but maybe when they're off on their own, they're all funny and playful like Peace?' Martha said, dropping down from the bank into the shallow water at the river's edge. Grit leapt off her shoulder and back onto the bank with a squeak of indignation as she crouched down to drink from her cupped hands.

'I guess I'll get to find out at some point,' I said. 'One thing is for sure though, we're going to have to reapply all of the ointment he's just washed off, because he's going to be sore and itchy if we don't.'

'It's not as if we have anything better to do, is it? Ahh, that's better.' Martha splashed water into her face. 'If it weren't for the current, I'd be tempted to go in and join him where he is now, the water is deliciously cool.'

Peace turned and began to wade in her direction. I grinned, knowing exactly what was coming. He sat down onto his hocks and leapt towards her, landing with a huge splash. It was as if the water rose into the air in slow motion before landing on top of Martha. She stood up, gasping and wiping water out of her eyes as Peace took another leap past her, splashing her from the side on his way to where I stood on the bank. He turned to stand next to me, snorted and then shook the water off himself and all over me.

'You're right, Martha, the water is indeed deliciously cool,' I said, laughing. 'And unfortunately, the load that Peace splashed over you had a decent amount of silt stirred into it.'

Martha coughed and wiped the pale brown water from her eyes. 'Did you tell him to soak me?'

'On the evidence of what you know of him so far, what do you think?' I said.

She laughed as she looked down at herself, dripping and dirty. 'I suppose I did ask for it. At least you won't be the only one walking into Greenfields looking as if you've been dragged through a ditch.'

I looked sideways at Peace, wondering if there had been more to his antics than just mischief, and was rewarded with the merest sense that wisdom and humour had been intentionally combined. I put a hand to his neck and rubbed it, and he looked around, his beautiful brown eyes holding mine. No thoughts passed between us. None were necessary. We both knew that he was looking out for me in the subtlest of ways as well as the more obvious ones. And he always would.

'Right, you go down and have a drink too, then we'll get ointment rubbed in wherever Peace needs it. Then we can rest in the shade over there, have something to eat, and get a good night's sleep. Thanks,' Martha said, taking my hand and allowing me to haul her up the bank.

'You're welcome, boss,' I said with a wink as I landed in the water with a splash.

'Sorry, I can't seem to help myself. I just want you to be prepared for tomorrow.'

'And you're right, as usual.'

'How are you feeling?' Martha asked.

I reached out into the river and cupped some clear water in my hands, splashing it over my head to wash off the silty water Peace had deposited on me. 'Nervous. I know everyone is furious with me and with good reason. I also know that my transgressions go far beyond those that are easily forgivable. I'm in for a hard time, but not nearly as hard as I made life for those I refused to help, so I just need to take what is thrown at me and try to make amends the best I can. I'm not sure I trust myself to be able to do it, though.' I took another double handful of clear water and just about managed to swallow a few mouthfuls of it as my throat tightened at the thought of the task ahead of me.

'You can do it, Adam,' Martha said quietly. 'You haven't underestimated how angry people are with you, but you have Peace.'

Instantly, I calmed. 'I do.' I turned to look up at him as he stood, dripping, on the bank where I had left him. He peered down his nose at me, his eyelashes sweeping together and then apart as he blinked. I felt safe, as I used to when my mother tucked me into bed when I was a boy.

I love you, Peace.

You need me. Because of that you feel affection for me. Love is an energy far more powerful than you yet fully understand.

I felt rebuffed and more than a little hurt, but then I had the same sense from Peace that I always had when he told me things; he was merely stating the truth. Whether I liked hearing it or not didn't change the fact that he was giving me answers to questions I didn't know I'd had, yet recognised once he had answered them. There was one question I did know I needed answering though. *Are you telling me that I didn't love Bronwyn? That she didn't love me?*

That is a question better answered for yourself.

It felt as if the ground were sliding away from underneath me, as if my view of my life, the whole foundation of what made me who I was, was the thinnest piece of glass and in danger of being shattered at any second. *Peace, please tell me that what Bronwyn and I had was real?*

Peace lowered his head and breathed warm air onto my forehead in long, slow breaths. Gradually, my panic receded and I remembered what to do. I grasped hold of the sense of him in my mind and allowed his calm reassurance to flood through me. It was okay to feel shaken when my view of the world was challenged. Panic began to rise in me again. So was I accepting that my wife and I hadn't loved one another then? That what we had wasn't what I thought it was?

Something began to wind its way through me. I recognised it. I had infused Peace's poultices and ointments with it, yet not in the pure form in which it was manifesting now. It lifted me, supported me, nurtured me and I felt as if nothing could hurt me while it filled me. But unlike when I had offered it, it asked nothing of me in return. It didn't need anything from me. I wasn't required to heal or respond or behave in a certain way. I didn't even have to accept it for it to continue being offered without limit or restraint. It offered freedom from worry, for there was nothing to worry about. It awarded a feeling of belonging, for it was all-inclusive. And it promised, unreservedly that everything was alright, for it was impossible to be otherwise. It was everything that my horse had shown me by his every thought and action.

I smiled as I suddenly realised why Peace had such an effect on me. Of all of those who had tried to help me, it was he who had got through to me, he who had got me to listen to him, he who had started me on the road to change and was keeping me on it. It made no difference how resistant I was, how rude, how violent – he continued to have such a powerful effect on me because he acted out of pure, unconditional love.

'Adam, are you alright?' Martha's voice drew me back to myself.

I opened my eyes. I was still standing in the river. Peace's muzzle rested gently against my forehead as he continued to breathe his love directly into me, helping me to identify it exactly, helping me to understand. What I had experienced with Bronwyn was as close to unconditional love as I had been capable of, as a human with all of the complications and opportunities for learning that came with it. And that was okay. I took a long, deep breath in and out.

'I think so, thanks, Martha.'

Chapter Twenty-Four

*M*artha was woken at dawn the following day by Grit running around in circles on her stomach. I was woken shortly after by her resulting shrieks, which quickly turned into laughter and then into a soft chatter of squirrel noises which Martha had apparently learnt, and to which Grit responded in kind.

I grinned, first at the two of them and then with affection for Peace as I realised that he had managed to lie down almost on top of me without waking me. His front legs were stretched out just in front of my face, and I could feel the warmth from his belly seeping into the top of my head. I sat up to find him fast asleep and snoring gently. My grin changed to a grimace as I realised that the fact that Peace had allowed himself to sleep meant that he had accepted Grit as part of our herd and clearly trusted him to keep watch, even though it had taken some time before he awarded me that level of trust.

'We haven't got much food, so we'll get going as soon as Peace wakes, shall we?' Martha said.

'Proper words, thank goodness. I thought for a moment that we were all going to be forced to speak in Grit's language,' I said with a wink.

She laughed. 'He likes it when I talk to him like that. I've no idea what I'm saying, but it's obviously the right thing because he makes the exact same noises back. Anyway, as I was saying, we should leave soon. We've only got a few scraps of food left and we have a good three or four hours of walking until we reach Greenfields, if we're still agreed on following the river south until we absolutely have to leave it?'

I looked up at the clear sky and nodded. 'It's going to be another scorching day, and I just feel happier knowing that Peace can cool himself down and drink whenever he needs to. I'm sorry, I know it's a longer route. You could always head directly to Greenfields from here and leave us to make our own way?'

Martha shook her head, a determined look on her face. 'You're my patients and I won't stop seeing you both that way until you're safely back in your cottage, Peace is grazing in your paddock, and you both have everything you need. I know you don't think you need me, but indulge me for my sake. Okay?'

'Safely back in my cottage? What do you think is going to happen to me on the way there?'

'Look at Peace with fresh eyes, Adam.'

I looked down at where my big, strong horse slept on. Only, now that I saw him purely with my eyes, he didn't look quite so big and strong. Although he had put on weight, I could still see his ribs, his hip bones still protruded and he was covered in scabs of various sizes. He looked like a victim of abuse and neglect. I put a hand to my mouth in horror. The villagers of Greenfields already saw me in the worst possible light and I wouldn't be able to blame them for thinking that I was responsible for Peace's condition, especially when they would be right.

'No one needs to know what happened,' Martha said quickly. 'You look every bit as bad as Peace does. You were both in the forest when the fire caught and spread so rapidly, and you both sustained burns and injuries whilst fleeing it. Morvyr and Felin found you and fetched me to help, since you were incapacitated. That's all true. The rest doesn't need going into, it's behind you. You've healed the injuries you caused and if Peace is happy that amends have been made then it's for nobody else to have an opinion to the contrary.'

I rubbed my forehead with the fingers of both hands, my eyes shut tightly. I wasn't going to be able to do this. I would have to either lie to save everyone hating me more than they already did, or I was going to have to tell the truth, and I didn't see how I could ever make them see me as anything other than the monster I had been.

Peace stirred and then let out a deep sigh. It was all the reminder I needed. I focused on the sense of him in my mind and held on to the calm it awarded me, with everything I had. I crouched down and put a hand to his shoulder, reassured by the constant warmth and strength that emanated from him.

'A forest grows back stronger for having come close to destruction,' I murmured.

'Sorry?'

'That's what Peace told me. He always tells it like it is, only in a way that I can't quite put my finger on until I really get it. And I think I get it. I'm not proud of what I did, of what happened, but you're right, it's behind us. I have to focus on being the person I'm trying to become as a result of it having happened. I'll just do that. Thanks, Martha.'

'Um, you're welcome, I think?'

Peace chose that moment to wake and heave himself up onto his elbows, all at once. I rubbed his neck and then his face as he blinked in the dawning sun.

'Morning, Peace,' I said softly and then moved out of the way as I sensed his need to get up. He got to his feet with a grunt and then stretched his hind legs out behind him in turn. Then he arched his neck, holding all of its muscles taught before loosening them again, shook his whole body, loosening a cloud of dirt particles, and headed for the river. He dropped his front feet down into it with an enormous splash and lowered his head to drink, leaving his hind feet up on the bank, his backside sticking up in the air.

Martha and I looked at one another, both shaking our heads and chuckling. 'There's no time to wallow or be downhearted with him around, is there?' Martha said. 'That bank is knee height. It can't be comfortable for him, drinking like that, surely?'

'He hasn't given it any thought, he's just in the moment, doing what he fancies,' I said. 'A horse doing a handstand in the river. Who would have thought that was a possibility? I'm interested to see how he's going to get out.'

I didn't have long to wait. Peace turned his body, allowing his hind legs to almost fall into the river, and then heaved himself back out.

'That's one way of doing it,' I called out to him, grinning. He squealed and bucked on the spot. 'You're feeling well. I get it,' I laughed.

Grit chose that moment to leap off Martha's shoulder, chittering in disgust that her attention was on Peace rather than on feeding him. It was all the incitement that Peace needed. He pretended to spook at the sudden movement, then leapt up in the air in a fly-buck, squealed again and took off at a gallop along the river bank. I felt his joy, his contentment and his enthusiasm for life and I couldn't stop smiling.

'I guess we'd better get going, then,' I said, stretching and feeling with satisfaction that my shoulder wound felt neither as tight nor as itchy as the day before. I lifted my back-sack onto my other shoulder and waited for Martha to take the handful of food scraps that she'd saved for Grit out of her own back-sack and wriggle her arms into its straps. When she had arranged it on her back to her satisfaction and Grit was happily perched on her shoulder eating one of the scraps, we set off after Peace.

He was a white dot in the distance, but I could feel that he had discharged his exuberance and was slowing down. I smiled as I felt him halt and begin grazing in one movement. It was a wonder he hadn't kicked himself in the chin.

'I don't think I've ever been so in need of a bath and a decent meal,' Martha said as we stumbled and tripped our way through the long grass that grew alongside the river. 'We need to head east now, otherwise we'll miss Greenfields. Another half an hour and we'll be there. Are you ready?'

I put a hand to Peace's shoulder as he walked beside me. 'As ready as I'll ever be.'

The time passed quickly. I was as hungry as Martha and my stomach rumbled loudly, but I couldn't have eaten anything; my throat was tight and my heart hammered in my chest. I held on to Peace with my hand and mind, and my feet continued to move, one after the other until the grey stone cottages of Greenfields loomed in front of me.

I swallowed, feeling as if I had a stone wedged in my throat. The home I had shared with my wife and had been desperate to share with my child, was there. I pressed my fingers into Peace's shoulder, desperate to hold myself together by holding on to him. He increased his presence in my mind. *Your memories will bring pain. Allow yourself to feel it for only then can you release it. If you attempt to hold it away from yourself you will follow the same pattern of behaviour as when you were here last. I will support you. You are not alone,* he reminded me.

I allowed the tears I had been attempting to hold back to pour, unchecked, down my face and I let out a sob. Martha took my hand, squeezed it and let it go. 'Stop any time you need to, okay?' she said.

I nodded, but stumbled on. I would do this. I would face the memories, the pain, the hate that I knew would be hurled in my direction. Peace was with me. I held fast to the sense of him in my mind and to the feel of him under my fingers.

Greenfields had begun as two lines of cottages facing one another across a cobbled street. Gradually, the lines had grown longer, with other streets and rows of cottages branching off at intervals. Each cottage had a large garden or paddock behind it, where vegetables were grown and animals were kept, so the cottages were spaced well apart, giving Greenfields a sprawling appearance. More cottages had been built in the time I'd been away, I noticed.

We approached a flock of sheep, most of whom were sheltering from the sun under a large oak tree. They watched us and a few began to bleat, unsure whether to rise and flee. We turned to walk a wider path around them and they stayed where they were, apparently deciding that we were no threat. I doubted that the villagers would be so easily reassured.

A child was swinging on a piece of wood suspended from a tree in the first paddock we passed. He stared at us, then dismounted from his swing and ran, shouting, into its adjoining cottage.

We rounded the cottage and set foot on the cobbles of Greenfields. I stopped in my tracks, remembering when I had arrived in Greenfields for the first time. I had been so excited at the thought of seeing Bronwyn again, so sure that she would allow me to court her and that eventually, we would make our home here.

I turned and rested my forehead against Peace's neck, holding on to his mind and to his instructions. I felt the pain. I allowed it to throb through me, to pierce my heart, to stab my stomach, and then I breathed it out and released it. All the while, I could feel a sense of strength and calm easing its way slowly through me, reminding me that I wasn't alone.

When my breathing had returned to normal and my tears had eased, I lifted my head and rubbed Peace's neck. *Thank you,* I told him.

Hold tightly to me and do not let go, he told me firmly. It was only then that I heard the low hum of voices.

Chapter Twenty-Five

a group of villagers had gathered in front of us and the group was steadily getting larger. Martha put a hand to my shoulder. 'Okay?' she whispered.

I nodded, biting my lip as I tried to focus on my sense of Peace through my steadily increasing anxiety. I had absolutely no idea what to say, so I stood there, looking from one villager to the next. They had been my friends. We had shared meals, conversations, triumphs and failures. I had treated many of them. Now, they were a blur of faces that I couldn't seem to recognise. To a person, they watched me with open hostility. Some stood with their hands on their hips, others with their arms folded. Mouths were held firmly in tight lines and eyebrows were scrunched into frowns. They were a human wall which I clearly wasn't to be allowed to breach.

Occasionally, they would glance at Peace and confusion would cloud their expressions, but it wasn't enough to distract them from their determination to keep me from entering the village, or from their hatred of me, which was palpable; I could actually feel it, almost as easily as I could sense thoughts and feelings from Peace.

Do not pay attention to it for you will be tempted to feel the same way. Focus on our bond, Peace told me.

I took a deep breath in and out, and tried to do as he instructed. *I believed you when you told me how behaviour is infectious, but seeing it, feeling it for myself is something different. How is it possible that my behaviour could be responsible for so much hatred and anxiety?*

Your ability to utilise the voice of your soul when you heal other individuals lifted the energy vibration of the human population as a whole for what affects one of you affects all of you. Your fellow humans may not have been aware of it in those terms but they had a sense that humanity was advancing. That lifted them and gave them increased hope for the future. Your aggression and refusal to provide healing threatened that hope. Your behaviour caused your fellow humans to question the foundation upon which the communities of The New were established and they are anxious and fearful as a result. But one who has the ability to corrupt so many also has the power to correct the mistake.

I find it hard to believe I can do that.

Belief is not necessary. Trust is all that is required.

I could feel his complete absence of doubt in both himself and in me. My shock began to subside.

'You've got a nerve, coming back here, Adam,' shouted a voice that seemed familiar, but which I couldn't quite place.

'So it's true then, you actually went to him in the woods and healed him, Martha?' someone else hissed from the middle of the crowd. 'After he refused to heal all of those who went to him for help? How could you? Some of them died.'

'Yes of course I healed Adam, and then he and I healed Peace, here. We're Healers. That's what we do. Adam needed some time away to come to terms with his loss but he's back now and, as you can see, he's Horse-Bonded. Everyone, meet Peace.'

There was uproar.

'HE'S WHAT?'

'A horse chose him? HIM?'

'You can't be serious.'

'You should be ashamed of yourself, Martha. It's bad enough Morvyr slinking off to the woods to see him every five minutes behind her husband's back, but you, Martha, how could you help him? You know the misery he's caused, flaming lanterns, you got lumbered with trying to help those he turned away. Then, at the first sign he needs help, you just go trotting off into the woods, leaving all of us – decent, respectable people – to fend for ourselves? And why, by the wind of autumn, do you have a squirrel on your shoulder?'

Martha flushed red. 'How dare you? I left Reeta in charge, and I don't even need to ask whether she's done a good job because I know she will have done. And I have a squirrel on my shoulder because he's choosing to be there, despite all of your shouting.'

The words of the ensuing argument washed over me unheard. I was consumed by horror. I'd had no idea that Martha would be vilified for helping me. And how much had Moryvr been putting up with over the past three years in her efforts to help me? The other villagers were clearly furious with her, and gossiping about her and Felin, all because of me. Shame rose in me, followed swiftly by anger.

Their behaviour is merely a consequence of yours. Do not take them further along the path to The Old than you have already. Hold on to our bond, Peace reminded me.

His mention of The Old pulled me up sharply in my mind. He was right. This was my fault and I had to try to make it right. I focused on his unwavering calm and composed myself.

'I suppose if any horse had to choose him, that one's a good match, I mean, look at it, it's in as much of a state as he is,' sneered someone. I swallowed down a burst of anger.

'I bet Adam did that to it,' said someone else. 'He threatened to beat just about everyone else who found him, looks like he actually did it this time.'

'Adam and Peace were both caught in the forest fire. They were both injured and they are both healing well, thank you for asking,' Martha said frostily.

'And we're expected to believe that they're Bond-Partners? We're supposed to look up to them? To listen to that… that creature passing on wisdom from what's left of his horse? Has anyone else seen such a miserable excuse for a Horse-Bonded?'

'Nope, and not for a horse, neither.'

The words almost seemed to hang in the air. Hurling abuse at me was one thing, but they dared to insult Peace? Anger flared in me again and I made no attempt to curb it. I took a step forward and several of the men in the front row shifted their feet further apart. They dropped their hands down by their sides and opened and closed their fists. The air was full of menace.

A loud squeal rang out and everyone looked at Peace. He had arched his neck and lifted his tail, making himself look even bigger than he was. The crowd shuffled backwards uncertainly. Peace walked forward and then turned to walk a line in front of them. He flung his front legs out in front of himself and allowed them to slap down to the ground in a parody of how horses normally walked. A few people sniggered. He moved up to a trot for a few paces, then stopped suddenly, performed a small fly-buck and squealed again. He turned to the crowd and snorted softly. He peered around at them all and I saw those who made eye contact with him begin to relax. A few were smiling whilst also frowning, unsure of what they were seeing.

Peace spun around to face the way he had just come, then leapt off the ground with all four feet. When he landed, he bounced on all four feet again and then looked back at his audience. There was laughter; not the sniggering of a few minutes before, but genuine, delighted laughter. He looked around at them all, his ears pricked, his eyes taking them all in; drawing them all in, just as he had me when I first met him. He reached out to a man, sniffed his face and then wiggled his upper lip under the brim of the man's sunhat, tipping it off. Then he let out another squeal and reverted to walking in his ridiculously exaggerated way, each front leg flung out in turn in front of him, before stopping and stretching like a cat, his belly almost touching the ground. When he stood back up, he peered back at the crowd, most of whom were now smiling and laughing at his thoroughly unexpected behaviour. He sniffed one of the men who had squared up to me, and then nudged him gently in the chest, pushing him into the man behind him. There were grins and chuckles all round.

Martha leant her head towards mine. 'There was me worried about how you'd be received,' she whispered. 'I knew Peace would help you but I had no idea he'd go to these lengths.' Grit looked at me solemnly from her shoulder, quiet for once.

'Well, at least they like one of us,' I said.

Peace turned away from the crowd and launched himself into a big, powerful trot. The crowd gasped as he transformed in an instant from buffoon to vision of magnificence. He circled behind Martha and me and then for once, came to a halt in a controlled and elegant fashion, his head over my shoulder. He nuzzled the side of my face and I smiled and reached up a hand to stroke his cheek.

The crowd stared uncertainly from him to me.

'His name is Peace?' The question came from a woman I didn't know, presumably a newcomer to the village.

I nodded.

'May I approach him?'

I could feel Peace waiting for me to decide how to react. He had diffused the situation, now it was up to me.

'Um, of course. Please do.'

There was murmuring as the woman came forward, and the whole crowd came with her. When she was close enough, Peace shifted closer up behind me and stretched forward to sniff her face. She slowly raised a hand and stroked his nose. 'He's... different from the others, isn't he? From the other bonded horses, I mean?' she said to me. 'They're normally quite approachable, friendly even to an extent, but they're usually more focused on their Bond-Partners than anything else, and they're more... more...'

'Dignified?' I said with a grin.

The woman smiled and nodded. 'No offence, Peace,' she said to him, reaching up to rub his forehead. 'I think you're wonderful.'

'He is,' I agreed. 'And yes, he's different from any of the horses I've met too, but then I suppose he would need to be. He's bonded to me, and I'm not exactly normal Horse-Bonded material.'

'You can say that again,' someone said and there was sniggering in the crowd.

Peace stretched his nose towards those jostling for position behind the woman, and she moved to one side to allow them to move closer, as did Martha. Soon there was smiling and laughing as more people took their turn at having Peace's attention. Every now and then, he would nuzzle my face or shoulder. When he cleared his nostrils, spraying the contents of his nose into my ear, there was uproar.

It wasn't lost on me that Peace was the opposite extreme of me. His antics, his humour, his exuberance, his carefully cultivated air of ridiculousness, balanced out the grief, anger and anxiety that I radiated. They more than balanced me out, actually; they swamped me. People were drawn to Peace. They wanted a share of his warmth, his enthusiasm for life, his ability to make them smile. And because of his obvious and frequently demonstrated affection towards me, their animosity towards me began to wane.

When everyone had had the opportunity to greet Peace, Martha fought her way through the crowd to stand in front of me. 'Okay, so I'm sure you've all heard how loudly Adam's stomach is rumbling, and mine isn't much better, so if you could all move aside and allow us to get to Adam's cottage? He and Peace need to get out of the sun, eat and rest. As you can see, neither of them have fully returned to health after their ordeal in the forest.'

'But I've just sent Ruth to fetch Sheena and Tom. They'll want to see their, what is Peace, their horse-in-law?' a voice near the back called out and was rewarded by laughter.

A shard of pain pierced my heart. Sheena and Tom were Bronwyn and Morvyr's parents. I swallowed hard and looked at the ground.

You have committed to correcting the corruption you have caused. Continue to feel your pain and release it. It is the only way to remain on the path you have chosen.

I can't cry in front of all these people.

It is imperative that you do. You have already learnt that telling the truth can bring comfort. Showing the truth can have a similar effect.

They'll feel better for seeing me suffering?

They will feel less hostile towards you if you allow them to witness your true self. You have spent much time masking your grief with anger. If you are to heal not only yourself but those around you then you must find the courage to be genuine.

I looked up to find that everyone was watching me. A lone tear escaped and trickled down my face. 'Tom and Sheena won't come. They won't want to see me,' I mumbled. The tear was joined by a whole lot more.

'What was that, Adam? We can't hear you at the back,' someone called.

I put a hand to Peace's shoulder and allowed myself to remember the last time I had seen my parents-in-law. They had knocked and knocked at my door, despite my yells for them to leave me alone. When I had finally flung the door open, I found Sheena holding a plate of food she had prepared for me, and Tom holding a bottle of his homemade chutney. I asked if they truly thought that either of their offerings was an acceptable replacement for my wife and daughter and railed at them to go away and never bother me again, before slamming the door in their faces.

'I said, they won't want to see me. And I can't blame them.' I let out a sob.

'Oh, so there are two people you don't blame for something then?' someone else said.

'Shhh, look, he's crying,' said a woman's voice.

'Good. He's caused enough misery to everyone else.'

Peace nuzzled the top of my head and everyone quietened. There was an awkward silence, only broken by the odd sigh or shifting of feet. I focused on my bond with Peace, on the sense of him, calm and strong within my mind. I held on to it with all of myself until his peace filled us both.

'I'm truly sorry for my behaviour.' My voice was soft but clear. 'From the moment I began my herbalism apprenticeship, everything went my way. I was respected for what I could do, and I loved that respect nearly as much as I loved my job. Then I found Bronwyn. When she agreed to marry me, I thought my life couldn't be any more perfect. When she fell pregnant, I was beside myself I was so happy, as many of you will remember.

'But then she and my daughter died while I just stood there, powerless, and watched it happen. I had no idea how to cope with their loss, or the fact that I wasn't as good a Healer as I thought I was. For three whole years, I behaved like a child having a tantrum at things not having gone my way, and the only reason I stopped was because Peace chose me as his Bond-Partner. He thinks I can make amends for all the pain and hurt I've caused you all. I'm not convinced that I can live up to being the person he says I can be, but I'm here because I'm very determined to try.'

There was a long silence. 'That's it? That's all you have to say? After everything you've done?' a man's voice boomed from somewhere in the crowd, making me jump and interrupting my focus on my bond with Peace. I felt flustered and opened my mouth to offer further apology.

Peace was quick to intervene. *Do not fuel righteous anger. Regain your focus.*

I did as he instructed. Then I said, 'I could stand here all day, in fact I could stand here for weeks, apologising, and it wouldn't be enough, I realise that. So, I'm going home to the place I wanted to share with my wife and daughter, and will now be sharing with Peace. If any of you would like to visit us at any time, for any reason, you will be very welcome.'

Peace let out a squeal and performed the smallest of rears. I just had time to marvel at the fact that, far from being worried by his behaviour, the crowd were, to a person, grinning at Peace as they parted, allowing him, me and Martha through. I kept my hand to his shoulder, still needing the strength and focus that physical contact with him gave me.

'Way to go, Adam,' Martha whispered as we walked away from the villagers.

I breathed out. 'Way to go, Peace, more like. I have no idea where that all came from.'

That is not the truth.

'Thunder and lightning, he's not letting up on me,' I said out loud. 'Okay, so I do know where that all came from, I just had no idea I'd be able to do it. Martha, you don't need to come with me, you're starving hungry and there'll be nothing for you to eat at my cottage. I'm more than grateful for everything you've done for me and Peace already. Please, look after yourself now and go on home?'

Martha shook her head stubbornly. 'I want to see you to your cottage. You don't know how you're going to react when you get there.'

'I've a pretty good idea, but if you're sure, then thank you.'

We walked the cobbles in silence. Every footstep that took me closer to the cottage in which Bronwyn and I had planned to spend our lives, was painful. I tried to remember back to when I had last been there. I remembered slamming the door on a messy kitchen with dirty dishes piled in the sink and more on the kitchen table. Everything I had thought of packing and then discarded had been left where I had thrown it. My last act before leaving had been to throw the mug from which I had been drinking, along with the remainder of its contents, at the stone hearth.

I had a big job ahead of me to get it all straight, I knew that, but first I would need to make sure that the paddock around the back would provide suitable grazing for Peace. I hoped the trees that were there when I had left were still standing, as they would provide him with shade. It wouldn't take much to clean the trough and fill it with water for him, but I hoped that weeds hadn't taken over and that there would be enough grass; Peace still had a lot of weight to recover before I would consider him fully recovered from everything through which I had put him. Once he had everything he needed, I would think about finding myself something to eat, and then work on my cottage would begin. We turned a corner and there it was in front of me.

The grey stone cottage was much like any other in this village and most others I had visited, with a window on either side of the wooden front door, and three along the top floor. The slate roof was covered in lichens of all different colours, as was the cobbled path that bisected the front garden as it led from the street to the front door. It hadn't been that way when I left – the lack of footfall on it had allowed the lichens to flourish as they did on the roof. Mine was the only front garden that didn't have a well tended appearance. In stark contrast to the mass of colour it would have been at this time of year under Bronwyn's care, it was an unattractive patch of short brown, green and yellow grass stalks. Someone must have cut it for hay, I supposed.

All of the other houses around mine had a lived in, well cared for feel about them, with brightly coloured curtains wafting out of open windows, flowers growing up around the front door and the windows of the lower floor, children's toys on front paths, and offerings of food and drink left on front steps as gifts from neighbours. My cottage looked dark, gloomy and miserable.

Grief tore at me, pounding at my head, tearing at my stomach and stabbing at my heart. I pressed my hand against Peace's shoulder and allowed myself to feel it all. Martha rested a hand on my arm until I had finished sobbing. 'Well done, Adam,' was all she said.

I nodded and attempted to smile. 'I need to get Peace around the back. He needs to get out of this sun.'

Martha nodded. 'We'll all go.'

Before we could move, my front door was flung open and for a moment, I thought it was my wife standing there, her arms outstretched in welcome. Morvyr hurried down the path and flung her arms around me. 'You're actually home, I can hardly believe it,' she said. 'I hoped I'd have another day to get everything straight, but never mind, I'm almost there.' She went to embrace Martha but took a sudden step back as she noticed Grit still in position on Martha's shoulder, watching the proceedings with interest. Morvyr grinned. 'Squirrel, what an unexpected pleasure.'

'His name is Git,' I told her.

Martha rolled her eyes. 'Adam,' she scolded, but then laughed. 'His name is Grit, Morvyr, for his tenacity and determination.'

Morvyr smiled. 'From what I know of him, you've named him well. You come in too, Martha. I've just been restocking Adam's food cupboards and from the sound of your stomach, you're hungry.'

I should have known. It was exactly the sort of thing Bronwyn would have done for a friend in need. 'Morvyr, thank you. Sincerely, thank you,' I said and was rewarded with a warm smile. 'I just have to take Peace to his paddock and check everything over before I come in. Is that okay?'

'Of course it is. I think you'll find everything to your and Peace's liking, Felin's been busy out there since we've been back. He's at work now, but he was planning to come back this afternoon and give it a last check for anything he might have missed. Come on then, Martha and, er, Grit, let's get you fed. I take it he'll come inside?' she asked Martha as they began to walk up the path to the front door.

'We'll soon find out, but I wouldn't be surprised. Yes, there he goes,' said Martha as Grit bounded through the front doorway and disappeared.

I rubbed Peace's neck and he turned to walk beside me. We went around the front garden and down a short, stony track beside my cottage. The wooden paddock gate was open in front of us and from what I could see, it was in good repair, as was the fence surrounding the large paddock that backed on to the cottage and stretched a good distance away from it, as well as several horse lengths to either side. The trees were indeed still standing, and there was a good amount of grass. There was a heap of weeds just inside the gateway and I could see the areas from which Felin had pulled them, leaving bare patches in his wake that would hopefully repopulate with grass now that the existing grasses had gone to seed.

I looked up to the clear blue sky, so intensely blue that the thought of rainclouds ever being able to obscure it seemed ludicrous. We needed them to, though. If the crops were to grow and the wells were to provide enough water to last out the summer, we would need more rain than had fallen during the rainstorm summoned by the Weather-Singers to extinguish the forest fire. That was for the Weather-Singers to worry about, though. They knew what they were doing and they never let us down.

A memory of a furious Bronwyn entered my mind; someone had questioned my normally sweet-natured wife as to why the Weather-Singers had allowed rain to fall on the day of his daughter's birthday party. He had been reminded in no uncertain terms how complicated a job it was to monitor the weather and all of its contributing factors, and to know when to risk influencing it for local gain without it causing a problem for others elsewhere. The Weather-Singers always took everything into account and did their best for as many people as possible, and they didn't appreciate being challenged over their decisions. I smiled a sad smile.

Your ability to feel and release your emotions is improving, Peace noted.

I came back to myself and blinked. Peace had dropped his head to graze by my side as I stood daydreaming. *Sorry, Peace, I'm meant to be checking everything is okay for you. There's shade over there and plenty of grass, and it looks as though Felin has already scrubbed out the trough and filled it, over there by the back door. I'll leave the gate open, shall I? So you can come and go as you want?* I felt his assent. *Is there anything else you need?* I asked.

I am content. You have no reason to further delay confronting that which you must.

I looked towards my cottage.

Chapter Twenty-Six

I walked in through the back door just as Grit was on his way out with an enormous chunk of cheese in his mouth, his eyes wide at the sound of running footsteps and Morvyr's annoyed voice that followed him. Irritating as I normally found him, the sight of him – a fellow newcomer in the place I had dreaded revisiting above all others – being his normal thieving self caused me to smile and relax slightly.

Morvyr appeared in the short hallway between the back door and the kitchen, looking flustered.

'He's long gone,' I said. 'By the time you reach the paddock, he'll be up a tree. Don't give him the satisfaction of being able to wave his cheese at you from where you can't reach him.'

'The little swine, I'd just cut that piece ready for you,' Morvyr replied. 'Come on in and eat.' She turned and led the way into the stone-walled kitchen.

I dropped my back-sack at my feet and looked around. Martha was sitting at the wooden table, upon which stood a vase of wild flowers along with two bowls of salad, a large loaf of bread and a cheeseboard. A saucepan almost full to the brim with what looked like tomato soup stood on the glistening wood-fired range. The stone floor had been recently scrubbed judging by the damp patches, and the pale yellow curtains at the window were new. It looked so different from the last time I'd seen it that I couldn't reconcile it with the place of pain and misery I had left.

'Adam, did I do wrong?' Morvyr said, holding the back of a chair tightly with both hands. 'I didn't want to upset you, but when I came round with some food ready for when you got back, and found the place in such a state, I couldn't bear the thought of you having to deal with it on your return.'

I shook my head. 'You shouldn't have done it, because you should have been resting, but it's... it's perfect. Thank you. I don't deserve your kindness, or Felin's, or yours, Martha. I was dreading this, but thanks to you all, and I suppose I should admit, thanks to Grit, it doesn't feel as bad as I thought it would.' I moved to the window and touched the curtains. 'Yellow was Bronwyn's favourite colour. You made these?'

Morvyr smiled and nodded. I turned back to look out of the window and my heart warmed at the sight of Peace grazing contentedly in the shade of the sprawling horse chestnut tree.

It hurt to be here without my wife but there were so many things making it easier. My Bond-Partner was with me. I had family and at least one friend who, despite everything, cared about me and had gone to incredible lengths to help me to come back. It was up to me to take the chance they were all giving me and do what I had promised.

I felt Peace's approval. He lifted his head and I thought he would acknowledge me with a glance, but instead, he looked around to his back just as Grit landed on it, using him as a stepping stone from the tree down to the ground. Peace watched the squirrel bound back towards us in the cottage and then dropped his head back down to graze.

I ran to the kitchen door and shut it.

'Err, Adam?' Martha said and when I turned to her, nodded towards the sink. Grit was perched on the edge of it, having just come in through the window. 'Good name, Grit,' she said with satisfaction.

We all laughed.

Once we'd eaten lunch and I had persuaded Morvyr and Martha to go home – Morvyr to rest and Martha to resume the life she had put on hold in order to help Peace and me, not to mention getting Grit out of my cottage – I shut the front door and there was silence.

I rushed to the kitchen and busied myself clearing away the remains of the food before washing the dishes. Then I explored the rest of my cottage. The living room was off one side of the hallway between the kitchen and the front door. Its stone walls were decorated with pictures made from tiny pieces of dried flower petals. There were four cushioned chairs arranged around a low table, upon which stood another vase of wild flowers. My consulting room was on the other side of the hallway. Two of its walls were masked by shelf upon shelf of jars of dried herbs. There were two chairs facing one another and a tall, wooden filing cabinet. The planters on the windowsill stood empty.

I climbed the stairs to find that the bathroom, like all of the rooms downstairs, had been recently cleaned and was immaculate. The door to the spare room stood ajar, allowing me to see that it was now empty of everything Bronwyn and I had gathered in anticipation of our baby's arrival. I slowly let out the breath I had been holding, and with it came tears. I rested my hand on the handle of the door until the pain had passed and then moved on to the bedroom. The room in which my wife and daughter had died. I felt Peace begin to weave himself through me, reassuring me of his conviction that all was well. Strangely, I didn't feel the urge to fight him over it.

I opened the door and walked slowly around the room, opening the wardrobe, drawers and the doors to the bedside tables. All of Bronwyn's clothes and personal effects had been removed. In their place were reminders of her that only Morvyr could have chosen. There was a small picture made in the same style that Bronwyn had favoured, the tiny pieces of coloured petals adding a texture to the picture that a paintbrush never could; new curtains and bedding in different shades of yellow; on my bedside table, a watercolour portrait of Bronwyn that had to have been painted by her mother. In the wardrobe and drawers were several sets of clothes for me, as well as a new pair of shoes.

I sat on the bed and took it all in. I had expected to feel devastated. I had been terrified I would be unable to cope, that rage and fury would take me over as it had when I was last here. Yet I felt a strange sense of calm. All was definitely not well – but it was okay for that to be the case. I did wonder, though, how I would ever be truly happy and at peace, the way I had been before.

You were not at peace. You were merely experiencing the absence of challenge.

Again, I surprised myself by nodding slowly as Peace's counsel settled in with what he had told me before. *Peace is a state of mind that doesn't depend on what's going on around me.* As I thought the words to myself as much as to Peace, I found that I understood them. This feeling of calm I had – even though my stomach was heavy, my throat dry and my head thumping – wasn't just coming from Peace. It was as if a little of it had found a place to settle within me. Although I needed to be very quiet in order to feel it, it was definitely there.

Morvyr had thoughtfully provided enough food to last me for several weeks, which allowed me time by myself to get used to living in a proper home again, with all of the daily routines that came with it; lighting the range as soon as I was up in the morning so that I had hot water and I could cook, topping up Peace's water trough and clearing his droppings into a pile in the corner of his paddock, eating meals at regular times, washing my clothes as well as clearing up after myself and keeping my cottage clean, so that whenever Morvyr came round to check on me, she could see that her efforts hadn't been in vain.

I never went for more than a few hours without venturing out to spend time with Peace. I needed his physical presence every bit as much as the sense of him in my mind, as a reminder that there was a good reason for my return to what was left of my previous life. He was the foundation upon which everything I was doing was built and without him, I knew it would all crumble again. As with everything else, he knew it. Although the paddock gate was left open, he never left to go exploring. Whenever I went to see him or rushed to a window for visual reassurance that he was still there, he was either grazing, snoozing under one of the trees, or resting by the back door. Occasionally, when he could feel me struggling, he would poke his head through the kitchen window. After pans and dishes left on the draining board had been snorted and dribbled over several times, I learnt to dry them immediately after washing them, and put them away.

As the days passed, people began to linger outside my home and wonder out loud to one another whether to venture into the paddock to see Peace. Eventually, the first of them did and the others soon followed. The initial murmurs of concern by adult voices and shrieks of children when Peace thundered over to see them would always change to exclamations of relief as he reached them without trampling them, and then to laughter and squeals of delight as he proceeded to welcome them in his own unique manner. I would watch from my bedroom window as a steadily increasing number of people arrived looking clean and tidy, then left some time later, smoothing their hair back down, replacing sunhats that had been knocked off or grabbed and thrown, and brushing bits of grass, soil, or globules of green saliva from their clothes. It seemed that Peace had enough affection for everyone – and they loved him.

Grit was every bit as popular, so Martha told me one evening during her daily "check on my patients" visit, as she insisted she was doing. Peace's scabs were rapidly crumbling and falling off, new hair was growing in their place, and he was filling out nicely, yet she would insist on performing a thorough inspection of his body whilst stroking his coat and chattering away to him, before turning her attention to me. I was every bit as well on my way to being completely recovered as Peace, a fact on which she remarked after the first week.

'You know, you actually look your age now, what is it, about thirty? You looked nearer fifty when I first saw you. No offence,' she said. Grit stared at me from his place on her shoulder, as if daring me to take any.

I sighed at him and then looked at Martha. 'None taken. I felt every bit that old. If I'm honest, I still do, but that's okay.'

Martha cocked her head slightly to one side, in an exact imitation of Grit. 'Are you alright, Adam? I mean, you look so much better, but you sound... different.'

I considered. 'I feel different. I've spent so much time either raging, feeling sorry for myself, or being terrified of coming back here. Now I'm here, I'm finding that although things aren't right, they're not so bad either and I don't really know how to feel.'

'You're like a storm that's blown itself out, aren't you?' Martha said. 'You know what that means?'

I shook my head.

'It's time to start doing what you came here to do. You need to start getting out and about and seeing people.'

I nodded. 'Peace told me the same thing this morning. I know who I need to go and see first.'

'Morvyr's parents?'

'Yes. I guess there's no time like the present.'

'Are you going to call in on Morvyr? She'll be glad to go with you.'

'No, she and Felin have suffered enough abuse already because of me.'

'Right, well, good luck then. I'll drop by and see you in the morning, okay?'

'Martha, you don't...'

'Yes, Adam, I do. Come on, Grit, oh sorry, Adam, you must have left the top off your biscuit jar.'

'No, I didn't.' I grinned as we watched Grit jump from the kitchen worktop to the table, holding part of a biscuit in his mouth, and then leap to the draining board and out of the window. 'Still think he's cute?' I said.

She laughed. 'I do, as does everyone else, and as I know you do, deep down. Adam, you came here to try to undo the upset you caused, don't you see that Grit is a part of that? You healed him. You were in a dark place and yet he managed to touch the part of you that was still you, and you healed him. As a result, he's here, helping Peace to lighten everyone up.'

'Peace, I understand. I've heard people out there with him and I've seen what he can do. But that thieving squirrel?'

Martha got to her feet with a grin and put her mug in the sink. 'One of these days, you'll admit how fond you are of him.'

I saw her to the door, and then went out to the paddock to Peace. He was surrounded by a group of people, each of whom were taking it in turns to offer him a piece of apple and then have the remnants of their offering ground into their hair along with a good amount of saliva. Those who weren't the current focus of Peace's attention were stroking whichever parts of him that they could reach. I envied him the ease with which he had ingratiated himself into the affections of the villagers of Greenfields and then remembered a time when it would have come easily to me too.

We have visited this several times. Had you not made mistakes you would not be looking to correct them. There would be no reason for you to try to be more than the man you were. The man that others will one day need you to be.

I remembered. *Does a real forest truly grow back stronger for having been almost destroyed?*

It is the way of nature. Catastrophe clears a path for possibility.

I don't think I'll try to convince Bronwyn's parents of that just yet. I'm going to see them now.

Peace cleared his nose over those people closest to him, who all stepped back, squinting and wiping their faces while their friends and children laughed. He walked into the space he had created, and nudged a few people out of his way until the crowd parted and let him through. They turned to watch him walk away from them, towards me. I nodded to them and made an attempt at a smile, unsure of what to say.

Say nothing. You extended an invitation to them when we first arrived. It is for them to decide whether they will accept it.

What if they never do?

It is only the present with which we are concerned.

When Peace reached me, I turned to walk away from the silently staring people, at his side. I put my hand to his shoulder and immediately felt stronger and calmer.

As we walked down the cobbled street, people came to their windows and doors to watch us go past. They pointed and smiled at Peace, but looks directed at me varied from unsure frowns to obviously hostile scowls. I was prepared for a confrontation similar to that when we had first arrived, but nobody shouted at me or attempted to get in our way. When we got to the end of my street, I turned right onto the main street, in the direction leading out of Greenfields. Peace knew where I was heading and walked by my side without question or comment. We came to the end of the cobbles and stepped into the pastureland. It was grazed down low as far as I could see ahead of me and to the left, but to the right were hedgerows separating the summer and winter pastures. It was to the winter pastures that we headed. As soon as we were through the gate, Peace dropped his head to graze the long grass. All around us were the wild flowers of which I had come in search.

I kept my hand to Peace's shoulder and allowed my sense of him to completely fill me. Then I thought of Sheena and Tom and began to pick flowers for them, infusing each one with all the love and positivity I could muster. They were kind people and loving parents. I had increased their suffering at the loss of their daughter with all of the abuse I had hurled at them, and I held firmly to my intention to put that right. When I had picked as many flowers as I could hold in one hand, Peace lifted his head and turned back to the gate.

When we turned the corner back onto the cobbles of Greenfields, there were villagers on their front paths and in the street, staring down at where they had last seen us. When we reappeared, they all made as if to look busy and one by one, disappeared back into their cottages to watch us from the doorways and windows.

They're as uneasy around me as I am around them, I observed.

Peace maintained his sense that all was well, as if that were all the reply that was required.

Sheena and Tom's house was on the main street and it felt as if we arrived there all too soon. As I felt myself beginning to get flustered and anxious, Peace nudged at my mind. I had let go of him a little. I retightened my hold and allowed him to be all of me again. Then I walked up the path.

The door was flung open before I was even halfway to it.

$\mathcal{J}$ stopped in my tracks. Tom looked more than ten years older than the last time I had seen him. His hair, grey when I left Greenfields, was now snow white and his forehead and temples were lined with deep gouges, as if his face no longer knew how to revert to the soft, smiling expression that had defined him when his family had been intact. When he first caught sight of me, he appeared confused, but then his eyes hardened to fury.

Sheena appeared beside him and he put an arm out in front of her to keep her there. She too had aged far more than the years alone could explain. Her grey hair had thinned and lost its wave and her eyelids drooped over her eyes, as if they didn't really want to open. They widened when she saw me, however, and she put a hand to her mouth.

Neither of them spoke. They stood, staring at me with occasional glances over my shoulder at Peace.

Guilt flooded through me. I should have been there to help them with their grief, but instead I had made it a hundred times worse.

It is the present with which we are concerned. Remember what we do here.

I blinked and came back to myself. I focused on my sense of my

Bond-Partner to the exclusion of everything else, then I looked back at Tom and Sheena.

'You brought two incredible daughters into the world and one of them isn't here anymore as a result of marrying me,' I said. 'Even with that being the case, all of your concern when Bronwyn died was for me, yet I behaved worse than appallingly. Your other daughter refused to give up on me, even though I'd given up on myself. She's spent years looking out for me, suffering my temper and lack of gratitude because she's been determined to see me through my grief, to look out for me for her sister's memory. There are no words I can think of to say that will make up for all of the hurt I've caused, but I wanted to let you know that from this point onwards, I will, with Peace's help,' I gestured to where Peace stood on the path behind me, 'be following Morvyr's example and honouring Bronwyn's memory, by being the man she deserved as her husband. She always loved it when I picked wild flowers for her, so I hope you don't mind, but I picked some for you.'

Tears ran down Sheena's face and she went to step outside, but Tom put his arm back out and blocked her. His grey eyes blazed with fury. 'It's taken you three years to come here and say that? We know exactly what Morvyr has done for you. Before she made her home with Felin, it was here that she returned in tears every time you lashed at her with that temper of yours. It wasn't enough that you used it to stamp on my wife's heart when it was already in pieces from losing Bronnie, and it wasn't even enough that you hurt Morv with it, as if you were the only one suffering, but you also turned it on the sick who came to you for help. You're one sorry excuse for a human being, Adam. And you turn up here, with that... fleabag in tow and think that a bunch of flowers will make everything alright?'

The venom in his voice knocked me off balance, and anger flared in me at his insult to Peace.

Peace nudged my back. *His anger is for him to feel. Do not allow him to provoke you into feeling it for him. He must feel his fury to its full extent if he is to be in a position to release it.*

Instantly, my anger subsided. 'I didn't for a moment think that the flowers would make everything alright, I just wanted to give them to you both, in memory of Bronwyn,' I said.

Tom spread his arms and looked around, welcoming everyone who had gathered in the street into our conversation. 'Did you hear that, everyone? Adam is here with flowers, in memory of Bronwyn! Three years after her death and that of our grandchild, he's finally realised that he isn't the only one who has lost her, he isn't the only one who will never see her smile again, he isn't the only one capable of experiencing grief. What about all of those people who are also experiencing grief, Adam, because their relatives died after you refused to treat them? Are you going to take flowers to all of them too?'

Each and every one of Tom's words pierced my heart. I reached a hand behind me to Peace's chest and felt his heart beating slowly and surely. I managed to slow my breathing, allowing the physical sense I now had of my Bond-Partner to strengthen the sense of him in my mind. I would stay calm. I could do this. 'Yes, I am.'

'He's going to take flowers to everyone who has suffered because of him. Behold, everyone, we're in the presence of Adam The Benevolent!' Tom cried manically.

There was sniggering from behind me.

'I'll just put these down here,' I said, and laid the flowers down on the path in front of me. I gave them one more burst of my love and intention to ease Tom and Sheena's pain, and then let them go. I stood up. 'I love you both and I'm so sorry.'

Sheena took hold of Tom's arm and tried to push it out of her way, but he held her where she was. 'Stay where you are, woman,' he growled. Shock lanced through me. He would never have restrained her or spoken to her like that before. Sheena's eyes held mine, a mass of pain and confusion. I wanted to go to her, to force Tom to let her go, but that wouldn't help them – from my place in my bond with Peace, I knew that. I turned to go.

'That's right, turn tail and run,' Tom sneered.

I didn't look back. I could feel Tom's glare on my back as Peace reversed down the path in front of me, for once careful where he walked so that he didn't stray onto the carefully maintained flower beds. Despite the situation, the sight of him lifting his enormous feet and placing them so carefully behind him, and the concentration on his face as he did it, made it hard for me not to smile. I wondered how I could possibly be in such an uncomfortable situation and yet feel so safe, to the point that it was an effort to keep a straight face.

Because all is well. Your current surroundings provide an illusion to the contrary yet through me you sense the truth.

An illusion?

Rest your mind. You have done well.

Peace reached the end of the path and turned to greet the people gathered there. Immediately, there were giggles and exclamations. There was the sound of a door slamming behind me and I turned to see that my flowers were still where I had left them on the path. I began to walk home.

I had taken no more than a few dozen steps when there was a clattering of hooves on the cobbles, and Peace appeared by my side. The sound of running footsteps preceded the appearance of a child on my other side. He had brown hair cropped close to his head and wide, dark brown eyes that were devoid of the laughter and mischievousness with which those of a child of his age – six or seven, I guessed – should have been filled.

'Dane, get back here now,' called a male voice. There was a sense of threat about its tone that I didn't like.

Dane glanced behind him and then looked up to me, squinting in the light of the setting sun. His lower lip trembling, he said, 'Mr Belson, my dad is angry with me and my mum all the time and it makes her cry. Can you ask Peace what I should do to make it better?'

My heart lurched. The malevolence that floated around Greenfields, in the air and through its people, had originated with me, and this child was suffering because of it. I blinked and took hold of Peace in my mind again, shaking myself out of my self-loathing.

Peace?

You have no need to ask me. You know the answer to his question.

I glanced behind me and saw a man who had to be Dane's father marching to catch up with us. I stopped and crouched down to look into Dane's sorrowful eyes. 'Tell your dad that you love him. It won't be easy, but whenever your dad is angry with you or your mum, look straight into his eyes, just as I'm looking into yours now, and tell him you love him. Can you do that?'

Dane nodded, his eyes filling with tears. 'Okay,' he whispered.

'Good lad. Peace and I need to go now, but you and your family can come and see us any time you like, okay?'

He nodded again and began to chew on a finger nail.

I rose and walked away from him moments before his father reached him. 'When I tell you to come back, you do it, you disobedient little idiot,' he told his son. 'What's that? Don't mutter, speak up.'

'I love you Dad,' Dane repeated, his voice shaking.

There was silence. I kept walking but when I turned to look back a few moments later, Dane's father had taken his hand and was leading him not ungently back to the other villagers, glancing down at his son every few seconds as if to say something, but then looking back in the direction he was going.

Peace and I visited Tom and Sheena's house every evening. I took freshly picked flowers imbued with my love and best wishes every time.

On the evening after our first visit, I found the flowers from the previous day where I had left them. I swept them to the side of the path with my foot and proceeded to the front door. It remained closed when I knocked, so I left fresh flowers on the doorstep in a jar half-filled with water that I had brought with me in expectation of needing it. I grinned as Peace patiently reversed down the path again, into a newly gathered crowd. When I turned for a final glance at the cottage before making my way home, I saw a curtain move at one of the upstairs windows.

The following evening, I found the path littered with wilted flowers and pieces of smashed glass. I warned Peace not to venture up the path behind me, then left a new jar containing fresh flowers on the doorstep.

By the fourth evening, people were waiting for Peace outside Tom and Sheena's cottage. They welcomed him with apples and carrots, squeals and laughter, whilst ignoring me. Peace stood with them, nuzzling and nudging, roughing up hair, spraying the contents of his nose over people and removing their hats as I walked up the path. I returned a few minutes later, having left a fresh jar and flowers. The door remained closed to me and the path increasingly littered with the remnants of my previous gifts.

As the evenings went by, it wasn't unusual for one of the crowd to peel away from the rest and walk with Peace and me as we returned home, wanting Peace's advice. Unbeknown to them, he rarely gave it, insisting that if I remained holding on to to him, physically as well as mentally if necessary, I would know what he would say. He was a relentless teacher.

He began to call for me to go to him in his paddock during the day, knowing that some of those who continued to visit him were wanting to ask him for advice or an opinion, but were either too scared of my temper or too furious with me to come and ask me to relay his counsel to them. To begin with, I couldn't seem to help walking out there with a somewhat furtive air, unsure what my reception would be and loathe to spoil the fun that Peace's visitors were very obviously enjoying with him; he had taken to resting his muzzle upon their shoulders, and occasionally on the tops of their heads, and then moving his own head around so that they were forced, laughing, to stagger around beneath him. No matter how rough he was with them, they were all relaxed in his company until I arrived. Then, silence would fall and there would be a lot of nervous shifting around until I managed to focus on the place in my mind where Peace resided, and that place became all of me. The resulting change in my demeanour must have been obvious because it was then that the questions for Peace would come, and he would continue to insist that I answer them.

I learnt to be at peace – by holding to Peace – before I left my cottage, so that however I was feeling when left to my own thoughts, it was only ever the version of me that was full of my bond with my horse, that anyone else saw. Gradually, the faces that had looked so familiar when I arrived back in Greenfields, yet had seemed to blur into one uniform face displaying nothing but loathing of me, began to come back into focus and separate back into those that I knew.

Three weeks passed before my evening visit to Tom and Sheena's cottage revealed an empty jar on their doorstep, the flowers I had left neither in it, nor strewn on the path.

My heart lifted and I wondered whether to knock on the door.

You have said all that is necessary. The relevant emotion has been felt and released. It is your love that they currently require in a form that they can accept. There will be a time for more words but that time is not now, Peace advised.

Okay then, I'll keep going with the flowers. I made my way back down the path, smiled at anyone looking my way, whether they acknowledged me or not, and then turned for home.

When Peace arrived next to me in his usual ungainly flurry, I noticed a pair of trousered legs on his other side. As I had learnt to do, I said nothing, allowing whoever had caught up with me to speak in their own time.

'I need help.' The voice was gruff and I instantly recognised it as that of Dane's father.

'Okay, well, ask away and Peace and I will do our best,' I said.

'It isn't the horse's help I need, it's, err, it's…' Steen cleared his throat. 'It's yours.'

'Mine?' I said.

'Martha said you would treat me, now that you've, err, well, now that you've calmed down.'

Hope flickered in me. 'You'd like me to treat you? Well, yes, of course I will. Do you want to come to the cottage now?'

'I'm here, aren't I?' Steen snapped. Then he sighed. 'I'm sorry. I'm in pain all the time and I take it out on everyone around me. My wife and son bear the worst of it and it isn't fair, I know that. The boy has taken to telling me that he loves me every time I get irritable, I imagine as a result of his talk with you and Peace. Anyway, it made me realise that I needed to do something about it, so I went to Martha a few days ago. She told me I had a parasite in my gut, but the preparation she gave me has only taken the edge off the pain. Martha expected more improvement than I'm showing, so she suggested I come to you. She surprised me, actually, because she didn't used to have much good to say about you.'

'She's a good Herbalist, but we all have areas of speciality and she obviously thinks that whatever you have needs mine,' I said.

'Oh, come on, Adam, we all know you're better than her. We all thought she'd leave here when she qualified, and go and practise somewhere that you aren't known.'

'She didn't leave because she's loyal to her family and to all of you here at Greenfields. She's devoted to her patients in a way I never have been, and I'm not sure I have the capacity to be. She gives you the security of knowing that she'll hang in there with you however bad things are, and she'll celebrate with you when you get better. I've learnt a huge amount from having been her patient, I can tell you. Greenfields is very lucky to have her.'

'But she could only help me so much.'

'So apparently, you're one of the few who need healing at a slightly deeper level, and Martha had the skill necessary to recognise it and refer you to me, just as I'll refer you back to her for what she can give you that I can't.'

'But if you can help me, why can't I just stay as your patient?'

'Because Peace and I won't be staying here for long. I have a whole lot of damage to undo, and that means I have a very large number of people to find.'

'But what if I need your help again once you've left?'

'We'll see what's wrong with you first, shall we? After you.' I beckoned for Steen to go ahead of me up my front path, and then turned to find Peace already making his way to his paddock. This would be the first time I'd had any dealings with anyone without the reassurance of his physical presence and I felt nervous. *Any advice?*

Peace stopped and turned his head to look at me. The evening sunlight glanced off the white of his coat, giving him an ethereal looking glow. His soft, brown eyes drew me in as they always did.

I sighed. *Okay, I know, hold on to our bond.*

You need not hold so tightly as has previously been necessary, was all the comment he made before continuing on his way.

'Adam?'

I blinked. 'Sorry, Steen, I just needed to ask Peace something.'

'About me?'

'No, about me. Go on in and take the first door on your left.'

Steen did as he was instructed and then when I indicated, sat down on one of the chairs in my consulting room. I focused on my sense of Peace as was becoming second nature, and then looked at Steen. 'Bear with me, and I'll see what I can find.'

I extended my awareness to Steen's body. The lining of his intestines was seriously inflamed as a result of the parasite, which had been left thriving due to Steen's resistance to finding out what was wrong with him. Martha's herbal preparation had killed the parasite and begun to ease the inflammation but its effects were being limited by something else. Intuition allowed me to know of Steen's extreme anxiety. I remembered that his father had died from a disease that had originated in his gut and could well understand that Steen had convinced himself that he was on his way to the same fate, leaving his wife and son to manage without him. While Martha's preparation had eased the symptoms, Steen's anxiety was preventing it from alleviating them completely. I would make some of my green paste, I decided. Its positive energy should reassure Steen and hopefully speed up his recovery if mixed in with the same preparation that Martha had prescribed.

'There's nothing to worry about. Martha's preparation has done its job – it's killed the parasite you had and it's easing your gut lining, but there's something I can add to it that should help it to work more quickly. If I run out now, I'll be able to collect the herbs I need to make up a new preparation, before it gets dark. Do you want to wait here?' I said.

Steen raised his eyebrows. 'You'll make something up for me right now?'

I nodded. 'Yes of course.' I stood up and reached for the basket I had always used for collecting herb samples. A stab of pain went through my heart as a memory surfaced of Bronwyn holding it for me whilst I crawled along on my knees, selecting what I needed. I felt the pain and let it go. 'You're welcome to go and relax in the living room or kitchen, or if you're up for more of Peace's attentions, go and see him and he'll be pleased to bestow them upon you,' I said.

'Thanks, Adam.' Steen's words followed me as I went out of the door.

Chapter Twenty-Eight

I woke suddenly, to a loud bang. My immediate concern was for my horse. *Peace?*

You have visitors. All is well.

The banging continued. 'Adam,' called an excited voice.

I went to my bedroom window, opened it and peered down to the doorstep. Steen's wife and son stood there, looking up at me. 'Keela? It's barely dawn, what's happened? Is Steen alright?'

'He's better than alright, Adam, please come down.'

I rubbed my eyes, pulled on my dressing gown and went downstairs, trying to wake up properly. When I opened the front door, there was a burst of movement. Small arms encircled me and clung on tight. 'He's alright,' Dane said, looking up at me. 'My dad's alright.'

'Steen was up early for work as usual, and he woke us both up with his singing,' Keela told me excitedly. 'Singing! Can you believe it? This is the man who has barely had a nice word to say to anyone for the past six months. When I asked him if he was okay, he said he was feeling better than he had in years, and that he was off to work but when he gets home this evening, he'll take Dane out to the paddock to fly his kite! Oh, Adam, thank you.'

I could hardly believe what I was hearing; the speed of Steen's recovery was astonishing.

It is human nature to underestimate the power of love and positivity. This is the first of many times that you will prove to yourself that which you know but have yet to discover.

How can I know it if I have yet to discover it?

Despite your sensitivity you spend a large proportion of your time drowning out the part of you that knows everything with the part of you that believes it knows nothing. It is normal for humans to exist in such a way. Do not fret. All is well. Peace went back to the doze that Keela and Dane's arrival had disrupted.

I frowned. It was too early for all of this.

'Adam?' Keela and Dane were both looking up at me.

'Sorry, Peace just interrupted. That's fantastic news, I'm so pleased for you all. I take it Martha dosed you both against the parasite that caused all this?'

Keela nodded. 'We've been fine, but she gave us a single dose of what Steen's been taking, just in case.'

'Okay, well if you're still feeling fine then I think you're in the clear, as I'm sure she's already told you.'

'What about our family and friends? Might they be infected too? Steen wouldn't let Martha or us tell anyone what was wrong with him but now he's back to himself, we ought to let everyone know in case they've picked it up too.'

'If any of them have any symptoms like Steen had, or if they would like to take a dose of the preparation as a precaution, tell them to go and see Martha straight away, or me if she's busy.'

'We will.' Keela reached out and put a hand to my arm. 'Welcome back, Adam,' she said softly.

I smiled. 'Thank you.'

~

The following days passed in a blur. As word got around that Steen had made a full recovery after coming to see me, I was inundated with villagers anxious to have a precautionary dose of whatever it was I had given him. I couldn't source the herbs and make up the preparation quickly enough and there was often a queue outside my front door. I was elated; each person who walked away with a dose was one who would hopefully contribute to the gradually lightening atmosphere in Greenfields, until it returned to where it was before I damaged it. Peace was left to entertain his admirers by himself during the day, but everyone knew that he and I would be walking to and from Tom and Sheena's cottage every evening, if they wanted to ask me for his advice. We were frequently accompanied by people wanting to do exactly that.

I was just taking a quick break for lunch one day when there was a knock on the front door. I sighed. I had closed it and pinned up a notice saying that it would be open to patients again shortly, but someone clearly couldn't wait. I didn't get the chance to rise from my chair before my visitor's identity was revealed by Grit bounding in through the open kitchen window. He leapt to the rim of the sink and then onto my kitchen table, skidding to a stop at the far end where I couldn't reach him. I rolled my eyes and grinned at him, then got to my feet, leaving Grit to help himself to what was left of my sandwich as I made for the front door.

Martha stood on the doorstep, holding a basket full of herbs in each hand. 'I hear you're run off your feet. Why didn't you tell me you could do with a hand?' she said as she stepped into my hallway and handed me the baskets. 'Here, take these, that's one less job for you.'

'Thank you, I didn't like to trouble you, I mean, I know you're always busy.'

'You didn't want to rub my face in the fact that you were able to help Steen where I couldn't, you mean,' Martha said. 'I thought we were past all that? Adam, you helped me to see my role here, and I'm happy with it. I help people, sometimes directly, sometimes indirectly. Today, I'm doing both.'

I stared at her.

'Err, are you okay?' she said eventually.

'You're everything I'm aspiring to be, you know,' I said quietly.

Martha frowned. 'I'm... what?'

'You're at peace with yourself. I'm not, but being around you reminds me that it's possible. Thanks for that, as well as for your help.'

'Okay... I think?' She grinned and then looked past me and grimaced. 'I'm afraid it looks as though you've lost some of your lunch.' Grit tore past me, leapt onto the consulting room door handle and then to Martha's shoulder, a crust and a piece of lettuce in his mouth.

'I expected it. I can make more sandwiches, if you'll join me?'

Martha shook her head. 'Thanks, but I've eaten. I can stay and help you make those herbs into more of the anti-parasite preparation, though, if you tell me what proportions you want them in?'

I nodded. 'Thanks, that would be great, come this way then. I've been using the same herb proportions you used in your preparation, just with an extra addition,' I said over my shoulder.

'And you're healing more than just gut inflammation as a result,' Martha said as she followed me into my consulting room. 'You're adding that disgustingly green paste, aren't you? And the atmosphere in Greenfields is improving; people are happier. You're not just healing them physically, Adam, you're healing them mentally too.'

I nodded and despite the warning I felt from Peace, I said, 'So does that mean you believe me? Will you let me show you...'

'No,' Martha said firmly. 'I know what I can do, Adam, and I'm happy and confident doing it. I just wanted to tell you how pleased I am that your courage in coming back here is being rewarded. Now leave me to it and go back to your lunch. Your stomach is rumbling so loudly, it's making me feel nauseous.'

'Okay, fine. I suppose I'll need to get extra bread out to feed Grit?'

Martha grinned. 'Accepting him into the fold at last, are you?'

I winked. 'Never.'

～

As Peace and I made our way to Tom and Sheena's that evening, laughter emanated from several open windows and a shrieking that initially alarmed us both, turned out to be a young mother being chased from the paddock of her cottage by her husband and young child. Both were laughing and carrying beakers of water that they evidently intended throwing over her in the heat of the evening. Nobody glared at me and many called out greetings, or smiled and waved at me, instead of only at Peace. The dreadful oppression I had caused was lifting, yet it wasn't making any difference to how I felt, I mused to myself. When I needed to interact with anyone, it was now as easy to find Peace and hold on to him as it was to scratch my own nose, but as soon as I stopped clinging to him and began to think for myself, I felt sad and hollow. I loved my Bond-Partner with a ferocity that I would never have dreamt possible, but I still felt the loss of my wife and daughter keenly. I couldn't get past wanting them with me, adding to my life with Peace. He was unwavering in his assertion that I would find the peace I sought by being a source of it for others and I believed him, but as the villagers of Greenfields began to forgive and accept me and it made no difference to me at all, I gained even more idea of the magnitude of the task ahead of me.

It will soon be time to leave, Peace told me as we approached my parents-in-laws' cottage.

Leave? But it feels as if I've only just started trying to make things right.

You need only reverse the direction of the path that you caused your fellow humans to take. The new energy vibration produced by your intervention will perpetuate and strengthen with no need of further input from you.

But Sheena and Tom still aren't even speaking to me.

Peace didn't answer but I felt a sense of anticipation from him. Instead of stopping to play with the villagers waiting to see him, he walked past them and followed me through the gateway to my in-laws' front path. I stopped. As had become usual over the past days, the flowers I had left on the doorstep were gone. Today however, the path had been swept clean of smashed glass and the many weeks' worth of rejected flowers that had previously been left rotting. Peace stopped close behind me and breathed his calm into my ear. The front door opened.

Morvyr had told me that her parents were looking better but as I stood open mouthed, staring at the pair of them, I couldn't believe what I was seeing. Their faces had softened and Sheena's hair had been coloured and swept up into a pleat. They both wore bright-coloured clothes, a stark contrast to the mixture of grey, brown and black they had been wearing when I saw them last, and they both stood smiling at Peace and me. They looked years younger and although their faces were still lined, their change of expression from angry, weary and anxious to smiling and serene, stretched out the lines, making them shallower and less obvious. This was more of the proof that Peace had ensured me I would find, I realised.

Tom moved to the side slightly to allow his wife past. Sheena held her hands out to accept the flowers I was carrying and I walked up the path and gave them to her. Cheering erupted in the crowd and Sheena and Tom both raised a hand to wave to their friends.

'Will you come inside?' Sheena said to me.

I smiled. 'Thank you, I'd love to.'

'What about… Peace, isn't it? Will he be alright out here?'

I nodded my head back to the crowd of people waiting on the street. 'He has plenty of entertaining to do out here, he'll be fine, thank you.'

Sheena gestured for me to pass her and go into the cottage. When I reached Tom, he did the same thing. As the front door closed behind us all, my heart thumped in my chest and I felt beads of sweat running down my back – far more than was necessary in order for my body to cope with the heat of the evening. Peace nudged my mind and I grabbed hold of my sense of him before anxiety prevented me from finding him at all. I breathed slowly, allowing his calm to fill me, and turned to Tom and Sheena to thank them again for allowing me into their home. As I opened my mouth to speak, Sheena held a hand up to me and shook her head. She opened her arms to me and when I went to her, drew me into a warm hug. I felt Tom's arm around me as he hugged us both.

There was the sound of a door opening. 'Is this a private cuddle, or can anyone join in?' came Morvyr's voice.

Sheena and I each extended an arm to include Morvyr, and big, strong arms from behind her almost managed to encircle us all. 'Thank goodness,' Felin's voice rumbled in my ear, full of relief.

When the five of us finally parted, the absence of the sixth and seventh people who should have been there hit me like a sledgehammer. I lost all sense of my horse as grief took me completely and I sank to my knees.

'Well, that's been a long time coming, better out than in,' Sheena said. I had been guided to the front room and now sat on a chair by the open window. Tom and Morvyr sat in chairs opposite me, Sheena was on her knees, holding my hands as I wept, and Felin stood with a hand on the back of Morvyr's chair.

'He's very loyal, isn't he?' Sheena nodded behind me and I turned to see Peace's head directly behind me; he was standing outside in the dark, his head through the window. I had thought that the warm air on the back of my neck was the evening breeze that blew in off the pastures, but I should have known that he would get as close to me as he could in order to support me. Immediately, as my grief subsided, I felt his serenity easing its way through me, comforting me and reassuring me that all was well. I reached a hand up to stroke his nose and suddenly realised that he had to be standing on Tom's flower beds.

'He's incredible,' I said. 'I'm so sorry though, I think he's probably trampled on a good number of your plants.'

'He brought you back to us all. We'll forgive him that,' chuckled Tom.

'I don't know what came over me,' I said, wiping my face on my sleeve. 'I'm meant to be here trying to make up for all of the hurt I've caused and instead, I've been bawling for... how long?'

'About an hour,' said Felin. 'It's okay, we all know you need to grieve, Adam, we're just relieved that you're finally doing it. Now we can all move on.'

'That's what Peace said, but I'm not sure I can.'

'As I understand it, he never said it would happen overnight,' Morvyr said. 'You've been back here, what, a month or so? You and Peace have contributed to the village, and people are laughing as well as feeling better, as a result. And it's changed you, Adam. You're already looking and talking more like the Adam we used to know. You just have to give it time.'

I nodded. 'Peace said that too. Thank you, all of you, for accepting me back into your family. I'll miss you so much.'

'Miss us?' said Sheena. 'Why will you miss us? You can't be going anywhere yet, you've only just come back to us.'

'I know, but I've hurt a lot of people and I have to find them all and make it right.'

Tom whistled. 'You were serious, then? You're actually going to try to find everyone you refused to help, and, what? Give them flowers?'

'They're not just flowers, though, are they?' Morvyr said, with a ghost of a wink at me. 'They're peace offerings. Look at you and Mum, Dad, they worked, didn't they?'

Tom and Sheena looked thoughtfully at one another and then at me. 'Yes, I suppose they did,' said Sheena. 'But, Adam, can't you stay just a little longer?'

'He's not going anywhere just yet. My baby is due in five weeks' time and he's going to be around until at least then, aren't you, Adam?'

My heart sank. More pain. Peace nudged both my mind and the back of my neck and I grasped hold of him, choosing his calm strength over the panic and dread that threatened to swamp me. I knew that Morvyr needed regular reassurance that I could give her now that Peace was there to ensure that I was in a position to detect any potential problems; she still succumbed to terror at times that what had befallen her sister and niece might befall her and her son. I nodded. I would be there to give her that reassurance and in the process, I would work through another aspect of my pain. I felt Peace's pride in me. 'Of course I'll stay until then. Peace and I can't leave without meeting my nephew.'

Morvyr and Felin both smiled. 'Thank you,' mouthed Felin from his place behind his wife.

'Well, I suppose that's settled then,' said Sheena. 'Adam, you look exhausted. Go home, get a good night's sleep and then come over for dinner tomorrow evening? We could have it outside in the paddock so that Peace doesn't have to stand with his head through a window to be near you?'

I chuckled. 'That would be lovely, thank you. I'm just glad he hasn't seen fit to snort all over your furniture. Would you like to come out and meet him properly before we go?'

'Yes, I would. Help me up, could you? My knees aren't what they were.'

'Of course. Sorry.' I was mortified all over again as I realised how long Sheena had been on her knees, comforting me. I leapt up and helped her to her feet, and then we all went out to see Peace. He was waiting for us on the path, as if his foray into the flower beds had never happened. He reached his nose out to sniff Tom and Sheena in turn, then he nuzzled their hands before resting his chin first on Sheena's shoulder and then on Tom's. They smiled as they stroked him and told him how beautiful he was. I loved him more than ever for his gentleness and for bringing such delight to two people who meant so much to me.

Morvyr and Felin left Peace and me at the gate, to go to their new cottage at the other end of the village. Peace and I walked home, the white of his coat appearing almost silver in the moonlight, the brown patches an inky black. I put a hand to his shoulder.

Thank you, Peace.

You are feeling a little better.

A little, yes.

Those you love are feeling much better.

Yes, thank goodness. And they look so different too. I knew the flowers would help them to feel better, but for them to make that much difference? I mean, it wasn't as if they were eating them, they just had them in the house. I can't even begin to imagine what else might be possible, it's mind blowing!

The power of love and positive intention is a recent introduction to your thought process. In time the knowledge of what is possible will be part of who you are.

So you keep saying. It's as if you've already seen who I'll be. How do you know? Can you see the future?

I know what I need to know at the moment I need to know it. It is always the present with which I am concerned.

You keep saying that too, yet it doesn't stop you dangling the future in front of me.

Humans find it difficult to remain purely in the present. You are driven by expectation and aspiration.

So you're giving me hope that someday I'll be this serene, knowledgeable person, so that I'll keep going? So I don't give up? You think I'm still that fragile?

Do you attempt to convince me that you are not? Peace's thought was gentle and loving, and accompanied by a surge of pride in me. It was impossible to feel deflated or to misunderstand his message; I was on my way to being more than the man I was but I still needed him desperately, and that was okay because he had every intention of being there for me.

I know I don't have to tell you how grateful I am to you, but I have to ask, why are you doing this? You're a horse, and yet you're living away from the rest of your species, in order to help me – why? Come to that, why do any horses choose Bond-Partners?

At present you would not survive as a species without us.

After all the damage our ancestors did to the planet, I would have thought that the rest of the species would be better off without us?

If it were merely a case of physical survival that would be true.

And it's not?

It is not.

Then what is it a case of?

Balance. Eventually you will understand. Rest now.

We had arrived back at my cottage and Peace continued on to his paddock without looking back as I stood frowning in confusion after him.

When I finally turned to go up the path to my front door, I realised that I could barely see either of them. I looked up at the sky in surprise. Clouds had moved in front of the moon. The night had become deathly still. A storm was coming.

I was woken by deafening claps of thunder. Peace was unperturbed, I could feel that, but I leapt out of bed anyway and rushed to the window at the back of the cottage to confirm with my eyes what I sensed in my mind. A bolt of lightning rendered my horse briefly visible; he was standing, resting a hind leg under the thick, drooping cover provided by a willow tree. How he could be dozing when rain lashed at everything around him, lightning flashed without warning and the subsequent thunder was loud enough to rouse those for miles around, I had no idea. But then I did. He had experienced storms before. He knew what they were and how to survive them. There was no reason for alarm. He would just be his normal, calm self and then continue in the same fashion once it was over. He was Peace. I went back to bed, cherishing the sense of him in my mind. I later discovered that of everyone in Greenfields, I was alone in having been able to sleep the rest of the night through.

Chapter Twenty-Nine

*T*he next five weeks passed quickly. I had a steady stream of patients coming to my door and when I wasn't with them, I was out in the paddock answering questions directed at Peace, but which he continued to insist that I answer by immersing myself in my sense of him. The answers I gave were authentic and from Peace, but in gleaning them from him in that way, as opposed to relaying a message from him, he ensured that no opportunity was missed for me to be in a peaceful frame of mind, even if it was his and not my own. His persistence, combined with the fact that I also needed to fill my mind with his way of being in order to be effective as a Healer, meant that feeling at peace became as familiar as it was blissful.

It was often remarked that my voice was softer than it used to be, and I noticed that my patients were sharing a lot more with me during their consultations, not only regarding their physical symptoms, but about how they felt and about their lives in general. I answered all of their questions from my place with Peace, and when they left my consulting room, even before they had begun to take their herbal preparations, all of which had been prepared with love and positivity for their bodies and minds to use in whichever way was helpful, they seemed to walk more lightly. I loved being a source of peace for them all and when I released my hold on my Bond-Partner to settle down for the night, I ached for the day that I might be able to feel it for myself.

I ate with Sheena and Tom every evening while Peace supplemented the grazing in his paddock with that in theirs. They loved him and I relished watching them dash out before dinner with carrots and apples for him, and then spend time stroking his forelock out of his eyes, rubbing his neck and teasing at the knots in his tail. More than once, I felt a pang as I thought how much I would have loved to have seen them with their granddaughter but seeing them with Peace, fussing over him and delighting in his attention, always lifted my heart.

When I arrived one evening, Sheena excitedly presented me with three brushes that looked like those for scrubbing the floor. They had handles looped over their wooden backs and each had a different bristle texture, from firm to very soft. 'Come on,' she said, 'we'll all go and give Peace a good brush before we eat. I'm assured that Rill's donkeys love it, so I'm sure Peace will too. He can't go around covered in mud and with his tail in a tangle all the time. We all prayed for a storm to break the weather and clear the way for more rain, but while it's suiting most of us, Peace looks like he's been dragged through a hedge backwards.'

'Let the man eat first, Sheen,' said Tom without much conviction and with a hopeful look in my direction, clearly as eager to go and brush Peace as was his wife.

'It's due to rain again later, we need to brush him now while he's dry,' Sheena called over her shoulder, already on her way to the back door.

Peace did indeed love being brushed. He stopped grazing and stood with a dreamy look on his face, occasionally indicating with his nose the areas that he considered needed extra attention.

'There,' Sheena said eventually, standing back with her hands on her hips to admire the results of our efforts. 'That's better, Peace, isn't it?'

The brushes had lifted away the last remnants of his scabs and his coat gleamed. The long hair around his lower legs, brushed until each hair moved independently of the others, rippled in the breeze, as did the hair of his mane, tail and forelock. His brown eyes, soft and knowing as ever, settled on each of us in turn, leaving none of us in any doubt that he knew how beautiful he was.

The breeze strengthened, carrying with it the faint sound of singing. 'The Weather-Singers are making sure the rain doesn't go around us, so it will be here soon. If you were going to be staying here longer, we'd have had a shelter built out here for when Peace comes, but at least he has the trees over in the corner to shelter under,' Tom said with a sidelong glance at me.

I knew that neither of them wanted us to go, and most evenings, one or both of them would allude to the fact that they would love it if we stayed longer, but I knew we couldn't. I felt badly for them, but I took comfort from the fact that they would soon have a new grandchild to occupy their attentions.

Morvyr and Felin often joined us for dinner and when they didn't, Peace and I always went to see them before returning home. They took to leaving the window of the front room open, knowing that he would announce our arrival by poking his nose through it and whickering to them as they rested in their large armchairs before bed, and wanting to include him as I went in to give them my daily dose of reassurance that their son was doing well and continuing to ready himself for his arrival.

I appreciated the efforts to which not only my family, but all of the villagers went, to include and attend to Peace, but I knew it wasn't for me that they did it; they respected and admired all of the horses who passed through the village with their Bond-Partners, but they adored Peace. They loved his lack of decorum, his willingness to include everyone in his affections, and his sense of fun, and that was on top of their appreciation for his advice and continuing presence in the village; normally the Horse-Bonded only stayed for a few days, a week or two at most. Everyone had had a chance to ask for counsel from Peace and although it was my thoughts that they received, he and I both knew that the counsel could have originated nowhere but from him.

Martha and Grit took to coming daily to my cottage for lunch. Since many of Martha's patients were coming to me for help with deeper rooted issues, she had a little more time and seemed more than happy to eat with me and then spend an hour or two after lunch going out to collect more of whichever herbs were running low on my shelves, exchanging pleasantries and laughter with those on their way in to see me, on her way out. Her willingness to help our patients either directly herself, or indirectly by helping me, was commented on often, and I sensed an increased fondness developing for her by the villagers of Greenfields, as well as an escalation in the trust and respect they had for her.

She's being the best she can be and she's amazing at it, I observed both to myself and to Peace as I stood at my consulting room window, watching her making her way towards the fields on yet another herb-collecting foray.

Yet she will find it difficult once we are gone unless we leave a source of that which she doesn't trust herself to provide.

Love? How do we leave that behind us?

Plucked herbs are not the only vessels available for transferring positive energy.

I considered, but not for long. *I can leave it in growing plants! So, if I find a bush or a tree and infuse it with love, how long will it stay there? How long will it last, I mean?* I sensed Peace's amusement and couldn't help but smile in response. *What's funny?*

It will be available for as long as the plant lives and afterward for as long as the components of the plant exist.

But that's forever. The plant will break down and its constituent parts will be recycled by nature into other... ohhhhhhhh, I see. Really? It will last forever?

You begin to understand the true nature of that with which we are concerned. Consider the love that you introduced to my body with your preparations. It did not merely heal my wounds but became part of my being. Even now it is part of the love that heals you in return. It can never be diminished. I could continue to give your love back to you for eternity yet I would always have the same reservoir from which to draw.

I fought to understand what he was telling me but the harder I tried, the less I understood. Then, when I finally accepted that I couldn't understand how a reserve of something could never be diminished when its contents were given away, I found that there was a part of me, deep down, that did understand.

It's because we're part of the same interconnected whole, isn't it? It helps to stop thinking about it and... feel it, I told myself as much as Peace. I sensed his approval.

When you allow understanding to come to you instead of chasing after it you open yourself to a far deeper level of comprehension. It will take time to become a habit, he told me.

And time is something I've run out of, because my first patient of the afternoon is just walking up the path.

Time is also not what you believe it to be but that is not a topic for current consideration.

There was a knock at the front door. *Are you trying to scramble my brain, Peace?* I asked as I went to answer it.

Were that the case I would have succeeded. Now that your patient is here you must put aside our discussion until your time is your own.

I know, I haven't forgotten the rule, all my stuff to one side. There, see? Already done. I opened the door and smiled at the friend of Sheena's who was standing there.

I took my time deciding what type of plant to leave for Martha, and where to put it so that she would have easy access to it. The more I thought about it, the more obvious the answer became and when Martha and Grit appeared for their daily lunch a few days later – her favoured cheese and salad sandwich and his pile of crusts were already on the table awaiting them – I put forward my suggestion.

'Move in here? Are you crazy? This is your home,' Martha said, her sandwich halfway between her mouth and her plate.

'A home that very soon I will no longer need.'

'But I'm not married,' said Martha.

'Having a cottage built when you marry is convention and nothing more. Grit takes up more space than anyone I know so you won't feel alone here, the consulting room is already set up and people are getting used to coming here for treatment. You can't tell me your parents won't appreciate having some peace and quiet from all the coming and going.'

Martha took a bite of her sandwich and chewed thoughtfully. 'But what about when you eventually come back?'

'I have a huge task ahead of me and I don't anticipate it being accomplished quickly. I may never come back here and in the meantime, this place will be left untended and unloved. You would be doing me a favour, taking it on for me. And don't worry, I won't be homeless, I'm Horse-Bonded so there will always be a place for me at The Gathering with all the others if I find myself needing somewhere to stay.'

Martha nodded. 'I suppose so. I must admit, it would be good for me to have more space and for my parents to have their house back.'

'That's settled then.'

'You're sure? You're really sure?'

I nodded and smiled. 'I'm really sure. You've been such a good friend to me and Peace, and I can't think of anyone I'd rather give this place to, especially since you're the only one who can make good use of the hawthorn growing along the back fence of the paddock.'

Martha raised her eyebrows. 'Really? I mean, I admit it will save me having to go very far to replenish my store of it, but it's pretty common, Adam, and there isn't a huge incidence of heart problems in the village.'

I took a breath and grasped hold of my sense of Peace, knowing that what I had to say next needed to be said from the right place and in the right way. 'If any of your patients have symptoms that seem obstinate in going away, like Steen's gut problem, then making a vibrant green paste from the leaves of the hawthorn out there in the paddock will really help. Use it if you want, or don't, but it will be there if you want it.'

Martha looked at me searchingly. Then she nodded. 'I'm sure there will be occasions when I'll be glad of it. Thanks, Adam. For everything. Do you know when you'll be leaving?'

'Shoving me out already?' I laughed and winked at her expression of horror. 'I'm joking. I'm just waiting until Morvyr has her baby, and then Peace and I will be off, so in a week or so, I should think. If you want to start moving your stuff in before then, and even better, if you want to start working from here, then go right ahead, it will give our patients continuity. Oh no, what am I saying, that means I'll be sharing my home with Grit again.'

Martha laughed. 'He's really very well behaved now that he's fed regularly.'

'Regularly being constantly, knowing him. It's a miracle he can still move.'

I jumped as a weight appeared suddenly on my shoulder. Grit chittered away in my ear but the noise was much softer than the tone he had used to adopt when scolding me. I couldn't help but smile and I put a finger up to stroke his back. 'You look after Martha, do you hear me?' I said to him. 'She's very special, but then I think you already know that, don't you.'

Martha wiped a tear from her eye. 'Look at you two, pair of old softies,' she said. 'I actually think you'll miss one another. I'll certainly miss you and Peace, Adam. I never thought I'd be sad to see the back of you, but I will be.'

'I haven't exactly made life easy for you here, have I?'

'You can't help being brilliant, but it's been hard, living in your shadow. I'm still in that shadow, but because you're different from how you used to be, it feels okay. Don't get me wrong, you were always a nice person, but now you're... you're...'

'Bonded to Peace. It changes a man, you know,' I said and we both laughed.

There was a hammering on the door, followed by Felin's voice shouting, 'ADAM!'

Martha and I looked at one another in alarm and both rushed to the front door.

Felin was already rushing back down the path. 'Come with me,' he said breathlessly over his shoulder, and ran back in the direction of his cottage.

'Morvyr,' Martha said to me and we both ran after Felin, leaving the front door to my cottage wide open behind us.

There was a clatter of hooves and Peace came cantering up behind us, slowing to trot next to me in a flurry of legs and swirling leg hair. Through my rising panic, I felt him nudging my mind. I seized hold of my sense of him and plunged into it, instantly relieved at the calm that swept over me. Whatever was happening, I could help. I would help.

When we reached Felin and Morvyr's cottage, Felin had already disappeared inside. I followed Martha as she raced inside after him and when she came to a sudden stop in the living room and I almost landed on top of her, I felt Peace's warm breath on the back of my neck. I barely had time to take in the fact that he had taken it upon himself to squeeze through the doorways and come in behind me, before I noticed Morvyr sitting in one of the armchairs by the fire, a bundle in her arms and a wide smile on her face. Felin was on his knees in front of her, stroking his son's cheek. He looked up at me. 'We wanted you to be the first to know,' he said.

Martha rushed to the two of them, put an arm around Felin's shoulders, and peered from the baby to Morvyr. 'You did this by yourself?' she said. 'He's okay? You're okay?'

'We're better than okay, thank you,' Morvyr told her. Then she looked at me. 'When I knew he was coming, I tuned into his body and mine and I knew we were okay but I don't even think it was me I was trusting, Adam, it was you and Peace. You've told me over and over that my son and I would be fine and knowing where that knowledge came from, when it came down to it, I found that I believed you. I felt so relaxed and confident, I didn't need any other help, my son was born quickly and easily, and, well, here he is! Do you want to hold him?'

Pain pierced through the sense of Peace to which I was desperately trying to maintain a hold. It lashed at every part of me and I bit down hard on my cheek to stop myself from screaming out loud at the welts it was leaving behind. Peace shuffled closer behind me and rested his muzzle on my shoulder. He breathed his warmth, his love, his calm into me, reassuring me that it was good to experience the memory of Bronwyn holding her daughter as she smiled an identical smile to that which Morvyr now wore. It was good to feel the resulting grief instead of running away from it as I once would have done. And now, it was good to let it go. I put a hand behind me to his chest and, as he breathed love and peace into me, I breathed out everything that hurt.

Morvyr, Felin and Martha were all looking at me, Morvyr and Felin hopefully, Martha with concern. A mountain of hurt had been felt and released in less than a minute, thanks to Peace, but it was a long enough pause to be uncomfortable.

I stepped forward and held out my arms. 'I would love to hold him.'

Felin very carefully lifted his son out of his wife's arms, his huge hands making the tiny bundle seem even smaller than he was, and handed him to me. 'Adam, meet Perry Adam Beech,' he said.

Before I could react, Peace leant over my shoulder, sniffed Perry and then very gently nuzzled the top of his head. As I cuddled my nephew, Peace cuddled us both, giving me the physical contact with him that I needed in order to not lose my hold of him as I clasped my namesake in my arms.

'He's beautiful,' I managed to say. 'Well done, all three of you, I'm so happy for you. And... thank you for naming him as you have.'

Felin took hold of both of my arms and looked into my eyes, his brown ones dark and serious. 'No, Adam, thank you,' he said. Then he raised a hand to stroke Peace's nose. 'And I never thought I'd be saying this to a horse standing in my front room, but thank you too, Peace.'

'He makes it seem normal, doesn't he?' laughed Martha.

I turned to look at Peace as he solemnly looked from one of us to the next, and I found myself laughing along with everyone else.

Martha slipped out, leaving me to cuddle Perry while his parents looked on adoringly. When she returned with a breathless Sheena and Tom, I allowed my nephew to be removed from my arms. Their happiness as they cuddled and cooed over their grandson made the happy event complete and I was stunned to find that I was enjoying myself.

Felin passed around glasses of his home-brewed wine for us all to celebrate Perry's arrival, and we took it in turns to cuddle the baby as we sipped and listened to Tom and Sheena regaling Morvyr and Felin with the trials and tribulations of parenthood. The stories they told of Bronwyn and Morvyr's escapades were hilarious, and when Felin collected our glasses and took them to the kitchen to be refilled, his shouts of horror at the rat moving around in the bread bag that subsequently turned out to be Grit, compounded the hilarity.

'You stay here with your family, Adam,' whispered Martha when our laughter eventually died down. 'I'll go to your cottage and see to your patients. I'll drop in to my house on the way and tell Reeta to deal with mine or send them on to see me at yours.'

I gasped. I had completely forgotten that I had an afternoon's work to do. 'Are you sure? Actually, come to think of it, it's now your cottage and they're your patients, so yes, Herbalist Evans, I really think you should get back there and be professional,' I said with a wink.

She laughed and nodded. Her withdrawal from the party was followed by Peace's, although his was a lot more conspicuous. To begin with, he attempted to turn around, but then, finding it impossible due to the furniture in his way, he opted for reversing instead. His solemn concentration as he walked slowly backwards out of the living room, down the hallway and out of the front door, was adorable. Everyone called out praise and encouragement, and when Peace's head appeared through the window, there were cheers.

'You might not be quite so pleased he's still here when you see the enormous pile of droppings he's left on your doorstep,' I said, but Felin waved a hand.

'I'll shovel it to one side and then spread it around the base of the apple tree I'm going to plant to celebrate the arrival of my son,' he said. 'Then there will always be a bit of Peace around here.'

His words gave me an idea. When more people arrived to congratulate the happy couple and meet the baby, I hugged the three of them, and Tom and Sheena, and made my retreat. I kicked aside the droppings over which everyone else had politely stepped, and as I did so, infused them with my love and happiness. The droppings would be broken down and their constituent parts absorbed by Perry's tree. I would not be there to see him grow up but my love for him and his family would always be there. They would absorb it when they walked past the tree and when they ate its fruit.

As Peace and I walked home, I couldn't stop smiling at the memories of my family's happy faces. A few people passed me, obviously on their way to see Morvyr and Felin judging by the baby clothes and toys they were carrying. They waved and called out to congratulate me on the arrival of my nephew as they hurried to meet him. Good news spread fast, I noted with satisfaction.

As does positive energy. You have done that which was necessary here. It is time to move on, Peace told me.

I sighed. *I know. I so dreaded coming back here, and now after only a few months, I'm going to find it hard to leave. Errr, what was that?* Someone I didn't recognise had just walked past me. He smelt as if he hadn't washed in some time, but it wasn't that which had pulled me up short to stare after him. I couldn't put my finger on what it was, but I knew I didn't like it.

You have moved on from who you were but your body remembers its old energy patterns. He who passed us by is carrying those energy patterns and they now chafe against you. Your discomfort is a positive indicator of the progress you have made.

He's like I was? What do we do?

He needs your help with another matter. When he visits you for herbs you would do well to question him as to where he has been. You will know what he needs.

You clearly know where he's been, can't you just tell me?

If I thought it helpful.

And you don't.

Do you tell your apprentices everything you know?

Well, no, I tell them a little and then set them exercises so that they learn the rest for themselves... okay, fine, I get it, this isn't just about helping that man, it's about me learning something.

It always is.

Always?

Everything is important and nothing is important.

Not that again, I still don't get what you mean.

You must keep learning until you do.

I was beginning to recognise those conversations with Peace that would never reach a conclusion but rather would go round and round in circles until I decided to accept that I wasn't capable of understanding what he was trying to tell me. This was definitely one of them.

Your tendency to try to think your way through that which confounds you is still strong, he observed. *Do not concern yourself. We have already agreed that allowing answers to come to you will take time.*

Okay, well for now, you need to go and catch up with all the grazing you've missed while you were busy helping me through what would have been a very tough time without you, and I need to go and help Martha with all those people queueing down the pathway, so that when whoever that was comes to me for help, I can set about learning whatever it is I need to learn this time. As Peace and I parted company, I sent a burst of love to him through our bond. *As ever, thank you for helping me.*

Gratitude is unnecessary. We do what we do, Peace told me and sauntered off to the paddock. Some of the children who had been queueing with their parents ran excitedly after him. I scratched my chin thoughtfully as I watched him go.

Chapter Thirty

I left Martha to work on in the consulting room and when she was in between patients, collected the files and supplies I needed in order to be able to consult with my own patients in the front room. When the queue finally petered out, I went to the kitchen to put the kettle on for us both. I pretended not to jump when Grit leapt from the top of the kitchen door to my shoulder.

'You've made yourself even more at home, I see,' I told him. It was when I was making my way to the biscuit barrel for a scrap for him rather than reaching for the kettle, that I realised how well and truly I had accepted him and his habits into my life. I shook my head, chuckling as he scampered off out of the window with his prize, his grey, bushy tail knocking the utensil pot over on his way past so that its contents crashed into the sink.

'Hullo?' called a husky voice.

I sighed. It looked as if tea would have to wait. I went back out into the hallway to find the man who had passed Peace and me earlier, standing just inside the front door. He was about my height, in his late forties, I guessed, with shoulder-length, greasy brown hair. He was dressed in a dirty green shirt, brown trousers and a thin, waxed brown cloak that was glistening with the drizzle that had just begun to fall outside. He wore a sullen expression and he smelt terrible. I was shocked at the realisation that if his eyes had been green instead of hazel, it would have been like looking into a mirror of my recent past. It was what I could feel from him that made my skin crawl, however.

'Err, go on through to your right and I'll be with you in a second,' I said, instinctively reaching for Peace.

The man did as I said. I immersed myself in the calm serenity that was my horse and instantly felt better. Peace continued to graze, but I felt his attention on me. He would step in if I needed him. I barely had time to congratulate myself on not needing him there physically with me in order to be able to deal with my disturbing patient, before I found myself in my front room, standing in front of the man.

'Um, you've clearly been travelling for some time,' I said, indicating for him to sit down. 'Have you been anywhere interesting?'

'I'm a flaming Pedlar, I'm always travelling,' the man snapped.

'Oh, I see, I'm sorry, I didn't realise you were a Pedlar, you aren't wearing your bandanna.'

The man fumbled in his trouser pocket and pulled out a frayed, filthy, red piece of cloth. He waved it at me. 'Here. My bandanna. Does this convince you? Now can we cut out the small talk and get on with why I'm here?'

I couldn't help raising my eyebrows. Pedlars usually wore the bandannas that advertised them as such with pride, knowing how crucial their role was to the continued success of the villages of The New. 'Um, yes of course. How can I help?'

The man held out his hands. 'I have a rash. I've had it before. It starts on my hands and then spreads up my arms, see?' He pushed up his shirt sleeves to show me that the angry red pustules on his hands did indeed appear to be spreading up his arms.

'What have you been handling recently?' I asked.

'Everything a Pedlar normally handles,' the man spat. 'I can't list everything, I can't even remember everything.'

'Okay, well then, where have you been recently?'

'I've come straight from one of the cities of The Old. I always get a rash like this when I go to any of them. I go to the Herbalist of the first village I visit next, they give me cream, the rash subsides enough that it doesn't hurt anymore but it never goes away completely, and then it flares up again the next time I go to one of the cities.'

'But all Pedlars go to the old city sites to collect supplies. I've had Pedlars come to see me for help before, but none of them have had this,' I said.

'Ah well, most of them are chicken,' the man said. 'They say they go to the cities, but they don't. They camp nearby, waiting for those of us that dare to go and dig through what's left, then they trade what they have for what we find, before going off to the villages with grand stories of how they found their wares. They never admit that it was me and a few others like me who found them. And then good old Bart,' the man sneered as he indicated himself with his thumb, 'has to go back and find enough stuff for himself to trade alongside what the other Pedlars gave him.' He looked away from me and his eyes unfocused. 'And all the time I'm there, I hear the ghosts.'

'Ghosts? What do you mean?'

He snapped back to himself. 'Ghosts? What are you talking about? There's no such thing as ghosts.'

'Err, right. Well I'm pretty sure the rash is caused by you touching something you're allergic to, but I'm just going to tune into your body to see if there's anything else going on.' I took a deep breath and checked back with Peace to make sure that I was in a place of complete calm, as he had taught me. Then I tuned into the man's body. I could feel the irritation in his skin and it wasn't just on his hands and arms, although those were the only places aggravated enough to have produced a visible rash. I shuddered as I intuited the cause of it. He was infected with the energy of the cities of The Old. The intense, all-consuming fear, hate and anger of the people who had lived there before being blown to dust, had pervaded his body and now wound their way through him. The negative energy was most highly concentrated in the parts of him that had come into direct contact with the earth as he dug around the ruins and into the old refuse sites, and his hands and arms were irritated to the point that his body was attempting to expel that which was so foreign, so toxic to the people of The New.

I held on tightly to Peace as the energy I could feel threatened to sweep me away. I identified with it. I had felt those emotions and expressed them with a force that had caused untold damage to our communities. However intensely I had felt and behaved, though, was nothing compared with the ferocity, the toxicity of the energy that was infecting Bart.

I felt a sudden admiration for him. He was dirty, smelly and grumpy, yet apart from his rash, that appeared to be the extent of how he was being affected by the energy which roiled through him. He must be one incredible human being. No wonder the other Pedlars left it to him to go into the cities – clearly, it took someone with the natural strength and positivity I suspected he possessed, to be able to tolerate being there as well as he could.

I felt Peace scrutinising my thoughts and observations, and then his satisfaction as I came to my conclusion as to how to proceed.

'Where are you staying, Bart?' I asked.

He chuckled slightly manically. 'Under my cart, where else? No one invites me into their homes anymore. I must be infectious, see?'

'Right, well I would like you to stay here. There's plenty of room for your donkeys in the paddock with my horse, and you can leave your cart by the side of the house. Where are your cart and donkeys, by the way?'

'Out on the pasture. Works better for me if people come out of the village to see me so my girls can graze, seeing as nobody wants to offer us lodgings. This serious, then? Am I going to die?'

'Yes it's serious, but no, you are certainly not going to die, in fact I'm going to get rid of that rash for good and when I do, we're going to need to have a chat about how to stop it coming back.' I looked past him, out of the window and could see nobody waiting outside. 'It looks as if we've finished for the day here. How about you go and fetch your donkeys and see them to the paddock, while I make up an unguent for your skin and also a draught I'd like you to take. You're welcome to stay here until you're better.'

'I suppose I could stay.' Bart frowned at me and then out of nowhere, exploded. 'Why are you doing this? What's in it for you? Are you going to rob me while I'm here? Is that it? You pretend to want to help me, but really, you just want what I've got?' I was almost blown back against the back of my chair with the force of his anger and suspicion. He was clearly more seriously affected than I had first thought. I sank deeper into my sense of Peace, briefly noticing his satisfaction that it had been my instant response to the malevolence hurled at me.

'If you would be more comfortable sleeping under your cart so that you can protect your things, then please do,' I said. 'It's your livelihood and I completely understand that you are protective over it. But do you see any harm in bringing it alongside the cottage here? Then I can give your girls a check over too, while they're in the paddock. When were they last wormed?'

At the mention of his donkeys, Bart calmed down. He sighed. 'Too long ago. I suppose they could do with a check over, they work hard for me.' He flared up again. 'But I'm sleeping under my cart. Don't want anything disappearing off it in the night.'

I didn't point out that if anyone wanted to steal from him – something that was unthinkable in our communities, when all of our goods and services were bartered or offered for free – then he was giving them plenty of opportunity while his cart was unattended now. He was thinking with the energy that infected him and there was only one way I was going to help him out of doing that.

'Okay then, that's fine. But just so you know, once I've given you the unguent and the draught you need, you'll be welcome to eat with me. And the door is always unlatched, so if you change your mind in the night and fancy sleeping in a bed, there will be one made up and waiting upstairs.'

Bart stared at me, long and hard, as if trying to find some sort of trickery in my suggestion. When he was unable to find fault with anything I had suggested, he nodded, got to his feet and stomped out.

Martha poked her head around the door. 'Phew, what a pong.'

'Um, you know I said you were welcome to move in straight

away?'

'Yes,' Martha said, stepping into the room. 'Why am I sensing a change of plan?'

'Would you mind at all postponing that for a few days? I need Bart to stay here until he's better. I also need to find him a bed.'

Martha came in and sat down opposite me. 'Who is he? And what's wrong with him?'

I told her everything. When I'd finished, she whistled. 'Okay, well there's a spare bed at my house, no one's used it since my brother moved out. I'll find a few willing bodies to bring it over and then it'll be there as a spare bed when I move in. I'm guessing you need sheets and pillows too?'

I nodded. 'The spare room was going to be a nursery. Morvyr removed everything we had ready for Alita. The room is bare.' There was no waver in my voice, no stab of pain, just a dull ache. I supposed that was progress.

'Of course, well we'll soon get everything over here that we need. I'll go and organise that now.'

'Thanks, Martha,' I called out as the front door slammed behind her. I got to my feet. I had work to do before Bart got back – the sooner he began his treatment the better, the poor soul.

I decided to kill two birds with one stone. I went out to the paddock and as I made my way to where the hawthorn bushes grew along the back fence, Peace sensed my intention and thundered over, his mane and forelock less buoyant than usual due to the moisture in the air. I reached out a hand to him and put my other hand to the first hawthorn bush. From my place with Peace, I gathered all of the love and positivity I could and sent it out through my hand to the bush, feeling it spread and take hold. I couldn't decide whether I was imagining the leaves looking a brighter shade of green in the dull light, and whether the brown twigs and spikes were more defined in my vision. I moved to the next bush and repeated the procedure. When I had imbued the whole hedgerow of hawthorn with as much positive energy as I could, I rubbed Peace's neck, picked several handfuls of the leaves and took them inside.

I ground them to a paste, a little of which I mixed into an unguent I already had in stock for soothing and hydrating dry, itchy skin. I mixed another small measure with raspberry juice, hoping that its sweetness and acidity would take away the bitter taste of the hawthorn leaves.

I had just poured the draught into a glass ready for Bart, when I heard the unmistakable rumble of cart wheels on the cobbles outside. By the time I reached the front door, the Pedlar was already leading his donkeys along the side of the house. The cart they pulled was piled high, covered with a dirty green tarpaulin, and didn't look particularly stable. I went out and helped him to unharness the four donkeys, taking the opportunity to tune into each of their bodies as I went. They did indeed need worming, and one of them was a little arthritic but apart from that, they were in reasonable health and condition. We took two each to the paddock and then shut the gate behind us.

Let me know if you want to go out and I'll come and open it, I told Peace. He barely acknowledged me, so absorbed was he in showing the four slightly bewildered donkeys how extravagant his paces could be when the situation called for it.

'He's something, isn't he?' Bart said to me as we watched Peace trotting back and forth in front of the donkeys, who were standing in a line, shifting nervously as they watched him. He stopped, spun around suddenly and snorted. The donkeys scattered in pairs, only stopping when they were as far from him as the paddock fences allowed. When it became clear that he had no interest in following him, they began to snatch at the grass, all four lifting their heads in between snatches to watch the huge, demented creature who resembled them and yet behaved nothing like them. Peace looked over at me and I felt his satisfaction at the stir he had caused. I grinned as he dropped his head and began to graze as if nothing had happened.

'Yes, he's certainly something,' I said.

'You're Horse-Bonded, then?' Bart said. 'So what are you doing with a house? Is The Gathering not good enough for you?'

'It's a long story,' I said. 'Anyway, your donkeys have all they need out here, so shall we go inside? Your unguent and draught are ready and waiting for you.'

'I s'pose,' Bart said. 'Or you could bring them out to me while I stay with my gear?'

'I can certainly do that.'

I waited with Bart while he drank the draught and massaged the unguent into his hands and arms as I instructed. 'I'll leave the salve with you,' I told him. 'Any time your skin feels itchy or sore, anywhere on your body, rub some in. If you run out, let me know and I'll make more. Ahh, here are Martha and her brother with their spare bed. We're going to put it upstairs in the room to the right of the stairwell, if you decide you want to use it.'

At the sound of voices, Bart leapt to his feet with a wild look on his face and stretched his arms out as wide as he could, protecting his cart.

'They're not here for your stuff, they're here with their friends to deliver a bed,' I repeated. 'I'm going to go in and help them, and then I'll bring some food out for you. Okay? Bart?'

He looked at me and for a second, I saw his eyes soften. They were kind eyes. Then, they widened again as the energy that roiled around within him rose to the surface and his paranoia returned. 'This is a trap, isn't it?' he hissed. 'You tricked me into coming here and now you've drugged me so you can steal my livelihood, you and those people.'

'How does your skin feel, Bart?' I asked him gently. 'That rash is already looking a little less angry to me.'

He looked down at his hands as if he had never seen them before. 'It is, isn't it,' he said. 'And did you mention food?'

'Yes, I did. Sit down and rest, and I'll be out with some as soon as I can.' I wondered whether he would be here when I got back.

I will prevent his donkeys leaving the paddock should the need arise, Peace told me. *Your treatments are already affecting him. It will not be long before he is back to himself.*

This isn't just gut irritation as Steen had, though, is it? The poor man is on the brink of insanity.

Peace merely lifted his head and stared at me.

Okay fine, I'll prepare to be amazed.

'Well, what are you standing there for?' Bart said, slithering down the cartwheel and landing on his bottom.

'Right, sorry, I'll be back shortly,' I said.

I flew through the door just as Martha's brother, Trent, and a couple of his friends were coming down the stairs. Trent was as slight and dark haired as his sister, with the same intense, blue eyes. 'Martha's just making the bed up ready for your, err guest,' he said. 'Are you sure about this, Adam? Bart has been here once before and he accused people of trying to steal from him when they asked what he had to barter. Some persisted because they could see he needed the food they had for him in return, but he's worse this time. He's not right in the head.'

'Thanks for your concern, Trent, but yes, I'm sure. Bart's a brave man who has been having a very hard time, but he'll be fine soon and then if you wouldn't mind, I'll need some help persuading everyone to trade with him.'

Trent looked at me as if I were crazy. 'I don't think anyone is going to do that this time, Adam. He's already scared a good number of them.'

'He's ill, but Peace has assured me that my treatment is working and he soon won't be.'

'Peace told you that?' Trent tilted his head from side to side as he considered. 'Okay, well then let me know when he's better and I'll spread the word. I can't make anyone trade with him, though.'

'No, but you can make them curious. Peace will do the rest.'

Trent shook his head, chuckling. 'That horse of yours, I'm already looking forward to seeing what he'll do. Count me in, I wouldn't miss it.'

I thanked him and his friends for bringing the bed, and they went on their way. I helped Martha to finish making up the bed – which involved me holding an angrily chittering Grit on my knee to stop him from diving under the sheet that Martha was trying to tuck around the mattress – and then invited her to stay for dinner.

'I would, but Grit has been unsettled since Bart showed up here, I think I'd better take him…'

'OUCH!' I shouted, releasing Grit and inspecting the bite he had left on my finger.

'Oh my goodness, are you alright?' Martha said.

'You were right, you need to take him home. I think Bart has reminded both him and me of a person we'd rather forget.'

'Can I dress your finger for you before I go?'

'No, you get on home, it's not deep. I think Grit wanted to get away from me rather than hurt me.'

Martha promised to let Tom and Sheena know that I would be unable to make dinner, on her way home. When she and Grit had left, I cursed myself. Bart had enough of an effect on me when I wasn't protected by Peace's energy, I should have realised that Grit would be affected by the familiar energy patterns too. I cleaned and dressed my finger quickly, and then heated up some leftover soup and took it out to Bart in a flask, along with a whole loaf of bread and a huge chunk of cheese. I checked on Peace and the donkeys – who were all grazing peacefully – and reminded Bart that both doors of the cottage were always unbolted and he could come in any time he wanted. He grunted in response as he tore huge pieces of bread from the loaf with his teeth. The poor man was famished.

I ate alone, thinking about everything that the day had brought. Perry was here safe and well, so I was free to go. Bart was also here, with symptoms unlike those I had ever come across before but which I was uniquely placed to recognise, understand and treat. I couldn't shake the feeling that the timing of the two events was no coincidence.

Peace interrupted my musings. *The voice of your soul grows stronger. Events are indeed unfolding as necessary. All is well.*

Before I could ask him to expand on his statement, he very obviously switched his attention back to grazing. I sighed. I would just have to wait and see what the following day brought.

Chapter Thirty-One

I woke in the middle of the night to the sound of footsteps thumping up my stairs. For a moment, I wondered who could possibly be banging around in my house when the whole village should have been asleep, but then I realised who it must be. I wondered whether I should go out to see if Bart needed any help finding the right room and the bed that awaited him, but I didn't want to frighten him by appearing suddenly, and risk him changing his mind.

He will not. He is much changed already. By the morning his memory of himself will be complete, Peace informed me.

I quickly lit my lamp and then opened my bedroom door just as Bart reached the top stair. He paused where he was, naked and dripping.

'I'll take up your offer of a bed for the rest of the night, if that's alright,' he said. Then he looked down at the puddle he was leaving on the floor. 'I've left my clothes outside. I was dirty and I stank so I washed in the trough. I'll refill it in the morning. In here?' He nodded his head towards the spare room door.

'Err, yes. Would you like a towel and a nightshirt?'

Bart shook his head. 'No thanks, I'm fine.'

'Okay, well do you need more unguent on your skin before you go to sleep? You've probably washed most of it off.'

'Nope. Goodnight.' He padded into the spare room and shut the door.

I heard the bed creak and then almost immediately, the sound of soft, rhythmical snoring.

There was no sign of him the following morning. I found his discarded clothes by the trough in the paddock and washed the worst of the dirt out of them in the water he had already soiled with his late-night ablutions. Then I cleaned out the trough and refilled it with fresh water, wormed all of the donkeys, and dosed the one with the beginnings of arthritis with a preparation I made up for her. I came in and washed Bart's clothes properly in the kitchen sink, before hanging them out to dry under the sun that was just beginning to appear as the clouds that had brought yesterday's drizzle moved slowly away.

When Martha turned up to help me with the day's patients, I suggested that she stay away, not knowing whether Bart would be recovered enough to not be a source of discomfort to Grit. She looked relieved as she left, telling me over her shoulder that she and Reeta would spend the day packing up the contents of her treatment room so that everything would be ready for when she moved her practice to my cottage.

Word had got around as to who I had staying with me and when I directed the few people who came to see me on to Martha's house, they looked as relieved as she had.

I spent the rest of the morning updating the files of the patients I had seen since my return, so that Martha would know exactly who had been treated with what when they transferred back to her. I ate lunch out in the paddock with Peace, and then when I climbed the stairs to check on Bart and could still hear his snores, I nipped out to see Morvyr, Felin and Perry, knowing that I was likely to find Sheena and Tom at their cottage too. With Peace's head poking through the window as always, I cuddled my nephew and chatted with my family.

We smiled, we laughed, we hugged and then I jogged back to my cottage with Peace trotting by my side.

He still sleeps, Peace told me.

That's good to know, but I want to be there when he wakes up. There's no knowing how he'll be.

There is every knowing. You merely require further proof.

Okay, fine, but I'd just like to get back there.

I was eating my evening meal when Bart finally appeared. He shuffled into the kitchen with a bedsheet wrapped around his waist, looking embarrassed. He was still a bit grimy and his hair needed a wash, but he smelt significantly less potent than he had the day before. 'Err, how long was I asleep?' he said, all trace of gruffness gone from his voice.

I grinned. 'Just the rest of the night and most of today. You must be hungry. Come and sit down. Vegetable pie okay?'

He nodded. 'Thanks.'

I fetched him a large plateful and then sat back down. 'There's bread and butter there too, if you want it, help yourself. I washed your clothes, they're on the stool over there. Sorry, I should have put them outside your door.'

He shook his head. 'I need to get properly clean before I put them on, but thank you for washing them for me.' He held my eye as he thanked me and I was stunned. His eyes, his face – he looked so much younger and I had a feeling that when he'd had a good wash and a shave, he would look younger still. His eyes sparkled and were full of the kindness that I'd glimpsed the previous day. As he chewed his first mouthful of pie, he nodded and smiled his appreciation.

'This is really good, thanks,' he said. 'Are my girls okay?'

'They're fine. I've wormed them and the oldest one has had the first dose of herbs to ease her stiffness.'

Bart nodded and said, 'I'll need to find her a retirement home soon, I know that. I'm just delaying it because I'm going to miss her so much and I'm worried she'll miss me and the other girls.'

'She's fine for a bit, yet. Peace was with me, trying to pinch the apples I was using to give her and the others their wormers, and he said that she and the others are all happy doing what they're doing for you. I don't think she's ready to retire yet.'

Bart's eyes lit up and he smiled a broad smile. 'Really?' When I nodded in response, he covered his face with both hands – whose skin now appeared normal. Then he rubbed his eyes and coughed. 'Sorry, I don't know what came over me, it's just that my girls are all that has kept me going these past years. They're everything to me. Thank you, and please, thank Peace.'

'Will do. Um, how are you feeling?' I said.

Bart frowned as he chewed. 'Do you know, I feel really well,' he said finally. Then he looked down at his hands and his face lit up. 'My hands! Look at them, they're clear! And my arms, and... the rest of me. What's happened to me? My skin has felt horrible for as long as I can remember and not just from the rash, it's felt like it's been kind of rippling, like something was crawling around on it and under it at the same time. All of a sudden, that's all gone and I feel... different. I'm thin, though. How did I get this thin?'

'I think you've been forgetting to eat,' I said.

He nodded thoughtfully. 'I've been frightening people away. The only ones who would trade with me for food were the other Pedlars. I feel like I've woken up from a nightmare. What did you give me yesterday?'

'Just something to rid you of what you picked up at the cities.'

Bart's eyes widened. 'The cities,' he whispered. 'I can't go back there, not to any of them. It was bad enough going before but now I feel better, the thought of being there again, with all the... the horridness and the g...ghosts whispering in my ear the whole time, driving me crazy, I can't do it.'

You can help, Peace interjected.

'Your cart is piled high with stuff. I can't imagine you'll need to go for a good while,' I said gently, 'and I'm hoping that by the time you do, I'll have found a way to make it easier on you. Do you feel able to answer a few questions about the cities, so I can try to work out how I can help?'

Bart swallowed hard and wrapped the sheet tighter around himself. 'I guess so.'

'Can you tell me about the ghosts?'

He shuddered. 'I hear them on the wind. It's like they can't bear happiness and they want everyone to be as frightened and as crazy as they are.'

'What do they say to you?'

'They whisper poison into me, trying to scare me so I'll run away. And I feel them in everything I touch – the soil, what's left of the buildings at the cities where anything remains, and everything I find there. This last year or so, I've been able to ignore them a bit more but now I'm wondering if that's because they drove me nearly as mad as they are.'

'You feel that they're people?'

'What's left of people, yes, I think so. The whole place reeks of them. The donkeys won't go there. I leave the other Pedlars to look after them while I go in with my handcart to bring out what I dig up.'

'May I go and have a quick look at what's on your cart? I promise not to move or take anything,' I said.

He waved a hand at me. 'Move or take anything you like, it's the least I can do after everything you've done for me. And I've never even asked your name.'

I stood up and offered my hand. 'I'm Adam. Don't get up,' I added hurriedly, nodding at his sheet.

He laughed and shook my hand whilst sitting. 'Thanks, Adam, for your care, your hospitality and your understanding.'

'You're very welcome. I'll just nip out and have a look at your wares, then I'll be right back.'

Peace was waiting for me at the back door and he accompanied me to the paddock gate. I climbed over it and lifted the bottom edge of the tarpaulin that covered Bart's wares. Immediately, I felt a faint sense of the same energy pattern that Bart had been carrying. I could feel that Peace was waiting for me to understand.

'The Pedlars are bringing that horrible energy out of the city sites and distributing it around our communities,' I murmured to myself.

I'm not the only source of negativity affecting the communities of The New, am I? I asked Peace.

You have been responsible for the largest disruption but there are other minor sources that we must address while we are about our main task.

Minor sources? This doesn't feel like a minor source to me,' I argued with a glance at the cart.

There are merely many objects all carrying an imprint of fear and negativity in one place. Inanimate objects each carry only a faint imprint of the energy to which they have been exposed. When they are worked into other objects by your people the energy put into them negates the negative energy in the same way that your positivity drove it from the scavenger but it would be better were they never exposed to it at all. It is the source of the negativity to which we must attend.

The source of the negativity? You mean the cities? How do we "attend" to them?

In the same way we attend to the negativity of which you were the source.

Love? We give love to the cities? How do we do that? I can't exactly rub unguent into the remains of a whole city, or give it a herbal preparation, and haven't we got enough to do, finding all the people for whom I have to make things right, without having to find all of the city sites that there must be? I don't even know where any of them are!

It is indeed a formidable task. It is fortunate that we are ourselves formidable. Peace turned and looked anything but as he wandered off, tripping over a tussock of grass on his way to the water trough, where he swirled his nose around and around in circles, splashing much of the water over the side before drinking.

'Where will we even start?' I called out somewhat hopelessly, the journey ahead of me having expanded far beyond my comprehension.

We have already begun. Do not worry for the future. Concern yourself with the present for that is all there is.

The present. Bart. He would have finished eating by now and I needed to run him a bath and give him another dose of the draught I had given him yesterday. Hopefully, that would take away the last of the panic he felt at the thought of the cities. I would make up a load of my paste for him to mix in with whatever he drank with breakfast each morning, I decided as I headed for the cottage. That should protect him from what I had no doubt he would be able to feel from the objects on his cart; having been subjected to the energy of the old city sites in such a potent way, he would be far more sensitive to it than most.

Bart was just mopping up the last of his dinner with a slice of bread when I re-entered the kitchen.

'Better?' I said.

He nodded enthusiastically. 'Much. Did you find what you needed?'

'I found a whole lot more than I consider I needed, but that's life with Peace,' I said and Bart looked at me with a blank expression. I grinned. 'Sorry. He tells me things in a roundabout way and now I'm doing the same to you. Yes, thanks, I found what I needed.'

I quickly mixed a measure of hawthorn paste with more fruit juice, and left him to drink it while I ran him a bath and looked out a nightshirt for him from my wardrobe. Then I sat on the bench under the kitchen window in the paddock and watched Peace and the donkeys mooching around, their tails flicking at biters as they grazed. The grass was getting low. It was a good job that we would all be moving on soon.

'Room for one more?' Bart said from the doorway. I had left scissors and a razor out for him and it appeared that he had made good use of them. I was shocked to see that he now looked closer to my thirty years than the late forties I had originally estimated.

I shifted up to the end of the bench. 'Sure. The nightshirt fits okay then?'

'Yes, thanks.' He sat down next to me and we watched the donkeys and Peace for a while in silence. Eventually, he said, 'I've been thinking. I'm a Pedlar. It's what I do, and what I used to love doing before I started visiting the cities. I don't want to go back there, but it's my job to bring all the resources they hold to the villages where they can be made use of. If there's a way for me to go and fetch what everyone needs without it driving me mad, I should do it. You mentioned you would try to find a way for me to do that?'

'Yes I did, and Peace thinks I have, but I'm afraid I can't tell you what we need to do because I don't fully understand it myself. For now, I'm going to give you a big batch of the paste I've been using to make up the draughts I've given you. Take a dose with juice every morning, and it will stop the rash coming back. By the time it runs out, I'm hoping that you will have traded all of your existing wares and that Peace and I will have cleared at least a few of the cities you visit of everything that has been affecting you, so that you can get more. I'm going to need you to draw a map for me so I that can find them.'

There is no need. I know where they are.

You do? How?

I feel them.

'I can certainly do that for the one closest to here, I've just come from it. But those further away? I'm not sure. I don't really take in my surroundings much, I just kind of know where I'm going and end up there.'

'Never mind. Apparently, Peace knows where they are. We'll visit the one closest to here first of all, so when you need more wares, make that your first port of call.'

'Are you sure you want to do that, Adam? I mean, if you haven't been there before, I don't think you can have any idea what it is that you'll be walking into.'

'You're right, I don't. Peace does though, and in his own words, he's formidable.'

Bart looked over to where Peace was grazing alongside one of the donkeys. He made her look tiny. 'He is that,' Bart agreed. 'I feel as if I should come with you both, to help.'

I felt Peace's response to that idea and shook my head. 'Thanks, Bart, but you've suffered enough. How you've resisted succumbing to the malevolence that you've been exposed to as well as you have is beyond me. You're much stronger than I am, but there's only so much anyone can take. Hopefully, we'll see you and your girls on our travels, but if we don't, take their lead where the cities are concerned. If they won't go near one, then we haven't reached it yet and it's to be avoided. Keep going until you find one they're happy with, and you'll all be fine. You could help us by spreading the word to the other Pedlars? Tell any who are affected as you were to find me and Peace for treatment, and the rest, let them know to follow their donkeys' leads as you'll be doing.'

'I can do that, of course I can. When will you and Peace be off?'

'I think we'll stay here tomorrow to make sure everyone knows you're healed and available for trading, and then we'll be off the day after.'

'I wonder whether I'd be better off just leaving. I seem to remember that I frightened a good few people when I arrived yesterday,' Bart said.

'You'll have Peace with you. Trust me, I have yet to come across anyone he can't win over.'

Peace did of course prove me right. When Bart and I had breakfasted the following day, we hitched his donkeys to his cart and then Peace and I accompanied them to the centre of the village. When Peace's admirers came out to see him, he trotted around the cart and the donkeys – who were by now used to his antics – and then stopped by Bart and nuzzled his shoulder. Bart grinned and rubbed Peace's nose, only for Peace to take the Pedlar's cap in his mouth, shake it and make off with it on his next trot around the cart. People began to laugh and more villagers came to their doors and windows to see what the noise was all about.

Peace stopped in front of Bart, who was still laughing as he accepted his slightly gooey cap back and put it back on his head. 'You're a chump, Peace, a lovable chump, but a chump nevertheless,' he said. Then he turned to the people watching. 'I understand completely if you're just here to play with Peace, but if anyone wants to see what I've got on the cart, I'm open for trade.'

'I thought we weren't trusted to look, in case we stole your stuff,' someone shouted.

'I apologise for my behaviour, it seems that I've been ill. I've had treatment though, and I can assure you, I'm as normal as I ever was,' Bart said.

'I'll come and have a look.' Trent appeared out of the crowd. While he was being thoroughly greeted by Peace, Bart untied the canvas from his cart and dragged it off. When Peace finally let him go, Trent smoothed his hair back and began to select items from the cart. While he was negotiating what he would barter for them, another couple of people stepped forward to fuss Peace, both of them ending up near the cart, from which they, too, began to select what they wanted.

Trent was as good as his word and on his way home, spread the word that Bart was healed and available for trading. Peace and I stayed there for an hour or so, but once it was clear that Bart was well and truly in the good graces of the villagers, we left him to it. I took him some food at lunchtime, which he accepted with copious thanks even though he didn't need it; there was a pile of food by his cart that he had been given in trade. He unhitched his donkeys and asked me to take them home so that they could rest in the shade, since his trade was showing no signs of slowing and the sun, clear of the clouds that had weakened its rays in recent weeks, was burning hot. I did as he asked and then spent the afternoon helping Martha and Reeta to move the contents of their treatment room, and the rest of their things, to my cottage; it seemed that Reeta would be taking the spare room for the last few months of her apprenticeship. I packed the sparse contents of my wardrobe and chest of drawers into a back-sack, leaving space for the food I would add in the morning.

'I feel as if we're pushing you and Bart out,' Martha said when we finally had everything organised.

I shook my head. 'Bart already has plenty of offers of lodgings, so he'll be sorted for tonight and as many other nights as he wants to stay in Greenfields, and I want to sleep outside with Peace for my last night here. The sky is clear so it will be dry, and it's still more than warm enough. I'm going to be doing a lot of sleeping outside from now on so I may as well start now. Besides, it will be easier for me to leave this place behind if I move out to the paddock first.' My voice shook a little and Martha reached for my arm. I managed a smile. 'I'm fine. I have Peace.'

'I hope you do someday, Adam,' she said. 'I really hope you do.'

Chapter Thirty-Two

I said my farewells to my family that evening. Saying goodbye to Perry and Morvyr, knowing that I may never see them again, brought with it more pain than I had experienced in some time, but with the help of my beloved horse, I was able to feel it and let it go. At least my tears weren't out of place since everyone, including Felin, spilt them too.

Word had spread that Peace and I were leaving in the morning, and we were stopped by pretty much the whole village in turn as we made our way home. It melted my heart to see how much Peace meant to them all and I was glad that they were unaware we were unlikely to return, as I had a feeling they would have found some way to try to keep us there.

It was hard saying goodbye to Martha and Grit, before we all retired for the night. Both of them had saved my life in their own way and although we'd had our difficulties and still had our differences, they had become friends whom I treasured.

I shouldn't have been surprised that Grit managed to have the last word as Peace and I left. We were up and ready to go with the first bird calls of the day, and as we passed through the paddock gateway for the last time, the squirrel's chittering attracted my attention to where he was perched atop the gate.

'You look after Martha,' I told him and he chittered softly back to me. 'And look after yourself,' I whispered, suddenly overcome with emotion at leaving the last link to my previous life behind.

He leapt onto my shoulder, chittered in my ear and then leapt onto Peace's back, ran towards his tail and leapt back onto the gate. I smiled at him with trembling lips and then put a hand to Peace's shoulder. *So, where to?* I asked him.

We will begin with those souls whose bodies perished long ago.

My heart sank. *We're going to the city site that Bart just came from?*

Peace answered with his feet. As we reached the end of my street, he turned left towards the opposite end of the village from that at which we had entered and marched purposefully forward, even though I knew – and therefore he knew – that some of the people I needed to find in order to offer healing, apology and anything else they needed, were in the next village along, in the opposite direction from that which Peace had taken. I sighed. Well at least, as far as I had gathered from Bart, the city for which we were aiming was nearly a week's walk from here; unlike the last time Peace and I had travelled any distance together, I had appropriate clothing, I was uninjured and, since the end of summer was fast approaching, the temperature was far more comfortable. I decided that I would enjoy the journey, if not necessarily the destination.

It is better to be free of expectation.

Huh?

When you allow your mind to fill with possible or even probable scenarios the voice of your soul has more through which to wade in order to make itself heard.

But I just immerse myself in you, then I can always hear my intuition.

There will be times when but for the voice of your soul you will not know that immersing yourself in me is necessary.

Because the voices might make me crazy first?

You are more sensitive than the scavenger and you will resonate more strongly with the energy patterns we will find than he did since you have owned some of them. You must stay clear of thought so that you are alerted to their reach at the earliest opportunity.

But you'll sense them before I do. Can't you warn me?

I could.

But you won't?

This is an excellent opportunity for you to find and retain the state of mind you seek regardless of that which exists and occurs around you.

Even if I go mad in the attempt?

The verge of insanity is an excellent position from which to choose peace.

Good to know. I'm just not that comfortable at taking the risk, I've lost my way once already, remember?

That was before we bonded. You merely have to choose our bond over that which will try to corrupt you. It will be a choice that only you can make and your mind must be free to make it.

Okay, so I need to clear my mind of expectations, even though I'm frightened almost witless already.

This is the first opportunity for you to make the choice.

Aaah. I understood. Instantly, I calmed without even reaching for Peace. He was preparing me. He had my back before I even knew that I needed him to have it. I remembered how I'd discovered the healing power of love in the first place – I had trusted him.

Your state of mind is improved yet not by the method I would have you improve it, I was informed.

You said I had to choose peace. I chose it.

You chose to see the absence of challenge. That is not the same as choosing peace.

Okay, sorry. So I need to practise keeping my mind clear of expectation, so that I'll be able to feel when I need to reach for you and then I have to choose to do it. Got it.

We walked on in silence for the rest of the morning as I did as he had instructed. I found it surprisingly difficult to keep drawing my mind away from imagining what we would find, but I managed it.

It's about being in the present again, isn't it? I said to Peace as I munched on a sandwich while watching him graze. *If I concentrate on the birds singing, or watch the clouds passing overhead, or count my footsteps or yours when we're on the move, I don't worry about what's ahead.*

I felt Peace's assent, but he was unimpressed, as if I had stated the obvious. Well, I was pleased with myself. It was one thing being told to focus on the present, but another to work out how to do it.

We journeyed on, sometimes in the late summer sunshine, sometimes in the dark, according to when Peace wanted time to graze or I needed to rest, but always side by side. Most of our journey was across grassy plains which at times appeared endless until the horizon was finally broken by trees or the odd hill, which we would negotiate before being back on the plains again.

We saw a herd of horses from afar one morning, and we were often passed at a distance by herds of deer. Rats and rabbits hopped through the grasses and the foxes that lay in wait for them ate well. As time went on, I found it easier and easier to stay calm and present, although as Peace warned me, that was as much because of the "absence of any challenge" as it was because of my attempts to do it.

It was during our fourth morning of travel that we finally left the plains and entered scrubland. I was relieved when we came across a stream, as I was on the last of my four water pouches, the puddles of water from which Peace had kept himself hydrated having been too shallow for me to refill them. I had been using the fact that my water supply was running low to practise remaining in the present as an alternative to worrying and, as always, had found that Peace was right; it was much more difficult to do in the face of challenge.

As I was filling the first of my pouches, Peace suddenly raised his head beside me, his chin dripping, and let out a shrill whinny. I almost dropped the pouch in the stream. *Peace?*

He was answered by a faint whinny. I stood up and squinted in the direction in which his ears were pricked, but could see only low hills and bushes. Then I saw something bobbing up and down in the distance, accompanied by a faint cloud of dust. As it got closer, Peace whinnied again, and was again answered. I could hear the thunder of hooves now, and was able to see that it was a brown, wide-brimmed hat bobbing up and down. I thought I recognised it and as it got closer, I knew who was wearing it.

When a tall, slender black mare appeared around the last of the bushes that had hidden her from my sight, I was already grinning, albeit slightly nervously. Risk slowed to a walk and Peace trotted an arc around some low-growing bushes to approach her slightly from the side. She stopped, they touched noses and then both horses stamped a front foot and squealed. Devlin laughed and jumped to the ground. He quickly unsaddled his horse, dumped his saddle and saddlebags on the ground and strode over to me, his hand outstretched. He was as tall as I remembered but where before his dark eyes had been serious and thoughtful, now they sparkled as he grinned at me.

'We'll leave those two to catch up, shall we? It's good to see you, my word you look different, and so does he, hasn't he grown and filled out?'

I shook Devlin's hand, feeling unsure of myself in the presence of someone who had seen me at my absolute worst. I was relieved when Risk and Peace provided a distraction by rearing, pretending to bite one another as they landed, and then thundering off at a canter, dodging bushes as they raced one another.

'He has,' I said proudly.

'He'll be strong enough for you to ride very soon. I must admit, when I first saw him, what was it, three months or so ago? I thought it would be a while before he'd be able to carry you, but he's grown into himself quickly.'

'Err, I have ridden him briefly already. It wasn't by choice though, exactly, it was because I couldn't walk.'

'Much like when I left you then?' Devlin said and clapped me on the shoulder. 'Sorry, you probably don't need reminding. Risk told me you've had a difficult time. By the looks of things, you're over the worst, though. What's his name?' He nodded his head in Peace's direction just as my horse chose to come to one of his signature halts, bouncing on all four feet at the same time.

I grinned and relaxed. 'His name is Peace and mine is Adam, I'm sorry I didn't introduce myself when we met. Thank you for saving my life and for taking me to him. And thanks for leaving me with what must have been pretty much all of your food and clothes, and for being kind enough not to mention how abominably I behaved towards you. The worst is indeed over, but I have a huge amount to do to undo all the damage I've caused.'

'Pleased to meet you, Adam. Peace, eh? Well, whatever it is that you're on your way to do, Risk and I are here to help. She hasn't seen fit to enlighten me as to what it is, exactly, that you need help with, only that your horse, sorry, only that Peace, asked us to be here, so here we are.'

'Oh, he did, did he? Well I'm glad it's not just me who gets kept in the dark. Does Risk give you answers that leave you with more questions too?'

Devlin laughed. 'Adam, welcome to the world of the Horse-Bonded. The rewards are huge, but they're equalled in magnitude by the frustrations of being guided by those so much wiser than we are. I see you've found water, good news, because I'm running low. Wouldn't you think that Risk would rehydrate herself before carrying on like that in the heat?'

We both looked to where the two horses were showing off their paces to one another, their ears pricked, tails held out horizontally behind and in Peace's case, with plenty of snorting. It was lovely to see him enjoying the company of another horse and for a moment, I felt bad about everything he had given up in order to be my partner. I still didn't see what he had to gain from it, but I found myself reverting to my practice of the past few days, and focusing on the present.

'Do you have food? I have plenty if not, and this might be a good time to stop for a bite?' I said. 'They can cavort as long as they feel is necessary and then have a chance to drink and graze. Not that the grass is as good here as on the plains.'

'It's good enough,' Devlin said. 'Yes, that sounds like a plan. It'll give us a chance to catch up.'

My heart sank. I wasn't sure I wanted Devlin to know everything that had transpired since I last saw him.

That which is truly behind you need not be relived. That which disrupts your thoughts may be further processed and released by sharing with one who will understand, Peace volunteered. I looked over to where he was doing little bunny hops while pretending to kick out at Risk and wondered for the hundredth time how one capable of being such a clown could offer such sage advice.

I told Devlin everything as we sat opposite one another, cross-legged in the shade of a large bush. He ate while I talked. Occasionally, he would nod, smile, or raise his eyebrows but other than that, there was no sign that I was telling him anything out of the ordinary.

Peace and Risk came to the stream to drink and then settled to graze nearby. I took extra heart from the nearby physical presence of my Bond-Partner, but I was surprised to find that I didn't feel the need to hold on to the sense of him in my mind in order to keep a hold on myself.

You have come far. I stopped talking for a moment to smile at Peace. His thought had been faint and not at all intrusive, but I just felt the need to acknowledge it. When I looked back to Devlin to continue with my tale, he looked from me to Peace and back again and grinned. He knew.

When I finally finished speaking, Devlin picked up his water pouch and handed mine to me. 'We should drink a toast,' he said. 'You've come further in these last few months than I have in the five years I've been bonded to Risk. To you and Peace, and all you have and will achieve. I'm glad to know you.' He took a swig of water as I sat staring at him.

'You are? How can you be after everything I've just told you?'

He shrugged. 'We're none of us perfect and according to what I've been able to understand from Risk, we wouldn't be here if we were. You've made mistakes, you're on a mission to correct them and hopefully, many will benefit from your efforts. Risk and I are here to help you in any way we can. You've been talking a long time. You should eat. I'll rub those two down now that the sweat's dry on their coats.' He got to his feet, pulled a couple of brushes from one of his saddlebags, and sauntered over to the horses. Risk whickered to him and Peace sniffed his hand, up his arm to his shoulder and then tipped off his hat. 'So you're a joker, huh?' Devlin said to him. He left his hat where it had fallen and rubbed Peace's forehead.

I sat watching them for a while, unable to believe Devlin's reaction to my confession of all the despicable things I'd done.

He is assisted in acquiring perspective in the same way as are you, Peace informed me.

I nodded slowly. *Risk counselled him as he was listening to me?*

She had no need on this occasion. We will not discuss their bond again.

I nodded. *Okay, I get it, it's private. Thanks for helping me to understand though. It's hard for me to remember I'm not the only one who is Horse-Bonded, even when I see it with my own eyes.*

It is customary for newly bonded humans to seek out and spend time in the company of those who have been bonded for some time in order to acquire help and support whilst they are adjusting to their situation. You have not had the benefit of time for such meetings.

So you asked Risk to bring Devlin to meet me here so he can help me to adjust to being Horse-Bonded? I thought I was doing okay at that by myself?

In most respects that is true.

Okay, so...????

You need him to teach you to ride.

What? I don't think Devlin thinks you're quite ready. I shouldn't have sat on you before, I know that, it was only because...

I am in the best position to judge when the time is right for me to carry you. That time is now.

But why do you need me to learn to ride right now? Don't I have enough on my plate as it is, trying to remain in the present all the time, without having something else to learn at the same time?

The two abilities are not mutually exclusive. When next we move on it will be with you on my back.

I sighed. *Okay, fine, as long as you promise me you'll tell me if you're getting tired and need me to get off?*

I do not foresee it being me who will be the first to require respite.

Challenge accepted. 'Devlin, the reason for your and Risk's invitation has been made clear,' I called out to him. He stopped brushing Risk and looked at me quizzically. 'Apparently, it's time I learnt to ride.'

Devlin looked from me to my horse and studied Peace's body appraisingly. Then he nodded. 'No problem. I'd have given him a little longer, but if he says he's ready, then he's ready.'

I heaved a sigh and then chuckled.

'What did I say?' Devlin asked.

'Nothing, I'm just finding it strange. Apparently, new Horse-Bonded spend time with those who have been bonded for some time, because it helps with adjusting to being bonded and all it entails?'

Devlin nodded. 'Most go to The Gathering, where there are always lots of Horse-Bonded in residence. You've missed that part of the process out.'

'I'm guessing that one of the things I would have been told there is not to argue with my horse when he tells me to do something?'

Devlin chuckled. 'You questioned Peace when he told you it was time for him to be ridden?'

I nodded, grinning.

'It's not so much that you would have been told not to argue, it's more that anyone who has been bonded for any length of time will tell you that there's no point. The horses are always right. If Peace tells you something then it's for a good reason. You can waste time proving that to yourself until you believe it, or you can accept the experience of all of those who have gone before you and just do as he tells you from the get go.'

'Okay, well he's told me that when we move on, it will be with me on his back. He's also assured me that I'll need a break before he does.'

Devlin grinned. 'I can tell you from experience that he's right. You don't appear to have eaten anything yet. You might want to, before we move on?'

'Right, sure, yes of course.' I suddenly realised how hungry I was. I felt lazy, watching Devlin brush Peace down while I stuffed my face, but I could feel how much Peace was enjoying covering Devlin in slobber while he eased the sweat and dirt out of my horse's coat in long, soothing strokes, and decided that they were enjoying getting to know one another.

When Devlin finally returned to where he had been sitting, his dark hair was ruffled and he had brown and green slime on the back and down one arm of his white shirt, a fact about which he didn't appear concerned. 'Risk tells me that she and Peace are ready. Are you good to go?' he said. I nodded and got to my feet, swallowing my last mouthful of apple. 'Marvellous. Let your first riding lesson begin!' There was a wicked glint in his eye and as I looked over at where Peace was pawing the ground as he waited for me, I felt excited but nervous.

You are concerned that you will appear foolish in front of your fellow human. Focus on each moment to the exclusion of all else and your disquiet will vanish.

Right, sorry, it's about choosing the present again, isn't it.
Always.

Chapter Thirty-Three

I didn't remember it being so difficult to balance on Peace's back when he had carried me before – but then when I thought about it, I had been bracing myself against his neck at the time, rather than sitting upright and balancing by myself. Devlin tried to reassure me that I was doing very well considering I had no saddle, I was carrying all my gear on my back and the terrain was far from flat. I had a feeling, however, that I would still have felt all over the place sitting on Peace whilst he moved in all four lateral directions at once as well as up and down, even in the best of circumstances.

I managed about half an hour before my back and leg muscles were spasming as a result of my efforts to stay in place whilst trying to follow Peace's movement, and I needed to get off.

'Okay, so now hold yourself still instead of following his body with yours, and he'll feel it and halt beneath you,' Devlin told me.

'Why can't I just ask him with my mind? Why do I need to give him physical signals?'

'Because there will often be times when you'll need to be conversing about other things while you're on the move. If you're used to turning your body so that he turns beneath you, squeezing with your ankles to ask him to push on faster, and stopping your movement when you need him to stop, he can respond quickly whilst you both carry on with your conversation. And if you're moving at speed and you see something ahead likely to cause him a problem, you'll be able to help him avoid it much more quickly if you just move your body instead of having to frame a thought and tell him. In the same way, if you can learn to follow his movements when he decides to turn or change pace, it will save you losing your balance and then causing him to lose his if he doesn't have time to warn you.'

I nodded and concentrated on trying to stop my body from following Peace's movement. Having spent the past half hour struggling to do the opposite, it was surprisingly difficult. I could feel that Peace knew what I wanted him to do, but he was waiting for my body to give his the appropriate signal before complying. When I finally managed to stop moving and sit completely still, he quickly halted beneath me. I lurched forward onto his neck and the weight of my back-sack prevented me from easily sitting back upright.

'While you're there, swing your leg over his back and jump to the ground,' Devlin said.

I did as he said but on landing, my legs gave way and the weight of my back-sack pulled me over so that I landed flat on my back on top of it.

Devlin chuckled. 'That wasn't the most elegant dismount I've ever seen but apart from that, you did well, Adam.'

Peace snuffled in my face, making me laugh. When he finally allowed me to wriggle free of my back-sack and sit up, I was able to smile, although as soon as I moved, my grin was replaced by a grimace. I hurt absolutely everywhere.

'How are you doing that?' I asked, squinting up at Devlin. 'You're carrying nearly as much weight on your back as I am, yet I'm in agony while you're sitting on Risk as if you were born there.'

'Practice. Up you get, you can walk for the rest of the afternoon so that you loosen back up, then when we stop for the night, I'm sure Peace won't mind if you hop on him for a little bit without your back-sack. You'll find it a whole lot easier then. Knowing exactly who you are now, I assume you have herbs with you to ease both your stiffness and bruising, and his?'

'Yes of course.' *Peace, are you okay? Did I hurt you?*

Peace peered down at me, his brown eyes reassuring as he waited for me to tune into his body and find out for myself.

Hmmm, you are a bit sore in places. I'm sorry, I'll work hard to get better at this.

My body will cope as long as you can provide appropriate herbs to support it when I cannot source them for myself.

I looked around at the surrounding scrub. *There's not much that will be of help out here, is there, thank goodness I have decent supplies with me. I'll be sure to replenish my stocks wherever I can so you'll always have what you need.*

Then there is no need for concern.

I dosed myself and Peace with herbs to ease our aches and then as they took effect, we continued onwards through the scrubland that stretched as far in front of us as our eyes could see. When Risk and Peace stopped and dropped their heads to graze, Devlin and I took it as our cue to stop for the night.

'I know we've had rain, but I've been avoiding lighting fires even so,' Devlin said as he rubbed Risk down, her sleek black coat gleaming in the evening sunshine.

'Me too,' I said. 'One wildfire was enough to last me a lifetime. How often do you do that?' I nodded towards Risk.

'I brush her saddle area whenever I take the saddle off, and in the summer, I remove the sweat and dirt from her coat whenever I have the opportunity, as she loves being groomed and hates to be dirty. When she has her full winter coat, I just remove the dirt from the saddle area so it doesn't rub, and brush any sweat off once it's dry. She'd love it if I groomed her as completely and as often as I do in the other seasons, but if I did, I'd be removing the grease and little bits of dirt that help to keep her warm.'

I sighed. 'I have brushes because my family got them for Peace, but I've only used them when he's looked really dirty. I've got a lot to learn about horse care, haven't I?'

Devlin grinned. 'Don't sweat it, you'll pick it up as you go. Peace will be the first to let you know if you misstep.'

I found my brushes, selected the one with the softest bristles and carefully brushed Peace's face before moving onto his neck and body. I copied Devlin's long, even strokes and Peace soon stopped grazing and closed his eyes. He loved it, and the more I carried on, the more I enjoyed it too. There was something very therapeutic about grooming my horse in this way, not just removing dirt and sweat but massaging his muscles and giving his coat even more of a shine than normal. When I had finished, I brushed his mane and tail, hair by hair as Devlin was doing with Risk's.

Once we had both finished, our horses were comfortable, gleaming and relaxed, whilst Devlin and I were tired, sweaty and wearing most of the dirt that we had dislodged from our horses. I smiled, feeling completely at ease. In focusing my efforts on grooming my horse, I had unwittingly joined him in his sense of himself; my mind was at rest from its usual frantic activity of either worrying or trying not to by focusing on the present... I was just there, with my horse, in the moment, at peace.

'We'll eat, shall we, while they do? And then if Peace is willing, you can have another ride?'

I nodded. 'And then I'll groom him again.'

'Yes, you'll need to make him comfortable before you turn in for the night. How have you been managing to get enough rest? I imagine Peace won't sleep while you do?'

I sat down where I was, in between two large tussocks of grass shaded by a clump of bushes, and began to root around in my back-sack for one of the many food parcels I had packed. 'I've just been sleeping for a bit whenever he stops to graze, then when I wake up, he tends to sleep before grazing a bit more and then we move on. So it's all horses who need someone awake to keep watch then? I wondered if that was just Peace.'

Devlin sat down beside me and began to rummage in his own back-sack. 'No, it's all of them. It'll be easier now there are four of us together, as we can take it turns to keep watch and we'll all get more rest. The horses give up so much of their natural way of life when they leave their herds in order to help us, but there are some instincts that they will always need to fulfil.'

'Have you been able to understand from Risk what it is that they get from helping us? When I asked Peace, he was obtuse, as he often is when I ask him things. I think he's like it when he doesn't think I'll understand the answer.'

Devlin chuckled. 'Good on you for cottoning on to that so quickly. No, I don't know exactly, but from what I can gather, the horses are in this for the long haul. They may not be gaining as much from bonding with us as we are at the moment, but there's a chance they might in the future, as might everyone and everything else.'

'So they're working towards something?'

'I think so. But in the meantime, how lucky are we to be two of the ones chosen to learn from them?' Devlin began to chew on some of the jerky I recognised from the food parcels with which he had provided me when he left me out on the plains with Peace. It was clearly a staple of his diet.

'I seem to remember Peace telling me that luck has nothing to do with anything,' I said thoughtfully.

It does not. Eat and rest. Then you will practise moving your body with mine once more.

By the time Peace and Devlin finally allowed me to get some sleep, I was exhausted but jubilant. Peace had walked circles around Devlin while I received detailed instruction on which parts of my body needed to loosen and which needed to tighten so that I could hold myself, instead of being a deadweight for Peace to carry. I learnt how to keep my balance while turning my body so that Peace could easily turn beneath me, and at the end of the session I even managed to signal to Peace to stop and then maintain my balance while he complied. I groomed him in the twilight, then gave him another dose of herbs to ease any soreness. I forewent my own dose, preferring to save the herbs for Peace in case I had trouble sourcing more.

Devlin nodded in approval as he watched me put my herbal pack back into my back-sack. 'You'll hurt tomorrow though,' he said.

'You'd do the same.'

'I would.' He lay back, propped his head up against his back-sack and tipped his hat forward onto his face. 'Risk will be grazing for some time, so we're free to sleep.'

The next thing I knew, bright light was burning through my eyelids and there was a munching sound by my left ear. I opened my eyes to see Peace towering above me. He stopped grazing the tussocks between which my head had come to rest after sliding off my back-sack, and nuzzled my face. I grinned and reached a hand up to stroke his soft, pink muzzle.

When he returned to his grazing, I sat up, wincing, and tried to get to my feet. A hand appeared in front of me and Devlin hauled me to my feet. 'Welcome back to the land of the living.'

'Flaming lanterns, does it always hurt this much?' I said, rubbing my back and then the insides of my thighs.

'To begin with, yes. As you get used to it, no not at all. The best medicine is to get back on and stretch those muscles back out.'

'What, ride again? Now?'

'Yes, just for a short while if Peace is up for it, which, judging by the fact that he's spent the last few minutes trying to wake you up, I think he is. You'll find it a lot easier to ride carrying your pack later if you can find your balance without it again first.'

I groaned.

'Come on, Peace wants you to ride, so ride.' Devlin went to stand by Peace and bent over, cupping his hands, ready to give me a lift onto Peace's back.

'I don't get any say in this at all, do I?' I moaned as I accepted the leg up.

'If you like, we can waste time while Peace tells you again why it's necessary and then you decide for yourself that you'll do it, but you'll get your breakfast much quicker if you just knuckle down and get on with it,' Devlin told me not unsympathetically. 'Okay, now ask Peace to move out onto a circle around me again, find your balance like you did last night and then ask him to change direction and walk around me the other way. Remember to keep some tension through your belly muscles and sit up straight, while keeping your lower back loose so you don't restrict him. That's it, now let your legs hang down a bit longer. If you stick them out in front of you like that, you won't be able to sit up straight…'

He was relentless. I thought I had found how I needed to sit the night before, but it seemed that there were always improvements to be made so that my balance and posture improved and I could be more of a help and less of a hindrance to Peace. I could feel that Peace was beginning to move a bit more freely beneath me and he was responding more quickly to my increasingly clear signals, so I trusted that all my pain and effort was worth it, but when I was finally allowed to slide to the ground and reminded to rub my horse down before I saw to my own needs, I could hardly believe that the day had barely begun.

'Smile, Adam, you're doing really well,' Devlin said.

I tried to make my grimace into a smile. 'Thanks. And thanks for your help, I can feel I'm getting a little bit better, I just had no idea it would hurt so much.'

'Just try to remember that it does until it doesn't, and the quickest way to get to where it doesn't is to practise. Come here, I'll finish rubbing him down while you eat and have a little rest. I've already broken my fast.'

I felt weak and useless, but did as I was told. 'How long have you been up?' I asked Devlin as he groomed Peace.

'About an hour, I should think. I always wake with the dawn.'

'So do I, normally. I can't believe how much this riding business is taking out of me.'

It is taking all of you. That is the benefit and the point.

I realised that I'd had no opportunity to think about what lay ahead of me. *Riding is like grooming, in a way, isn't it? It's relaxing for the mind, if not for the body.*

The better aligned are our bodies the better aligned are our minds. Our emotions. Our souls.

Suddenly, my body's aches and pains didn't seem so bad.

The next few days and nights followed a similar pattern to that when Peace and I had been travelling on our own. We stopped for slightly longer when the horses decided it was time to rest or graze, however, in order for me to have a short but more intensive riding lesson from Devlin than those when he and Risk were either separated from or forced to walk behind Peace and me by the seemingly endless bushes, and when I was encumbered by my back-sack.

I threw myself into my attempts to be a better rider whenever I was astride Peace, and I began to feel bereft every time I landed back on my own two feet; my body's protests faded into insignificance as I came to yearn for the deep, effortless sense of connection with my horse that riding gave me, and it wasn't long before it was Devlin calling our sessions to a close, rather than me. I was glad that his experience ensured I never rode Peace for longer than was appropriate for his young body, as Peace was every bit as keen as I.

We counted ourselves fortunate that the weather held for us. The nights were dry, if cool, and the days were filled with blue skies and gentle, late summer sunshine that warmed and eased my aching muscles.

It was just as the horses stopped for a mid-morning graze on the eighth morning after Peace and I had left Greenfields, that I began to feel uncomfortable. I was standing next to Peace, having been walking by his side to give us both a break from my continuing attempts to improve my riding. When I touched his mind, he seemed content, so I shrugged, wriggled out of the straps of my back-sack and then pulled out of it the brush I would need to groom the area of his back where I had been sitting.

As I brushed his coat and then his tail, I was lost in a feeling of calm contentment. Within minutes of sitting down to rest against my back-sack, however, I felt odd again. I had washed thoroughly in the stream by which we had camped the previous night, and my brushing of Peace's already clean coat had merely smoothed the hairs back down rather than caused the release of any dirt, yet I felt as if I wanted to scrub my skin of some unseen filth that I knew couldn't be there. I rubbed my bare forearms and then my sleeved upper arms and shivered.

Devlin looked up from a sketch he had just begun of the horses. 'You're not cold?'

'Not really, no, I just feel a bit... strange, I think.'

'You think?'

'I don't know.'

'Adam, are you alright?'

'Do I sound as if I'm alright?' I snapped.

Devlin held a hand up. 'Take it easy. Can I get your herbs out of your back-sack? Are there any that might help with... whatever it is that you're feeling?'

'When I want your help, I'll ask for it. It's always the same with you, isn't it? You poke your nose in where it isn't wanted and then just keep on and on.' I got to my feet and scowled at him. He frowned at me and then turned suddenly to where Risk had been grazing, but was now staring at him. Peace was nearby, staring at me.

I shook my head and blinked. There was something I had to remember. What was it? I didn't know and I began to feel panicky. I felt a pressure from deep inside of me, as if something were trying to get out, trying to reach for Peace. Reach for Peace! I found him within my mind and instantly, relief flooded me as I remembered. I had to choose him over that which would corrupt me from the city that we must now be nearing. I had to choose Peace over insanity.

I rushed to his side and put my hand to his shoulder, feeling the need to hold on to him physically in case I wasn't strong enough to do it mentally against that... whatever it was. I shuddered and rubbed Peace's neck as I turned back to Devlin. 'I'm sorry, I felt something nasty from the city and I let it affect me before I remembered to hold on to Peace to protect myself. We must be almost there.'

Devlin nodded. 'Risk tells me that she and I will need to wait here while you and Peace go on. Apparently, I'm unprepared to withstand what's there. We're not abandoning you, we won't go anywhere until you both come back, but it seems that this is something you and Peace will have to do alone. I'm sorry, I wish I could be more help.'

I shook my head. 'Don't be sorry, you've done more for me than I can ever thank you for already. When Peace is ready, if you don't mind, I'll have one last riding lesson to send me on my way, and then we'll be off.'

Devlin nodded. 'Sure.'

'Will you be alright staying here?' I asked Devlin as I went to sit back down by my gear.

He grinned. 'I'm well used to, and very happy with, Risk as my only company for weeks at a time. I'm sure I'll manage.'

'No, I mean, do you not have that horrible, skin-crawling feeling? Do you not need to back-track a bit to a more comfortable place to camp?'

Devlin shook his head. 'I don't feel anything.' He hesitated and looked over to where Risk was grazing and then added, 'Risk assures me I'm okay here. I'm obviously not as sensitive to things like that as you are.'

I nodded. 'All the same, I'll be back as soon as I can.'

'You'll be back when you get back,' Devlin said.

Peace grazed well into the afternoon, much longer than he normally would have; I could feel that he was preparing himself for what lay ahead. I followed his lead and ate a large lunch. Then I tried to rest, but couldn't completely; I didn't trust myself to drop off to sleep in case I couldn't find my way back to Peace when I woke up. When he stopped grazing, I got to my feet. 'It's time,' I told Devlin.

He gave me another riding lesson on Peace, reminding me again of all the parts of my body to which I needed to pay attention so that I was sitting in as balanced a position as possible, and therefore in the best place to give Peace clear signals. We hadn't yet gone any faster than a walk and I asked Devlin whether he thought I was ready to try a trot.

He nodded. 'It won't be easy without a saddle, but I think it's worth a try in case you need a bit more speed at some point.' He looked in the direction in which Peace and I would be continuing on alone and then blinked and looked back at me. 'Sorry, what was I saying? Yes, more speed. I'm sure Peace won't mind you taking hold of his mane with both hands. Then, keeping your position exactly as you have been, ask him for more speed with a squeeze of your ankles. Keep your lower back relaxed and follow his movement, just as you have been in walk. Peace, if you could take a bigger circle for now, that would be helpful. Adam, I want you to count Peace's steps. Count ten in walk, ask for trot, count ten in trot and then ask for walk by stilling your body until you feel him respond, just as you would when asking for halt from walk.'

I did as I was told. I was surprised to find that, busy as I was counting steps, I didn't find the different rhythm and movement of Peace's trot much more difficult to sit to than his walk. As soon as I asked for walk, Peace obliged.

'Good, keep going and now ask for fifteen steps of each pace at a time,' Devlin told me.

It wasn't until I was doing thirty steps of walk and then trot that I began to bounce in the trot.

'Okay, ask for walk again. You've found your limit with regard to how much trot you can do before you begin to tense up, so when you practise trotting next, keep to twenty-five steps at a time, with the walk breaks in between. It's important for you that you develop the muscle memory of how to sit to the trot smoothly, but even more important for Peace, as having you bouncing on his back will unbalance him, not to mention being uncomfortable.'

I nodded. 'Peace knew what he was doing asking for you to meet us, didn't he? You're a good teacher.'

Devlin grinned. 'I didn't find riding easy to begin with. I think it's easier to teach when you've struggled yourself.'

I grinned as I dismounted. 'Modest too.' I held out my hand to him. 'Thanks doesn't seem a big enough word for everything you've done for me, but in the absence of anything better, thanks, Devlin.'

He shook my hand. 'It's what I'm here for and what you're here for. It's what we do, Adam, we're Horse-Bonded.'

I nodded. 'I'm beginning to have a better grasp of what that means, thanks to you.'

'Don't mention it. Do you want to sort through your stuff and pack what you want to take with you, while I rub him down?'

'Yes, thanks.' I tossed him one of my brushes and then set about emptying my back-sack and selecting what I thought I might need, so that I didn't have to carry the full weight of it.

With my attention on my gear, the quietness of mind that always accompanied riding slowly subsided. My stomach began to churn horribly as Devlin's words from earlier went around and around in my mind: "…in case you need more speed at some point." I had told him what I was facing at the city and he was expecting me to need to flee, I knew it. He didn't think I was strong enough to cope with what I would find there. Well, who was I kidding, I probably wasn't. What was I even doing here, anyway? Why was it up to me to heal the cities of The Old? Why couldn't someone else do it? I selected a spare set of clothing from the stack I had with me and a long, white hair dropped to the ground from between two shirts. Peace's hair got flaming well everywhere, I thought to myself irritably. It was a miracle that his tail remained so full when he shed so many of his tail hairs over me and my clothes. Something pushed at me from within. Peace! I had to choose Peace. I could have slapped myself with frustration but as I sought him where I knew I could always find him in my mind and immersed myself in his conviction that all was well, I felt his approval.

Twice now the energy of the city has reached for you and twice you have found your way to me. It will become increasingly difficult but you are doing well, he told me.

I couldn't remember to do it by myself though, could I? You stared at me the first time and it was only because one of your tail hairs was in my stuff that I remembered this time.

You did not remember. The voice of your soul nudged you and you heard it. You are ready.

Chapter Thirty-Four

*a*s Peace and I walked away from Devlin and Risk, I put a hand to Peace's shoulder as I so often did. As always, his warmth and strength seemed to flow up my arm and into my body even as his mind provided a sanctuary of peace and tranquillity for my own.

It wasn't long before trees came into view in the distance. We were walking towards a forest? Had the city been replaced by trees? I wondered to myself. Would I have to fill each and every one of those trees with love? That could take forever. My musings were all the opening they needed to latch on to me.

'Our city. Leave or you die,' said the first whisper. 'Not safe here. Nowhere is safe. You're doomed. We're all doomed,' said the next. 'Leave us alone.' 'Kill you.' 'Going to hurt you.' 'Cut you, slash you, make you bleed.' 'Kill everyone before they kill us first.' 'Do it, press the button, kill them all.' 'Go away. We want to be left alone. Just go away.' The whispers filled my head and roiled around in my stomach. I felt sick and yet strangely comforted by the familiarity of their intentions. I identified with their impulse to hurt others, whether with words or with violence, to give them respite from their own hurt. I identified with the need to frighten others so that just for a little while, their own fear would recede. It worked, I had done it myself often enough. And I could do it again.

I stopped walking and glared at Peace. 'LEAVE ME ALONE,' I screamed at him. The whispers in my head turned into a wild cackling. 'I NEVER WANTED YOU. I NEVER NEEDED YOU. ALL I EVER WANTED WAS TO BE LEFT ALONE!'

Something was wrong. Shouting at people had always made me feel better, but all I felt was empty and… scared. Peace was standing calmly, staring at me, his soft, brown eyes drawing me in.

'Peace,' I whispered. I ran to him and flung my arms around his neck.

'Kill him. It's the only way,' the whispers urged me.

I took a step away from Peace. 'LEAVE US ALONE,' I shouted to the whispers.

My shoulder was nudged and I turned back to Peace. He nuzzled my face and then stared at me again. A familiar pushing from within caused me to blink and shake my head. Peace. I had to choose Peace.

Peace, I'm sorry, I don't remember letting go of you but they got into my head.

All is and will always be well.

I latched onto his thought and allowed it to fill me. Instantly, the whispers were no more.

What happened? I asked. *I was totally with you, and then I wasn't.*

You considered what is in front of us instead of confining yourself to that which we are about now.

Aaaaargh! Why can I not stop doing things like that?

It is the nature of humans to use the past and future as a distraction from the present. There are instances when it is a useful strategy but they are few.

And this is definitely not one of them, I agreed.

Yet each time you find your way back to me you gain strength.

I do? Because right now all I feel is weak and shaky.

The effort and intention required to choose peace is significant when on the brink of insanity. It does however award you a degree of strength that could never be achieved in the absence of difficulty.

So this is good for me?
All is well.

As we walked on through the scrub towards the trees, I began to feel a little chilly, despite the warm sunshine. I stopped to take a thin, green pullover from my back-sack, focusing extra hard on keeping my mind with Peace now that I no longer had the extra reassurance of being in physical contact with him. I managed it, but hurried to get my jumper on and my sack back on my shoulder so that I could put my hand to his shoulder once more.

By the time we reached the trees, I was cold again. I cursed. I had left my warmer clothes in a pile by Devlin's gear, not foreseeing that I would need them before my return.

'Hate you. Kill you.' The whisper was gleeful as it reached the piece of me that had pulled back from Peace in order to pass judgement on my discomfort. I threw all of myself back to where his mind was lodged within mine, before any more whispers could find a way in. I had a spare shirt with me that I decided would have to do. I stopped again, removed my pullover, donned the extra shirt and then put the pullover back on. As soon as I put my hand back to Peace's shoulder, he walked onward.

We weaved our way through the trees for several hours. It was eerily silent. No birds called, no animals rustled through the undergrowth and the leaves hung completely still from the branches of the closely packed trees. Whenever I had to leave Peace's side to go around a tree trunk, I would reach my hand back out to touch him at the earliest opportunity. On one occasion, I found him several trees away from me when I reached for him and despite focusing everything I had on holding to the sense of him within my mind, I felt a bolt of panic.

'He can't protect you. No one can. You're mine.' The whisper was accompanied by a sense of intense delight. I shuddered.

'Flee while you can. Get away from here,' another whisper urged me. But then Peace was there, angled across my path so that I bumped into him, jolting me out of the fear that was fast turning to anger.

Choose Peace. I put my hand to his shoulder and the part of me that had allowed the voices in was back with him.

They didn't miss an opportunity. When I stumbled over a tree root, they assured me they could cause me unlimited pain. When my sunhat snagged on a low branch, making me jump, they told me they would poke my eyes out. And when I was startled by a lone crow calling out somewhere in the distance, they told me they would rip off my head with their bare hands.

'YOU DON'T EVEN HAVE HANDS,' I roared back at them. 'You're pathetic. You lived lives full of fear and hate and you can't even stop being vile now that you've annihilated one another. Your threats are empty. You can't hurt me but I'm going to get rid of you.'

The cackling in my head was deafening. I put my hands to my ears to try to block it out as I stumbled between the trees, but it just got louder and louder.

'Get rid of us? That's what others said and look what we did to them.'

'You can't get rid of us, you're ours.'

'We can't hurt you? We're already hurting you.'

'We shouldn't play with him. We should just kill him.'

I stumbled out of the trees into a vast area of... nothingness. My hands still over my ears, I squinted around at the barren landscape, shivering despite my extra clothes and the sun that shone down from above. It wasn't completely empty, I realised. I could see what looked like the remains of buildings in the distance, and what was that, some sort of tree? But it was wrong. It had curled back down itself, as if desperate to get back underground with its roots.

The cackling continued.

I staggered onward, the soft, dusty soil lifting around my footfalls and floating in the air around me. Where it came to rest on the skin of my arms, neck and face, it felt as if the fingers of those who wished me harm were closing around me. Revulsion swept over me and I felt dizzy. A familiar emotion began to bubble up from deep down inside of me. I felt my lips curl into a rictus as I recognised it. Rage. A large white mass threw itself in front of me and I felt warm breath in my face but I pushed past it and ran further into the desolation of the old city, throwing my hands in the air. 'COME ON THEN, DO YOUR WORST AND SEE WHERE IT GETS YOU. THERE'S NO HURT YOU CAN DO ME THAT'S WORSE THAN WHAT I'VE ALREADY SUFFERED.'

The cackling went silent. 'Want to bet?'

Pain exploded inside of me as they crammed my body with their agony. I felt the fear that had driven them to wall themselves into their city, that had driven them to hate any who weren't as fearful as they were and to commit atrocities that I could barely comprehend. I felt their confusion and terror when they were left adrift, their bodies having been incinerated while their hate still drove them on. And I felt their loss. Through all the animosity they had felt to those unlike them, they had still been capable of feeling intense need for those they considered to be their own, many of whom had passed on completely instead of hanging on to the earthly existence to which they clung. I knew how it felt to suffer loss. Immediately, they homed in on my memories of my wife and child and the cackling began again. I shook my head. I couldn't have them in my head at the same time as my beautiful family. They didn't belong together. My loss was different from theirs. My suffering was different from theirs.

'No it isn't, no it isn't,' they all sang. They poked through my memories, prodding at them until I was screaming with the pain. I began to run, but kept tripping in the soft, deep, dusty earth. When I fell, I scrambled back to my feet and ran on. Then I fell and landed across something soft and warm. It moved beneath me, until my feet were no longer in contact with the ground.

I was upside down and blood was rushing to my head. I was swaying in a rhythm that seemed familiar. *Sit up.*

Peace? Thank goodness but I can't keep them out...

'They died and it was all your fault,' screeched a voice.

'Leave me alone,' I sobbed. 'Please, leave me alone.'

'Bronwyn would still be alive if it wasn't for you,' crowed another.

The movement beneath me changed rhythm, jolting me. *Sit up,* I was instructed again. Peace. He was trotting. He slowed to a walk and

I tried to swing a leg over his back so that I could do as he said. I had to choose Peace.

'You'll never find peace.'

'You know what you did.'

'People have died because of you.'

There was a jolt beneath me again and I nearly slid off. The movement had stopped. *Sit up.* There was no urgency about the instruction. I could feel Peace's intention to keep making the same suggestion until I followed it. Even now, he held to his conviction that all was well. That realisation allowed the sense of him in my mind to swell. I grabbed hold of it, at the same time taking hold of a chunk of his mane. I swung my leg over his back and sat up.

Oh thank goodness, Peace.

They will not give up easily.

I need to get away from here. I can't keep them out of my head.

They have no way to reach you as long as your mind is with mine.

But I can't sustain it. The second I lose concentration, they'll be in my head again. You said I have to heal the cities, but how do I do it when I can barely keep my own sanity?

In the same way that you healed my wounds.

What? I make up a paste in this... this desert where nothing seems to be able to grow, and then smear it... where?

The paste was merely the carrier of that which was required for healing.

Love. Okay, so somehow, I try to stay with you in my mind so that I can stay sane, and at the same time, I have to try and find a way to give them enough love to heal all of this misery and fear and hate and...

Hold on to me. Do not let go.

His advice held. I did as I was told, quickly calming before the voices could find an opening through which to torment me again. I breathed in and out slowly. I put my hands on either side of his withers, feeling his strength.

Okay. I'm okay. But, Peace, why can't you heal the city? It doesn't seem to be affecting you like it is me. Surely you could do a better job than I can?

Humans were the cause of the damage. Humans must redress the balance. It is necessary for you personally and for your species that you do this.

I sighed. *I have to be a source of peace for others if I am to find it for myself.*

They are one and the same.

They are?

Focus on helping the souls who would torment you. You resonate with them because you identify with choosing fear and pain over love and peace. You can help them by showing them how to choose differently.

But how? They're ready and waiting to tear me away from you at the slightest opportunity.

The better aligned are our bodies the better aligned are our minds.

So I ride you? Now?

Our last lesson will serve you well.

I gathered myself together and sat as Devlin had taught me to. Then I asked Peace to move towards the ruined buildings in the distance, and began to count. After twenty-five steps of walk, I asked him to trot. It wasn't easy for him due to the depth of the silty soil beneath his feet and he had to take shorter, more lurching steps, but he willingly obliged. Within ten steps, I had lost my balance, unable to sit to the bouncier trot. I just about managed to ask him to walk, without falling off. I decided to try five steps of walk and five of trot at a time instead. I immersed myself in feeling what my body needed to do in order to stay in harmony with Peace's, and when I was achieving five steps of trot at a time with ease, I increased it to eight and then back to ten. Soon, I was smiling.

We began to weave between piles of rubble and the remains of what must have been enormous buildings, judging by the stubs of walls, none higher than my waist, that outlined multitudes of rooms and corridors. The ruins poked out of the grey dust and stretched as far in front of me as I could see, completely unclaimed by plants, birds or any of the natural life that would normally reach out and fill in areas left vacant. I focused on the evidence of what humans could both achieve and destroy and sent my love out to it, just as I had to the plants I had ground down to make my healing paste. Then, keeping my body and mind with Peace as he continued to alternate between walking and trotting, I sent my love out further to infuse the air, the ground and everything buried within it. I sent it down as deep and out as far from me as I could. It was limitless, powerful and all consuming. It permeated the city, asking nothing, giving everything.

I have no idea how long we continued so, absorbed as I was in keeping with Peace and sharing all that we were, but when his steps began to falter slightly, I immediately asked him to slow to a walk and then to a halt. I leant forward, swung a leg over his back and dropped quickly to the ground.

Peace's sides were heaving. Pink skin showed through the drenched white fur of his coat and sweat ran off him in rivulets, making dark streaks in the deep, grey surface beneath where he stood. I rubbed his shoulder and noticed for the first time that I was as sweat-soaked as he was. I pulled both shirts and the jumper over my head together, to find that the air that reached my skin was now warm. We were both exhausted, and we needed water. I had brought four full water pouches with me, but I remembered dropping them when I stumbled out of the trees. I could see the forest in the distance; Peace must have circled around to head back at some point. Immediately, Peace and I began to walk slowly back to where shade and water awaited, no communication necessary.

When we finally made it to the trees, I spotted where I had dropped my water pouches and back-sack. I had brought my largest cook pot for Peace to use as a small bucket in case water proved difficult to come by. I emptied the whole of the first pouch into it, followed quickly by the second as Peace drank, and then the third. Only when he lifted his head, his thirst satiated, did I allow myself to sink to the ground and drink from the last pouch.

Did it work? Have they all gone? I asked.

You already feel the warmth on your skin where before it was chilled. We have done enough for now. We both require rest and your herbs in order for our bodies to recover fully from our exertions.

I nodded and scrambled to my back-sack for the herbs that would ease Peace's body. *I don't mind hurting, but I'm sorry you are,* I told him.

It was necessary. I will recover. We may rest together. There is little here capable of bothering us.

You're sure? I asked as I held out the herbs to him that he needed.

Peace took them and looked at me as he munched them, his brown eyes tired, but as calm and sure as ever. Then he moved to a space between two trees, dropped to his knees and lay down with a grunt.

I sat down on the ground next to him, relieved to be back in the forest. The smell of the trees, the fallen leaves beneath me, the slightly damper feel to the air all felt so familiar. I leant back against Peace's belly and was asleep within seconds.

When I woke, all was quiet except for the sound of Peace's deep, slow breathing as he slept. Night had fallen and everywhere was dark. I got to my feet, grimacing at the pain in my muscles, and staggered the few steps necessary to clear the trees and stand in the site of the old city. The dust that I disturbed no longer clawed at me as it settled on my skin and the whispers were gone. I looked up at the sky, marvelling at the multitudes of stars shining brightly and imagining that they were the souls who had finally passed on and were now at peace.

I jumped at the faintest of murmurs. I frowned and focused my ears and my mind, listening. Nothing. I tottered out into the bleakness, looking around myself in the pale light of the moon. I sank down to my shins in places, and marvelled at how Peace had carried me for so long. He had responded to my every signal immediately, never faltering in the deep, fine soil until we had done what we needed to do. No wonder he was so exhausted. I looked back to where I could just about make out his large, white rump, his magnificent tail splayed out behind him. He gave everything of himself, always. How was I so fortunate as to have him in my life?

I heard another murmur behind me. I swung around, but everywhere was quiet again.

Do not concern yourself. Your love gave those souls the energy to find peace and move on. You merely perceive the faintest echoes of some of the events that occurred here. Those too will shift with a little help.

I turned to look back to where Peace had heaved himself up to rest on his elbows. I couldn't see his stare but I could feel it.

I'm not sure about riding you again any time soon, Peace, your body hasn't recovered fully from the last time.

I am in better condition than you. I ingested the herbs my body needed, Peace informed me accusingly, his scolding softened by his appreciation. He knew exactly why I hadn't taken any myself. *Even were it necessary for you to infuse our surroundings with more of your love you would not need to ride me. There is little left here to distract you from keeping your mind with mine of your own volition. It is a more permanent source of positivity that is required here however.*

A more permanent source? Like the hawthorn bushes at home?

You will have help transplanting the bushes required now that your friend can be comfortable here. His Bond-Partner and I will assist.

Will anything grow here though? I kicked my foot through the silt. *This doesn't look very fertile.*

On the contrary it has much to offer now that life here will no longer be thwarted by the dead.

I ambled back to Peace and crouched down by his head. He whickered as I stroked his cheek.

Your coat needs brushing now that your sweat has dried, I told him. *I should never have fallen asleep without covering you with the contents of my back-sack, or at least with some of the forest floor. You could have got a chill.*

Were I at risk of that I would have rolled in the remains of the city.

Even so, Devlin would never let Risk go to sleep in that state.

You need not emulate your peers in order to feel worthy. They have their voyage to make through life and you have yours.

I sat down and crossed my legs, frowning in thought. *Everything you tell me seems so obvious and yet I'd never be able to think that way without you.*

Peace rested his muzzle on my knee with a long sigh. *Your efforts here have propelled you closer to being able to do so. You have done well.*

Chapter Thirty-Five

*T*he next time I awoke, the top of the sun was peering over the horizon, its rays skimming across the vast expanse of the ruined city to reach us before fading to almost nothing in the depths of the forest. Peace was lying flat out again and I had somehow ended up curled in the crook of his head and neck, my head on his shoulder. I sat up and to begin with, I couldn't decide what it was that was different... Birds! I had heard a single crow in the distance the day before. Now, I could quite clearly hear a multitude of birds calling to one another as they questioned whether it really was time for the day to begin. I was amazed that any had ventured into the area so soon after the departure of that which had kept them away, let alone the number I could hear – and for them to be chirruping sleepily now, they must have arrived before darkness fell the previous evening.

They were drawn by your energy. The ground animals are on their way. Those who fly will be further attracted by the bushes you will plant and their energy will complement yours in helping everything to return to the way it should be. Peace heaved himself back up onto his elbows and I moved quickly out of his way.

I'd best get to it then, hadn't I? I got to my feet and stretched, ignoring the pain and stiffness that I felt was absolutely worth having.

I brushed Peace down and then ate quickly, mindful of the fact that there was little here for him to eat. Then we made our way back to where Devlin and Risk awaited our return.

Since the trees were so closely packed, branches low enough for Peace to reach were few and far between, but he pulled at leaves from the odd few that were, as we walked. When we reached the scrubland, I suggested to Peace that I leave him to graze and rest whilst I went to fetch Devlin and Risk.

No need. They approach, I was informed.

Sure enough, within minutes, I heard hoofbeats and Risk and Devlin appeared around a large clump of bushes. Risk's saddlebags were jammed full, as was Devlin's back-sack; I was relieved I wouldn't have to walk back to retrieve my stuff.

'I gather it's good news,' Devlin called out with a grin. He leapt to the ground almost before Risk had halted, and strode over to me, offering his hand. 'Well done, mate,' he said. 'According to Risk, you "demonstrated enormous trust and courage, and many have benefitted as a result." So, you've cleared the city of its ghosts?'

I told him everything that had transpired, whilst he unsaddled Risk and rubbed her down. 'I could just do with your help now, to dig up some of these bushes and plant them throughout the city. Peace assures me that they'll grow and if I infuse them the same way I did with the hawthorn bushes in my garden at home, they'll be a constant source of positive energy to help clear the last of the energy of The Old, and will allow nature to reclaim the area,' I finished.

Devlin stood upright and nodded. 'Sure. We don't have shovels with us though. Spoons?'

'Yes, so we'll have to make do with seedlings. Peace has said he and Risk will help, so I think if we empty out Risk's saddlebags and find a way to bundle some seedlings together for Peace, they can carry a load each, as can we. We should be able to take hundreds.'

'Okay, well let's get digging, then when the horses have finished grazing and are ready to go, we will be too.'

'Great.' I wriggled out of my back-sack and then bent down to look for my spoon.

'Ouch. You don't look so great,' Devlin said, watching my slow, careful movements.

'I'm fine, I've just stiffened again from standing still. It's all good. No really it is,' I assured him with a smile when he raised his eyebrows at me.

He gave a short nod. 'Good on you,' he said and turned to his own gear.

~

'If anyone had told me that I would spend any amount of time in my middle years digging around in the dirt with a spoon, I would never have believed them,' Devlin said with a wry grin as he brushed the last of the dirt from his trousers.

It had taken the rest of the morning and half of the afternoon, but we finally had enough shrubs to fill Risk's saddlebags and both of our back-sacks – allowing a little room for a few food parcels each – and to make up two evenly sized bundles tied up with a rope belonging to Devlin, which Peace had assured me he was happy to carry. I put a thick wad of my clothes under the middle section of rope as it passed over his back, the bundles suspended on either side of him. Then I attached the two ends of the rope together underneath him to stabilise everything.

Remember to give yourself extra room between those trees, they're close enough together as it is, I warned him. He merely turned to look at me, blinked and then set off for the forest. I grinned.

'Peace is obviously keen to get going, we'll let you two lead the way,' Devlin said with a nod towards Peace's departing backside.

It wasn't pleasant, forcing my already protesting muscles to get back to work and carry the water pouches I had refilled and attached to the outside of my back-sack, plus the shrubs packed within, especially since several of them were poking me in the back. I couldn't have cared less though. I hadn't dared to allow myself to believe that I could actually heal the city – I had gone along with trying because Peace had insisted upon it – and yet here we were, on our way back there with our friends, carrying the ingredients for the last part of the process. The birds were singing in the trees and the forest seemed lighter, somehow. It wasn't – the light that penetrated the canopy of the closely growing trees was the same as before – but it felt that way to me.

'Hey, look over there, to your right,' Devlin whispered behind me. Lots of dark shapes were moving at speed. A fallen tree provided a gap in the canopy, allowing a beam of light to reach the forest floor and illuminate the deer who jumped over its trunk one by one whilst appearing to be one long, flowing animal. Then they were gone. My smile stayed on my face until we reached the bleakness of the city site.

That too will change rapidly once we have finished our work here, Peace told me. His thought was accompanied by a sense of satisfaction that pleased me no end.

I found where I had left the cook pot that I had used as a water bucket, emptied a water pouch into it and offered it to the horses, refilling it as they drank. By the time they had finished, Devlin had relieved them of their loads. Before we could brush them down, they took themselves into the sandy, silty soil of the city and rolled, over and over. When they got up, they shook, a cloud of dust hovering above each of them. Peace snorted and Risk squealed and stamped her foot. They blinked at one another, their eyes seeming excessively bright in the dull grey dust that caked them both from head to tail.

I grinned and Devlin chuckled. 'Now see what you've done to yourself,' he said fondly to his horse. She responded with another squeal and then wheeled around and took off, her tail held high. She was a lighter build than Peace and found it easier to move through the deep soil, but still she cantered no more than five large circles before she was blowing. She slowed to a trot and made her way back to us, her nostrils pink and flaring, little flecks of sweat giving her dusty coating a dappled appearance. She stopped in front of Devlin, her ears pricked and eyes shining.

'She knows what you and Peace did here. She's just added a little joy of her own,' he said to me as he rubbed her forehead. 'Are you going to stand still and let me brush you down now?' he asked her.

She jumped to the right with her forelegs and then trotted past him to stand in the trees. Peace joined her and they settled down for a doze.

Devlin looked back to me with a wry grin. 'Apparently there are other things more urgent than my obsession with my own and Risk's appearance. I'll just grab a mouthful of water and get back to digging then, shall I?'

I laughed. 'It won't take as long to plant the seedlings as it did to dig them up, and by the look of those clouds in the distance, they'll have a good watering in. Maybe it will wash the dirt off the horses too.'

'Wishful thinking, my friend, wishful thinking,' said Devlin. He took a mouthful of water, wiped the opening of the pouch with his shirt and then handed it to me. 'You're right about the clouds though, we'll be pushed to get this lot planted before the rain arrives.'

Immediately, I focused on my sense of Peace, went to where Devlin had left his back-sack and saddlebags and infused all of the shrubs within them with a strong burst of love and positivity for the future. 'They're ready when you are,' I told Devlin.

'Where do you want me to plant them?'

'Just space them out as far and wide as you can. Peace tells me that they'll grow and spread quickly with all that the soil has to give them, so we don't have to get right to the far reaches of the city, but if you start over on the left and work your way away from here, and I start on the right and do the same, our loads will get lighter as we go and we'll see how far we can get.'

'Right you are.'

I held effortlessly to Peace as I planted my share of shrubs, infusing each of them with love as I lowered them into their holes. As I packed the soil around them, I imbued them with my intention that they continue to provide energy to the city site so that the last traces of The Old could be laid to rest and nature welcomed back.

When the first drop of water landed on my head, I looked up and around me. I was almost at the ruins and Devlin was a small dot in the distance off to my left. When I looked behind us, it was gratifying to see all of the little dots of green in the mostly bare landscape between us and the trees where the horses still snoozed. I was halfway through my share of plants. Since all that was left of the buildings was walls, it was a case of either running back to the trees for shelter, or carrying on in the rain.

Devlin changed from a dot to a stationary vertical line and I supposed that he was probably considering the same options. I shrugged. It wasn't cold and if I worked faster, I would be moving more and generating more heat. I would carry on. Devlin would either decide the same, or he would head back, the choice was his.

Having exhausted the bundles that Peace had carried for me, I now had only the back-sack to drag behind me. I nodded to myself and got back to work.

Within minutes, the sky had darkened to purple and the rain was falling too heavily for me to be able to see what Devlin had decided to do. I worked as quickly as I could, but it was never quite enough for me to be warm. Water sheeted down my back and poured off my forehead as I crouched down to plant each seedling in the streets of The Old before running, stooped over, to the location for the next. A part of me registered that I was wet, cold, uncomfortable and increasingly hungry but from my place in my bond with Peace, I was protected from forming any sort of judgement about my situation. It was a liberating way to be.

It wasn't until I was packing soil around the stem of my last seedling – a satisfyingly large one – that I was distracted from my place of tranquillity by the ground vibrating. All of a sudden, there was movement in my peripheral vision and I was sprayed with clods of the soaked and now heavy, sticky earth.

I will take you to shelter, Peace informed me.

I grinned and tried to blink the rainwater out of my eyes so that the white blur in front of me could resolve into my horse. My world. He was always there before I thought to need him. *You're a sight for sore eyes, thanks, Peace. I'll get on from that wall over there.*

As soon as I was on his back, he walked a couple of paces and then began to trot. I grinned. It felt easy. The ground was firmer now that it was wet, so Peace's trot was smoother than when I had ridden him the day before. My vision was blurry due to the rain, but I didn't care. I could do this. I felt a sense of challenge from Peace. It was all the warning I had before he leapt into canter. I stayed with him, keeping my lower back loose, not gripping with my legs, just allowing my body to follow his movement.

'WAHOO!' I shouted into the rain. Peace took my shout as encouragement and increased his speed. I loved it. I could barely see at all now, all I could feel was rain slapping into my face, and my own and my horse's enjoyment as we tore back to the trees.

We seemed to be racing through the rain forever. How far had I travelled? I wondered to myself.

Far enough. The city will now thrive, Peace told me, at last beginning to slow down.

When he stopped, I came close to going over his head but just managed to shift my weight back far enough in time. I slid to the ground, my muscles screaming in protest at their continued abuse, and rubbed my eyes. The trees were just in front of me and Risk was halting beside me. Devlin jumped to the ground and the four of us darted under the dense cover of the trees.

'I stand corrected, the horses have indeed been washed clean, as have I. I actually think I've lost a layer of skin,' Devlin grinned, tilting his head back in order to see me from under the drooping brim of his sunhat. 'Did you plant all of yours?'

I grinned back. 'Yes. You?'

He nodded. 'I don't think Risk would have come for me if I hadn't finished, she's pretty stirred up about all this. I take it that white streak that converged on us was you and Peace?'

'It was. Before you say I'm not good enough to ride at that speed, I had no say in the matter.'

Devlin took his hat off and wrung it out, leaving his dark hair stuck to his scalp. 'After what you did yesterday, I don't think I have any right to tell you anything. It's phenomenal, what you and Peace have done here, Adam.'

'It was Peace far more than me. I'm just a parasite who hangs onto him in order to feel better about myself.'

'Far be it from me to comment on what goes on between you and your Bond-Partner, but for what it's worth, I think you're selling yourself short.'

'Well, thanks for that, and for your help. You've done as much as I have today; if it weren't for you and Risk, Peace and I would be having to go back for another load now.'

'We're done here then?'

'Peace says the city will thrive now.'

He clapped me on the shoulder. 'Great news. We'll make our way straight back then, shall we? The horses need to eat and we could all do with keeping moving while we're soaking wet. Then we can chat about where we're heading next.'

'We?' I said as he and Risk walked past Peace and me to take the lead.

'You fancy transplanting the millions of shrubs that it's going to take to transform all of the old cities, with a spoon by yourself, do you?' he said over his shoulder.

'But don't you have other things to do?'

'If anything comes up, Risk and I will have to attend to it but in the meantime, if you want our help, we're at your disposal. And I was joking by the way, the first village we reach, I'm getting us each a hand shovel.'

'You know we're not just travelling to old city sites, though, don't you? I have to find all of the people I chased away when I was living in the woods, and make things right.'

He raised a hand up to shoulder height. 'We won't get in your way. When we're near a village you need to visit, Risk and I will leave you to go on alone. When your business is done, we'll accompany you onward.'

Peace? I asked him, feeling suddenly unsure. Whilst Devlin and Risk were good company and had been a massive help, I didn't know whether I wanted them with us all of the time. I didn't know whether I would be able to learn all I needed to from Peace while we had the distraction of company, and whether it was cheating, somehow, to have help and support.

He is the first of many who will offer their assistance. Your path will be easier to tread if you allow others to walk it alongside you.

But I have you. You're with me.

You have already discovered that you have more to learn than I alone can teach you.

I considered for a few moments more while Devlin walked on in silence. 'Your help, and Risk's, would be appreciated. Thank you,' I said finally.

He put a hand up to wave without looking back at me. 'No problem.'

So where are we heading next? I asked Peace. *To another city, or to find someone living whom I've hurt? I know where a few of them are but I don't even know where to start finding the rest.*

We will begin with those whose location you know. The rest will find you as we travel.

They will? How?

They know not what it was exactly that you took from them but when they hear that you are providing it for others they will be drawn to you nevertheless.

Chapter Thirty-Six

The sun had gone down by the time we arrived back where we had stored our packs underneath some bushes. The rain had stopped, so we changed into dry clothes, ate a hasty meal and then settled down for the night to the sound of Peace and Risk munching contentedly nearby. I was asleep within minutes and the sun was well up by the time I woke the next morning. Immediately, I felt guilty for not having taken a turn at watch.

Your body and mind needed more rest than any of ours, Peace informed me matter-of-factly and then turned his attention elsewhere.

'Sorry,' I said to Devlin, who was piling up refilled water pouches, having clearly already washed and shaved.

'Don't be, you obviously needed the rest,' Devlin said, his answer as devoid of accusation as Peace's had been.

I grinned. 'That's kind of what Peace said. Is this what happens, the longer we're Horse-Bonded – we start answering in the same way as the horses?'

He smiled back. 'It would be nice to think so, wouldn't it? Now, where are we heading today?'

'Peace has told me to head next for people whose location I know, and the closest of those are at the next village along from Greenfields.'

He nodded. 'That village in the hills, Uptown, I know it. The views from up there are stunning. Risk and I will camp an hour's ride out, I'll be more than happy sketching for as long as it takes for you and Peace to do what you need to do.'

We arrived at Devlin's chosen spot in less than half the time it had taken to travel from Greenfields to the city site; I was able to ride for longer at a time and at greater speed, and Peace was more than willing and able to carry me.

I envied Devlin as he settled down with his sketch pad next to his grazing horse. Since Uptown was so close to my home village, I was well known there, as were my life choices of the past few years. Several of its inhabitants had made the mistake of seeking me out in the woods and had been on the receiving end of both my rejection and my temper as a result. I anticipated my and Peace's reception there being very similar to that which we had experienced at Greenfields.

The present, was all the reminder Peace gave me, all the reminder I needed to settle into place with him in my mind. He turned away from Devlin and Risk, and carried me onwards.

In no time, we had crested a steep hill and were looking across at Uptown, its grey stone cottages built into the side of the next hill, its single cobbled street zigzagging from left to right as it wound its way from the highest cottages down to those near the valley floor.

I dismounted from Peace and offered him water in my cook pot, which he accepted readily. While he drank, I brushed him down, enjoying the warmth of the sun on my arms and face, and the sound of the birds chirping as they looped and swooped in the sky, catching flies. When Peace had finished, I took a few swigs from my water pouch, repacked and shouldered my back-sack, and put a hand to his shoulder. We would walk on together from here.

The shouts of outrage began as soon as we set foot on the cobbles of Uptown. Immersed as I was in Peace, I could see that the best way to begin to undo the damage I had caused was to be quiet and let the villagers discharge whatever they needed to. I found myself nodding in agreement with everything they said, for it was all true. The crowd grew, the shouting got louder and louder as more voices contributed to my berating, and then gradually, it quietened down.

'And he has the gall to show up here with a horse, like he's one of the Horse-Bonded,' a man said before silence finally fell.

Peace took a step towards the man and stretched his neck out, reaching for him without imposing on his personal space. The man frowned, unsure what to do. He looked about him, saw that all eyes were on him, and flushed red. Peace turned his head onto one side, his neck still outstretched, and wiggled his top lip. There were some giggles and the man grinned. He tentatively reached out a hand and was rewarded with a whicker as Peace sniffed him. I grinned as the man stepped closer, receiving a gentle nuzzle to his shoulder before his cap was knocked off.

Peace made his way around the villagers, making each in turn the object of his affection. Once the tension had well and truly lifted, he gently manoeuvred his way back to my side. As had happened at Greenfields, the villagers looked from him to me, their expressions alternating between smiles and frowns of confusion.

'So... are you Horse-Bonded then? For real?' someone called out.

'I am,' I said. 'This is Peace, my Bond-Partner. I realise how unexpected our presence is here, and I fully understand why mine, at least, is unwelcome. I've behaved unforgivably towards some of you and unfortunately, I can't take that back. What I can do is tell you how much I regret my behaviour and how sorry I am for the hurt I've caused. I'm here to help in any way I can. Obviously, I don't expect any of you to offer lodgings as you normally would to visiting Horse-Bonded, so Peace and I will camp down in the valley, by the oak tree. As you will have noticed, he loves people and will welcome visitors who want a fuss and a play every bit as much as those of you who would like to ask his advice.'

They watched in silence as we turned to go, and began to whisper as we walked away but no one shouted abuse at me or tried to stop us leaving. I breathed out slowly and let go of Peace in my mind.

I was surprised by how easy I had found it to keep my mind with his through it all, and how calm I felt now, despite all of the anger and hostility that had been directed towards me.

Your experience at the city prepared you well, Peace observed.

Which was why you wanted us to go there before visiting any more villages, I told him, realisation dawning. *If I could hold to you through everything they threw at me, I would be better able to do it with living people. I wonder if any of them will come to see us.*

I didn't have long to wait to find out; Peace had his first visitors that evening, followed by more the following morning. I kept my distance as I had at Greenfields, allowing them to enjoy his warmth and sense of fun without interference. I did, however, spend some time infusing the oak tree whose branches gave us shade and shelter, with love.

It wasn't long before I was being hailed to act as Peace's voice so that visitors could ask him for advice. Eventually, it was a relative of one of those who had come to me for help when I lived in the woods, who was doing the asking. Her name was Chel. She was tall and thin with a stern demeanour, accentuated by a heavy, slightly masculine brow over intense blue eyes. After passing on Peace's counsel to her – now that he knew I could find and stay with him more easily, he was actually giving the advice himself instead of insisting that I do it – I enquired after her cousin.

'She's the same,' I was told stiffly. 'Ungol's remedy keeps her stable but he can't seem to cure her. You were her last hope and when you turned her away, she was devastated.'

'Do you think she would allow me to visit her?'

Chel shrugged. 'Gina doesn't put up much argument to anything, she can't find the strength.'

I almost let go of Peace but the moment I felt myself sliding into shame and self-loathing, I held on fast. I would be no help to anyone if I let my old patterns re-emerge.

'Would you be so kind as to tell me how I can find her home?' I asked.

～

It felt all too familiar to be walking a cobbled street of an evening with grey stone cottages either side, one hand clutching a bunch of love-imbued wildflowers, the other at Peace's shoulder, he on the receiving end of warm words and smiles whilst I was either scowled at or ignored. The similarity to events in Greenfields ended, however, when I knocked on Gina's door. It was a while before anything happened but eventually there was a thud, as if someone had come to rest against the door. The latch was lifted and the door slowly creaked open to reveal a grey-haired, wizened old lady. She was almost bent double as she braced herself between the doorframe and her walking stick.

'Chel said you would come,' she wheezed, squinting up at me through cloudy eyes. She had used a stick the last time I had seen her, but she hadn't been bent over with the effort of breathing as she was now. Peace's head appeared over my shoulder, reaching out to Gina, reminding me to do the same.

'Thank you for opening your door to me,' I said. 'I'm truly sorry for the way I spoke to you when you came to visit me, and that I refused you the help you needed. I realise that I've caused you to suffer and I'm more ashamed of myself than I can ever convey to you. Will you allow me to try and help you now?'

I was shocked when a grin spread across her face. 'It's been a while since a man brought me flowers,' she wheezed and then began to cough. I stepped forward, wanting to support her but she held a hand up to me and shook her head. By the time she had finished coughing, she was shaking and her legs were trembling. Her bout had, however, given me the time to perform a full inventory of her body. Both my training and my intuition told me what I needed to do. 'Come in,' gasped Gina, 'you can put those in a vase yourself.'

I rubbed Peace's forehead, then left him on the doorstep and followed Gina as she walked, one painfully slow step at a time, down her dark hallway and into an even darker kitchen at the back of the cottage. As she shuffled to a chair, I looked up at the ceiling where it met the wall that was built into the hillside. I couldn't see anything out of place, but I knew it was there. At that moment, the front door banged and Chel came bursting in. 'So, can you help her?'

'Yes, I think so. Chel, does anyone else here have the same breathing difficulties as Gina?'

'No. I seem to remember mention of the fact that some people did in days gone by, but not anymore.'

'And are all the cottages built in the same way?'

'Yes, apart from the newer ones which are built with decent ventilation, now that the Rock-Singers and Glass-Singers have worked out how to do it. They've built their solution into most of the older cottages too, but old stubborn here refused their offer of putting it into this one, saying she couldn't be doing with the mess. Is that what's causing the problem with her breathing? Stale air?'

I shook my head and sat down next to Gina, bending to look into her eyes. 'Gina, your airways are constricting and producing excess mucus as an allergic reaction to mould that's growing in here somewhere.'

Gina's eyes widened. 'I keep a clean house, there's no mould here,' she gasped.

'I can't see it either, it's possibly the same colour as your paintwork, but I know it's here, probably on that back wall or up on the ceiling. Ungol's remedy has been working to keep mucus production down and your airways open as much as possible, but they're having to work against your body's ongoing response to the spores of the mould being allowed to grow by the damp air in here. I bet you felt better when you made the trip to see me in the woods, didn't you?'

'She did! She was that much better by the time she got back here that to begin with, we all thought you'd healed her, but then she got much worse again. So all she has to do is have ventilation put in?' Chel said excitedly, her brow lifting to reveal a much softer expression.

'She can speak for herself,' rattled Gina.

'Chel, would you be so kind as to put these flowers in water?' I asked, handing them to her. When she leapt to fulfil my request, I looked back to her cousin. 'You will need to move out of here while the walls and ceilings are scrubbed and ventilation is installed, Gina.

In the meantime, there is a little adjustment I'd like to make to the preparation you've been taking and something I would like to add to it. By the time you move back in, you'll be feeling a whole lot better.'

I swallowed as she reached out a shaking, blue-veined hand and laid it upon my own. 'Better late than never,' she wheezed and winked at me.

'I'm humbled that you're so open to allowing me to help,' I said.

'Evie sent word...' She began another coughing fit. By the time she had finished, my surprise was subsiding and being replaced by a warmth that permeated my body before coming to rest in my stomach.

'Evie Dennison? From Greenfields?'

Chel put the vase of flowers down on the table and sat down the other side of Gina. 'Yes, she sent word to several of us that you've changed and that you and Peace helped practically the whole village with one thing or another. Most people here didn't believe it. I was one of those who wanted to, as were those who have already been to see you. Gina believed her, didn't you G?'

'And I was right, like always...'

'Except about having ventilation installed. You'll come and stay with me until we have this place straight and Adam has healed you. Okay?'

Gina nodded. 'Okay.'

Chel looked back at me, all of the hardness I had witnessed in her before, gone. 'The flowers are beautiful, Adam, I'll take them back to my cottage with Gina, it's four down from here.' She held my gaze. 'Thank you.'

I shook my head. 'Thank you, both of you. For your trust and your forgiveness.' I stood up. 'I'll go and make up your new preparation, Gina. I have most of what I need in my pack, and it won't take me a minute to find the few herbs I'm missing. I'll bring it to you at Chel's, before dark. I must warn you, the new preparation will be a more vivid shade of green than anything you've been asked to take before.'

As Peace and I wandered back down to the oak tree, I wondered about the fact that I had been forgiven so quickly. Peace was noticeably silent on the matter, as he tended to be when waiting for me

to realise or remember something. All of a sudden, it came to me –
something he had told me, what seemed like years ago. *One who is
capable of creating disturbance to the extent that you have done is
capable of creating harmony to the same degree.* Just as the effects of
my dreadful behaviour had spread out far and wide, the same was
beginning to happen now that I was trying to make things right.

This is what you were meaning, isn't it? I asked Peace. *Word is
spreading and it won't just mean that people will come to find me
instead of me having to find them all, it means those I do find may be
more open to forgiving me. So maybe as time goes on, it will gradually
get easier?*

Easier. Yet not easy.

Nevertheless, I felt lighter, as if I had a bit less of a burden to
carry.

The following morning, I had barely washed and breakfasted
before a steady stream of people began to arrive to see Peace and me,
mostly to ask for Peace's counsel but some to ask for my help as a
Herbalist; it seemed that Gina was already doing much better and Chel
had wasted no time in passing the word around.

By the afternoon, I had received several offers of lodging, for
which I was grateful but which I refused; since none of the cottages
had paddocks, I preferred to camp in the valley so as to be near Peace.
Those whose offers I refused brought me freshly cooked food instead,
for which I was immensely grateful.

When Peace and I visited Gina at Chel's cottage that evening, she
had colour in her cheeks and her breathing was deeper and easier. She
managed to hold a conversation with me without coughing once,
telling me of how her neighbours had rallied and were scrubbing her
cottage from top to bottom, and that the ventilation system was being
installed the following day. She also told of how she had spent a good
part of the day sitting on the front doorstep, watching the comings and
goings to her cottage, and how cheerful everyone seemed to be.

Over the days that followed, most of the villagers came to see
Peace and me for one reason or another. Many left with preparations
that included my green paste and all were exposed to the positivity

emanating from the oak tree and to the peace I was able to provide from my place with Peace. I was stunned when our visitors included those who, like Gina, had sought me out at my hovel in the woods and been turned away. I had fully intended to seek them out as I had Gina and was humbled, delighted and relieved that not only had they come to me, but that they allowed me to give them the help for which they had been forced to wait far too long.

Peace and I left Uptown after just five days. Five days to lighten the darkness I had caused, where in Greenfields it had taken weeks, I mused to myself.

You are not the man who returned to his home village, Peace observed as he carried me back to Risk and Devlin.

But I'm not who I want to be, either. I'm envious of those who can take from me what I can't feel for myself.

There is yet much to do, agreed Peace.

Chapter Thirty-Seven

*P*eace and I visited two more villages as summer gave way to autumn. Both times, we left Devlin and Risk a short distance away while we went on alone. Both times, we returned to them four or five days later, leaving a village healed of the damage I had caused, and either a bush or tree infused with my love and positivity, behind us. Devlin collected herbs to replenish my stores, and continued filling his beloved sketch book while we were absent.

By the time the oranges, reds, yellows and browns of the trees proclaimed that autumn was in full progress, the four of us were on our way to the site of another city of The Old. I felt confident that Peace and I could help those poor souls still intent on doing harm, to move on, yet sometimes, when I was on watch by myself at nighttime, I would succumb to feeling nervous that I would be distracted by them initially, as had happened at the last city. I needn't have worried. Peace and I were now strong enough that I was riding him for most of the time that we were on the move, and the ever increasing harmony with which our bodies moved and communicated meant that my mind sat ever more effortlessly within his. I only became aware that we were close enough to the city to be within reach of the souls that lingered there, due to the sudden drop in temperature and my consequent need for extra clothing; apart from that, I was immune to their influence, so secure was I in my place of peace.

As Peace and I moved together in harmony around what was left of the city – on this occasion, merely a massive crater of dust, with large pits dug here and there by the few Pedlars willing to excavate anything that could be of use – I found it easy to hurl our love and positivity out to those who had suffered for so long. Our energy pervaded the atmosphere, the sand and everything buried beneath it. The temperature gradually rose to that of the ambient temperature and when Peace came to a halt, I immediately slid from his back, knowing our job was done.

Devlin and Risk arrived within the hour, each dragging a massive bundle of tree saplings to add to those that Peace and I had brought; Devlin and I had dug most of them up on the way, the rest, he had unearthed whilst Peace and I had come on ahead to "work our magic," as Devlin insisted on calling it. The saplings were infused with positive energy and planted in the dust of the city before the day was out and we left feeling satisfied that another site was now safe for the Pedlars.

The rest of that autumn was spent travelling from one village to the next. A couple were only a few days' ride apart from one another, but it took weeks to travel between the others. Some villages knew I was on my way and many of their inhabitants received me well, however I was met with anger and resentment by those who had merely been given time to refocus their disappointment and their hurt. Other villages were unprepared for Peace's and my arrival. Whether their inhabitants included those who had been directly affected by me or not, the simmering unpleasantness that I encountered on arrival was the same at each. Peace and I followed the same procedure at every one of them as we had at Greenfields and Uptown, with the same happy result.

When the leaves had all fallen and the chill winds of winter arrived, Devlin suggested that we retreat to The Gathering before the snows came. I appreciated that Risk didn't appear able to grow as thick a coat as Peace, and Devlin was, unlike me, unused to living with the barest of shelter during winter, so after consultation with Peace, I agreed.

It took us nearly a month to get there. Despite the plentiful warm clothing pressed upon me by the last village I had left and which, obviously, I had shared with Devlin, despite the fires we lit each evening and took turns to keep roaring all night, and despite the fact that we kept moving all day in order to keep warm, all four of us were glad when, as we walked alongside a wide, fast-moving river one day, paddocks full of horses, livestock and winter crops came into sight through the sleet which had been pounding at us all for the past hour.

Devlin sighed. 'Thank goodness.' He leant forward and rubbed Risk's neck. 'Almost there,' he told her. 'We'll soon have you and Peace standing in a nice, deep straw bed with a big pile of hay.'

My stomach began to churn. 'Will we be staying far from the horses?'

Devlin chuckled. 'No, don't worry I can guarantee that one of the paddocks closest to the buildings will be empty, they're always left for new arrivals. The anxiety you're feeling right now is completely normal.'

'It is?'

'Since you bonded with Peace, you've never been far from him and the thought of it now is worrying you. I know that because it's something that bothers all of the newly bonded when they arrive, and they've usually only been bonded a matter of days or weeks. You've been bonded for months, now, so I imagine your jitters are even worse than normal. Adam, don't worry, you'll be among people who understand you here. People who are automatically your friends.'

'This is me, though, isn't it?'

'What do you mean?'

'I can't imagine any of the other new arrivals here will have been as well known as I am for causing hurt and upset.'

'You're forgetting that they're all counselled by Bond-Partners every bit as wise as Peace.'

'Do they always listen to them though? Even if they or someone they know has been hurt?'

'Admittedly, it can take time for them to act on their horses' counsel sometimes, but they always listen, Adam.'

You have merely to take your place with me and their reactions towards you will be irrelevant. As always it is your behaviour towards others on which you need focus, interrupted Peace.

Yes, sorry, I don't know what came over me. I've got used to how I need to be when we visit the villages and old cities, but I guess I'm feeling a bit overawed by the thought of so many Horse-Bonded in one place.

This is merely a further opportunity to practise making the choices that serve you instead of those that do not.

I sighed. *Focus on the present. On our bond. Of course.* My worries disappeared in an instant.

As we turned off the river bank to ride between the paddocks, I was thrilled to see so many horses of all builds, sizes and colours. Some were peering out of grey stone shelters at the worsening weather, but many were grazing the rough, winter grass despite the sleet that was fast turning to snow. A few in one paddock were cantering around, bucking and squealing as the cold wind whipped up behind them.

Devlin stopped at the last paddock before some enormous grey stone buildings, far bigger than any I had seen before. As I dismounted, I wondered at the strength of the Rock-Singers who had managed to lift rocks four and five storeys high with purely the strength of their voices and intent.

'Thanks, Peace,' I said, rubbing his back where I had been sitting so that the chill wouldn't cause his muscles to stiffen.

'Now we're finally here, you can get a saddle made for him. That broad back of his will be a challenge, but our Pinafer will love him,' Devlin said.

'Pinafer?' I asked as Peace and I followed Devlin and Risk through the paddock gate.

'The resident Saddler here. She's great,' Devlin said, stepping to the side and peering into the water barrel. 'That's full, good, but we'll need to break the ice on our way out. Come on, Risk, and you, Peace, let's get you to the field shelter. Hopefully there'll be hay in there already, if not, we'll haul some for you.'

Thankfully, there was hay shaken up in a huge mound along the length of the back wall of the shelter. Peace and Risk immediately tucked in. I checked that there were no stones lodged in Peace's hooves and then went outside with one of my wooden-backed grooming brushes, to hammer at the ice in the barrel until it gave way to the water underneath.

If you need water, Peace, now's the time to come and drink, this will freeze back over in no time, I told him. It seemed he didn't and neither did Risk.

'We'll come out every few hours to rebreak the ice,' Devlin said, appearing in the shelter doorway. 'Ready to come and claim a room, and then meet everyone?'

I almost strayed from Peace, but I checked myself in time. 'I'm ready.'

~

The grey buildings were arranged around a currently deserted cobbled square with a statue of a horse and person in the centre, upon which snow was beginning to settle. Devlin hurried towards a building on our right. 'You'll take up residence in one of the healing rooms, as you'll be needing to be free with your talent while you're here, just like you would be in a normal village.' He held a door open for me and then hurried along a long corridor. Warmth and laughter spilled out of a room with its door open and as we passed several others, I could hear voices within. A door opened just in front of Devlin, and a middle-aged woman stepped out.

'Oh, Devlin, hi, you made me jump! Good to see you back. Can I help you at all?' Her brown eyes were warm and friendly.

'No, I'm good thanks, Jess. This is Adam, he's newly bonded and a Herbalist, so I'm just looking for a room for him to work from. I take it there are some free?'

'Oh my word, you both look frozen. Adam, it's lovely to meet you, we've been waiting for you and have prepared a room ready. You have quite a queue waiting to see you once you've settled in.'

I shook her hand. 'Err, I do? I mean, sorry, it's lovely to meet you too. You have a room ready for me? There are people waiting to see me?'

'Of course. Bart passed through here a few weeks ago, his cart piled even higher than normal and full of how you not only healed him, but how somehow, you've managed to make the old city site he had just come from, safe for him to visit too. We had no idea they were such dangerous places for the Pedlars. And a few of the bonded passed through villages on their way back here that are apparently much different as a result of a visit from you and... Peace, isn't it? We assumed you'd turn up once the weather worsened, and there's been a lot of excitement to meet you and your – if reports are true – very friendly and exuberant Bond-Partner. Anyway, we don't need to get into that now, follow me and I'll show you to your rooms, then Devlin can show you where the baths are, you both look as if you need a hot one.'

Devlin winked at me as, stunned, I followed Jess to a room whose door was slightly ajar. She pushed it open and beckoned for me to go in. 'The other Herbalists have all donated some of their stores, so it's fully stocked.'

One of the stone walls was lined with shelf after shelf of jars containing dried herbs and there were planters on the windowsills containing live herbs that upon inspection, appeared to have been recently watered. There were armchairs arranged in a circle in front of the fireplace and a filing cabinet for my notes. A door stood open to an adjoining room with its own fireplace, a bed and another armchair.

'I'll get those fires lit while you're having a bath, so it'll be warm in here by the time you return,' Jess said.

I shook my head slowly. 'I don't know what to say, other than, well, thank you.'

Jess smiled. 'You're welcome. I'm a Tissue-Singer, by the way. There are some things I'd like to discuss about some of the healing

I've heard that you've been doing recently, when you have time. No rush,' she said and breezed out of the door.

I looked at Devlin. 'Did that just happen?'

He chuckled. 'You're among the Horse-Bonded now, Adam. I can't promise they'll all be quite so welcoming, but from the sound of it, it seems likely. Dump your stuff, I'll show you where the bathrooms are in this block and then when I've claimed a room in the general accommodation block and had a bath of my own, I'll be back to take you to the dining room for dinner.'

Not all of the Horse-Bonded were as pleased to see me as Jess – initial reactions varied from friendly and welcoming, as she had been, to suspicious and wary – but once again, it was Peace who wasted no time in softening attitudes towards me. On my first morning, I was sitting eating breakfast at one of the many long tables in the cavernous, stone-walled dining hall with Jess and some of the other Healers, when a clatter of hooves caused us to look towards one of the huge, almost floor to ceiling windows that usually let in light from the cobbled square but was now filled with Peace. He put his upper lip to the window and dragged it downwards so that the pink lining of his lip was visible as it left a trail of saliva down the window. Delighted laughter immediately filled the room and there was a scraping of chairs as some rushed to crowd around the window, while many, including those who had watched my entrance to the dining hall with thoughtful stares or frowns, ran to the door to go out and meet the new arrival.

'I'm pretty sure I shut the paddock gate behind me after Devlin and I replenished his and Risk's hay and water this morning,' I said with a grin.

Jess chuckled. 'The horses all know they're not confined to their paddocks and they often change to different ones, but they normally call for us to open the relevant gates first, rather than jumping them.

And I can't remember ever having seen a horse come to the square to meet everyone, as appears to have been his intent?'

I grinned as Peace turned around to greet his crowd, filling the window with his backside. 'Oh, that will definitely have been his intent. Shall I go out there, or leave them all to it?'

'If it were me, I would do whatever it is that he is trying to help you to do,' a fair-haired woman who had introduced herself as a Bone-Singer named Mable, said with a wink.

I laughed as I got to my feet. 'I can't tell you how good it is to be here. I'll catch up with you all later?'

'We're counting on it,' said Mable.

Within a matter of days, Peace had managed to meet every human resident at The Gathering – no small task since there were hundreds – as a result of frequent visits to the square, peering over the fences of other paddocks to meet people visiting their horses within, and, when he was actually in his own paddock, cantering to the gate to greet anyone passing by. He was loved and adored by all and by association, I became a universally accepted member of the Horse-Bonded.

Jess hadn't been exaggerating when she told me that there was a queue of people waiting to see me. I was given a few days' grace to settle into my rooms and the routines of The Gathering – which included being assigned my share of the chores that everyone willingly undertook so that the home of the Horse-Bonded could operate as one enormous home, contributed to by all – and then the knocks on my door began.

My visitors ranged from those wanting help with chronic ailments to curious Healers wanting to know what it was that I did differently from other Herbalists for my preparations to be successful where previous ones had not been – one of whom, I was thrilled to find, was open to the information I had to share in its entirety and left my rooms in excitement and with the intention of producing her own version of my green paste – and those Horse-Bonded wanting more details as to what, exactly, Peace and I had done at the two city sites we had managed to heal; apparently Devlin was being circumspect when asked about it and insisting that people asked me.

It was partly, yet not entirely, down to this last group of visitors that Peace and I remained at The Gathering for only the absolute worst of the winter weather, leaving only four weeks after our arrival; when my fellow bonded learned that Devlin and I had been transplanting hundreds of plants at a time using spoons and hand shovels, I was inundated with offers of help and encouraged to lead them on a mission to heal more cities as soon as possible. That alone may not have been enough for me to leave the warmth, comfort and comradeship of The Gathering before the end of the winter, however; it was my restlessness that ensured our departure.

To begin with, I thought that maybe I just needed time to adjust to the easier way of life that on the face of it, I was thoroughly enjoying; I had become so used to needing to take refuge in my bond with Peace for so much of each day that maybe, being able to make it through an entire day whilst resident in my own mind was something that would take time to feel normal. As the weeks went by, however, my restlessness only increased and Peace refused to give me counsel as to the cause. He refused to comment at all, actually, meeting all of my questions regarding my state of mind with the silence that I had come to learn meant I already had the answers I needed. When I finally arrived at the answer for which I had been looking, as expected, I found it in counsel that Peace had given me on many previous occasions. The absence of challenge did not result in peace.

Peace's response to my realisation was immediate. *A period of rest and recuperation is helpful but the voice of your soul will not allow you to rest for too long. We have taken significant steps along the path we must tread but it is a long path.*

I can leave tomorrow, Peace, but what about you? There's still snow on the ground, and there may be more to come. You've become used to shelter and a constant supply of hay, don't you want to wait until spring?

I felt his amusement. *This is not my first winter.*

I chuckled as I sat in the armchair by the fire in my bedroom. *No, I guess it isn't.*

Chapter Thirty-Eight

*W*e left the following day, along with three other Horse-Bonded whose horses were, like Peace, of the hardier type and willing to leave the comfort and shelter of The Gathering come what may. Others, Devlin included, promised to find us once the weather was kinder, insisting that their horses would always know where Peace was, and that catching us up would be no problem since we would be stationary for days at a time.

The weeks and months passed quickly as Peace and I travelled between villages and city sites, always in the company of my fellow Horse-Bonded and their horses, apart from when they paused to allow us to go on to the villages alone. Our group varied in number and composition as different partnerships arrived and left, with Devlin and Risk being our most frequent companions; my fellow Horse-Bonded were stalwart in their determination to ensure that Peace and I had help to heal the cities of The Old.

When winter approached, we made our way back to The Gathering again, but as was the case with my last visit there, I couldn't settle for long. It frustrated me that however many times I had witnessed the effect of telling the truth from a place of peace over the past year, however much I had come to appreciate just how powerful an energy love was from having given it repeatedly in the form of flowers, words and herbal paste, and seen it replace pallor with colour, lethargy with vitality, hurt with comfort and turbulence with calm, I felt little different in myself. From my refuge in my horse's mind, I could speak with absolutely no attachment to the outcome of a conversation and thereby say the exact words needed to provide comfort and relief to others. Wherever we went, whether to cities of the dead or villages of the living, my horse's calm strength enabled me to infuse trees and bushes, dust and rubble, with love and positivity. I was able to undo the damage I had done, to be a source of peace for those I had hurt, because through it all, I had Peace... yet not peace.

Again, we left The Gathering before winter was done with us. With our friends at our side, we travelled to villages and city sites through the blossom and hope of spring, the heat and joy of summer, the colour and reflection of autumn and then the crispness and introspection of winter before arriving back at The Gathering – a cycle that we repeated over and over again. The further we travelled, the more it amazed me just how far the effects of my behaviour had spread; the ripples were smaller the further they were from their source, yet they were there.

As the years went by, I gradually found that I needed to reach for Peace less and less. His calm strength stayed with me for longer and longer at a time after I ventured out from the refuge of our bond, and I was able to withstand the anger of those I had hurt, to apologise and to provide healing when requested, from a place of peace in my own mind... except when loss was involved. Any questions asked of Peace regarding the loss of loved ones, any allusion to it during healing consultations, or any commiseration for my own losses would cause me to instantly reach for Peace. Only from my refuge in his mind could I cope with the subject without aching for my wife and daughter.

As I aged, I would get panicky every now and then, feeling as if time were running out, not just to repair what I had broken, but to find what I still sought. My inability to cope with the issue of loss without continually diving for the refuge that Peace never denied me left me beyond frustrated. I just couldn't seem to find the missing ingredient, the final step to being totally at peace by myself.

From time to time, I would sigh and say, 'I just want peace.'

My horse's response was always the same. *You merely affirm your belief that you do not already possess it.* Then he would very obviously divert his attention elsewhere, signalling that the conversation was over.

The villages and cities to be healed grew fewer and further between. Our travelling companions gradually changed from those who had been ageing alongside Peace and me, to younger, more newly bonded partnerships. Devlin hung on longer than any of the others who had joined me from the start, but when Risk reached her thirties, the two of them finally bowed out.

Eventually, there were no people left to whom I had to make amends, no more discarnate souls who needed help to move on, and Peace and I found ourselves arriving back at The Gathering earlier in the year than we ever had before. As I walked at Peace's side, a gnarled hand to his shoulder, I smiled at the sight of people riding in the sunshine along the riverbank, of horses snoozing nose to tail under the trees, and of wild flowers and grasses waving in the breeze in those paddocks that were unoccupied. Then I felt sad that so many of those horses who had been our companions over the years had passed on, never to grace the paddocks of The Gathering again. It had been years since Peace had been able to carry me but I was immensely grateful that he still remained when so many were no longer with us.

As we settled back into The Gathering, it took a while for me to accept that I had run out of opportunities to be a source of peace for others – that the path on which Peace and I had embarked forty odd years earlier had finally come to an end. When I did, finally, I despaired.

I've been in search of peace for so long. I'm never going to find it, am I? I asked Peace, leaning back against him whilst he lay dozing in one of the paddocks at The Gathering.

You are closer to your goal than you realise.

But how can it possibly be taking so long for me to find that which I've helped so many others to feel?

It is one of the drawbacks of being as sensitive a human as you are. Your ability to sense and feel so deeply and intensely leaves you vulnerable. You cannot always rationalise that which you feel and without someone to ground you, you become unstable. Your parents kept you steady until you met the partner you assumed would be with you for life. When it was her time to go she left you in peril but with an opportunity you were unable to see.

So you called me to you, but I was too unhinged to respond.

When your family made their transition your pain rang out through the ether and I heard its call.

And I'll always be beyond grateful, you know that. But may I ask why you didn't pull me to you earlier, so that I didn't get into such a state?

To achieve a state of peace from a position of insanity endows a degree of strength that someone who has never experienced severe challenge could never possess.

So it was necessary for me to do so much damage that it's taken us a lifetime to mend it? That just seems crazy. Look at us, Peace, I'm seventy and you're, what are you now, forty-five? That's beyond old for a horse and yet you're still here with me, still helping me to be at peace so that I can find a way to be okay with loss. We've run out of villages to visit. We've run out of cities to heal. We've watched old friends depart from this world ahead of us but we're still here, and I still can't be completely at peace without you. What is there left to try?

That which would always be the final step.

Which is?

You must let me go.

Chapter Thirty-Nine

*T*he world spun around me. He couldn't leave me. I wouldn't allow it.

It is beyond time for me to move on. You know that. Yet I will not go without both your agreement and your acceptance. Our journey together was always leading to this point. You are ready. When you agree to let me go you will find that which you have always had yet could not recognise.

But I don't agree and I don't accept it. I can't lose you, you know I can't. I sat upright and began to rock backwards and forwards, holding my head in my hands.

He Who Is Peace. Look at me.

I spun around. *What did you call me?*

He gazed into my eyes with his own brown ones, now surrounded by white hair where once there was dark brown. They were tired eyes. *I know you will do this for me. You see that my coat is thicker than it should be. You see that I cannot keep the flesh on my bones. Without your healing ability I would not have been able to stay with you this long. With your healing ability you could keep me here longer and I would gladly stay if I thought it necessary. It isn't. You are ready but I*

will not leave my body until you have realised the potential you saw
for yourself when you chose my name: He Who Is Peace.

But I can't be here without you. I... just... can't.

You can although you do not have to be.

I don't?

Once you are who you have always had the promise to be I could
take you with me if you truly desire it. But as He Who Is Peace you
would be in a position to help others make great strides forward.
Others who have the potential to advance and take the rest of the
human race with them.

You want me to do that, I can feel it. But how will I be able to even
think about helping anyone else when you won't be here?

Because you will have accepted that loss does not and has never
existed.

But how do I accept that? I've tried. All these years, I've tried.

You have not tried. You have merely prepared. You are stable and
strong. You act and speak from a place of peace. You have come to that
place by experiencing over and over the power of love. It is from that
same place that you must make your decision now.

So you're telling me that if I love you, I'll let you go and then
somehow, I'll be okay with loss?

No. Make no mistake. I am telling you that if you choose love over
fear you will know that you could never lose me for loss does not exist.

His eyes never left mine. They were as soft as ever, as full of
knowing and of love. Through my panic, I felt a flicker of something
else. I trusted him. Out of that flicker blossomed my love for him. We
were Bond-Partners. We had grown so close that I couldn't tell where
he stopped and I began. We were both strong and calm. We both knew
that whilst everything was important, nothing was important; we knew
that all was well. Always. My brain tried to interrupt and ask how it
could be well when I had lost my family and I would shortly be losing
Peace, but I pushed out the interruption. I chose love. I chose trust. I
chose calm. I chose strength. And I knew. I couldn't lose Peace
because he was part of me. I couldn't lose him any more than I could
lose myself.

We are Peace, my horse agreed.

Do you need to go soon?

That would be preferable.

Now?

That would be best.

Would you come with me to our favourite place?

You would like my body to be buried there. And eventually yours. He Who Is Peace you have chosen well.

I have had the very best of teachers.

I fetched a shovel and then we walked together slowly out of the paddock and down to the river, past the paddocks of horses, sheep, cows, goats and crops. When I was hailed, I lifted an arm to wave back but we didn't stop. We sauntered along slowly, peacefully, my hand on his shoulder as always. When he stopped to graze a while in the warm sunshine, I sat down and watched him. When he was ready, we carried on along the river bank. When we were clear of The Gathering, we turned to meander up through the hills until we reached the brow of one from which we could look back down over the sparkling river, as if we and it were all that existed.

Peace lay down with a grunt. I knelt down at his shoulder and replaced my hand.

This isn't the end, for it can't be. I love you, Peace.

He lay flat, breathed out once and was gone.

Do not be sad for it is as you knew it would be. I will ask a final time whether you would like to come with me. Since he was no longer confined to his body, he filled my mind and, it seemed, the air all around me.

I shook my head, blinded by the tears that filled my eyes before brimming over to soak my cheeks. *I would love to come with you but I won't. Not yet. I'll do as I know you want me to do.*

Part of me will be with you throughout.

But you need to move your focus further away, I know, I can feel the pull on you. But I also feel the thread that still connects us. I know where you are and I know I'll join you there some day. I love you, Peace, and I'll be okay. Please, go to wherever is pulling at you.

When you are ready to follow I will be waiting. His thought faded and I was alone in my head... yet not alone, for that was not possible.

In letting go of Peace, I had found peace.

Epilogue

here were times when I missed Peace so much, I wondered whether I had made the right decision, staying in my body when he left his. Almost immediately, though, I would smile, knowing that all was well because I was Peace and he was me. I didn't feel that I wanted to stay on at The Gathering without him, though. Some who had lost their horses did stay on, wanting to be around other horses and people with whom they had so much in common, and happy to contribute to the running of the place whilst sharing their experience with any of the Horse-Bonded community who wanted it. I felt the need to be somewhere quieter, somewhere I could rest and contemplate my life so far and prepare myself for whatever was to come.

I chose Coolridge in which to settle, partly because it was a village that Peace and I had passed through many times and always found ourselves reluctant to leave due to the beauty and warmth of both the residents and its location, and partly because it had recently found itself without a resident Herbalist.

When I arrived at the village nestled into the side of a valley so that wherever one stood, one could see the most beautiful lake sparkling from the valley floor, there were tears of sadness from the villagers for the absence of Peace and then smiles and laughter when I asked whether they would allow me to be their Herbalist. I was immediately and excitedly hustled along to the empty cottage of the previous Herbalist, who had left to marry into the family of a neighbouring village, promising to return at regular intervals in case she was needed. I was assured that she would be only too happy for me to occupy her cottage for the time being and within only hours, its rooms, bare when I first entered, were furnished and the kitchen cupboards were full.

I had only been there a matter of months when, just as the sun was peeping over the hilltop to the east one morning, I awoke to the smell of paint. Who could have been painting during the night? I wondered. And why, when I put my head out of my bedroom window, did the smell seem fainter outside than inside my cottage?

There was a familiar squeak and the sound of a latch dropping into place; someone had just shut my front door. Strange. There was never a need for me to lock it, but it was unusual for someone to pay a visit without knocking.

I dressed quickly and made my way downstairs, the smell of paint becoming steadily stronger. I followed it to the front room just as the sun's rays burst through the window and onto Peace and me.

The mural of the two of us as we had been thirty odd years previously had been painted by a talented artist, who clearly knew us both very, very well.

I rushed to the front door and opened it. There was no one there. I hurried down the path, opened the gate and went out into the street, looking both ways as it curved around the hillside. A familiar figure was shuffling away and almost around one of the bends.

'DEVLIN!' I shouted.

He stopped and slowly turned, careful to lean on his walking stick so as not to overbalance. A wide grin spread across his face as he began to shuffle back towards me. I jogged to meet him.

'All right, you don't need to rub it in, you young whipper snapper,' he said.

I laughed and drew him into a hug. 'Where do you think you're going? You break into my home that isn't even really mine, you vandalise the front room and then you leave without even saying hello?'

'Steady on, you'll have me over,' he said, laughing. 'No seriously, Adam, let me go.' When I complied, he steadied himself with his stick and clapped me on the shoulder. 'I didn't want to wake you. I'm staying at Boffy and Teela's. I arrived late last night and Teela told me where you were, so I came on over with my paints and had a little play.'

'A little play? Devlin, the mural is stunning and you've been up all night doing it after travelling here? I can't find the words to tell you how much I appreciate the gesture, your skill and the fact that Peace is right there where I can see him again. Thank you, old friend, thank you. Very much.'

He squeezed my shoulder with surprising strength. 'It's me, Adam. After all our years travelling together, do you think I need you to find words to tell me anything? I knew how much it would mean to you and that was why I did it. Help me back to that comfortable little cottage of yours, then, and get the kettle on. It's taken me months to track you down after arriving at The Gathering and hearing of Peace's departure and then yours – you have some explaining to do.'

'And you have some sleeping to do.'

'Now don't start getting bossy, I'm older than you and I was bonded before you.' He looked sideways at me as we walked at his slow, shuffling pace, and winked. I grinned at the attempt to pull rank he had always tried to use when we disagreed, and that had become a standing joke between us.

It had been five years since we had seen one another, we agreed over breakfast. We reminisced and caught up with one another's news and I finally got around to telling him why I was in Coolridge.

'So you've found peace, and it still isn't enough?' Devlin said with a wink.

I grinned. 'It's enough for me, but Peace wanted me to do more. So now I wait to see what life has in store next.'

'And you think that whatever it is, it will find you here?'

I nodded. 'I do. I can't explain it but I feel that something is coming and I'll know it when it gets here.'

'And until then, you wait?'

I nodded. 'Until then, I wait.'

Other books by Lynn Mann

**Humankind is ready for change and
Adam has a further part to play...**

The Horses Know Trilogy

The Horses Know

Amarilla is one of those chosen by a horse as a Bond-Partner. She looks forward to a lifetime of learning from her horse and of passing on the mare's wisdom to those seeking help. But then she discovers that she is the one for whom the horses have all been waiting. The one who can help them in return.

In order to give the horses the help they need, Amarilla will have to achieve that which has never been attempted before. Only her beloved mare can give her the motivation, the courage and the strength to believe she can succeed. If she does, a new era will dawn for horses and humans alike...

The Horses Rejoice (The Horses Know Book 2)

Amarilla and Infinity have been the catalysts for change that they agreed to be, but they know there is more to be done. If they can befriend the Woeful and persuade the rest of humankind to do the same, then the destructive ways of The Old will forever be in the past.

Amarilla, Infinity and their friends set out on a journey to find the Woeful but their search becomes something so much more due to a courageous chestnut mare, a lone Woeful youngling and numerous herds of wild horses who seek their help along the way. But the friends never forget what they agreed to do. They must reach the heart of the Woeful community. And then they must be willing to risk losing everything...

The Horses Return (The Horses Know Book 3)

It has been more than twenty years since the Kindred came to live in Rockwood. Most of the villagers have embraced the Kindred and all that they have to teach, but there are those who fear the Kindreds' influence, and so have drifted away to live as outcasts. The outcasts suffer, living as they do, but they refuse help, even from the Horse-Bonded.

Will is adamant that he can succeed where the Horse-Bonded have failed, and bring the outcasts home. But his forceful personality constantly gets in his way. He is the key to the future, but if he is to play his part, he must allow a herd of wild horses to show him how to be the person he needs to be. Only then will he fully understand the lengths to which Amarilla and Infinity have gone to ensure that he can fulfil his destiny and reunite the human race...

Horses Forever (A Sequel to The Horses Know Trilogy)

It has always been believed that the people of The Old obliterated themselves generations ago, but when horses begin to amass at one of the city sites of The Old, the villagers of Rockwood discover the truth – an underground city, full of people, has survived.

Supreme City's inhabitants have been waiting for the conditions to be right for them to come up to the surface and claim dominion. They believe the time has come. They are genetically enhanced, armed and aggressive, and they are certain that nothing can stand in their way. But they haven't counted on Will, Maverick, the Horse-Bonded and several hundred horses...

The Strength Of Oak (A Prequel to The Horses Know Trilogy)

Unloved and unwanted by her parents, Rowena is desperate for a way out of the life she hates. When a horse chooses her as his Bond-Partner, she thinks she has found one – but she soon discovers that while she can leave her family behind, there is no escaping herself.

With patient guidance from her horse, Rowena begins to accept the truth of her past, and to believe she can change. But then her past catches up with her at the worst possible moment, leaving her with a choice. She can be the person she was, or she can find the strength to be the person her horse has shown her she can be. One choice will give them both a future. The other will be the death of them...

A Reason To Be Noble (A Prequel to The Horses Know Trilogy)

Quinta is crippled with anxiety and can barely leave the house, so she is terrified when she senses the touch of a horse's mind on her own and realises that he has selected her as his Bond-Partner. She manages to find the courage to leave her home and her village, and meet the horse whose mind calls to hers. A bond settles into place between the two of them, and Quinta's outlook on life begins to change.

With her horse's guidance, Quinta's confidence slowly increases, but she has a long way to go if she is to leave all of her fears behind, and her horse is a relentless teacher. When it seems as though he has pushed her too far, Quinta must find a way to trust that everything he has taught her still holds true. Their lives and that of a young boy will depend on it...

Tales Of The Horse-Bonded
(Companion Stories to The Horses Know Trilogy)

A collection of short companion stories to The Horses Know Trilogy, Tales Of The Horse-Bonded is available to download free. To find out more, visit www.lynnmann.co.uk.

Did you enjoy In Search Of Peace?
I'd be extremely grateful if you could spare a few minutes to leave a review where you purchased your copy. Reviews really do help my books to reach a wider audience, which means that I can keep on writing!
Thank you very much.

I love to hear from you!
Get in touch and receive news of future releases at the following:

www.lynnmann.co.uk

www.facebook.com/lynnmann.author

Acknowledgments

When I sat down to begin writing each of The Horses Know books, my husband, Darren, asked for one of the horse characters to be based on Braveheart, his partner in mischief of more than twenty years. The trouble was, Braveheart is such a big personality that I didn't have anywhere to put him that would allow me to do him justice. As soon as Adam and Peace's story began to unfold in my head however, the realisation dawned that at last I had a character crying out to be based on our big, lovable clown. Thanks, Brave, for putting smiles on so many faces with your antics over the years, and for being our Peace.

As always, huge, heartfelt thanks to my editorial team: Fern Sherry, Leonard Palmer, Rebecca Walters and Caroline Macintosh – I know how lucky I am to have you all.

Jon Morris of MoPhoto has once again generously provided the fabulous photographs that have allowed designer Amanda Horan to produce a cover that melts my heart – massive thanks to you both.

While Peace's character is one hundred percent Braveheart, I couldn't seem to help aspects of his partnership with Adam being influenced by my relationship with a certain blue-eyed, piebald mare. She is no longer with me physically, but her influence remains. Thank you for reading and allowing me to share our horses with you!

Made in the USA
Coppell, TX
09 December 2021

67693215R00187